RED WATERS RISING

ALSO BY LAURA ANNE GILMAN

The Devil's West
Silver on the Road
The Cold Eye

The Vineart War Trilogy
Flesh and Fire
Weight of Stone
The Shattered Vine

As L. A. Kornetsky
The Gin & Tonic Mysteries
Collared
Fixed
Doghouse
Clawed

LAURA ANNE GILMAN

THE DEVIL'S WEST, BOOK THREE

RED WATERS RISING

SAGA 🔱 PRESS

LONDON SYDNEY **NEW YORK** TORONTO NEW DELHI

SAGA PRESS
AN IMPRINT OF SIMON & SCHUSTER, INC.

1230 AVENUE OF THE AMERICAS, NEW YORK, NEW YORK 10020

Text copyright © 2018 by Laura Anne Gilman
Jacket illustration copyright © 2018 by Emma Ríos

SAGA PRESS and colophon are trademarks of Simon & Schuster, Inc.
For information about special discounts for bulk purchases, please contact Simon & Schuster Special Sales at 1-866-506-1949 or business@simonandschuster.com.
The Simon & Schuster Speakers Bureau can bring authors to your live event. For more information or to book an event, contact the Simon & Schuster Speakers Bureau at 1-866-248-3049 or visit our website at www.simonspeakers.com.
Jacket design by Greg Stadnyk
Also available in a Saga Press paperback edition
The text for this book was set in ITC Galliard Std.
Manufactured in the United States of America
First Saga Press hardcover edition June 2018
2 4 6 8 10 9 7 5 3 1
Library of Congress Cataloging-in-Publication Data
Names: Gilman, Laura Anne, author.
Title: Red waters rising / Laura Anne Gilman.
Description: First edition. | New York : Saga, [2018] | Series: The Devil's West ; book 3
Identifiers: LCCN 2017040212 | ISBN 9781481429740 (hardcover) | ISBN 9781481429757 (softcover) | ISBN 9781481429764 (eBook)
Subjects: LCSH: Teenage girls—Fiction. | Magic—Fiction. | Devil—Fiction. | GSAFD: Western stories. | Fantasy fiction. | Occult fiction.
Classification: LCC PS3557.I4545 R43 2018 | DDC 813/.54—dc23 LC record available at https://lccn.loc.gov/2017040212

They say

after

there is silence.

They are wrong

i hear you in everything.

AARON L. GILMAN

1933-2016

Northern Wilds

Unclaimed Lands

Junction

Flood

De Plata

The Mother's Knife

SPANISH PROTECTORATE

THE DEVIL'S
WEST

0   200   400

Miles

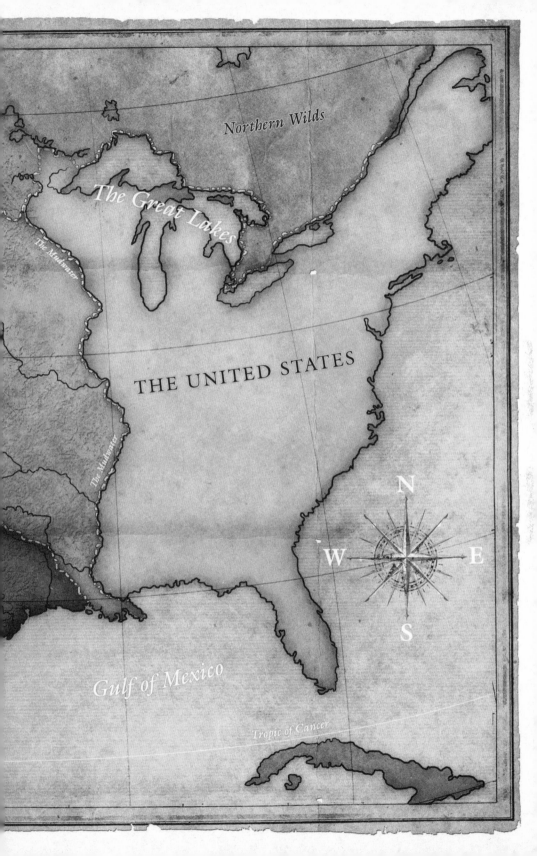

THE DEVIL'S WEST, BOOK THREE

RED WATERS RISING

PART ONE

A PROPER VAGABOND

ONE

Isobel had traveled from the low plains to the high reaches of the Mother's Knife, through storm and sun and snow, but the past few days had found her limit. "It's winter," she said, not for the first time. "Why is it still so warm?"

"Welcome to the southlands," Calico Zac said with a shrug. "You get used to it." Both Isobel and Gabriel gave him a side-eye at that, and he laughed.

They had met up with the native Rider a week earlier, traveling through Nanatsoho lands. He had proven a fascinating companion, especially for two Riders well and truly sick of each others's stories, but spoke little of himself, saying only that he'd been gone from home for some time, and offering to keep them company along the Road if they were heading in the same direction.

They had been. Although Isobel was having deep second thoughts about Gabriel's insistence that the winter months would best be spent traveling the southern swing of the Territory, if it was all like this.

The morning sun dappled through still-green branches overhead, the Road stretching clear and flat ahead of them, following the slight curve of the stream that Zac said would lead them to their destination. But despite the shade, the air was thick and heavy with moisture, making the simple act of breathing exhausting and leaving Isobel with the constant urge to scrape at her skin. She knew it had not in fact begun growing moss to match the sides of the trees bunched up alongside the road, but knowing that and believing it were two vastly different things.

Gabriel made a rueful noise as he mopped the sweat from his brow before tugging his hat back down over his forehead. "He's right, Iz. You will get used to it. Eventually. And summer's worse."

Isobel glared at them both then, using the edge of her own kerchief to wipe the sweat gathering along her hairline. It didn't help; within minutes, her face was again lightly coated, matching the wetness under her blouse and settling around her waist. Her hat hung from its cord down the back of her neck, the weight of its brown felt too much to bear, even if it meant she had to squint in the occasional spars of bright sunlight coming between the trees.

She glanced at the men riding on either side of her. Gabriel had shed his jacket and rolled up his shirtsleeves, but Calico Zac seemed utterly unaffected, save for a faint sheen of sweat on his face. Their horses, and the mule following behind, seemed likewise unaffected, their tails swishing lazily at the insects but otherwise showing no signs of distress. She hated them, just a little, just then.

Still, it could have been much worse without their companion to show them what leaves, rubbed on the skin, could dissuade the worst of the insects, and how to tie their bedrolls off the ground at night to catch even the faintest breeze.

Isobel had spent the first sixteen years of her life in the high plains, where storms left the air crisp and clear, and summer heat could be avoided until night fell and things cooled again. Even in the months she'd been on the Road, they'd traveled up into the mountains, where the high summer sun might pink her skin, but never felt particularly warm. She felt as though she'd passed into another world. Maybe the one folk said the devil came from, infernally hot and filled with suffering. *Damp* suffering.

"We'll keep the southland for last," she muttered, mocking Gabriel's deeper voice. "'Avoid the snows, you'll see enough in your time, no need to rush it.' You didn't say anything about the air pretending to be water, or the insects."

He ducked his head just enough that she knew he was hiding a grin. "Oh, now, they're not so bad . . ."

"There are beetles. Everywhere." Specifically, large back beetles in her clothing when she woke up in the morning, and a massive brown spider in the grain she'd been cooking for breakfast.

She had not screamed, but she might have used some words that might have gotten her ears boxed, back home.

"You'll get used to it," Calico Zac said again, just as a brightly colored darner swooped and fluttered in front of her, seeming to alight between Uvnee's ears before shooting off again.

Isobel scowled down at her hands, staring at the ragged edges of her nails, the sun-darkened skin and the dirt ingrained into the leather of Uvnee's reins, then glanced sideways and saw that Gabriel was smiling, his gaze following the darner as well.

It was the first time she'd seen him smile in days, she realized suddenly. That particular smile, the one that wasn't about something funny, but a good thought, that made him happy. They'd ridden together long enough that she could tell the difference, and she wondered why—and when—that smile had become rare.

She looked up to see more darners, diving singly and in pairs, skimming low before disappearing into the foliage. Darners were as pretty as butterflies, maybe even more so, Isobel had to admit. And didn't bite or sting.

"All right," she admitted, letting the reins go slack on Uvnee's neck long enough to cross her arms and direct a glare at Zac. "Maybe there's something to be said for this part of the Territory, too. Still doesn't make up for finding a widder in my boot this morning."

The two men glanced at her, but didn't respond, and she shifted in her saddle, terribly aware of the weight of her skirts and the close fit of her boots. She'd rolled down her stockings the day before, choosing one discomfort over another, but the heat still prickled on her skin, damp and uncomfortable. Uvnee snorted, and she eased on the reins, aware she was holding too tight and the mare was becoming uneasy. "Sorry, girl," she said. "I'm just . . ."

"The word you're looking for," Gabriel said, "is 'cranky.'"

She couldn't deny it. Nor could she avoid the reason for it, far more than the too-damp air or the increase in biting insects.

They weren't only heading south. They were heading toward a place called Red Stick. A city.

Isobel had never been in a city before. She couldn't quite imagine it, no matter how many times she'd asked Gabriel, and now Zac, to describe it to her. That many people, all in one place . . .

With all that had been happening in the past few months they were on the Road, all the things they'd dealt with, it was sometimes easy to forget that she was riding for a reason. This was her mentorship ride: She was the Devil's Left Hand, the physical form of his judgment and protection, and the people of the Territory needed to know her—and she them. She did not have the freedom to say where she might go or where she might stay; she went where she was needed, same as any of the devil's tools.

And the southernmost corner of the Territory was important. The Mother's Knife held the silver mines and kept the Spaniards from invading in force from the west, but they were inhospitable, even for the native tribes; few people lived there year round. The plains were kinder, but the largest town they'd visited had held no more than a few thousand souls, and more often they saw farm-groupings, two or three families gathering together for protection and company without quite forming a town.

The southern edge of the Territory was different.

Isobel unhooked her canteen, taking a mouthful of the warm, flat water, and thought glumly of frost-covered fields and the snap of snow in the air. Not that she wanted particularly to be caught in a blizzard or even wake up covered in overnight snow—a thing that had happened once, which was once too often for her—but those options seemed more pleasurable than this.

She took another mouthful of water, forcing it down her throat. The mule, who had been following behind at a sluggishly resigned pace ever since the native and his dun pony had joined them, came up alongside and nipped at her sleeve.

"You want some water, boy?" she asked, and squirted a little onto its muzzle. Long ears flicked at her, and he pushed his muzzle against her arm before moving off, his dusty sides rippling with a shudder. She would have to give him extra attention when they made camp, she decided; he was as sulky as a small child.

"Zac. Tell me more about your people," Gabriel said. "You said your tribe was small?"

"Small, and likely gone by now," the other man admitted, the saddle under him creaking as he shifted, and Isobel thought that he was uncomfortable with the question. "We did not have enough to offer other tribes to join with us, and so my cousins made families elsewhere."

"And you took to the Road."

"And I took to the Road," he agreed. "And now I return."

Neither Gabriel nor Isobel pressed further. A man's—or woman's—past was their own.

Before they could change the subject, the horses walked around a thick clump of thick-trunked trees whose branches spread out like something with far too many arms, and the sparse trail they had been on was crossed by a much wider road, ruts in the packed-down dirt indicating that wagons had passed along here often enough to leave wear.

Isobel exhaled, pressing down through her heels, letting her awareness sink slowly into the deep, rich soil beneath her, the way Gabriel had taught her. Something pulsed in response, the feel of it as strong and familiar as Uvnee's hoofbeats.

"Not so much a greenie anymore," Gabriel said, watching her with an odd smile. "Stretching for the Road like a proper vagabond."

The Road: not a single road but the interconnected trails and paths, the ever-running medicine that ran the length and width of the Territory, looping and turning on itself, power constant and free—save where it bottled up at a crossroads. A Rider could never be lost, so long as they could feel the Road beneath them.

But with the Road came crossroads.

Calico Zac reached into his pocket, as though searching for something, but Gabriel put a hand out to halt him. "No need," he said, and nodded at Isobel.

A wise Rider always checked the way with silver. Crossroads caught power, and even a sparsely traveled one such as this could hold danger. Silver warned, and cleared. It wasn't foolproof, but if you were not a fool, it was safe enough.

But Gabriel called her the devil's own silver for a reason.

She dropped from the saddle, feeling the ache in her hips and knees as she did so, the weight of her skirt almost surprising, after so many hours in the saddle. The moment her boots touched dirt, the feeling of the Road ahead of them intensified, and she let herself reach out, not deep but along the surface, half-braced for the tingle of something pooling within the crossroads.

"It's clean," she said, pushing down the faint feeling of disappointment. "A marshal must have been by recently to clear it out." That was what marshals did; they kept the Road clear and safe, as well as sorting any rumblings of trouble or mischance off the roads.

"Or a magician," Gabriel said. "Can you tell?"

She shook her head. "It's just clean. No trace of anything left."

Clean but not empty, not the way the northern hills had been, where magicians had done such damage. She tried not to think of those places; she had left them warded, but it would take the devil himself riding out to put them to rights, she thought, if even he could.

"Then back up in the saddle," Gabriel said, "and let's move on. Zac, how much farther until we reach the limits of your peoples' lands?"

"Not far, I think." He shrugged when they both looked at him. "It's been many years. Landmarks change. Look for marked posts. That will tell us who claims an area."

"Individual tribes, not the confederation of tribes as a whole?" Gabriel sounded fascinated, so Isobel tried to pay attention.

"The confederation is, how you say it, política? Politics. Boundaries are personal."

"That's not . . . How can that be? Borders are inherently political . . ." Gabriel shook his head, kneeing his gelding closer to argue with Zac. Isobel left them to it, letting them lead the way as she traced the Road forward and back, as far as she could reach before the feeling faded into dusty nothingness.

The Mudwater should run just a few days southwest of them, she thought, remembering the map Gabriel had laid out the last night they'd slept under a roof, tracing the path they'd come and the route they'd take. The Mudwater, where the Boss had first stood, so long ago, and told conquistadors, 'Go no farther.' Although, knowing the boss, Isobel thought he'd used rougher words than that. . . .

To the east of the river lay the United States. Farther south, she knew, Spain claimed both the spread hand of the delta itself and the waterways beyond, demanding a high price for any who tried to sail them. And both nations eyed the Territory like it was their birthright, sticking fingers to test the boss's resolve.

She had slapped several of those fingers back herself but never once seen the Mudwater itself. Gabriel had taken them north, and then west, not south or east. Not until now.

Not until she was ready, she supposed. And still, he told her nothing of what to expect.

Gabriel was her mentor, her teacher, as well as a friend. But she'd learned that he had too much in common with the boss in that they both seemed to think that teaching her to swim meant tossing her into the creek so she could figure out how not to drown.

But Zac was with them now. He was neither teacher nor guardian but a fellow Rider. He might give her a different answer.

"You grew up here," she said, into a moment when neither of them were speaking. "Tell me about Red Stick."

She had difficulty reading natives as easily as settlers; they had different expressions, different tells, the boss called them, and a few days' riding together was not enough to learn his particulars, but it seemed almost as though he hesitated before giving a sideways shrug.

"I'm not sure what much more I can speak to. As I said—"

"It's been a long time since you were home, I know. So, what was it like then?"

"Busy. It was always busy. Boats using the Mudwater stop there to sell and buy, then go back up- or cross-river, back and forth. There are always strangers coming and going."

"That means if something's happening, Red Stick knows it first," Gabriel added, and Zac made a hand gesture of agreement. "Gossip is one of the things bought and sold."

Isobel rested her hand on Uvnee's neck, feeling the rough warmth of the mare's coat, the coarse, scratchy hairs of her mane passing over the tops of her fingers. Traveling by boat sounded terrifying; she'd never seen anything larger than a trapper's dugout, never even stepped in one of those. The Americans claimed the river as theirs. The boss just laughed and said they could try to hold it, for all the good it would do them. The Mudwater was its own.

"Who do they trade with cross-river?" They had seen a few farmholdings as they traveled but nothing that might interest traders, she thought.

"There's an American fortification just on the other side, and of course there's Liberdad."

Isobel nodded, feeling something tighten in her gut. Those were two very good reasons for her to become familiar with this area: any place where American military gathered could become a problem at any time, and Liberdad could be the spark that lit that trouble.

Back home, Iktan told stories about Liberdad, although she didn't believe he had ever been there. Beholden to no one, the city rested between a bend in the Mudwater and a massive lake that was fed by the sea itself, and was home to pirates, freebooters, and whatever navy paid them enough for berthing—Spanish, American, even the English and French. And once through their gates, the entire Mudwater—and the Territory's less-defended border—could be laid open.

The boss stepped carefully around Liberdad, and they paid him the same respect. She had never questioned the stability of that—until now.

The thought was uncomfortable. Too many of her thoughts were uncomfortable these days. She pushed it down with the others and reached back to pull her hat up, settling it firmly on her head as though to protect her from further distractions. "But what is it *like?*"

Gabriel's gelding turned his arched neck to look at her; her voice might have gotten a touch high-pitched in her exasperation. She made a face at the horse, and one of its ears flicked at her as though it were laughing.

"Large," Gabriel said finally, when their companion was silent. "Nowhere near the size of a city in the States, of course, but larger than anything you've ever seen before. Crowded. And crowded with people who came here from all different places, for all different reasons. All sorts of people, not all of whom would be given pause by that sigil in your hand."

The native Rider glanced at her hands where they held Uvnee's reins, and she let go with her left hand, pressing the palm flat against her thigh instinctively, as though to hide the markings there. The thick black lines were a reminder of what she had asked for, the Bargain she had made for it nearly a year earlier. Power, and respect.

The devil didn't ask for more than you could pay. But all she'd had to pay with had been herself. And while power might rest in the palm of her hand, respect had to be earned. Face-to-face, and hand-to-hand.

She'd never had to face so many people at once.

"This is a test, isn't it?"

She heard a faint, familiar huff of laughter from Gabriel. "Everything's a test, Isobel. Red Stick's a port city, for good and for ill, and a frontier town into the bargain. You don't control places like that, you just hope for the best."

"Thank you for your reassurances," she said tartly, knowing that it would only make him laugh more. She looked up to see Calico Zac watching them curiously, and for a second she wondered what he might look like out of his standard-issue rider's gear of dustcoat and trou, if his people wore deerskin or woven cloth, if the beaded hatband he wore was the style of his tribe or something he had acquired in his riding, if his people wore their hair longer, or if his short-cropped hair was more usual.

Her thoughts made her frown, wondering where they came from, and Gabriel misinterpreted her expression, moving Steady over a pace so his knee bumped up against hers.

"You're ready for this, Isobel. Learn it. Learn them. Let them learn you. Local tribes, too." He cast a glance at Zac, who was still watching them both. "We'll spend the winter here, then ride the Muddy back up north in the spring."

She heard something odd in his voice, but before she had a chance to ask, Calico Zac stiffened, lifting his head as though he'd heard something, and Gabriel put a hand on her leg, a warning pressure to be still and silent.

"Sit ready," he said, squeezing her leg once before pulling his flint-lock, a short-muzzled carbine, from its saddle holster. Steady's reins were dropped almost casually across the gelding's neck as Gabriel reached with his other hand for the powder and shot, loading the weapon with dexterity she'd yet to master.

By the time she'd heeded his command, gathering her own reins up in a firm grip and unhooking the strap that held her blade against her own saddle, she heard what had alerted them: hoofbeats, coming hard down the road toward them. Three horses, she guessed, light and fast. Isobel thought of the letter still tucked into her pack, waiting to be handed off, and wondered if the approaching horses carried a post-rider she could hand it over to.

That hope was quashed the moment they came into view. Post-riders were often young, but these were mere boys, riding neck and neck with no regard for anyone else who might be sharing the road with them.

Only at the last minute did one of the riders realize they weren't alone, and pulled his horse, a tall bay, up hard enough to make Isobel wince. The horse danced under him, exuding resentment that it had been forced to stop, and the other two riders followed suit, if a little less abruptly.

She could practically feel Gabriel's desire to shoot them, simply for mishandling their horses, and the curl of Zac's lip suggested he felt the same.

"Easy . . ." she said, soft as though she were speaking to her mare, and Gabriel's arm eased slightly, the carbine no longer pointing in their direction, although still held ready in the crook of his arm. She could not see what Zac was doing on the other side of Gabriel and Steady's bulk, but she did not doubt that he had a weapon at the ready as well, likely the horn-handled blade she'd seen him sharpening.

Trusting them to stay calm, she shifted her focus to the newcomers. They were young and male, their heads bare, skin pale enough to tell her they did not work outside, that this was a jaunt for them, briefly released from counter or desk.

There was a tense silence. One heartbeat, then another.

"*Bonjou!*" the first boy finally called out. "*Konmen lé-zafè?*"

The words sounded familiar, but meant nothing to Isobel.

"Better for not being knocked over," Gabriel said tartly, clearly having no trouble understanding them. "Does your papa know how you're mistreating his cattle?"

That stung, as he'd clearly meant it to, and the boy drew himself up, pushing his horse closer in a high-stepping sideways dance, showing off his control of the beast. "Bo Argent's mine, and I'll have a whip to you for presuming otherwise, *étranger*."

They'd been speaking French, Isobel realized, although with an accent she had never encountered before. Odd, to hear it spoken this far south, where Gabriel had told her that Spanish or Portuguese, or even Inka-Quechua was more common.

Closer, she could see that the boys were likely near to her own age, their leader wearing a fine white shirt with a banded collar like Gabriel's, but white as though it had been dipped in bleaching powder only that morning, and his trousers were black and clean, with boots shining underneath.

Money, she thought, Marie's training allowing her to estimate the cost of everything he wore, likely down to a quarter-coin. Money, and careless with it.

Acadians, she realized. Gabriel had mentioned them briefly. Settlers from the Northern Wilds, where his own people came from; refugees from the war between France and England. While his folk had lingered just within the Territory's border, Acadians had gone downriver, as far from the remains of war as they could reach.

They had taken their wealth with them, clearly, or rebuilt it in the decades since then.

Isobel wasn't impressed by her first encounter.

"Peter, hush," a second boy said, his voice lower, and in English, his desperate glances up at Gabriel making it clear he intended them to be understood. "We near ran them off the road, riding reckless as we were. And if you'd injured Argent, your papa would be the one to lift the whip and land it on your backside, not his."

"He insulted me," the first boy retorted, never dropping his own glare from Gabriel. "He and his boys, and their mule," he added with a sneer, "should be along the side, not taking up the full of the road."

Isobel sucked at the inside of her cheek to keep from responding, but the third boy did it for her, his cheeks flushed with embarrassment. "My apologies for my brother, mademoiselle. We only now realize he is blind in one eye and half-witted to boot."

Only then did the first boy's gaze flicker to Isobel, then down, finally taking in the fabric of her skirt tucked around her legs, then up to note the swell of her blouse over her bosom. Isobel lifted her chin, eyes narrowing as though to dare him to make further comment.

None of them apologized to Calico Zac, however.

"Pah. Boy or girl, it makes little difference. They are in our way and they must move. After this man apologizes for giving insult."

There was a pause, letting his words sink in. Giving insult was serious business. Isobel had judged and carried out sentence for that crime, could still feel the drip of their blood on her fingers, for all that she'd never laid hand on them. For this . . . boy to claim Gabriel had given insult . . .

Breath gathered in her mouth to speak, when she glanced sideways and saw that corner of Gabriel's mouth that had twitched earlier was now pressed flat, not in anger but the need to suppress laughter, and across Steady's neck she could see Calico Zac's hands open and close, the trade-sign for "infant" clear in his fingers. And suddenly her own chest was tight with the same, the absurdity of the moment like cool water on her skin, and her temper.

They were only boys, full of themselves and their self-importance, no more a threat than a cattle-hand with one whiskey too many in their belly and hands prone to wander without asking.

"Ah, *oui*, an apology you have, then," Gabriel said, and if his words were placating, his voice was merry enough to be taken for further insult. "We are most sorry to have encountered you on the road, and will endeavor to not do so again."

Gabriel had been trained to the Law, in the States, and when put in the mood could speak circles around his opponents. She had heard him go on in similar manner once, when they'd unwillingly shared a camp-fire with bandits, insulting all within earshot with such graceful language they'd been taken for compliments. But from the way the boy's eyes widened, he had education and wit enough to recognize it, and pride enough for it to go down the wrong way.

He pulled his shoulders up, staring down his nose at them. "Your name, étranger."

"Gabriel Kasun." Names had power, but her mentor gave his as though no power could touch him, as though giving it to these boys was less than whispering it to a tree. Her lips parted in awe at the subtlety of the insult, worthy of the boss at his worst, and tucked it away if she ever needed use it herself. "And these are my companions, Calico Zac"—and the native inclined his head gravely at them—"and Isobel née Lacoyo Távora."

She tipped her hat at them in perfect mimicry of Gabriel when he played at being card-sharp, taking her cue from his tone.

"But you would best know her by her title," Gabriel went on. "The Devil's Hand."

Isobel had learned that there were three general reactions to settlers when they heard who she was. Most pretended unconcern, watered by a faint respect. Some were impressed, or awed. And some few pretended as though they'd never heard the phrase, had no idea what the Devil's Hand might have to do with them, or they the Devil's Hand.

Rarely did anyone attempt to kill her.

TWO

Gabriel had been in more fights than he cared to remember, with guns and knives and fisticuffs, and he knew it was already too late, the throwing knife cutting air, aimed at Isobel's unprotected chest, too fast for her to react, too fast for him to intervene. He was cursing himself for becoming complacent, for dismissing boys merely for their youth, for every mistake ever made.

But while his heart raced, the world around him seemed to slow, his thoughts a second ahead of his actions, logic rather than panic determining how he reacted. Even as his carbine dropped back into ready position, finger curled under the guard, pulling the trigger, he was kneeing Steady forward, knowing the shot would go wide but hoping the noise would spook the horses, cause them to unseat their riders.

A high-pitched whinny followed by swearing in Acadian patois told him at least one horse had done just that, and his lips stretched in an ugly grin even as he reached the boy who'd thrown the knife. Steady barreled into the side of the other horse, while Gabriel lashed out with his free hand, grabbing him by the hair and yanking him out of his saddle.

Off to his side, he was vaguely aware of Calico Zac reining his dun out of the way, and gave a momentary prayer of thanks for that—the last thing this needed was for a native to get caught in the fracas.

The boy—Peter—went to his hands and knees in the dirt, scrambling to avoid Steady's hooves, hissing words Gabriel'd wager hadn't been learned at his mother's knee. Breathing heavily, Gabriel slotted the firearm back into its holster and wheeled Steady around for another go. He'd show this boy how to give insult.

"Don't kill him," a voice called out in French, then English, "please, do not kill him." He was tempted to ignore them, the blood rushing in his ears louder than their turnabout pleas, until he heard Isobel call his name.

"Gabriel, no!"

He reined Steady in before the gelding could trample the boy under his hooves, but kept within reach, the gelding between the boy and Isobel and her mare. His chest was heaving, sweat itching his eyes, and the urge to violence thrummed under his skin like the roar of a waterfall.

Something still sane warned him that this was not him. The violence was not entirely his own: there was a snarl of something unworldly within it, hissing for violence and retribution.

No, he thought. No. These were children. Foolish, posturing children, but children. Get thee from me: I do this *my* way.

He forced the rage down, sending it under water and mud to cool. It was harder than it should have been, but it went, snarling resentfully. He shuddered once, as though a haint had touched his skin.

"Gabriel?" Isobel didn't touch him, didn't reach out, but he could feel her there, waiting, her own breath a harsh rasp. She was unharmed.

The other two boys were off their horses now, watching him the way you might watch a ghost cat up on the rocks, reasonably certain it won't leap but not willing to lay bets on it, aware that you won't have time to shoot if it changes its mind. He moved Steady a step away, then another, until there was room for them to get their companion, hauling him to his feet with little care and much haste.

Peter was still snarling, fighting their hold, ready to lunge the moment they let him go.

"Easy, boy," Gabriel said, as much a warning as advice. "Don't go being further foolish."

The rage was gone; he was his own man again, and he didn't wish to hurt the boy any longer, but he would, if it came to that. "Whatever maggot lodged in your brain, to make you behave that way?"

There wasn't a particular rule of hospitality on the Road itself, not the way there was once you'd made camp, but there was a certain courtesy, if you followed the law. You didn't assault a man—or a woman—without cause or insult far greater than anything this boy could have claimed. And if you did, and survived the attempt, a marshal might come pay close attention to you. The sort of attention that typically ended with a bullet between your eyes, and your family burying you for a fool.

"Listen to the man," one of boys said urgently. "Think, you idiot. She's too young to be the same one."

"Je m'en fous."

"The same one what?" Isobel sounded confused, then she said "oh," even as Gabriel realized what the boy was nattering about. Isobel was not the first Hand ever; there was Marie, the Devil's Right Hand, but as far as Isobel had said, she never left Flood. It was only the Left Hand who rode: but the last one had died . . . long ago. Before Gabriel had been born, much less these youths. So long ago that there were only stories left, and none who could tell them firsthand.

It was possible, though, that those stories had been handed down. And equally possible that those telling them had originally come out on the wrong side of the Hand's judgment.

That was a complication he had not anticipated.

"I've offered you no harm," she said. "And I came here with no intent—"

"You're all the same," the boy spat, although he had ceased to fight against those holding him. "All instruments of the devil, the stick that beats us to nothing, the fist that knocks us into the dirt. Your master and you both should have been burned to the ground and your ashes thrown back into the pit from where he came, long ago!"

At that, Isobel went very still. Gabriel was no magician, to sense the winds rising or power gathering, but he knew Isobel, and he knew storms.

"Your papa should have taught you manners, if he could not teach you wisdom," she said, and he could hear the words crackling in her mouth like lightning. "Or sent you across the border, if you refute the Agreement. Nothing holds you to the Territory, if it displeases you so."

"The Territory is ours! You're not wanted, you and yours. Some day—!"

His companion on his right clogged him across the head, and the boy slumped forward midword, unconscious. "His papa and mama will forgive me, even if he does not," his assailant muttered, hauling the body backwards, while the third stood between them and Gabriel, as though to guard their escape.

"Teach him to mind his manners before power," Gabriel told them, one wary eye on Isobel, who was rubbing the fingers of her right hand across her sigil-scarred palm in a manner he did not trust. "Or the next time he opens his mouth, it may be in front of someone less lenient than she, like a magician—or the devil himself."

If that didn't put the fear into them, their deaths would be a mercy to the world.

The horses shifted uneasily but allowed them to remount, the unconscious boy draped forward over his horse's neck, his legs quickly tied to his stirrups.

And then they were gone, riding back the way they'd come, leaving only churned-up dirt and dust, and a swirling, burning sensation in Gabriel's stomach. He turned to his charge, pushing all else aside for the moment.

"Are you all right?"

Isobel took a moment to consider his question, then nodded. "He had terrible aim."

The knife he'd thrown lay point-down in the dirt, only inches from where she'd been.

"Fortunate for him," Gabriel said tightly. He realized his fists were clenched, and thought of cool water, a river in late summer, deep and slow. "Killing them would not have served us well, going into town, no matter how justified it was once he took first blow. It's good warning, though. If well-heeled young fools like that have bought into that nonsense, others here will as well."

He turned to look at Calico Zac, who had dismounted at some point, watching them with wide, cautious eyes. "Did you know anything about that?"

Isobel was using her hat to brush dirt off the back of her skirt, sticky strands of black hair that had escaped from her braid now clinging damply to her face and neck. She frowned down at her boots, then replaced the battered hat firmly on her head. "What nonsense?"

"Free Territory nonsense. The idea that the devil's holding 'em back, keeping 'em from . . . god only knows what. Getting into trouble, most likely. We've seen it before." He waited until she nodded, remembering. Even close to Flood, there were those who saw the devil as, at best, an overly protective parent they'd outgrown.

Most of them had never stepped foot more'n a mile from their homestead, much less knew anything about the world outside. He couldn't blame folk for ignorance, but he assuredly did for foolishness.

"There were some, even before I left," Zac said, slowly. "But your people are often unhappy when told no. They called themselves the . . . organized offense?"

"Organized Offensive," Gabriel corrected him. "That's what they call their pamphlets, the organized offensive. Yeah, I've run into them once or twice. Claiming that the devil's Agreement should not bind the Territory or those within it, who believe that the devil's hold on the Territory corrupts it and them."

He'd not come across any of those pamphlets in recent travels; he'd half-hoped they'd fallen out of favor or otherwise been silenced. But no; it seemed they'd come here, raising a new generation to follow them.

"Organized Offensive?" The name sounded even more laughable in Isobel's mouth.

"Names make small men feel better about their smallness."

Isobel pursed her lips. "Anything with a name also has power."

He couldn't argue that, and yet . . . "Less than they wish to believe, else they'd have made far more inroads than they have."

She nodded but seemed less than convinced. Fair enough: he was less certain than he'd been a day before as well. That much bile in one boy's heart had to be planted early and watered often. And the two with him had stopped him only because he would clearly lose, not because they disagreed.

"Do you know anything more—" he asked Calico Zac, not expecting anything.

Sure enough, the native made an empty-hands gesture. "As I said, I did not pay much attention then, and it has been a long time since."

"They're less of an issue deeper in the Territory," Gabriel said, reaching into Steady's saddlebag for an apple and biting down on it, the crunch of the fruit between his teeth oddly satisfying. "The borders call to 'em, I suspect. But they're not alone here. Everywhere there's an opinion, they pop up like prairie dogs. Folk who don't understand the Agreement protects 'em as much as it restricts 'em, think they can have everything without giving up anything."

"But . . ." Isobel took the apple core from him when he would have tossed it to the ground, and fed it to the mule, who belched in contentment. "Like April."

"Like her, yes." Isobel's childhood friend, who longed for electric lights and cobblestone streets, thinking they came without a price she would have to pay. Gabriel had been in the States, had tried to live that life, and he knew, firsthand, deeper than blood, the price that was asked.

Nothing came without a price. Not power, not freedom, not comfort.

"April never spoke against the devil."

She'd been careful not to, Gabriel remembered. Not that close to Flood. But Isobel, for all that she'd learned and grown, was still innocent to some things. "April knew your boss," he said. "Folk out here, they don't know him 'cept as a name, or maybe someone who rode this way when their grandparents were pups. It's easier to blame him for everything, even things that he's got no hand on." He snorted. "They'd blame him—or you—for their own skinned knees, if people hadn't seen them fall down on their own."

He hated that her eyes still had a wide, shocked look to them, her mouth tight with tension. They'd faced monsters both human and beast, and she hadn't looked that way in the aftermath. She'd sorrowed then, or been angry, or afraid and angry for that fear. But never shocked.

Growing up in the devil's house had protected her. And his job had been to undo those protections, one layer at a time.

Lacking more words that might ease her, Gabriel reached over and chucked her under the chin, pleased when she scowled and knocked his hand away. "My point being, Isobel, you can't do anything about what other people think inside their own heads. You've got enough work dealing with what they *do*."

He could see she wasn't convinced, but he wasn't entirely sure he was, either. So, he left it at that.

"Come on, mount up, both of you. Daylight's wasting, and we've still got a ways to go."

THREE

Isobel slept restlessly that night, her dreams filled with scowling faces and charging horses, and she woke before true dawn feeling as though she'd not rested at all. She could see the long lump of Calico Zac under his blanket, and the shadow of Gabriel sitting upright against the trunk of a tree, the carbine across his knees. She suspected he had not moved since he relieved her at watch around midnight, the way he breathed and the drape of his arm telling her that he was awake, in that odd haze he fell into while on watch that she hadn't been able to learn.

If anything larger than a chicken came near them, he would have been immediately alert.

Sure enough, his head turned as she shifted out of her elevated bedroll, the noise drawing his attention, and she lifted a hand to tell him all was well.

The air was cooler with the sun yet down, but her skin still felt sticky, and there were itches that told her bugs had been to feed while she slept.

They would see the River in a day or two, Gabriel had said. The Mudwater, what the Americans called the Mississippi, and the Spaniards the Espiritu Santo. Gabriel said the Natives who lived on its banks called it Grandmother Waters. It was very near here, long ago, that the devil had told the conquistador de Soto that he could not have these lands, that no mortal would enter the Territory with conquest in mind, and used the power of the river itself to make that oath into truth.

The boss never spoke of it, but there were stories told, when he wasn't around. Of how he'd stood alone, his voice carrying over the waters, and the men who tried to cross anyway all sickened and died, until the remainder turned tail and fled.

Remembering this, remembering that the devil's will was that strong, should have made her feel better. Instead, it shifted her thoughts to the people across the river, pressing up to the banks, forever looking into the Territory and seeing . . . what? What would she see, looking back across the water at them?

Gabriel had studied there, had told her a few stories about the great cities, larger than a dozen Floods, with more people than she had ever seen in her life living in one place. A city of people, like a massive herd of buffalo, left in one place, day in and day out. . . .

Isobel's imagination failed her. She took a fresh dress from her pack, shaking it out before fastening it, then reached for her boots, carefully checking them for visitors before lacing them on. If she wasn't going to sleep, she should water the horses, and rebuild the fire for breakfast.

The horses were sleeping when she approached them, their bodies swaying against each other, heads down as though they'd wake up and start eating again automatically. She pushed at Uvnee's shoulder with her own, letting the mare's warm scent and weight chase the uncomfortable thoughts away. The mare whickered sleepily in response, head lifting to nudge at her rider, while Steady's ears twitched, but otherwise ignored the familiar presence.

The mule, already awake, ducked and backed away like a puppy when she tried to put the halter on, a clear invitation to mischief.

"You're feeling frisky this morning," she said. "You like this heat?" Her fingers wound into the coarse mane hairs, and the skin below twitched under her hand, but the mule's hide was smooth and cool, same as the horses. "If I didn't have to wear clothes, I might feel better too," she grumbled. The sun at high noon in the mountains had been intense enough to bake her skin, but she could wipe away the sweat. Here, even when it was cooler, the damp air made her aware of every breath she drew in, as though her lungs resisted it. "You might not be so happy once the packs are back on, though."

The mule snorted, and tried to eat the edge of her sleep-mussed braid before she pulled it back, hitting the tip of his nose gently with the end in playful scolding. "What have I told you about that?"

The shift of air and the faint crunch of dirt underfoot warned her, seconds before Gabriel came up alongside them. His collar was undone and his hair a sweat-damp mess, and she resisted the urge to finger-comb it for him, the way she might a wayward child's. The brown strands were long enough to curl behind his ears now, and fell over his forehead when he wasn't wearing his hat. She supposed she didn't look much neater, and wondered if them being shorn and clean would have changed the boys' reactions the day before.

Likely not. Pretty was as pretty did, Marie used to tell them, but being pretty wouldn't change a mind convinced you were already ugly.

"You didn't sleep well," he said, less an observation than a statement of fact.

She shrugged, pushing the mule away when it tried to nose into her jacket pocket for a treat. "Well enough. Some dreams, but nothing that woke me. You?"

His throat clenched as he swallowed, but his voice remained steady. "Peaceful as a babe."

Isobel had grown up in a house of women, which meant babies, occasionally. Babies slept no more peacefully than any other creature alive.

"It wasn't your fault." She should have said that the night before. "What people think of the boss, what they think of me, and especially what they do with what they think, none of that's your responsibility."

Especially when it was true. The devil ran an honest house, never forced anyone to the table who didn't choose to play, but there was a difference between bargains and agreements, and the Agreement was one everyone signed just by the fact of living in the Territory. You either lived by it or you left.

Or you died. And there was no recompense for death if you died by foolishness. If Gabriel had killed that boy, it would have been the boy's fault and no one else's.

"That's not . . ." He paused. "I suppose to you that's true."

She nodded, watching the mule trying to pull up a low brush that seemed to be its match in stubbornness, and hoped it wasn't anything that would give the beast a stomachache later. "I've been trying to remember anything I might've ever heard about the boss coming down here, but he never told stories about it, and neither did anyone else. Or . . ." She had never thought about there being a Left Hand before her, but that was foolish, of course. Of course there had been. But . . . when? And what had they done, what had happened that left people so angry even now? "What do you think happened here? To them, I mean. I should have asked . . ."

"If you had, nothing they told you would be useful," Gabriel said. "Bitterness teaches people new words, and they use 'em too much."

She had no idea what he meant by that, but he was still speaking, so she held her tongue and waited. The mule's scarring had turned into pale white stripes along its side, and Steady's lameness had nearly disappeared by now. Uvnee alone seemed unchanged since the morning she'd come out of the saloon to see the brown mare waiting for her, eyes as bright and mouth as soft as that first ride. Isobel suspected the same could not be said of her.

"I think, rather than head directly into town, we should detour. Pay our respects to some of the local chiefs, see if we can't do some trading rather than rely on what the mercantile might have." He nodded a greeting to Calico Zac, who had walked over to join them in time to hear that last bit.

"You'll need something particular to win them over, as I doubt trade has fallen off since I left. They won't be easily bought."

Gabriel made a face, then nodded agreement with Zac's observation. "I should have thought of that. Other than the sheepskin we picked up, that I don't think Isobel will want to give up—"

She scowled at him; she'd traded fiercely for that, and she intended to keep it, short of the devil himself asking for it, and maybe not even then.

"No, but I think you were right. Not about trading, but . . ." Her words trailed off, and she pulled on the end of her braid, as though that might pull what she wanted to say out of her head and into her mouth.

"They will know you rode through." Zac shaped her thoughts for her. "It would be rude to not allow them to offer hospitality."

There was that, and also the thought that if there was trouble brewing between the folk of Red Stick and the boss, she should get a feel for how the local tribes felt, too.

"And I should have thought of that as well." Gabriel sounded downright disgusted with himself. "Coffee might help me wake up. Is—"

"Get the fire going again so you can have your coffee."

The coals had stayed warm overnight, and it was a simple matter of giving them air and some fresh twigs before setting water to boil. Zac brought out a skillet and set it on the fire, the comforting smells of lard and cornmeal combining making her mouth water.

She sat across the fire from him and used a rag and soap powder to wash her face and hands, giving extra effort to her knuckles and nails. By the time the water had boiled, she was, if not clean, certainly presentable by Road standards. But that simply made her aware of how much grime must be on the rest of her skin. A quick whiff of her sleeve made her cringe slightly, and a glance at Gabriel's shirt, with its faint sweat stains at arm and collar, confirmed her suspicions.

"If we're going to go visiting, we might want to look for a place to wash up, first, though."

∾ ∾ ∾

They'd barely gotten back on the Road when it split, forking at an angle deliberately formed to avoid a crossroad.

"If you go that way," Calico Zac said, pointing toward the wider road, "it will take you to Red Stick by way of what was—at least once—a series of larger villages. But this will be where our roads change."

"Your people are along the other road?"

His mouth twisted slightly, a shadow falling over his expression. "They were, once. Now . . . I will find out."

You did not say goodbye on the Road. It twisted and turned and you never knew when you might meet again. But Isobel was aware that they had rarely met anyone twice, and it was with oddly mixed feelings that she watched him ride away.

"Don't you start pining," Gabriel warned her, and she glared at him, then turned Uvnee's head and pushed her into a brisk trot, forcing Steady and Flatfoot to catch up, the mule braying a gentle protest all the while.

The trees around them changed as they rode on, the ground rising and falling in gentle swells that reminded her of the plains near home, although they looked nothing alike. There were too many trees, for one, and far more streams, mostly narrow ditches cutting deep in the loose soil, but one came up wide enough that the water lapped at her knees as they rode through, the current pushing firmly against them, trying to sweep them with it. She held her breath until they reached the other side, keeping her eyes firmly fixed on the rise and fall of Steady's rump ahead of them, reins soft in sweat-slicked hands, aware of the mule swimming alongside.

"A little deeper, and we'd have been swimming too," Gabriel said when they came out the other side, and there'd been an odd tone in his voice, tight and low, that made her hold any questions she had about how they'd *know* if they needed to swim.

They then had to stop and check the animals' legs for leeches, pulling a handful of the wriggly black shapes off and dropping them into the mud.

"Ugh." She flicked the last one off her fingers and double-checked her hands to make sure none of them had somehow found their way back onto her or Uvnee.

"I haven't missed that," Gabriel agreed.

By mid-day, she was noticing a gradual change in the terrain. The ground was still soft and dark, but the trees were different, branches spreading out rather than rising up, and the deep green of leaves and moss made the afternoon sunlight seem particularly eerie. Isobel wasn't sure if the air was becoming dryer or she was simply accustoming herself to it. Since her skirt had still not dried entirely from the creek, she suspected the latter.

She also noted that Gabriel's mood was shifting, although she couldn't quite place a finger on how. They were both quiet, but that was not unusual for them, especially after having a third person with them for days. There simply wasn't anything to say.

And yet, the silence felt oppressive rather than comforting. There was the occasional movement of something in the brush, and the flutter of things overhead, but nothing had shown itself long enough to be identified that she could ask about, and he'd already told her that he didn't know what the massive trees overhead were, beyond "looks like some kind of oak, and the moss is lady's beard. Makes terrible-tasting medicinal tea; if anyone offers it to you, tell them you'd rather be sick."

"Zac said that the local tribes formed a confederation, because they were too small to stand alone? How many tribal villages are there?"

"That's an excellent question, and I can't tell you with any surety."

She made a face at him for that: Gabriel, who made a point of knowing everything about everyone he'd ever met?

"Don't give me that face," he told her. "I can only remember so much, and I can only learn what folk are willing to tell me. There're a dozen tribes in these parts, maybe more, but some of 'em claim lands small enough they've never been marked on a map, and some of 'em are probably small enough settlers never stumbled in on 'em, and they like it that way.

"And then there're those like his cousins, who marry into another tribe and disappear, or splinter off, like your friends in the foothills, who won't have a proper name for a generation or more. And some—"

A shriek cut through his words, causing all three animals to startle and both riders' hands to drop to their knives instinctively. Nothing rushed out to attack them, though, and the sound wasn't repeated.

"Please tell me that was a bird," Isobel said, her voice shaky.

Gabriel was scanning the trees overhead. "Either a bird or a particularly upset haint," he said, and she wasn't certain he was joking. She realized that her fingers were pressing against the sigil in her left palm, and she forced them to ease and open. The power she could draw upon wasn't any use against a haint—they had to be trapped and dismissed with a purely ordinary ritual—and she thought if she used it against a bird, of all things, the entire Territory would know and mock her forever.

There was no cause for her to be on knife's edge. Except she was suddenly aware that she *was*. And if there was a thing she'd learned, it was to listen when her nerves itched.

"Odds are we will run into a haint or two while we're down here," Gabriel said, as though that had been their previous conversation all along. "Some reason, they linger here. Maybe they like the damp, maybe people just don't mind them, maybe something else. But we should restock your salt sooner rather than later."

The supplies she'd been given when she left Flood had included a stick of salt longer than her palm. She'd used enough now that it was barely a stub; silver might tell you where power lingered, and help clear it out, but pure salt scoured, and kept things at bay. He was right: they would need more.

The thought of shopping was a welcome distraction. "There are mercantiles down here?" There'd been none worth the name for weeks past, and while they could always trade work or coin for dried meats or beans, or hard soap, other things were in rarer supply. Like pure salt. And stick candy.

"Red Stick's a trading town, Isobel," he reminded her. "I've a suspicion anything you need, you can get, and if you can't, someone will bring it in from Liberdad, for a price."

Isobel's curiosity about the free city flared again. "Do you think . . . will we get to go there?"

Gabriel sucked in his cheeks, thoughtfully, then said, "I'm not sure that's a wise idea just yet. Or ever. Not for the Devil's Hand, anyways. You've an itch to see the free city?"

She looked at him sideways, then rolled her eyes. "Any reason I wouldn't? It was always . . . just a story before. All sorts came to Flood, but never once anyone from there, never anyone who'd ever even been there. And the boss would just laugh when we asked him about it. Like we'd told him the best joke ever."

"I can imagine he sees it that way," Gabriel said. "It's outside his purview, but it's also a thorn in the sides of both the States and Spain, thumbing their nose at the laws of both. Anything that irks them likely pleases him. City's got the reputation for trouble, but it's more that most of the folk living there are either deserters from the Spanish fleet or slaves escaping from—pretty much everywhere. That makes them prickly about anyone trying to tell them what to do. Every military attempt to bring them to heel's ended miserably for the would-be invader."

"Because they hold the only safe harbor along the coast," Isobel said wisely.

"The only large, safe harbor," he corrected her. "And mayhap more. There's a rumor and it's only far as I know a rumor, that Liberdad's home to medicine folk equal or more powerful than anything within the Territory."

That made her shoulders straighten in reaction, Uvnee coming alert under her. "Even magicians?" What they gave up in sanity, those who went to the winds gained in strength, as they knew from too much firsthand experience. If they gathered there . . .

"Less crazy, more sociable," Gabriel said. "But as I said, it's only rumor. They're powerful enough to not show themselves. Like your boss: folk in need go to *them*."

Everything he said just fed Isobel's curiosity—and her worry. But it was outside the Territory and not particularly friendly to it, either, so the Hand showing up would likely be unwanted at best. Isobel slumped back in her saddle, resigned to the fact that she would likely never see it, save across the banks of the Mudwater.

"Oh." She had a sudden thought. "There'll be a post station in Red Stick?"

"Most likely, yes. You'll be able to send your letters on, probably straight up the River." Her letters, and the packet she'd been carrying for someone else, for what felt like forever. Time to wash her hands of that burden, at least.

"Liberdad may be more interesting, but Red Stick's still the largest settlement in the Territory. If there's anything you need, anything you need sent, any gossip you need to know, it'll be there."

"I'm not sure if that was meant to be an enticement or a warning," she said dryly, and he laughed, adjusting the brim of his hat to shade him from the sun as the road curved into the full glare. "Neither am I, Iz. Honestly, neither am I."

The trees grew more sparsely there, and Isobel caught sight of a wide, slow creek appearing and disappearing behind them. She felt her heart leap in excitement before recognizing that it was nowhere wide enough to be the Mudwater, never mind Gabriel just having told her they were still days away from reaching it. Still, it was wide and looked slow compared to the one they'd crossed earlier, and she wondered if it would be safe to bathe in, if she could convince Gabriel to make camp earlier than usual.

But before she could say anything, he reined in his horse and lifted his hand above his knee, two fingers outstretched. "Ah, look there, do y'see?"

Distracted, Isobel followed his pointing finger, squinting to make out the distant shape of something not too far down the road, where it dipped down into the river. Three thick poles, pale red against the greens and browns of the heavy growth behind them.

"Tribe markers he told us to look for," he said. "There should be a village nearby." He glanced up at the sky, gauging the sunlight remaining. "We'll ride to their border and camp there, and announce ourselves officially in the morning."

"And bathe?" If there was an established ford, the current should be safe for washing, too.

He closed his eyes, likely checking with his water-sense, then nodded. "And bathe."

Gabriel was in trouble. He knew where they were, more or less: although he'd only been this way once before, when he was much younger, the maps he carried in his head and his connection to the Road made getting lost nigh impossible. But he knew better than most how quickly details could change: fires or floods, tribal squabbles or border incursions—or illness, monsters, or malign medicine. Not to mention the not-insignificant risk of wildcats or demon. A wise Rider kept their eyes open; a foolish one became a lesson to others.

And the Road only told you where you were, not what to expect.

That had to be why his nerves were rag-edged, the hairs on the back of his neck prickling, his stomach sour as though he'd eaten too many apples. It had nothing to do with uneasy dreams, or the sense of something pressing against him, watching him out of the corner of their eye . . .

He shook off the unease, forcing his attention entirely onto Isobel, who was currently investigating the remains of what had once been a bridge of sorts.

If it had, however, he suspected it hadn't been intact during

Isobel's lifetime. Rough, water-worn splinters of wood stuck upright on either bank, but there was no sign of where the beams themselves had been, the waters having long ago swept them downriver.

He would have assumed that a storm had made this crossing unsafe, save that the road was still well-marked where it went down to the water's edge and then picked up on the other side, while the slopes themselves were covered in sparse grass and tall stalks of some plant he could not identify, brown and narrow, without flower or leaf. If the ford had been abandoned, vegetation would have taken over by now.

"What do you think?" he asked Isobel when she turned and looked an inquiry at him, expecting him to tell her if it was safe to cross. She made a face at him but turned back to study the water. He waited with the animals while she walked along the riverbank, her hands clasped behind her back. The edge of her skirt dragged a bit, he noted; her hem had come loose. Neither of them were anything more than indifferent menders, but with luck, they would find a seamstress in Red Stick who could put them to rights.

His mind drifted a bit, marking off the items they would need to replace: salt, obviously, and a packet or two of pine tea to ward off scurvy, a new saddle pad for Steady, more powder and shot . . . and hopefully a broadsheet with news fresher than a month past, to know what was happening back East, and in the world beyond.

He might have turned his back on the States, but he didn't for a moment think that they had returned the favor. Jefferson was plotting something, and while knowing in advance wouldn't help any, it would make him feel better to have some sense of the disaster to come. And it would do Isobel good, too, to start looking beyond the borders. He wasn't certain it would help her, but more knowledge was better than less, in her case. Likely.

He hoped, anyway.

And if he could find a smith to sharpen his blades, as long as he was making a list of wishes, that would be useful, too. A whetstone only went so far.

"Gabriel?"

She was calling to him from the edge of the bank, crouched next to the waterline. He joined her, reining in his instinctive reach toward the water, and waited for her to go on.

"Not there," she said, tilting her head toward the wooden shards a few yards upstream, "but here. I think."

He waited, and she blew out an exasperated breath. "All right, fine. Could you please check and make sure I didn't miss anything?"

He grinned at her, then reached out, placing his hand just over the surface of the water. But then he hesitated, something in him screaming caution.

Dowsing, they called what he could do, back in the States. Witch, they would have called him once, and stoned or hung him. Here in the Territory, he was just one of many, one with an almost-ordinary skill that paled before what Isobel could do, with the devil's mark on her. But this was his, born in his blood and bone.

Gabriel would have torn it from his body if he could, for all the trouble it had caused him, but if he couldn't, he'd be a fool not to use it. Still, when instinct advised caution, only a fool ignored it. Water was life, but water could drown, too.

He reached forward with his senses gently, barely an exhale to ripple the surface, and waited, then nodded approval. "There's a tricky current toward the center, but should be safe enough, if we're careful."

It would be embarrassing to survive beasts and ancient spirits and malicious foreigners only to drown fording a creek. Not to mention, explaining that to Isobel's boss would be . . . awkward.

They'd enough practice now reloading the packs that it took them only a brief pause, then Isobel, taking the lead without being told, moved Uvnee down the bank and into the water. The mule snorted and flopped its ears at getting wet yet again, but followed, not wanting to be left behind.

Gabriel gave the water one last glance, making sure that nothing moved under the surface save the flicker and splash of fish and the occasional flop of frogs, then eased his hands on the reins, giving Steady his head to cross at his own speed. The creek was as sluggish as it had seemed on the surface, but the bed below was thick with mud that sucked at the horses' hooves with every step, making it as difficult to cross as its swifter-moving cousins.

And if Gabriel was more tense than expected as they pushed through, the water lapping at the animals' bellies and swirling under their tails, that prickling sense of *something* making him more cautious than usual, he saw no need to mention it.

But there was another lesson he could teach her here.

He waited until they were through the center where, as he'd felt, the currents tried to tangle them up, and almost to the other side before getting her attention. "In the spring, the banks will flood," he said, pointing to where the ground lifted from the water in a gentle incline. "Probably, oh, six feet, maybe more. Good for the soil, bad if you're foolish enough to build there. Even in winter, I wouldn't trust it; one good storm and it could wash you away before you knew there was trouble."

He watched her study the banks, obviously trying to memorize the look and feel of the ground there. It *looked* inviting, the gentle slope giving easy access to the water, easier washing and fetching, or to cast away night soil or refuse. That was the danger, and he had learned the painful way not to trust it. They would make camp farther in and haul the water to them.

Gentle slope or no, without a bridge it wasn't easy to reach the bank; the grass was slick and the brown-stemmed plants were sharp. Even the mule, typically surefooted, slid back a bit as they scrambled out before bounding ahead of them, packs jouncing in its eagerness to get back on dry, solid ground.

Isobel let her skirt fall back over her boots and praised Uvnee for being so good and brave, laughing when the mule came up and shoved its heavy head against her leg, asking for similar praise.

"Yes, and you're even braver, because you didn't have someone on your back to reassure you," she told it as she got down to fix the packs they'd rearranged for the fording, then scratched behind one long, fuzzy ear until the mule's head drooped in pleasure.

Gabriel leaned in his saddle, watching them with amusement. He'd traveled with that mule for years, and it still barely paid him heed, but it was like a puppy around her, greying ears and white-scarred hide practically quivering when she praised it. When they finally parted ways, he might have to accept the mule would likely be going with her, not him.

"Maybe we won't bathe in that, after all," Isobel said as she looked at the mule's legs, then glanced at Uvnee and Steady in turn. Mud caked their legs well above the knee, and nearly to their flanks in the back.

"We weigh less than the horses," he reminded her. "But let's read the poles first and see what's waiting for us before we make any plans."

The markers had clearly, deliberately been placed where anyone crossing the river would see them; no rider or settler would be able to claim ignorance of whose lands they were now on. Gabriel slid out of the saddle, keeping one hand on Steady's reins while he stepped closer to investigate.

With so many languages spoken, the tribes had long ago worked out a way to say, "This is my space, you are—or aren't—welcome here," and when the settlers came in, they'd adapted to it, using sigils and carved words to make their own mark. But the markers there bore only a passing resemblance to the sigil-posts he was familiar with farther north. Rather than stone or ax-shaved wood, these were full sapling trunks, faintly reddish bark intact, the heft of them thicker than he'd expected, thicker around than his hands could span, and scratched from years of claw marks reaching as high up as his chest.

He reached out to touch one long scoring, remembering the claw of the spell-monster that had nearly killed him, the starving fury of the ghost-cat that had attacked them. From the slight intake of breath next to him, Isobel was remembering it as well.

"Nearly three feet long, back paws to front, stretched out," he said, judging the distance from ground to marking. "Long and drawn out; it was sharpening its claws, not attacking. Big beastie. I wonder if that was what we heard scream." He'd rather a live cat than a haint, if possible. Haints were damned unpredictable.

"Or whatever it was hunting," Isobel said, which wasn't actually a more comforting thought. She'd reined her mare in alongside him, and the mule snuck between their horses as though for protection, although there was nothing he could sense, and both horses were calm. Still, Flatfoot was often wisest of the five of them, and Gabriel let his hand rest on the hilt of his knife, sliding under the leather latch of the sheath as he checked around them, letting all his senses take in their surroundings.

Nothing. The road behind and ahead was clear, no dust rising to indicate recent travel save their own, and the now-familiar chirps and trills of the local birds sounded, where if there had been danger, they would have stilled. He'd trusted his instincts for decades; he had no cause to doubt them now. But still, he watched the mule, and was uneasy.

"They're like the post on the road to Clear Rock?"

"Close enough." The marker post there had been taller, unpainted, and the carvings words he'd recognized, but the intent was the same: this is our place, and we have the right of say. Intruders be warned. Or, possibly, ride no farther or be filled with arrows. The inability to read a warning did not negate the result of failing to heed it. Ignorance was not only no excuse, it was a good way to get killed.

"What do these sigils mean?" Isobel asked, pointing to a deep-carved marking showing creamy white against the reddish bark, two horizontal lines with a shorter wiggle between them, wrapping a finger's length across one of the poles.

"The one up top is a confederacy mark," he said, although he was less than certain, himself. "Remember what Calico Zac said about the tribes banding together. Based on this"—and his finger traced a different mark, then another, then the two of them overlapping just below—"I think it tells us that two tribes share this area. And before you ask, I have no idea which tribes." He had a map carried in his memory, but in some places, it might as well be marked "Here there be dragons." "Shall we go find out?"

He was relieved to see her grin, the grim melancholy that had wrapped around her lifting, if only for the moment. She might be the Devil's Hand, but she was a rider, too. And a Rider on the Dust Roads never said no to a journey and always yes to discovery.

The Road on this side of the river was less worn; it had clearly seen fewer riders since the bridge had collapsed—or been removed—and the vegetation had taken advantage on one side, creeping back over the dirt, setting root and spreading branches, while the other side of the trail ran along the river's bank, occasionally crumbling at the edge. Both horses and the mule kept edging toward the middle, which caused a series of ongoing collisions.

"All right, fine," Isobel finally said in disgust, and with a glance back at Gabriel, took the lead, while he and Steady took the rear. Riding single file had more disadvantages than it did advantages, but not enough to argue about.

He frowned at the way the animals shied away from the vegetation, though. Even the mule was staying clear rather than reaching out to take a clump of grass or leaves on the off chance it might be tasty.

Gabriel reached out, fingers stretched, to touch a branch spreading itself over the road, feeling it tremble under his fingers although he barely brushed it.

He kept his hands to himself after that. Some places were uncanny, some more than others, and all a wise rider could do was ride on.

❧ ❧ ❧

They passed three more markers as the daylight shifted toward the west, glinting off the water still flowing sluggishly alongside them. These were different from the first set: where those had been slender poles, these were squat logs about a man's height, set upright, the bark scraped off and the flesh underneath painted red. But the sigils and figures etched into the wood looked to be the same.

Isobel dismounted to better study these, her mouth thoughtful. Gabriel waited; if she had something to say, she would say it in her own time, and they were in no particular rush. The pricking along the back of his neck had subsided, and the mule and Uvnee were both reaching down to grab at bites of grass as they walked, so he presumed—cautiously—that they had passed whatever was making him uneasy. Or it had gotten bored with them and wandered off. Either was possible, and equally probable.

"Stop borrowing trouble," he told himself, reaching forward to pluck a stray brown leaf out of Steady's mane, watching it float slowly to the ground.

Three poles suggested that at least three tribes shared this road or laid claims to the lands around them. Likely, all of them were small populations, like Calico Zac's people, and he wondered how the confederacy he'd described worked, if each tribe sent a representative for a set term, the way they did in the States, or if it was a looser agreement, called on only in times of need, either in defense or to raid other tribes with less risk.

None of Isobel's concern: the devil's Agreement only bound how they dealt with settlers, not each other, but it was an interesting development, and he wondered if the devil was aware of it, or cared.

Isobel was still focused on the marks in front of her. "That says…'Blackwater'? Is that the river or a tribe?"

"Could be either or both. Nearest tribe I know of should be Three Moons, but down here, maps are as much guesses as anything. And even when you know, you don't always know what's happened since you were by last."

She nodded; he'd made a point of reminding her how many tribes there were in the Territory. Her boss likely knew them all, but even he might miss some. Especially if they were small or wanted to be left alone.

She mounted up again, tucking her skirts down with a practiced hand even as she urged the mare forward. He should test her again on her saddleback skills, he thought. Maybe pick up a net somewhere, see how she handled a surprise attack from overhead. A rider wasn't a rider until they could drink coffee and load their weapon while at a full gallop, cursing in at least two different languages. Or so his mentor had told him, many years ago,

He grinned to himself at the memory and let his legs stretch down into the stirrups, feeling Steady shift under his weight, smelling the deep green and wet browns around them, sliding into the awareness where he could practically *feel* the world around him without being aware of any one thing.

Then the short hairs on the back of his neck prickled again, and he rested his hand on the nearest knife, index finger touching the silver inlaid in the hilt. It was still polish-bright; whatever he was feeling, it was not gathering power near him. And Isobel seemed to feel nothing.

He forced his hand away from the blade and let Steady follow the others.

The sky was a deep red behind them, the moon already rising in the low east ahead, when they finally came within sight of the first village. The outer buildings were square-sided and glimmering a smudged white, with sloping roofs made of some sort of thatching. They could see the sparks from fires deep within the village, and the shadows of figures moving along the outskirts of the structures, but no one came their way or hailed them.

"They have wards up," Isobel said, her voice hushed, a hint of hesitation threading through it.

Gabriel couldn't blame her for being leery. Her experience with the mountain town of Andreas and their ancient wards had left her cautious of native wardings; they had learned through experience that not all reacted kindly to the devil's mark crossing them, even when invited.

She let her hat fall back off her head and dangle against her back by the leather cord, and wiped her forehead with the edge of her sleeve. "Should we—"

"We're strangers here," Gabriel said. "We wait until they decide to notice us."

"I knew that," she said under her breath, even as Gabriel dismounted, leading Steady to a slight rise in the ground where they could make camp, well within sight of the village.

"Keep the beasts close by," he told her as they unloaded their gear. This close to Spanish lands, it was likely that horse acquisition by friendly raiding was common, and he didn't have enough trade material to regain them in negotiations on the morning, if that were so.

While Isobel watered and groomed the horses and mule, Gabriel set the coalstone in the center of the ash of previous fires and piled a circle of grass twists around it. A gentle press of the coalstone, and sparks snapped, flying out to catch the tinder, then the dried wood he built around it. The last scraps of the turkey they'd caught riding through Wishita lands would sweeten the taste of the usual soaked beans.

He missed Calico Zac less for his company and more for his spice bag. He should have thought to barter for some before they parted ways.

Waiting for the fire to settle, he rose from his crouch and stretched, fingers reaching for the sky, then bent forward, hearing and feeling something creak. Isobel would want to bathe before dinner, most likely, while there was still light to see by, and he couldn't deny he would too. Turning in a circle, he let his senses creep out again, feeling for the sweet, bright taste of fresh water, tracing it from rivulet to stream, searching for a source steady enough to be useful. It would be outside the village but nearby. . . .

His nostrils flared, and he set off toward the scent, all their water sacks and canteens slung over his shoulder.

His route took him past where Isobel was pushing at Steady's hindquarters, getting him to lift a leg for her.

"How's that haunch doing, hmmm? I saw you favoring it, yes, and so did he, so don't pretend you're fine."

Steady snorted heavily, turning his neck to nip at her backside while she was bent over.

"And none of that, you, or I'll bind up your tail so you can't swat at the bite'ems," she warned. Gabriel's lips twitched; Steady knew better than to bite a presented backside, but knowing better didn't mean he wouldn't, occasionally.

One hand held Steady's hoof, while her other ran up and down his leg, looking for unusual warmth or sign of swelling. "All right, you take it easy tonight, and we'll check again in the morning."

Between that, and Flatfoot's scars from the ghost cat's attack, and Uvnee's wet-eye, the horses were starting to show a bit of Road-wear. As were their riders. Gabriel thought a stay somewhere civilized for a few weeks would likely be good for everyone. Relaxation, regular meals, softer beds and maybe even a bath . . .

Yeah, they'd all feel better once they were in Red Stick.

Isobel watched her mentor over the low remains of the fire, her hands methodically scraping grease off the pan. He was looking up at the sky—what they could see of the sky, she amended—one hand rubbing at his neck thoughtfully, as though considering using some of the left-over water from their sponge baths for shaving. Except he'd shaved not two days before, and his usual pattern took him a week before he decided the scruff had grown enough to be irritating.

Whatever he was looking at, she thought, it wasn't in the sky or trees above them but somewhere inside.

She'd noticed him doing that more and more. If she spoke to

him, he would respond, but always with a sense of reserve, as though she'd pulled him from worrying thoughts. It was recent, but Isobel hadn't been able to finger when or where it had started. Not Andreas, which had been her first thought. The deaths and revelations that had happened there had shaken them both, but they'd talked about it, during the endless hours of riding, and she'd thought she—they—had managed to put it aside, at least for now. Then she'd thought that he was growing tired of her company. He'd said he'd mentored people before, but surely not for this long. He was accustomed to riding alone, after all, not tied to whatever lessons he and the boss felt she needed to learn.

Then they'd joined up with Calico Zac, and it had gotten better for a bit, or maybe she had been distracted from noticing, with the change, but ever since Zac had left, it was back again.

No, it was back worse.

She worried. But she would not ask.

Isobel listened to the noises around her: past the shuffling and breathing of the horses, past the slow sound of Gabriel's breathing, noticing the noises she'd become accustomed to, the squeak of frogs and the low click and rustle of insects, the occasional yip of something hunting along the river. She didn't know the nights there, but it sounded peaceful. Good sleeping weather. They'd set a salt circle around the campsite, invoking hospitality protection but nothing else, not wanting to risk offending the village, who were undoubtedly watching them, waiting to see what they would do.

She dropped her hand to the ground, feeling the grass prickle against her skin, grains of dirt cool and damp. Pressing deeper, she felt the bones, deep below, a soft grinding hum.

She had thought, once, that everyone could do this, the way everyone could feel warnings around a town, or riders could feel the Road. Learning otherwise had thrown her, uncertain if she remembered her memories from before becoming the Hand properly, or if this was something else the devil had given her leave to do.

It was as natural as breathing now, calming the way her favorite doll used to be.

Gabriel finished whatever he was doing and knocked the remaining sticks away from the coalstone. It glimmered sullenly in the ashes, a reddish glow, enough to illuminate their bedrolls slung above the ground nearby, leaving the horses darker shadows in the night. She looked up and saw the faint glimmer of stars splayed like countless coalstones, the moon a near-empty curve hanging low over the trees.

Distantly, she could hear noises coming from the village, the clatter and rumble of people living in proximity. Three weeks on the Road, sleeping under the open sky, and she had almost forgotten those homely sounds. It caused an ache in her chest, but she wasn't sure if it was longing or simply the memory of some time long ago, of a person she no longer was.

The Devil's Hand had no home.

"It may be a long day tomorrow," Gabriel said, his voice rough and graveled, as though he'd forgotten how to use it. "People. Talking. Making nice. Probably a late night, if we're welcomed. Get sleep now."

She nodded, her body in agreement, as a yawn caught her off guard, and he laughed.

Isobel threw a rude gesture at him, then stripped down to her chemise and pulled off her boots before climbing into her bedroll, where the chorus of insects accompanied her down into sleep.

FOUR

She was running. Her feet slapped against the ground, the dirt rough and warm, her heart pounding in her chest, breath whistling through her mouth, heavy forms warm against her sides, a musky stink filling her nose.

Something chased them, but they did not care. The ground was forever, and they were forever, and the sky was forever and they were forever.

And then the sky went black and the ground disappeared, and they were falling, falling . . .

Isobel woke to the smell of a wood fire and meat sizzling, and opened her eyes in panic at the thought that she'd overslept, that Gabriel had let her oversleep. Sitting up, she blinked in surprise at the elder crouched by the firepit. At first, she thought him a continuance of her dream, the long grey hair and bare skin of his upper body not quite real to her eyes.

Another moment, and she recognized that the smell of something warm and spicy cooking came from their own fire, now built to a crackling blaze. She was awake. This was real.

She couldn't see from where she'd slept if their warding circle had been disturbed, but cooking over someone's fire wasn't a particularly hostile act. Still, Isobel glanced sideways at Gabriel, who was already awake, his feet bare under his trousers and his shirt loose over his unmentionables and open at the neck as though he'd just rolled out of bed.

The last time an elder had appeared at their fire like that, he had been a useful guide, if beyond frustrating, since he spoke neither English nor Spanish, and Isobel did not speak enough French to join the conversation between him and Gabriel. She hoped this would not be an echo of that; she might scream.

The old man pulled a pot off the fire, frowning at whatever was in it, then used a fingerling knife to pull several palm-shaped objects out, dropping them onto a plate.

One of *their* plates, the battered tin immediately recognizable, as on second glance was the pot the old man was using. Isobel sighed. If this individual could cross over hospitality wards without setting them off, it was to be expected their supplies would be considered fair taking.

She didn't recognize what now rested on the plate, reddish-brown and soft from boiling, but Gabriel clearly had no such hesitations, picking one up with his own blade, polished and far deadlier, and taking a bite out of the tuber.

"Groundnut," he told Isobel without looking at her. "Taste a bit like turnip. Can give you the belly, though, so be careful. Only take enough to be polite."

There seemed to be no rush, so, unlike Gabriel, she took the time to dress properly, pulling her skirt up over her stockings and fastening the shirt she'd slept in so that it covered her properly at wrist and neck, then shaking out and pulling on her boots before joining them at the fire. Her hair she left unbraided but pulled over one shoulder to keep it neat.

The old man looked up as she joined them. His face was pocked skin pulled tight over hard bones, but his eyes were soft, and the faintest hint of a smile eased his stern expression. He reminded Isobel of Iktan, the bartender back in Flood, although they looked nothing alike save they were both old and male.

She dropped her gaze politely and took the plate from Gabriel, using a fork from their kit rather than her knife to claim her tuber. It opened easily under the prongs, the skin soft and the insides nearly mush. She popped half into her mouth and chewed. It was bland but warm, and Isobel had eaten far worse, before. Even discounting her own early attempts at trail cooking.

"Por que você está aqui?"

The old man's accent was odd, but his words were mostly recognizable. Isobel felt a twinge of disappointment that she would not be called on to test her much-improved trade-sign, at the same time feeling relieved that she would not be called upon to test her trade-sign. She waited for Gabriel to respond, then realized that he was looking to her.

Oh.

She licked her lips, and put down her fork, giving all her attention to their company, focusing on the edge of his collarbone and the sharply-wrinkled line of his neck.

"Mi nombre es Isobel née Lacoyo, de Flood." She paused, waiting to see if he understood. The way his eyes narrowed at the end, she thought he had.

"Mulher do diabo."

She had no idea what he had called her, but he'd gotten the important part, at least. She lifted her hand and made trade-sign for "good enough," and the old man broke into an unexpected grin, showing pink gums and crooked teeth.

"O diabo é ben-vindo".

That, she understood. The devil was welcome.

The old man was called Xaquin, and he had been sent to bring them into the village. The younger children flocked around them as they entered, staring and giggling, while the women called out mocking comments that earned them a flick of Xaquin's wizened fingers in return, making them cackle like geese.

Isobel watched as Gabriel's ears turned red under his hat at something one of the women called, and giggled until he turned to glare at her.

"I'm sorry. It's only that they seem so . . ."

"Casual?"

"Unworried," Isobel said softly, watching the children dart about, bare feet dirty and faces scrubbed clean. The last children she had seen lived where an ancient, enraged spirit shook the ground, and the Territory itself could barely keep it constrained. They would grow up knowing uncertainty, not ease.

"Don't look for trouble where there is none," Gabriel warned her, his blue eyes squinting at her in mock reproof. "Not every corner of the Territory is in need of the Devil's Hand, Isobel. They got along perfectly well with marshals and riders and their own sense for years before you were born."

Isobel pulled a face at him, then turned her attention back to the villagers. The few men she saw had the same pock-marks on their skin as Xaquin, while the children and most of the women were clear-skinned. A disease that struck only the men? Or a ritual scarring? Impossible to ask without offending, so she tucked the question away and simply took it all in as their guide took them to an open-sided, high-roofed structure at the center where four figures waited for them. Their hair was long, like their guide's, but bound up with long feathers in a way that looked formal.

"Chiefs," Gabriel said quietly, as though she hadn't already figured that out. Closer observation showed subtle differences in their appearances, although she couldn't place a finger on them without staring rudely.

"I am Breaks the Branch," one of them said, his hands open and palms facing them. "This is my village. With me stand Elijah"—and the second man, with a stern, drawn face and surprisingly green eyes, nodded gravely at them—"Seven Toes"—and Isobel managed not to smile at the name, even as the third man raised a hand in acknowledgment—"and Bitter Storm.

"We speak for those who sleep and hunt these lands."

Isobel glanced at Gabriel, her own thoughts reflected in his eyes. Runners must have been sent out the moment they were spotted, and Isobel doubted they did that for any stranger who wandered into their territory. Which meant they knew who and what she was well before Xaquin had entered their campsite.

They had been readying themselves for a visit from the Devil's Hand. Had Calico Zac warned them? And if so—what had he said?

Isobel did not know if they were expecting some show of magic or power; if so, they would be woefully disappointed. "I am Isobel née Lacoyo Távora of Flood, also known as the Devil's Hand. This is my mentor, the rider Gabriel Kasun, known as Two Voices."

There was a moment of stillness, but it was considering, not shocked, confirming her suspicion that they'd known full well who she was when they sent an elder to greet them. Typically, in native campments, once introduced, she and Gabriel were treated simply as two more riders, welcomed to the fire with due ceremony and—often—some small jabs or mockery that Gabriel told her was a compliment, not insult.

None of that was present here. Instead, a fifth man, draped in a cape made of feathers and white fur, came forward to speak in an unknown language, Xaquin stepping forward beside him to translate softly.

"The people of the Moons Confederacy have heard of the hawk that flies to the Old Man's hand. They have heard that she bears feathers of her own, the regard of other People. That she speaks fiercely and fights bravely but does not seek quarrel where there is none. These things we hear of the one named Little Sharp Beak."

Gabriel made a noise that might have been a muffled laugh, but his expression remained seriously intent, and she worked to do the same, biting the inside of her cheek to stay still.

"The people of the Moons Confederacy abide by the Agreement made with the Old Man. We have offered no insult to the settlements, nor made harmful treaty with Those-Across. We acknowledge Little Sharp Beak and Two Voices, and welcome them to our fire, that they may extend safe protection over our people, too."

Safe protection from what, Isobel presumed she was already supposed to know, from the expectant look on the medicine man's face.

When in doubt, imply you know everything. She could see the boss in her memory, unlit cigar tucked into his vest pocket for once, his hands busy not with the expected deck of cards but with a small lump of silver, flowing and reshaping itself under his touch. *That way, they will tell you whatever you need to know, thinking you already know it.*

Isobel still wasn't comfortable with formal speech; she tended to be more eloquent when angry, which Gabriel said was probably a mark of the Left Hand as much as the sigil, but that didn't help here and now. "We are comforted by your words and your hospitality," she said, pausing long enough for Xaquin to translate her words in turn. "A long road is made easier by shared fires."

Accepting hospitality, yes. Implying a desire for a longer relationship, yes. And no mention of the boss, so this wasn't official, unless they chose to make it so; good.

The welcoming concluded, two young women came forward, their faces flushed and eyes bright, to usher them to a small but well-built hut with a firepit in the center, rafters along the sides for storage, and a hole in the roof for the smoke to rise through. Their belongings were brought in after them, while they were informed in slow but clear English that the horses and mule were to be turned out with the tribe's own small herd of horses.

The older of the two women then turned to Isobel. "Do you wish to bathe?"

Isobel would have been offended by the implication that their sponge-baths the night before had not been sufficient, save she was driven near to tears by the offer. "Please. Yes."

It wasn't until she reached the steam-house and encountered other women within that she realized that the offer had been made only to her, not Gabriel, and why. The women within were all older than she, their hair graying, their bodies wrinkled, and they had no shared language, but they giggled and smiled much as the girls Isobel had grown up with, cautious but not frightened of this stranger in their midst, and any awkwardness on her part was quickly washed away with the sweat and grime.

She walked back to the hut they had been given, her thoughts drifting to the saloon. Practical Catie, and Sarah, Rosa, Peggy, Lisabeth, little Alice . . . She couldn't remember their faces, only the sounds of their voices, chattering at each other, almost indistinguishable. Even Marie and Ree's faces were blurred, she realized, and she could not be certain Iktan was as she thought she remembered him, or if she'd replaced him with another bronze-skinned expression.

She thought it should bother her more, that she was losing memories of her childhood. But they would still be there when she returned, and she could relearn them then.

Back in the hut, Gabriel was sitting cross-legged on one of the sleeping pads, cleaning his boots. They had been dark brown once, a design tooled along the heel, but now the leather was a beaten, faded tan and the designs merest hints. Still, he cleaned them carefully. His hair was damp and his skin warmly flushed, so she determined that there had been a steam-bath for men as well.

Gabriel took one look at her, seeming to recognize that she felt off-balance, though he could not guess the reasons for it. "They wouldn't have welcomed us if they meant us ill."

"I know that," she snapped at him, then sighed. "We should have asked Calico Zac more. Do you know anything at all about their customs?"

"No more than you," he said, not looking up from the oilcloth in his hands. "And expecting one tribe to be like another is like expecting a Spaniard to be like a Statesman, Isobel.

"I do know that confederation doesn't make 'em all one family group; just allows them privileges and obligations that would normally only be given to family. More likely to intermarry, too, I'd suspect. Them being anxious to make nice makes me think they're feeling spooked about their other neighbors."

That matched her suspicions, too. "Settlers?"

"Maybe. Or the folk cross-river. They mentioned 'em specific, so there's an issue there, trust me. I'd be surprised if they didn't see raiders every now and again."

"But not the local settlements, not from Red Stick, else they'd have requested aid."

Gabriel did look up at her then. "Are you sure they haven't? Or that they won't, once we've eaten at their table?"

It was a fair, if cold, question. The boss hadn't told her anything before sending her out, and it was entirely probable that she'd not seen, or not understood what she had seen, any requests that came in while she was still indentured. The boss played his cards so close to his vest, they might as well be underneath.

She combed out her hair, feeling the smoothness of the wooden comb and the dampness of her hair under her fingers, and tried not to worry at things she didn't even know yet.

"They left you clothing," he said, nodding to a small bundle tied with cord by the door. "We're expected to put on a show for each other, so if you have any gewgaws or jewelry you brought along, wear it now."

"Any gewgaws other than the ones you told me not to pack, 'cause I wouldn't need them on the road?"

He grinned, not even a little abashed at her comment. "Those, yeah."

When their escort came for them at dusk, Isobel was wearing the skirt she'd been given, the dark blue cloth draping softly over her hips, tucked with neat darts at a loose waist and falling to the toes of her boots. She had braided her hair into two plaits, the way the women in the steam hut had, and fixed her two small feathers in one braid so that they fell just behind her left ear. In addition to the brightly polished silver ring on her hand that she never took off, a small carved cameo dangled from a dark red band at the hollow of her throat, and thin, polished wooden bracelets jangled on her wrists. She'd glared at Gabriel when she drew the cloth bag hiding the jewelry out of the bottom of her kit, but he'd looked toward the ceiling and said nothing.

He had dressed in his own clothing, trou and tab-collar shirt, boots shining with polish, but a double-banded necklace of polished white beads and blue shell now hung around his neck that she was reasonably certain he'd not had before.

Unlike earlier, their escorts were three men, two older and one younger than Isobel, who blushed when she looked at him. All three were bare-chested, their faces painted with black stripes, and their hair cut short on the sides and twisted into a knot at the back. Their voices were soft, but their postures were stiff, their gazes flickering everywhere but her face. Gabriel pushed his elbow against her side, speaking softly, out of the corner of his mouth. "You're making them nervous, Isobel."

"I'm making them nervous?" She kept her voice low and even, her hands loose, her eyes downcast, as they were led through the gathered crowd, and offered seats. "They're acting like I might bite or sting at any moment. That makes me nervous."

That wasn't what was making her nervous, and they both knew it.

Gabriel would be the first to admit that he had not been expecting an elder to not only greet them but feed them, nor to meet not with one chief but several, nor to be escorted to dinner by men who likely belonged to their medicine society. But he chose to take this as a positive thing, not a warning. Even when the tribes were unhappy with the devil, which was often enough, they were not foolish enough to attack his Hand without cause, and Isobel was not foolish enough to give them cause now.

And yet, he was uneasy. The feeling of being watched, of being pressed by something, had not returned, but in its place was a more familiar concern that only grew as the meal went on.

He took the offered plate of food from the young woman and nodded politely in acknowledgement, not meeting her eyes or smiling. Next to him, Isobel made a game attempt to eat, but he could see that she wasn't tasting the food, her throat working too hard to swallow.

They had known who Isobel was. Knew *what* she was. And yet they had said nothing directly save polite chitchat that would have been as at home in a parlor in Philadelphia, teacups balanced on knees, as it was in a shagwood pavilion in a summer camp on the banks of a Territorial river.

There were many things Gabriel had learned, riding the Road. The first was that when things were bad, you shouted the danger and worried about niceties later. The second was that when things were particularly bad, you eased your way into it, in the hopes that someone else would be fool enough to step into the mess instead.

He said none of this to Isobel. She knew enough; adding to her worries would only make her hesitate, doubt, when she needed to be decisive.

And their staring could not help matters any. Not all, but enough, particularly those seated along the sides, were staring and then recollecting themselves before it became insult, then looking back as though unable to stay away.

He looked sideways at his companion, trying to see her as they might. Her hair was in two braids, not quite as dark as theirs but just as long, tucked forward over her shoulders, the two feathers she had been given by the dream-speaker months before woven into the strands by her left ear; the edges of the small brown feathers were bedraggled by now, fluttering as she breathed. Her jawline was tense but strong, the skin stretched over it a healthy brown. Her hands were steady on the wooden utensil, the rise and fall of her chest a little too fast, but other than that, no one would know she was not completely calm.

Enough, he decided. The longer this facade continued, the more her unease—and theirs—would grow. Best to call their bluff and see what cards they were holding.

He waited until there was a brief lull, then coughed politely, indicating that he wished to speak. When the elders nearby tilted their heads toward him, he put his platter and utensil down and rested his hands in his lap, fingers pressed together, until Xaquin stepped forward and nodded at him, indicating that he was ready to translate as needed. "Respected elders. We thank you for your welcome and your hospitality.

"I am Gabriel Two Voices, and I have been given the care and protection of this person." His hands made the sign for brother-uncle, then guard dog, and one of the chiefs' lips ticked upward. Arrogance—that he might consider himself the Hand's guardian—and humor, that he took the role of dog, and the confidence to bring them together. That was the road to follow. "I have brought her here, and she wishes to speak with you."

Gabriel hoped she was ready.

And then he wasn't sure why he'd even worried.

She stood as well, and her voice was soft, but it carried over the space, her even tone more impressive than a shout. "As my companion says, we thank you for your shelter and care. I would give a gift of equal value but have only my humble skills." She did not open her palm; she had no need to. "If something troubles your thoughts, I would offer my ear to hear them."

That was all. That was all she needed to say, to ask. To make the offer, so that they were not requesting aid but accepting her gift. Gabriel realized he was holding his breath and forced himself to exhale normally.

The hosting chief looked at his companions, then all there turned to a figure seated off to the side, the fifth man from earlier, still clad in his cloak, who . . .

Gabriel would not have sworn under oath that the man rolled his eyes, but the man rolled his eyes.

"Thank you for speaking so plainly," the man said in English. His voice was stronger than Isobel's and deeper, but he spoke as softly, as though this were a conversation between the two of them, not cast over the distance of the dais, or listened to by dozens around them.

The fact that he was likely not being ironic, that to them that had been plain speaking, would have made Gabriel smile in any other circumstance.

The cloaked man did not look at anyone for permission, but went on. "We have always lived here. The two rivers feed us, the ground holds us, the winds free us. This is our place, our bones the bones of the earth."

The familiarity of storytelling—different words but the same rolling tone—did make him smile, even as his mind sorted the words, looking for what would be important.

"The people have always lived here, although we have been called many names. When the first pale men came, we welcomed them. They abided by the Old Man's words. They built their homes by the break in the river. They hunted the smalldeer and the pheasant. They learned our words and taught us theirs. It was good. Some of their children came to live with some of ours. Some of our children chose to live with theirs. This was good."

Gabriel was the son of a métis woman. Marriages between settlers and natives weren't always good or easy.

"Across the border-river, the Mudwater, other people live. They do not know our words. They trade with our settler-cousins. They speak words with them."

Next to him, Gabriel felt Isobel straighten, although she hadn't seemed to move.

"I do not know what words they speak to each other. But when we trade with the towns now, there are looks. There are whispers. We do not know what the other people say, but the winds and the waters hear these whispers. The winds and the waters become uneasy."

"Bluecoats come look at us," one of the warriors interjected, looking only slightly abashed when the medicine man glared at him for interrupting. "They only look from their flatboats, but they look long."

Soldiers, on barges, remaining within the running waters of the river-border. That would be enough to make the devil restless, if he felt it, but nothing that could be considered a challenge.

Yet.

Isobel's breathing hitched; she was likely thinking the same thing. Particularly after their encounter with the US Marshal, and the warning Gabriel had received of a "corps of exploration" sent by the new President to survey the Territory.

Looking. Poking. Setting words to do what they could not with weapons.

One of the chiefs, the one named Elijah, lifted his hand, palm up, and the medicine man nodded at him. His hands were badly scarred, palm to wrist, as though he'd grasped a burning log at some point.

"My grandmother was a pale rider," he said. "She has gone back to the bones"—died, Gabriel translated in his head—"but as she weakened, her dreams became stronger. Her last dreams, this winter, were of a fish on the shore, an owl covered in snow, and the river waters rising red."

Gabriel swallowed, his mouth dry. Not all dreams meant something. Dreaming true was a gift—a curse, mayhap—and dying did not grant someone gifts they did not have before. Mostly. But the image of fish, of red waters rising . . . Had he dreamed something similar recently? If he had, he did not remember it. But he was no dream-walker, for all that Old Woman often walked in his, and water did not tell him all of its secrets.

What he did know was that water did not care about humanity. Like the winds, it flowed as it would, over bone and under sky, and if flesh stood in its path, it washed over and around them without pausing. Flesh came from bone and water, but only bone cared.

Water is, he heard in his memory, Old Woman Who Never Dies's bent and wrinkled finger an inch from his nose, crooked as though to pull his stubbornness from him. *Water is.*

Everything is, Old Woman, he thought back at the memory, then realized suddenly that the young chief had finished speaking and there was silence.

The silence lengthened, and someone in the crowd coughed, quickly shushed. A child in the distance raised its voice in a yell, and a dog barked. Gabriel's skin prickled, deeply aware of every speck of dust, every rustle and exhale, the smell of the food left uneaten on his platter, the faint familiar stink of Isobel's skin and clothing next to him. His knee itched, and his back ached, and he felt the urge to spring up, to stride around the camp, to gesture and make as much noise as he possibly could.

"You have welcomed us into your home, shared your hearth, and spoken of your concerns," Isobel said. "And we have heard them."

There was no roll of thunder, no sudden silence, but Gabriel, watching the faces of the men sitting opposite them, knew they too heard the power that rested on her tongue when the Devil's Hand spoke. If they intended to ask for . . . anything, now was the time.

"It was our honor to welcome you," Breaks the Branch said. "And our honor that you heard our words."

The moment passed. Isobel nodded, and picked up her platter and utensil once again. Around them, others began eating as well, the small hum of conversations resuming.

Gabriel stared at his own platter, his appetite gone.

The story they'd been told was tacit acknowledgement that the tribe—the confederation of tribes, so probably every village in the area—knew something was wrong, something that involved them. But they would not ask the devil for help in dealing with it.

Why? What stopped them?

Gabriel was afraid he knew the answer.

FIVE

Isobel could feel a scream of frustration rising and strangled it through sheer force of will, fists clenched tightly enough she could feel her nails digging into the flesh of her palms. "I can't do anything for them if they won't ask!"

There wasn't enough room in the space they had been given to pace, and nothing she could throw, or hit, that would not end badly.

Seated in a comfortable crouch across from her, Gabriel's fingers were restless on his thigh, tapping and stretching and tapping again, the only sign that he felt even a hint of her own frustration and irritation.

The meal had been over long enough for them to have been escorted back to their hut, and for the sounds of a full village to gradually fade to quieter noises, human voices subdued under the weight of the night air. Despite scrubbing her teeth with cleaning powder, she could still taste the fish they'd eaten between her teeth and on her tongue, the tangy-sweet flesh lingering as a ghost, and she wondered if she would be required to salt herself to be rid of it. Tea would help, or whiskey. They had neither.

Something was wrong there. Something that disturbed their dreamers, made their hunters uneasy, their chieftains uncertain. But even with pale rider blood in their veins, it was not enough to call her officially. Isobel could feel that as she felt the devil's sigil in her palm, the black lines still and cool in her flesh. They had to *ask* before she could do anything for them.

If there is a threat, I need to face it, she wanted to rage at it. *What use am I if you will not wake when help is needed?* But rage was useless. They would not ask for help, for whatever reason. But she was aware that something was wrong. That was a place to begin.

"You know water," she said. "They spoke of the river, of fish on the banks, of people across the river. Did you . . . Have you felt anything . . . off?"

She thought he would have told her, if he had. But maybe he didn't realize what it was, or that it would be important.

She realized her leg was starting to twitch in sympathy with the tapping of his fingers, and she forced it to still, tucking it underneath her and rearranging her skirt to give her hands something to do. The fire in the center of their—hut, she supposed it was, although better made than any hut she had ever seen, the ground firm-packed and the walls well-chinked—crackled and popped, and sparks rose with the smoke, drifting slowly out the hole in the center of the roof. A dog howled somewhere in the camp, but otherwise, the night was still.

"No," Gabriel said, finally. He seemed to realize his hand was tapping, and made a fist with it instead, thumb rubbing over his knuckles. "But that . . . doesn't mean anything. They're here; they're going to feel it first. A fish on the banks, an owl covered in snow. They're not the most troubling of omens, but they're definitely omens. What do your . . ." He hesitated, then went on. ". . . your instincts tell you?"

"The sigil's quiet; I haven't . . ." She bit back what would have been an excuse. He hadn't asked what the sigil or the whisper was telling her, but what *she* felt. "They're screaming at me," she admitted. "But screaming is remarkably unhelpful." Her tone became acerbic with that last, and he chuckled, releasing some of the tension that had filled the air.

Gabriel shrugged. He had stripped off his jacket and thrown it over his pack when they retired for the night, pulling off his boots and placing them by his bed, but otherwise had not prepared for bed. They were both exhausted. Surely, this conversation would be more productive in the morning?

But she didn't want to think about the dreams she might have if she tried to sleep now.

There was the sound of something scuffling the ground outside their hut, then a voice. "Little Sharp Beak. May I speak?"

The voice was vaguely familiar. Gabriel glanced at Isobel. "It's your dwelling," he told her. "You have to allow him in."

She made an "oh" face and stepped forward, lifting the flap to reveal one of the chiefs from the earlier gathering. Bitter Storm, she remembered. Not much for talking, but a very intent listener. He waited, dark eyes intent on her face, his body practically singing with apprehension.

"You are welcome to here," she said, stumbling a little over the formality of the language despite all Gabriel's coaching.

Bitter Storm made a gesture of what she thought was either thanks or acceptance, then ducked his head to enter. Only when the door flap closed behind him, hiding him from view, did some of that tension seem to ease.

His hair was loose rather than roached or braided like the others, and this close the lines around his face looked to be of tension, not age.

Isobel waited, then glanced at Gabriel, realizing that he was not going to take the lead this time. "It is late," she said, turning back to Bitter Storm. "You have something to say that could not be said by the fire?"

"The words spoken by the fire were truth," Bitter Storm said. His

hands rubbed against the sides of his legs, that nervous tension returning. Or a new tension, she decided, studying the man. Before, he had
simply not wanted to be seen entering the strangers' dwelling. Now
something else bothered him. Was he uncomfortable speaking to the
Devil's Hand in private? Or was there something else?

"They spoke the truth," she said carefully. "But not all the truth?"

"The confederation was a good thing; it saved our people from
being washed away until we were nothing more than memory. But
my village, we live closer to Red Stick than most. When the white
men first came across the river, we were the ones who welcomed them.
They learned our names, and we learned theirs. It was good between
us for many years."

"And now something has changed between you?"

He made a sideways gesture with his hand, meaning uncertainty,
hesitation. "A shift in the current. Nothing we can speak of, nothing
we can touch and say, 'This is wrong.' But yes."

"Why come to me?" Isobel needed him to say it. Someone had to
ask the Devil's Hand for aid; she could not offer it.

He looked sideways, the shadows on his face deepening. "You
know their ways. You know their words. You may understand something that we do not."

Gabriel leaned forward then, breaking what seemed to be an
impasse. "You wish her to go into Red Stick and determine . . ."

"Learn what they mean with these new words, these looks they give
us!" The words were an exasperated explosion, and she realized that
he understood the roles they had to play but resented them, resented
having to ask a woman—an outsider—to do what he could not, to
help his people.

But she needed him to speak the words. "And then?"

He glared at her then, and Isobel glared back, aware of how very
much the two of them likely looked like two hens squaring off over a
corner of the scratch-yard. If so, she'd show them a little sharp beak. . . .

"And mend it," Bitter Storm said, biting his words off. "Whatever it is. These are your people acting wind-knocked, Devil's Hand. Find what ails them, and heal it."

The sense of the chieftain's presence lingered after he'd left, turning to shoulder through the door-flap like the storm of his name.

"Be careful what you ask for . . ." Gabriel said softly. "It's not only the devil who answers, sometimes."

"You're no help whatsoever," Isobel said, collapsing onto her pallet in a sprawl of exhaustion that would have had Marie scolding her for indelicacy back home. There was a faint dark stain on the skirt, and Isobel rubbed at it with one finger, wondering if she was expected to return the garment or if it was hers to take, and who she could ask, how much offense the question itself might give.

"You don't want help; you want someone to tell you what to do."

She made a face but could not contradict him. She did, rather desperately. She also knew he wasn't going to be the one to do that.

"If we were to play with the law," Gabriel began, rubbing his fingertips thoughtfully, as though missing the feel of reins between them, "Bitter Storm may not speak for the confederation, but as a representative here he may be considered the voice of his particular village. In such a case, his request that you *do* something about the situation could be construed as a formal request for aid from that village, as it is more directly affected by . . . whatever it is he feels is happening."

"Don't advocate at me," she said. "This isn't a courtroom, a judge isn't here, it's just me."

"Your authority is equal to that of judge and marshal," he reminded her, voice softer than before. "And, in this situation, would take precedence. Ignore the sigil. Ignore the restrictions of the Agreement."

She opened her mouth to tell him that was impossible, when he held up a hand, stopping her. "What do you *feel*, Isobel?"

"Confused. Angry. Worried. Tired." She ticked them off on the fingers of her right hand, then folded all four fingers back into her palm, curling them around the thumb. Gabriel wasn't the only one accustomed to worrying the reins while he thought, she realized, and almost smiled. A proper Rider, indeed.

"Tired is a given. Worried, too. Confused . . . well, yes. But why are you angry, Isobel?"

This was familiar, this back-and-forth, Gabriel leading her along the dual paths of logic and emotion. She held on to that familiarity, let it guide her.

"Because if I choose wrong, if I do the wrong thing, or I fail to do the *right* thing, the people here may decide I am not to be trusted, that the devil is not to be trusted . . . that the Agreement is not to be trusted."

And trusting the Agreement was what kept the Territory safe for everyone. It was not just a single rule but a nest of them, guiding and shaping how the Territory grew.

But what of those in between? The Agreement bound only settlers, taught them how to behave. But tonight they spoke of intermarrying, settlers and native. And Isobel had seen the children of such families before, up in the mountains: cast out of tribes, unwelcome in settlements. Were they bound by the Agreement as well or protected by it?

"I'm angry because I don't like it when things are muddy."

He laughed a little—at her, at her words, at himself, possibly, and nodded. "Then un-muddy them," he said, and, as though that were all that needed to be said, knelt down to bank the small fire to coals. Once the inside of the hut was cast into shadows, he poked once at the pallet he'd claimed, then lay down on it with a soft groan, knuckling the flat pillow under his head into a better semblance of comfort, and closed his eyes without a further word, leaving her to her problems.

Isobel scowled back down at her hands, feeling the weight of all that she was, all that she had bargained for, press against her chest from within, and she pushed her hand between her breasts as though to force it back. Wisdom told her to go to sleep, that whatever would come would come in its own time, and being well rested would only aid her thinking.

Nonetheless, she hesitated. Rather than crawling under the blanket in imitation of Gabriel, now lightly snoring, she instead sat on her pallet with her legs crossed underneath her, tilting her head back against the bark-rough wall and letting her eyes fall shut. The pressure within her chest eased but did not entirely fade, and the black-inked sigil on her left palm itched slightly, although it might only have been her imagination.

Formal request or no, there was a need. And whatever the boss might have intended, whatever the wording of the Agreement said, Isobel found that she was not capable of ignoring that need.

And if the people would not tell her what they needed her to do, perhaps the village itself would.

The floor beneath her pallet was covered with a mat of woven reeds, the texture rough to the touch. Below that, ground hard with winter, resting after the rigors of growth and harvest. She had never tried to reach the bones through another surface, always reaching skin to soil, but the reeds didn't seem to interfere; her eyes went hazy and her arm tingled, a vague numbness reaching past her elbow, across her shoulder, holding her still no matter what she might have desired.

Down, down to where the bones waited, heavy and still. She could feel the *sense* of something, less than the awareness of someone breathing across the fire, or even the horses shifting in their sleep at a distance, but a prickling within her own bones, a twinge of recognition as it slipped over her senses.

And then nothing. She waited, floating in the strange sense. There was no warning, no alert or alarm, but no reassurances, either. The bones rested, alert but silent, uneasy, but without a direction to point. The lines of the sigil itched but did not flare into heat or cold, and the whisper that had warned her before remained silent, non-present.

Whatever rested within the Territory knew no more than Bitter Storm. Or could tell her no more.

When she resurfaced, eyes opening to see the shadowed interior of their dwelling, Gabriel was sitting up on his pallet, the whites of his eyes glinting in the banked coal-light.

She licked her lips, somehow surprised to find them dry and cracked, with an additional tang of sourness. It had felt only moments, but she knew that she lost track of time when she touched the bones.

A glimpse up through the smoke-hole told her that it was still night, but the sky was lighter than it had been; closer to morning but still not yet dawn. Hours, she had been listening, waiting.

When her voice could work again, she asked, "How long have you been watching me?"

"A while."

His stillness reminded her of the cardsharp she had first met, who understood that the cards could only be managed so far, that every-thing after that was managing other players—and yourself.

They both waited in the shadows, but there was no noise from the campment beyond, no movement at all save the night air breathing outside, the occasional call of something hunting in the brush, and farther beyond, the faint hum of water. Isobel was unsure, in the way that often lingered after she touched the bones, if she was feeling with her own awareness or another's.

Finally, Gabriel asked, "Did you learn anything?"

That was an excellent question, and she wished she had an answer. "Something is wrong," she admitted. "But the bones don't know what."

"Well, that's useful." Gabriel's voice was dry, wry, and some of the tension singing through her body coiled itself down, still present but less ready to strike, in the face of his resigned humor.

Nothing had been easy up until now; why would she think that would change?

"What do you want to do?"

Isobel closed her eyes again, rubbing at them with one hand as though to erase her exhaustion. "We were already going to Red Stick. We will continue on. If there is more amiss than rumblings and staring from across the river, maybe I will find evidence of it there."

And do what then, she had no idea.

PART TWO

WALLS AND FRONTS

ONE

When the sun had risen enough to reveal a clear blue sky, they rebuilt their fire until it warmed the air enough to dress, then went outside to discover fresh water waiting in a reddish clay pitcher, and warm food on a covered platter made of the same material.

Isobel traced her fingers along the lines cut into the rim, noting how the simple curving lines echoed the ones in her palm. Gabriel was teaching her how to identify the beading styles of different tribes, although she despaired of ever being able to remember them all. Some patterns meant something, others were simply what someone had found pretty, and been kept for generations, until it was tradition.

Tradition was important. It told you what you needed to do, what you needed to know.

The marshal's sigil was the tree-and-circle; everyone knew what it meant. No one, far as she knew, had ever asked the boss what the looped circles meant, but the boss did nothing without purpose, and certainly not in choosing the sigil he marked his Territory by. She would ask him when she went home.

Along with the many other things she had thought of, written in her journal so she would not forget. What the whisper was that spoke to her ofttimes. Why buffalo hooves struck the bones so much louder than elk or deer. Why some folk were touched by Territory medicine and others not. How a child of two races fit into the Agreement. Important things that should be known.

Placing the pitcher back down on the ground, Isobel looked up to watch the folk moving about in the dawn light, going about their morning chores or duties with only the occasional sideways glance at the two strangers in their midst. It was a harsh reminder: she was not Izzy to these people, nor even Isobel, but the Devil's Hand. She was not here to be their friend; the welcome last night had been ceremonial, not personal.

Still, the feeling of being isolated in the middle of the village made her uncomfortable and oddly melancholy.

"We should make our farewell and be on the road," she said, reaching for her pack. "You said it's still two days to Red Stick, and I'd rather not make it three."

They rode all day without incident, Gabriel pointing out the plants that he knew, and occasionally stopping to make a quick sketch of ones he did not. Isobel knew that someone was watching them; she could feel it, prickling along her skin: not a worrying unease but an awareness that came and went, possibly one set of eyes giving way to another. But human, definitely human. They hadn't seen even the hint of a demon in weeks. Isobel wasn't sure if that was good, or bad, or simply that demon as a group had decided they weren't worth the bother of bothering.

"I'd be fine with that," she decided, looking up as something large passed overhead, the shadow of it darkening the morning sun and making a shiver run down her spine.

The ancient spirit she'd encountered in the high valley still visited her nightmares when she was particularly tired. She knew it was still bound, she would have felt the reverberations deep in the bones of the territory if it had broken loose, but the memory of it still made her wake with sweat-soaked skin and a rasping howl in her throat.

This land, scattered with branching trees and clumps of odd, waist-high plants, seemed unlikely to host anything like that, or anything fierce at all, although Gabriel warned her that there were reptiles the size of a horse who would consider her and Uvnee both a good-sized meal, although he'd never seen one of the creatures himself.

The closest she came to it was a turtle, its shell patterned in browns, that poked its head out of the underbrush, looking at them with tiny, beady black eyes and a heavy, beaked maw.

Mid-day, they passed two red-hued pole-markers set in the middle of the road, with it splitting directly after, one narrow road meandering toward the river, the other turning away. Some of the markings were similar to the poles they had seen before, while others were new. Both seemed nearly identical to each other save for direction, with no suggestion where either might lead.

"We'll go inland," Gabriel decided after his eyes went distant, checking with the map he carried in his memory. "The river curves north, and we want to head south."

Calling it "inland," Isobel soon decided, was a lie of the basest sort, as the ground soon became even more damp, with tangled, lumpy tree roots snaking across the trail, all the better to catch an unwary hoof, and the heart-stopping sight of one of the beasts Gabriel had told her about crawling across the road ahead of them. Although it showed no interest whatsoever in them, the mule had stamped its hooves and refused to go forward until it was well out of sight, and Isobel decided she was in complete sympathy.

But the beast was of a lesser concern to Isobel than the way Gabriel was behaving. He had laughed at them for their reaction to the alligator, but there had been something off about it that had made her look twice, and then a third time.

She couldn't say exactly what worried her; something in the way he rode, the way he ran his fingers through his hair, the way he stroked the scar on his cheek, the way he kept checking the tie-down of his knives and touching the stock of his carbine. It was as though he were expecting an attack at any moment, but save for the alligator, there had been no hint of a threat. Even the sense of being watched had faded, since taking the fork in the road.

"Does it snow here?" she asked, less because she was curious and more to break the silence and get him talking.

"Never that I've heard. Cold rain's about the worst they'll get, well, that and the witch storms. Come up off the coast, full of sound and fury, take out anything in their path. Those they get, reasonably often."

"Witch storms?"

He frowned, and she could almost *see* him sorting through what he knew. "Huricán, they're called, too, or wilding winds. Worse than any storm you can think of, rain coming at you sideways, winds that pick up trees and hurtle them through the air . . . They're just storms, near as I can tell, but it's not surprising folk think there's bad medicine behind 'em."

"Worse than a blizzard?"

Gabriel considered that for a while. "Blizzards, mostly, if you're inside, you're safe," he said finally, pushing a low-hanging branch out of the way as they rode under it. A small red bird raced down the limb and scolded him, then flew off before he released the branch. "In a huricán, you could lose the roof off your house."

She wasn't sure if he was teasing her or not. "And people live here anyway?"

That seemed to finally break his mood, and he laughed. "Never judge a man's home, Isobel. It won't ever end well for you. And there are folk who'd say that Flood's the ass-end of all creation, too, so there's that."

She was busy trying to think of a response to that as they came up over a rise, taken by surprise when Gabriel reined Steady in, turning the gelding so that she had no choice but to stop as well. His hat was pushed back from his forehead, his eyes squinted, and there was an odd smile on his face she'd never seen before. "Isobel, may I present to you the Mudwater."

She blinked, then turned to look. The road ahead was clear, looking out over a valley, and she could see a broad, twisting flow, like a massive flat ribbon curling through it, a few patches of clearing visible along its banks. "That . . . That's . . ."

"Yes. Yes, it is."

He was enjoying this. Isobel would be irritated, if she could spare enough attention from the view. There was nothing about it, particularly, that should make her chest feel so tight, her gut clench as though from hunger, and yet...

It couldn't be that large; it must be a trick of distance or light.

This was the edge of the Territory. Across that shining ribbon, the devil held no sway.

Finally, Gabriel reached out to touch her elbow, a gentle pressure against her skin, recalling her to herself. "Are you all right?"

She had to think about the words a moment before she could understand the question.

"I think so?" She hadn't intended for it to be a question in return. It wasn't anything more than running water, she reminded herself. Larger than any river she'd ever seen before, true, but she'd waded across water up to Uvnee's belly, had swum in currents faster than what she could see from here, and hadn't felt this . . . shock? No, she decided. Not shock. Awe. She had known it was long, and that it was wide, but she hadn't realized it would be quite so . . . quiet.

Which was nonsense; it could have been the roughest of white water and they would not be able to hear it from there, but she knew, somehow, that it was quiet. Quiet, and deep, and powerful. This was a river that kept its own counsel.

She said as much, and Gabriel tugged at one ear, then half-shrugged. "I told you some call it Grandfather Waters. Or Grandmother, depending on the tribe. There's a reason for that."

He sounded odd, and she tore her gaze away from the river, turned in the saddle to look at him, luxuriating in the stretch of her spine as she did so. That odd smile was gone, but the tightness around his eyes remained. "Are you all right?"

He scoffed, looking away, then down at the reins in his hands. "I've seen it before," he reminded her.

That wasn't an answer.

She looked again, trying to pick out more details. She wondered if the clearings were single families, or folk banded together, if it was the seeds of a village to come, or a farmstead that would die out if the children chose to move on. For a flutter of her eyelids, she could see something moving within it, rising over the banks, like the floods Gabriel had told her happened.

"Another day, we'll be in Red Stick," Gabriel said, and the vision was gone, the rump of his horse followed by the mule, until Uvnee gave her head a shake as though to ask why they were still standing there.

They were both tired, the lack of true sleep the night before making itself known, but Gabriel couldn't bring himself to suggest making camp. Not until they were safe in Red Stick, where the noise and bustle of the city might provide some kind of distraction from their worries.

It was foolishness, and he couldn't have found the words to explain it had Isobel asked. Thankfully, either she caught some edge of his urgency or else she was humoring him: when they pushed on past when they normally would have stopped, she only nodded as though this was a perfectly logical thing to do.

He could justify it to himself: the weather was dry, the moon bright enough overhead in the wide-open sky to illuminate the road, and the road wide and smooth enough to keep the horses safe as they ate ground in a slow, steady walk, the mule staying close at their heels.

An owl cried as they passed a long, low-slung barn, dappled shadow against darker shadows, and Isobel lifted her head, listening for another call. An owl, covered in snow . . .

Owls were harbingers; stories differed on if for good or ill. Gabriel put no stock in most stories like that, but he'd also seen too many beasts that carried something more within.

They'd been accosted by no spirit-animals recently. He spat to the side and hoped he hadn't just gathered the attention of some nearby spirit, bored and in search of humans to befuddle.

When the second call came, it was high and long, lingering even after the sound itself ended, and he found himself reaching for silver. "That's no owl, Iz. Don't listen to it."

"A haint?"

"More likely a fetch, or it could be something else entire. Wait until—" There was another cry, this one harsher, more a triumphant bark, and then silence.

"Was that a fetch-fox?" Isobel had stopped her mare and was looking around as though expecting to see it appear before her. "I didn't think those were real."

"I've never seen one, but I know riders who swear they are. They say you can tell them by the blue of their fur where a regular fox would be white, and the blue of their eyes."

"And they eat fetches." She sounded fascinated and horrified.

"Fetches, haints, poor-wills . . . anything that's not entirely flesh. They've no interest in us, and we should have no interest in them, Isobel." Fetch-foxes were tricksters in some stories, and Gabriel had no desire to see what one might make of Isobel, or she it, were they to encounter each other.

They rode on, an occasional true owl calling its hunting song from overhead, and once he saw the flash of movement that told him deer were nearby, but other than that, the night was still, the stars overhead now hazed by clouds, the moon still full and bright. The road dipped away again from the river eventually, the flat landscape and trees—incredibly tall, with gnarled branches that looked disturbingly like arms or legs—hiding the water from view again. Something in his gut shifted, and he pressed a hand into the small of his back, as though to push out an ache. He considered changing his mind, finding a place to rest for a few hours, at least, but he could see nowhere that would suit, and when they passed smaller farmsteadings, the windows were dark and silent. In more isolated areas, he might have taken refuge in a barn and asked permission in the morning, but closer to civilization, they risked being woken with a musket.

"Sleep," Gabriel told Isobel when she was finally unable to muffle a yawn. "I'll keep us on track."

She made a noise that might have been a protest but loosened Uvnee's reins to give the mare her head, and settled deeper into the saddle, her weight seeming to slump from shoulders to knees.

In the pale darkness, with only the horses and mule for company, Gabriel let his own thoughts slow and settle, trusting Steady and Uvnee to mind their riders, and Flatfoot to sound the alarm if anything came near them.

And if he, too, fell half-asleep, lulled by the steady *clop clop* of twelve hooves echoing under the moonlight, the horses were not going to tell.

The first time she had seen Gabriel fall asleep while riding, she hadn't been able to imagine doing the same herself without falling off or otherwise disgracing herself. But when Isobel slowly woke, the sky a pale red, telling her she had, in fact, slept several hours in the saddle, her only thought was that she had no idea where she was.

"Almost there," Gabriel said, as though he could hear her thoughts.

She sat upright in the saddle, stretching her spine up and her legs down, feeling things crackle and pop pleasantly. Her backside ached, and her eyes were gritty with sleep, but it was no worse than some nights when she'd slept on the ground.

There was a cluster of farmhouses in the close distance, their roofs red-hued in the sunrise light, a few small fields cleared around them. A small herd of shaggy brown cows grazed nearby, regarding them incuriously, while a few goats wandered by. Farther along the road proper, penned by a low wooden fence, a handful of horses milled about, clearly waiting for someone to come and fetch them.

It reminded her so much of the farmlands outside Flood that something scraped behind her eyes, causing them to water. But even that was forgotten as the road took another curve over a small hill, and Isobel's first, overwhelming thought was *oh*.

Where the farms had been a loose cluster, this was a massive knot, dark and glittering along a curve in the river. And their road led directly to it.

"You all right there, Devil's Hand?"

There was laughter in his voice but also concern. She forced the fluttering panic down, making sure her voice was controlled before asking Gabriel, "How many people live there?"

"No idea." Gabriel sounded far too calm, and when she was able to tear her gaze away from the view, his expression was amused, although she'd give him credit for trying to hide it. "Haven't been here before, only hearsay from other folk. More than you've ever seen in one place, I'll tell you that much."

He seemed to suddenly realize that she was having trouble breathing. "None of them will be any different from any folk you've met before, Iz. Some of 'em will be fine, some of 'em will be rude, all think they have something to prove. And some of 'em might become friends; we're there long enough to make 'em."

He was right; she knew he was right and wise. But with every step Uvnee took toward the sprawling mess of buildings that was Red Stick, the more Isobel wanted nothing more than to put heels to Uvnee and send her running back in the opposite direction.

❧ ❧ ❧

You didn't enter Red Stick. It engulfed you.

Even with Gabriel at her side, it was worse than Isobel could have imagined. The noise hit her first, the roaring beast of voices raised and wagon wheels clattering, the ringing and hammering from shops, the calls of animals in the market they passed, chickens and ducks in crates, cows and sheep in pens. After weeks on the road where often they saw and spoke only to each other, it was worse than a physical assault, forcing her to cling to Uvnee's mane like a child until the dizziness passed.

The smells hit her when she tried to take a deep breath to calm herself; sweat and smoke and sawdust, and things she could not identify, pungent enough to make her eyes water and her throat clench in a gag. She pulled a kerchief out of her pocket and held it to her mouth, unashamed.

"You'll get used to it," Gabriel said, although she noted that his face was pinched in distaste as well. "Just wait until you smell low tide."

From his tone, she didn't think she'd be rushing to do that anytime soon.

They dismounted just inside the gate, and while Gabriel went to speak with someone who looked official, with a pressed coat and slicked-back hair, Isobel held the horses, the mule now on a lead tied to Steady's saddle, and tried to look as though she were perfectly at ease, even as she could feel her bones quivering.

It wasn't fear; she knew that there was nothing to fear there. And yet, every inch of her screamed to *do* something, to strike out against a threat that did not exist, or hide, that the threat could not find her.

She had wondered, when she was younger, what it might be like to travel to one of the eastern cities. Ree, the cook back home, had made it sound horrible. Gabriel's stories of his time in Philadelphia, of the noise and the smells, made it sound fascinating, if a little sad. This wasn't sad. This was *terrifying*.

Steady was the only one of the five who seemed not at all disturbed by the clamor around them; Uvnee was rolling her eyes nervously, only Isobel's hand on her neck keeping the mare calm, and the mule stayed close to Steady's flank, occasionally pressing against it as though for reassurance, uttering low, unhappy noises every now and again.

"We need to find a stable for them," she said, when Gabriel came back, having exchanged a number of coins with the man and shaken hands.

"Should be one a ways over," he said, taking Steady's reins from her. "Most folk prefer to keep their cattle on the outskirts of town."

"Less noise?" she guessed.

"Easier to get them out, if'n there's fire," he said.

She looked around as they walked, noting the two- and three-story structures all made of wood, and could see the wisdom of that. Then her thoughts went to the idea of them catching fire, how quickly it could spread, how it would be to be caught in the center of the city while it went up in flames, and she thought her heart might explode, it started beating so fast.

"Isobel, breathe."

Gabriel was next to her, his hand on her arm, warm and tight, and she focused on that, on the feel of Uvnee's hot breath on the side of her neck, the smell of Gabriel, that blend of water and leather and sweat she could identify in a dark room on a moonless night, that said comfort and safety and not-alone.

"If there's a fire," he said, conversational as though they were talking about anything else, "they've got water crews. Folk pull the water from the river, send it where it's needed."

She focused on his words, the sound of his voice. "Folk like you?" Gabriel was a dowser, could sense where water flowed, where it went. But she'd never heard tell of anyone who could *move* water.

"Stronger than me. Or better-trained, at least." There was an odd tone in his voice, one she couldn't place. "Water likes least effort. Divert a stream, send it through the streets. See the channels dug there, along the sides?"

Once she knew to look, there were in fact narrow troughs in the hard-packed dirt of the road. "They can hold enough water to put out a fire?"

Gabriel shrugged. "Never seen it myself; only heard folk talk."

She was ashamed that he'd been able to read her fears that easily, but thankful as well, and the combination made her snappish. "So, you don't know if it actually works?" The river was so close, but fire could move so very fast.

Gabriel shrugged, hands and elbows rising in a too-familiar gesture. "Folk who live here seem to trust it."

Snappish and childish. She felt the urge to stomp her feet, something she hadn't done since she *was* a child. She wasn't that child anymore, hadn't been since the day her indenture had ended, the hours before the devil had accepted her offer, had drawn up the contract that ruled her now. She could not indulge in such things.

"My apologies," she said, forcing a calm she did not believe. "I didn't mean to—"

"Isobel." Gabriel squeezed her arm once, gently, and then let it drop, but he didn't move away. "It's all right."

The stable was small but well-built, with a handful of youngsters caring for the beasts while an older man in the spark-stained leathers of a blacksmith took Gabriel's coin, counting out three nights' stay. Isobel, once she'd seen that Uvnee would be well cared for, found her attention caught by something across the narrow alley: the familiar, unexpected sight of a wooden box, twice as wide as a man and about as high, painted bright yellow, with the devil's *infinitas*—the same mark that rested on her palm—burned into the wood.

"I'll be right back," she told Gabriel, grabbing a packet from her saddlebag. He nodded, distracted by the stablemaster's offering of a discount for the whole week paid up front.

The last postal drop they'd come to, she'd been acting for a post-rider down with stomach-flux.' There'd been a packet there for Gabriel, and another for someone named Smith, in a place called Tallahatchie. She'd taken them both, been carrying the second around with her ever since, the sense of responsibility for this man's letter weighing on her like a persistent itch.

The envelope was wrinkled at the corners now, with ink stains from having been tucked within her journal, but it hadn't gotten damp or ripped, or gotten lost.

"You're to be someone else's problem now," she said, tipping the letter in through the narrow slit. A courier came through regular, Gabriel had said. Mr. Smith's letter would be on its way again soon enough.

"Isobel?"

Gabriel came out of the stable, their packs slung over his shoulder, and saw her standing there. "Ah. Good idea." He dropped the packs and reached into his own, pulling out a series of smaller envelopes.

He had read the contents to her as he wrote them. One was to his old friend Abner Westbrook, in the States, and another to a mutual friend Abner had mentioned. Cautious, careful, never mentioning Isobel or anything of what Gabriel was doing at that moment, but seeking any news the men could pass along of happenings in the States.

"I asked Rufus inside, and he said a courier hadn't been by in a few weeks, so they're overdue. Maybe two, three days, someone should swing by. He also said there's a hostería, cheap but clean, a bit further in he recommends. No bathhouse, but real beds and pillows."

Isobel allowed herself to be distracted. "If they have a basin I can wash my hair in, all will be forgiven," she said, resisting the urge to scratch at her scalp. For some reason, staying awake all night—or at least, staying in the saddle all night—made her feel grubbier than making camp did. Likely because she'd not had a chance to unbraid her hair or brush it out.

The fact that people around them seemed to take their disheveled appearance in stride somehow only made her feel worse. She studied the clothing worn by several of the women they passed by, noting the finer fabric of their skirts and the puffed sleeves of their bodices.

Sadly, she suspected such things were deeply unpractical for the road. She looked down at her dark brown wool skirt, thought of the lighter-weight clothing she had been given to wear for the feast, and thought she might just be impractical, for once.

"Silver for your thoughts," Gabriel said, leaning close to be heard over the rumble and surge of the noise around them.

"Clothing," she admitted, and he laughed, grinning up at the sky with a lightness she hadn't seen on him in days. "I'll own to thinking it might be time to acquire some muslin shirts, better suited for this clime," he admitted. "You're past due your pay, so it's not as though we can't resupply."

"Oh." Isobel stopped dead in the street, then had to rush to catch up, ducking around two older gentlemen holding a heated conversation in the middle of the street. She hadn't even thought—but of course, her bargain with the boss had included the means by which she—and Gabriel—would live while she was in the boss's employ. "How—" She stopped her own question. "You think the post-rider will bring it? Or a courier? But how would they know we're here?"

"He's your boss," Gabriel said cheerfully, still grinning. "You tell me."

TWO

"How many nights?" The woman at the counter of the hostería was ancient, the wrinkles on her face falling over themselves, her eyes rheumy and ringed with blue shadows underneath, her hair thin and white. But her equally wrinkled hands were steady as she wrote into the ledger book, the quill pen scratching smoothly across the page.

"Names?"

"Gabriel Kasun, Isobel née Lacoyo Távora."

The pen scratching paused. "Not kin?"

"Road companions," Gabriel said.

"Humph." The woman clearly wasn't happy, but she didn't say anything more. Isobel felt a tinge of heat touch her cheeks. She knew what some folk thought, they'd faced it before, but after so many weeks on the road, making camp together, she forgot sometimes that Gabriel was male, in that way. And she was reasonably sure he didn't think of her as female, in that way. It wasn't an issue for them, and it hadn't been an issue for most of the folk they'd met along the road. But here, she realized, it might be different.

"Is this a problem?" she asked the woman, and something in her tone must have changed, because the woman lifted her head and looked directly at her.

"'T'ain't right, a young girl like you traveling with a man not her kin. Since you asked."

The urge to put this woman in her place, to break her down and make her acknowledge the foolishness of her words, struck Isobel. She was the Devil's Hand, not some child to be protected from her own mentor. Instead, she merely smiled at the woman, and if the smile was one she'd stolen from the boss, rather than Marie, she need not admit it to herself.

"I'm a woman grown and make my own decisions."

"Humph," the woman muttered again, but finished making the ledger entry and held out her withered hand for the coins.

The hostería was different from the one they'd stayed in before, back in Patch Junction. This was more like the saloon back in Flood, with a main area where residents might gather, and rooms for rent above. The floor was a smooth planking that made a *shhhshhh*ing noise when she swept the toe of her boot across it, and Isobel noted with approval that it had been swept clean recently and the corners cleared of cobwebs and dust. She might be a rider now, and firsthand proof that the Dust Roads were aptly named, but she'd spent her childhood chasing after dirt and dust as though they were personal offenses.

The room a young girl showed them to was just as clean, with a single window covered in light curtains that trembled in the faint breeze, a pale yellow rag rug on the floor, and two beds, each narrow as a bedroll, pushed up against the walls on either side of the rug. A small table with a pitcher and a bowl on it completed the room, the walls bare of anything resembling decoration, and washed a pale white from floorboards on up to the ceiling.

Isobel suddenly wanted nothing so much as to drop her kit and fall face-first onto the nearest bed, and find out if the pillow was as soft as it looked, the mattress as firm. Instead, she carefully placed her packs at the end of one bed and turned to investigate the pitcher. There was water in it, and a cloth towel folded next to it, so she washed her hands and face while Gabriel puttered about behind her, his boots soft on the rug, then louder when he stepped onto the floor.

"What now?" she asked, not turning around, bracing herself for whatever he was going to say. Go find the local badgehouse for her to check in, maybe, or visit the mercantile . . .

"Now we find somewhere to eat where someone else has done the hunting and the cooking and the cleaning," he said. "And possibly find a decent drink."

Gabriel would be lying if he said he wasn't more amused than worried by Isobel's reaction to Red Stick. For all that she'd grown immeasurably since they rode out of Flood, her green as a greenie could be, she was still a child of small towns and wide-open spaces, the mercantile town of Patch Junction the largest thing she'd ever seen.

Not that most Territory-born were much better. There was something about the sheer vastness of the Territory that should have caused folk to clump together; instead, they seemed to stretch as far away as they could get.

Except here, and a few other places along the River. Trade was part of it, and the convenience—you could ride a barge faster than you could ride a horse, especially if you were moving merchandise—but for some folk, it was more than that.

A shudder ran down his spine, and he covered it by tipping his hat and mock-bowing toward a pair of women who were giving them slightly scandalized looks. He supposed they were a bit of a road mess, even without their gear over their shoulders.

Still, the occasional curious once-up-and-downs they were getting here were nothing compared to the looks he'd gotten when he landed at William and Mary, barely older than Isobel and rough as the backside of a nopal. The folk of the Territory, for all their flaws, took the wild and the weird as just one more thing in the day, not something to be gawked at from behind a cage.

He poked at that thought, a bit surprised that the bitterness lingered when he thought of his college days.

Water doesn't like being boxed up, he heard a dry voice crackle in his thoughts. *You try'n cut it off, it always finds a way out.*

Hush, Old Woman, he told the voice, only to hear it cackle again, not unkindly, but with a definite edge.

Old Woman Who Never Dies had a tendency to wander his dreams often enough even when he wasn't twitchy, and nothing he could do would keep her out if she was determined to say something, save hope she couldn't find him in the mass of dreams doubtless being dreamed here.

That, or not sleep until she got bored of his stubbornness, and wandered off again.

"Have you seen a place you might like to try?" he asked Isobel, focusing back on the issue at hand.

She turned to look at him, her fresh-scrubbed face not lit only by excitement but also apprehension. "I wasn't expecting choices."

He hadn't thought that would be what daunted her. He likely should have: half or more of the time they rode into a settlement, there was only the one resthouse and maybe an attached kitchen, or at best a saloon. Red Stick seemed to host a handful of eating establishments within their walk from the hostería, and easily twice as many saloons, each of them no different from the last save for the sign outside.

"I suspect they're all going to have the same sort of food and the same sort of folk," he told her. "Close your eyes and pick one."

Much to his surprise, she stopped and closed her eyes, tilting her head slightly and lifting her hand. Her right hand, he was relieved to see: he didn't think the devil would have a preference in where she should eat, but the devil was a particular sort, now that he thought of it. . . .

"There." Her voice cracked a little as she opened her eyes and looked at where she was pointing. Across the street, a simple front painted pale blue, with an open arched doorway under a sign that read SULLIVAN'S.

"A cat-licker out here?" he said in surprise, then huffed at his own surprise. "Well, we could do worse, I suppose." He offered her his arm, making an excess of gallantry of it, and after a long stare as though to ask what he was doing, she took it as daintily as any Philadelphia miss.

Sullivan was, in fact, the owner of the establishment, a low-ceilinged, roughhewn place, with half a dozen slab tables and a cook the size and shape of a small mountain, who took turns shouting with the owner, to the obvious entertainment of the guests.

"You've no more sense than the good lord gave a cheese."

"Aye, and a cheese is a thing of satisfying nature, and no shame to be sliced thus." The host's voice had a rhythm to it that told Gabriel he was not Territory-born, not American-born either, although he looked barely old enough to have made the journey, much less set up his own shop.

"Born of cow farts and moldy rocks," the mountain returned, laughing far too hard at his own joke, even as he rattled a pair of dishes onto the counter, a slender figure racing up to catch them and cart them to the table. Whatever it was, it smelled worth eating.

"Two for a meal, or are you here to wash the road dust from your throats, my good friends?" the proprietor asked as he caught sight of them, abandoning his repartee to greet them.

"Both," Gabriel said, reaching up to remove his hat, running his other hand through his hair. Even on the short walk over, the damp-ness had plastered it to his scalp uncomfortably. "But a table, please."

"You've come to a foul place."

"Beg pardon?" Gabriel turned to face the woman who'd come up to them. She was nearly as tall as he, whipcord-thin in her face and torso, draped in a man's shirt laced at the neck, and vest over her skirt. Working clothes, practical rather than fancy, to match the worn look on her face. There was a man standing behind her, in similar roughhewn clothing, but where her face was stirred up in bile, his was softer, as though trying to blend back into the shadows, despite her hand being locked in his.

"You've come to a foul place," she repeated.

"Grace, leave these folk alone," the host said, trying to slide between them, but the woman stuck out an arm, stopping him in place.

"The streets are befouled with pride, the wheat sickened with contamination. This is not the truth; this is not the way—"

"Grace, enough! I put up with your nattering because you likely mean well, but I won't have you bothering visitors. Johnny can stay if he's a mind to, but you need to go."

The woman glared at him, then glared at Gabriel and Isobel for good measure before turning on her boot heel and marching herself and the man with her out the door, letting it swing shut behind them.

"My apologies," the host said, rubbing a hand over the top of his head in what looked like a mix of exasperation and embarrassment. "Grace, she's not a bad sort, nor's her brother Johnny, but she's taken some queer ideas into her head. And likes to tell folk about 'em."

"Queer ideas?" Isobel asked, as she took her seat at the table they'd been shown.

"Ah, there're folk here as don't take kindly to growing larger, think we shouldn't let folk build more storefronts, more warehouses, whatnot. It's nothing, just foolishness."

There were three men sitting at the table they joined. They had clearly finished their meal already, the battered tin platters in front of them scraped clean, their glasses half-filled with a smoky amber liquid. "You're too kind to them, Sully," one of them said, an accent similar to the boys they'd encountered on the road. "They'd run you out of town, and me the same, if they could."

"Why?" Isobel turned to him, her head tilted in curiosity.

"My mother's mother was White Hill tribe and 'Cadian," he said, "but my papa came upriver from Freetown. These folk, they don't like Freetown much."

"They don't like anyone's not Territory-born," a second man said. He was paler, slighter, with long narrow hands that reached for the pitcher on the table and refilled his glass. "And they've got a point, to a point, but after that, they become damned fools. You should have kicked her out weeks ago, Sully. Her and all her ilk, they're enough to put a man off his feed."

"They're harmless," the oldest of the three said, waving a hand in dismissal. "Don't frighten the travelers; Sully needs their coin. Just don't order the thing he claims is stew, and you'll do fine."

"It's because I've not the cooking of it, that's the problem," Sully muttered with a glare back at his cook, then handed Gabriel a hand-printed sheet, the ink brown but readable even in the dim light. "Two glasses of nature's neat for the weary riders, yeah, and coming up swift." It wasn't a question, but Gabriel nodded agreement anyway, even as their host was turning away, shouting something in an unknown language to the cook.

Anti-Acadian sentiment? After encountering those boys on the road, Gabriel couldn't find it in himself to blame anyone, not if they were a sampling of what went on around here, but it was still troubling. A glance at Isobel's expression told him she was thinking much the same.

"You're northerners," the first man who'd spoken said now. Now that Gabriel was looking, his features were darker than the natives they'd met so far, his features slightly broader, but he had the same raven's-wing sheen to his hair and could have easily passed for any of half a dozen tribes from here to the Wilds. "Down to avoid the snows?"

"Among other things," Gabriel agreed. He waited, but Isobel was too-carefully studying the menu, leaving the conversation to him. "Been on the Dust Roads a while now, thought it would be good to sit the winter out rather than risk chilblains or frostbite, and lose a toe—or worse."

"No fool you," the older man agreed. "Was back, oh, too long ago now, I was still trading upriver, got caught in a snowstorm the likes I never want to see again. Managed to survive—"

"By slitting his horse open and hiding inside," his companions finished for him, and he scowled, while Gabriel smiled into the glass the host brought to them, letting the mild ale hide his amusement.

Isobel had put the menu down and was having an intent discussion with Sully about the merits of the roasted chicken, the ale was more than drinkable, and they'd seemingly stumbled onto that most useful of things—talkative locals. Gabriel stretched his legs out under the table and picked up the pewter fork by his plate, twirling it gently in his hand and watching the candlelight splash against it with each turn.

Despite everything'd they'd ridden in with, Gabriel felt himself starting to relax. Mayhap there were folk stirring dissent, like that woman, and mayhap that was what Bitter Storm was hearing ripples from, but it seemed like most of the town were reasonable sorts, not prone to kicking up trouble when there needn't be any. Work more for the local marshals than the Hand.

Which reminded him: Isobel would need to check into the local badgehouse, let them know she was in town. He'd remind her, if she forgot. But it could wait until morning.

THREE

Gabriel's first conscious thought was awareness that he was in a bed, a roof over his head, a pillow under it.

Not a roadside camp, no wide sky above him. The resthouse. Red Stick.

The thin coverlet had been pushed down to his feet, and a thin film of sweat clung to his skin, making the faint breath of air coming in through the window more tease than relief. The room was too dark even for shadows; only his awareness of where Isobel had laid down to sleep allowed him to recognize the soft noises to his left as her breathing, familiarity telling him she was deep asleep, whatever dreams she might be having peaceful enough not to disturb her.

His dreams had not been peaceful.

Water doesn't like being boxed up.

"Old Woman, I say this with the utmost of respect, but for the love of all, hush."

The shuddering in his chest when he took a deep breath was no answer, nor was the sudden need to be out of this bed, out of this room.

He reached into his pack, left as usual by the foot of the bed, and took out the coalstone. The small lump lay inert and cool in his hand until pressed, then it began to glow with a faint pinkish light. It would become too warm to hold within minutes, but a minute was all he needed to gather his clothing from the night before and dress, sliding his smaller knife into its sheath on his belt and catching up his boots and hat before extinguishing the coalstone and putting it back, then closing the door gently behind him.

The hallway was cooler, if only slightly, and lit by tin sconces hung at odd intervals along the walls. He padded down past closed doors, politely ignoring the sounds coming from some of them, down the stairs, and out into the street without encountering another waking soul.

It was too late for revelers, too early for morning chores; even the street curs that were curled under the wooden sidewalks slept, legs kicking as they dreamed of offal and chasing cats.

He looked up, but the sky was overcast, the moonlight muted and the stars no help. Red Stick had not installed streetlamps yet, and he waited until his eyesight had adjusted enough to see. His fingers touched the hilt of his knife, less for reassurance than habit, and he sat down on the stoop to put on his boots and fix his hat on his head before stepping down into the street.

He would have sworn he had no purpose other than to escape the stuffy air of their chamber, but Gabriel found himself walking without hesitation, as though something pulled him by the reins. He supposed it had been inevitable, no matter his own intentions or desires.

Water doesn't like being boxed up.

There were three powers within the Territory, three sources of all medicine. The winds were powerful, and cared nothing for mortal life. This was a fact all in the Territory knew. The wind fed magicians power, and took their minds in payment. Bone and earth were what humans came from, formed and shaped and forever belonging, and bone was powerful but stingy with it. It would touch you but once, and you chose what you would do with it.

But water, water did not care, and cared for everything. Water *was* everything, consumed everything, and woe to the mortal who forgot that.

Gabriel had tried to forget once, and been reminded. Forcibly, painfully, at the price of weeks of his life he could no longer recall.

So it did not surprise him when his steps took him away from the two- and three-story buildings with their well-maintained fronts to wider streets with lower buildings, and then, inevitably, to the very edge of the city, where the banks of the Mudwater lapped up against the shore, and a series of wooden docks extended into the water like short fingers reaching into the darkness.

A bird called out, and something splashed, there was a low cry of something in the thicket beyond what humans had claimed, and Gabriel stopped, trying to breathe through the panic clutching at his lungs.

He had stepped off the road at some point and not realized it. Reddish-brown mud clung to the edges of his boots, heels and toes sinking deep and pulling loose only with an effort. The night-dark waters lapped quietly, nearly within reach, surface smooth but roiling below with currents and devil-knew-what beneath.

The Mudwater was no meadow creek nor mountain river, no underground stream passed through cleaning stone. It was a Power, complete within itself.

Gabriel was Territory-born; he did not fear it, nor any part of it, as such. And yet, the memory of the creature that had attacked him in the hot springs far northwest was never far from his memory, the scarring still visible on his ribs and face, though faded to pale white lines against darker skin now. He still felt the marks on his face every time he shaved, every time he washed his face, every time he caught his own reflection. It didn't bother him; he had never been handsome enough to be vain. But he knew they were there, under incautious fingers, even half-hidden by the scruff of his beard. A reminder, for when he forgot: the world was not gentle, was not kind.

Wind and bone and water; none of them were kind. They did not understand what it meant to be kind, only to be. Only humans demanded kindness. Only humans demanded fairness.

He stared out across the water, unable to see the other shore, only trusting that it was there, and exhaled.

"I'm here, Old Woman. What now?"

The air remained silent, the faint sounds of night birds muted, the occasional splash as something breached the surface of the waters. His head felt fuzzy and sharp all together, as though he was suffering from too much drink and too much coffee all at once, and the fact that the sensation was a familiar one made it no less unpleasant.

"Grandmother?" He could not have sworn, at that moment, if he queried the medicine woman who had taught and tormented him, or the River itself, or if he could tell the difference betwixt the two just then.

His blood heated, vapor rising from his skin. The waters were not black-blue but black-red. He could see the currents swirl, the surface popping although nothing rose beneath it, the pattern of the current stilling and reversing, then reversing again, red overtaking black, until the entire river ran in streams of carmine, crimson, and rust.

Silt from the banks, he told himself. The rains had washed it into the waters, carried it downstream, or sifted it upstream. The local tribes made their pitchers from clay that color; it meant nothing. Bone and earth, mixed with water, nothing he had not seen in a hundred streams, a thousand times.

Or he was imagining this, was dreaming, still in his bed in the center of town, still wrapped in a coverlet, head on a pillow, dreaming of dreaming. He would wake now. He would turn to go, turn his back, walk back up the embankment, back onto dry dirt and wooden structures.

"A fish on the shore, an owl covered in snow, and the river waters rising red."

Gabriel closed his eyes, but the blackness there was red-tinged as well. His fingers twitched, and he felt the air shift around him, the sweat on his skin cooling until it became clammy, the sensation of tendrils wrapped around him, pulling him forward, urging him into the currents themselves.

"No." Revulsion rose in him even as desire swamped his senses; need and fear shoved down his throat, the sense of infinite patience countered by a single hard, dry thought.

Isobel.

Isobel's first thought was that there was someone in her room. Her second thought was to wonder why she had been sleeping in a room. In a bed.

Her third thought was wondering if there was coffee, and if she was going to have to get out of the comfortable bed she was in to have it.

"Out of bed, lazybones," a familiar voice said, drawling with amusement. "You've slept past the morning birds and through half a dozen wagons clattering past."

She could hear the noises now coming in through the window from the street below, the clatter of wheels and the rumble of voices, male and female, and for a moment she was sick for the saloon, the voices and noises she had grown up with. There were days and weeks she went without thinking of who she had been, where she was from, but those sounds brought it all back.

This wasn't Flood, though. This wasn't home.

She pushed the covers back and sat up. Her rail clung to her back with sweat and tangled oddly around her legs; civilized nightclothes felt awkward now, after so many nights sleeping on the road.

That thought made her realize that Gabriel was already dressed, his hair wet and slicked back, his face newly clean-shaven. The points of his jaw were paler than the skin above, making it obvious the beard had been there, and the jagged line of the scar on his cheek was now entirely visible.

She squinted at him, still oddly sleep-hazed. "There's a bathing room?"

"Down the hall," he said. "Fresh towels and soap, too."

She didn't wait past that, slipping out of bed and grabbing her one remaining clean dress from her pack. Even if it was only a bucket and cold water, fresh soap was a thing of glory and she wouldn't risk someone using the last of it before she got there.

There was a hip-basin—nearly the size of a tub, large enough for Isobel to stand in it while she rinsed the soap away, then dried herself with towels that were soft, not sun-dried and rough. Another thing she had nearly forgotten to miss. There was even a second towel, which she used to dry her hair. She took up a handful of it, frowning at the ends. It was nearly down to her waist now, unbraided, and ragged. Peggy used to cut it for her back home. She would need to find a pair of scissors somewhere, or surely there was a barber in town.

For now, she braided it into a single plait, the damp weight of it barely noticeable in the equally damp air of the bathing chamber. Staring at her reflection in the tiny silvered mirror hung on the wall, she squinted at the face squinting back at her. Her skin was darker than she remembered it, her face leaner, her mouth . . .

Isobel made a moue, the reflection doing the same. Her teeth were still crooked, her eyes still brown, the pinprick mole at her hairline still there. If Peggy were to see her now, would she look the same? Or would the other woman be able to see what Isobel had done?

She looked down at her left palm. The black lines of the sigil hadn't changed either, the double loop within the circle clear sign to anyone that she was the devil's own. At first, that had given her pride, a flush of power. When she'd realized it was not her power, that the respect people showed was not given to her but to the devil through her, she'd still learned to take satisfaction in it.

Then they'd ridden into the mountains, drawn by a whisper of pain, of need, and she'd . . . she'd come face-to-face with something older than the boss. Something of such power, in such pain, she'd had no choice but allow it to be locked away forever, lest it destroy others.

The weight of that still rested heavily on her, no matter what she might pretend to Gabriel. She had done that, and she had executed two magicians. Never mind they'd been maddened beyond control; never mind they'd been dangerous to everything around them. They had been human still.

She had been the devil's judgment, the cold eye that did not flinch, and the weight of it was on her alone. And the worst weight was not that she felt guilt but that she felt none at all.

She touched the memory of the boys on the road, reassured by the ache there, like a sore tooth wobbling in its socket. She was angry still, and worried, and a little scared, and somehow, feeling those things made her feel better.

Still human.

She left the towels in a pile by the sink, and closed the door softly behind her.

The hostería offered a morning meal laid out on platters covered by yellow cloths. Isobel poked under a few and found sweet corncakes in one, rice dumplings, black sausage, and something an older woman in front of her said was called speckled hominy. Isobel watched as Gabriel loaded his own plate up, and followed in his path, then joined him at one end of a wooden table at the far end from where other guests were already seated.

"You'll be wanting coffee." It wasn't a question, but Isobel nodded when the young girl held a battered tin pot up for inspection. As the black liquid poured into cups, Isobel's nostrils flared, and her mouth began to water. "Oh, proper coffee," she said, and when the girl, teeth flashing in a bright smile, produced a small pitcher of milk, Isobel felt the need to restrain herself from hugging the girl, if only because it might spill her drink.

"Are you saying my coffee isn't good?" Gabriel asked, pausing with spoon halfway to his mouth.

"Firepot coffee," Isobel said, watching as the color changed from black to milky brown closer to the color of her hat. "'Good' isn't usually the word I'd use to describe it." And it was worse when she made it.

He made a face but couldn't argue that, and didn't, going back to his meal as the girl poured him a cup as well.

"You folks come down the road?"

"We did." Isobel glanced up at the girl, taking in the round face, short curly hair cut tight against her head, dark eyes bright under thick eyebrows. Thirteen, maybe. The daughter of the hostería keeper, or an indentured girl like Isobel had been. "What's your name?"

"Ana."

"Hello, Ana. I'm Isobel, and this is Gabriel. We've been traveling a long time, and your coffee is very good."

"Papa makes it with chicória, the way Grandpapa did."

Isobel nodded wisely at the imparting of that secret. "It is very good. It reminds me very much of how it is made in my home, too." She cast a sly sideways glance at Gabriel, then leaned forward, the girl tilting her head forward as well, as though to share a secret. "Gabriel makes very bad coffee."

Ana giggled. "Road coffee is very bad," she said. "Papa said so."

"Ah. Was your papa a rider?"

"I was a marshal," a deeper voice said, and Isobel looked up to see an older man with Ana's brown eyes standing nearby. "Emphasis on 'was.'"

Gabriel leaned back in his chair, arms crossing over his chest. "You can take the sigil off but you can't ever put it down," he said. "Else you wouldn't be eyeing us like you're thinking of tossing us back into the street rather than keeping our coin."

The man eyed him, then Isobel, and then turned to his daughter. "Ana, go look after the other tables."

The girl pouted but did as ordered, while her father took the empty chair across from Gabriel, turning it around and sitting in it, his elbows resting against the back.

She took careful measure of the man. He was square-shouldered, broad-faced, and stern, but there was no violence in him that she could read.

"You stink of trouble, the both of you," he said. "So, tell me why I shouldn't toss you back."

He wasn't a marshal any longer; Isobel owed him nothing. But it was manners to check in with the local badgehouse, when there was one, just to let them know the Devil's Hand was in town, and he was the first of that kind she'd seen in this town. So, she lifted her left hand, turning it so that he could see the sigil, then curled her fingers over it. Although the rest of her skin was still lightly slicked with sweat, her palm where her fingers touched it was dry and cool.

"Huh." He didn't sound surprised, or particularly impressed. "I'll be keeping your coin, then. And offering you better coffee in my office, as well."

Gabriel watched Isobel watching the former marshal as they followed him from the dining room down a hallway to a room at the back of the building. She was cautious but calm. The office was a corner of the stillroom, a smooth-planed board set up on trestles for a desk, covered with two heavy ledger-books and a dish holding a cake of ink next to several hard-used quills and a battered reservoir pen. As they passed through the doorway, Gabriel noted a smoothly etched shape in the doorframe overhead: the tree-and-circle sigil, plus a shape he did not recognize. Protection runes, he supposed, although he'd never heard of them being useful for more than keeping the superstitious away.

The man gestured them at the mismatched wooden chairs opposite the desk, while he refilled their cups from the pewter pot simmering over the grate.

This coffee came with a bolt of something stronger. Isobel sipped at it, her nose wrinkling slightly at the taste. Gabriel had noted a while back that despite growing up in a saloon, or maybe because of it, she'd never developed a taste for liquor. Gabriel took his bolt in one shot, feeling the shock of smooth fire burning down his throat, settling somewhere in his chest before plummeting into his stomach. Not good stuff, but it would do the trick.

Ana's papa's name was Rafe Bernal, and he'd quit the road when his daughter was born. There was no mention of a mother, and Isobel didn't ask.

"Settled in here, took over the badgehouse when old Durgin died. Been here nearly fifteen years now, since just before Ana was born." He shook his head, as though surprised at the time passing.

"Haven't seen a sigil like yours in more than that. Never did make it up to the Old Man's part of the Territory when I was riding; never felt the need, I suppose. Kept to the river roads, mostly."

"And there's no marshal in all of Red Stick?"

Isobel's question carried a tinge of surprise. There wasn't a requirement that one be there; marshals took oath for the whole of the Territory, and most of them were restless as riders, but it did seem odd.

"Was a young marshal came in, three, four years back, then one day he just up and disappeared. We do have a judge, though he doesn't see much business. Mostly, things take care of themselves around here."

Rafe paused, then looked down into his own mug, the first time he'd dropped eye contact. "Suppose I should tell you now. I did my time in the Mud."

Gabriel felt his eyebrows rise. That would explain the whiskey in their cups, then, if he thought he was going to have to talk on that. Not a memory a man faced stone sober.

There was silence, and Bernal lifted his gaze again as though expecting Isobel to have . . . done something, Gabriel supposed, although he had no idea what, and suspected Isobel didn't know either. He had no idea if she even knew what the Mud was, or had been, rather. He turned his head slightly, to check on her.

She was very still, her expression set in soft lines, as though she were listening to something else, far away. Gabriel didn't think she was; she'd told him that when she *knew* things, it wasn't so much hearing a voice as feeling like she'd always understood but just forgotten for a bit, but he could understand why the man's face went a shade green at just the idea that she might be talking direct to the devil.

"Do you feel the need for judgment?" Isobel finally asked, and her voice was her own, nothing echoing deeper. "Are you asking for the Master of the Territory to weigh your sins?"

"No." He held her gaze this time, two pairs of dark eyes, unblinking, and Gabriel felt something inside his chest jump, then still. "I know my sins and the weight of them."

The Mud was a long time ago, but he supposed to someone like Rafe, it was the same as yesterday. Heavy rains and flooding up and down this stretch of the Mudwater, and most of the crops that hadn't drowned had been frost-blighted or otherwise destroyed. People panicked. Gabriel had been far north then, but even they'd heard whispers of it. Nobody knew how it started, or who started it, but when it was done, there was blood to go around on everyone's hands, settler and native.

The Agreement had failed, utterly, and no matter who started it, it would have been well within the rights of the native tribes to sweep every settler into the river and watch them drown.

They hadn't. Life went on. The Mud was only spoken of in whispers, as though to speak was to summon the haint of that failure, and the names of those who'd survived were buried deep in the bones.

Gabriel studied Bernal. He couldn't have been more than a boy himself when it happened, likely only a few years older than Isobel, likely only just made a marshal. A long time to carry that weight, no matter what he'd done.

Isobel only nodded once, then sipped her coffee again before placing it down on the low table between their chairs. "I am more concerned with now," she said, and there was the echo he'd been half-listening for, the deeper tones in her words that told a careful listener the speaker was more than she appeared. Bernal's gaze flickered, and then he nodded once. The matter was closed.

"Tell me about the people here," she went on, and it wasn't a request.

Bernal took a moment to refill his cup—this time straight from the bottle set on the floor, foregoing the coffee entirely. "I don't get much beyond my front door these days. Ask me the going price for trout, or how the saloons are handling the issue of drunkards deciding to settle issues mid-street, and I've first-hand knowledge. But past that . . ."

"You run a boardinghouse," Gabriel said, refusing him that escape. "I suspect much of what's past your front door comes *in* it on a regular-enough basis."

"Some, and regular enough," Rafe admitted. "So long as you understand that this is none of what I've seen myself, nor experienced."

Isobel nodded once, waiting, and the man took a moment to gather his thoughts.

"Past decades, the town's changed. Time was, once you'd've heard more Spanish or Portuguese than French—along with the English, and now, what with the Acadians settling here, their patois's all over the place."

"That's caused troubles?" Isobel was thinking of the boys they'd met, along with the gossip from the saloon, it didn't take any skill to see that.

"Nah. Or not so much. Mostly the 'Cadians are fine folk, if a bit prideful, but you gather too many of any folk in one place, there are bound to be differences. Mostly they get settled by a quick round of fisticuffs, or the occasional out-and-out brawl."

"Or drunken fisticuffs in the street," Gabriel interjected.

"That's more a sport than an argument, but yeah. We're not much for long tempers here, any of us. Particularly in the winter—summer, it's too warm to do more than make rude gestures."

"So, the town's quiet?" Isobel leaned forward, chin resting on her folded hands.

He snorted. "Red Stick's many things, but quiet's never been one of them. But it was . . . peaceful, for the most part."

Isobel's dark eyebrow lifted, and for a moment Gabriel saw an echo of the devil's golden eyes in her own brown ones. "Was?"

He looked at his cup, then set it down on the desk. "Wasn't a thing I could put a finger to, not clearly. Not like . . . back then, when we knew there wasn't going to be enough food for all of us. Weather's been fine, harvest was decent enough, by all accounts, and if fishing's been off a bit, that happens. Nothing to spike prices or make folk foolish over. But there's still . . . something."

"What sort of something?" Isobel's head cocked, and it might have been intended to make him more inclined to confide but instead made the man retreat, picking up his mug again and taking a long drink.

Isobel waited.

"I mean I don't know, something," he snapped at her, then suddenly seemed to remember who—what—he was speaking to. "I don't know how to explain it better than that, because nobody else has been able to either. But folk who passed through, they don't linger long as they used to, and the locals . . .

"It's like being squeezed," he said, finally. "Or pushed, maybe. Nothing sudden, just this sense of being tense all the time, but there's nothing actually happening, and it's annoying you but there's nothing to be annoyed at?"

Bernal seemed to like that explanation, although the shrug he gave when he finished told Gabriel that he knew it was still less than helpful. "There's some, gossips and old men, who thought it might be magicians working mischief, or demon, though they don't as a rule wander down this far. But we've a few medicine folk here who warded the town twice over, and worked their rituals, and couldn't find anything in particular, so . . . And the local tribes, they're good folk, smart fishermen; word had it they were feeling the same thing.

And they couldn't point a finger at why neither."

For a man who swore he didn't know much past his front door, he seemed to know quite a bit. Gabriel bit the side of his cheek to stop himself from pointing that out.

Bernal's eyes narrowed, as though he'd heard Gabriel's thoughts, and his gaze flicked between the two of them before coming back to rest on Isobel. He opened his mouth, rubbed his knuckles across his chin, then shook his head. "But you're here, and my eyes tell me you're a slip of a girl, but that sigil tells me something different. You're here and you're asking questions and that means there's something actual happening. Or something fixing to happen."

Isobel opened her hand—he wasn't even sure she was aware she'd been curling her fingers so tightly—and rested her hand palm-down on her knee. She had no obligation to tell him anything; he was no longer a marshal, held no power in this town save that within these walls. But Gabriel hoped she would think to the need for allies, for ears that could hear what they would not . . .

"The second, we think," she said. "Nothing that I may act on yet."

Mood was not an offense. 'Something' told her nothing.

"But thank you for sharing this with me. Being aware of . . . something may allow me to ease tensions before actual trouble occurs."

For once, Gabriel heard, even though Isobel did not say it. He sympathized.

There was silence between them again, less uncomfortable than watchful, waiting. Rafe had been drumming his fingers on the back of his other hand, then slowing until only a single finger tapped, slowly.

"We have some ideas," Gabriel said, watching him, playing a hunch that if they only kept the former marshal talking, he would say something useful, watching him the way he would a bench of jurists, looking for the crack that would make his case. "But nothing we could hang a man on, so—"

Tiny, tiny, but a definite flinch. Gabriel noted it, and knew that Isobel had as well.

"Tell me," she said, and it was not a request.

He sighed again, pushing back in his chair and looking as though he wanted to be anywhere but where he was. "This isn't a rough town, understand. Mostly folk who live here, they . . . There are all kinds of folk who land here, and we have our own agreement, if you will. We remember the Mud. Wasn't just us against them then; it was everyone against each other, trying to survive. We remember how that went and we don't want it again."

Isobel's voice was soft, just the right side of coaxing, the way she'd talk to a skittish horse or Gabriel would have used on a frightened witness, once upon a time. "But something happened."

"Last week. But it's been brewing for a while. Two months. Group came into town, got some folk worked up about nonsense, how we was living wrong, that sort of thing. They were from downriver, one of the settlements that trades across the river regularly."

Downriver, and trade, meant they dealt with folk from Liberdad, Gabriel surmised. Which was . . . not illegal, seeing as how there weren't what passed for laws of that sort in the Territory, and nobody had a problem with the Free City in and of itself, but the city was in lands claimed by the United States, even if Liberdad itself disputed that. Which made things . . . potentially prickly.

"I think we encountered one of them last night ourselves," Isobel said dryly. "And they brought trouble?"

"They *were* trouble. Claiming we'd sullied ourselves—no, sullied the land, that was it. That letting the Acadians in, letting the freemen settle here. As though letting had anything to do with it. Territory's free to anyone who needs it, I'm right?" He didn't wait for their confirmation. "So, yeah, they were annoying—all right, they were worse than annoying, they were like mudflies in summer—but killin' 'em? That wasn't right."

"Last week?" Isobel was sitting upright now, her jaw tense.

"Two of 'em, aye. Man and a woman."

"Who did it?"

Rafe shook his head. "No idea."

Gabriel wasn't sure if the former marshal was lying or not—he didn't have enough sense of the man—but Isobel would know. That was the kind of thing she did.

"I swear, I've no idea. If I did . . ." The man touched his lapel, an almost instinctive gesture, as though to reveal a silver sigil he no longer wore.

"If you don't know who or where," Isobel went on, "how do you know what happened?"

"They found the bodies outside the city wards, hunting party heading out just before dawn. Rope burn around the neck, neck cracked, nothing else. No bruises, no . . . no anything."

"They weren't raped, you mean." Isobel said it flat enough that he didn't have anything to react against. Gabriel might know how protected Isobel had been, but to this man, she was not a young woman who might be prone to vapors, or even a Road-hardened rider, but the Devil's Hand.

"No. They didn't seem to've put up a struggle, either, and neither of them were delicate creatures. I heard about it this morning, before breakfast. By then, most of their people had up and gone. Gotten the message they aren't welcome here, I guess."

"I guess," Gabriel echoed, his brittle sarcasm wasted on the room. "These folk they were . . . haranguing. Where are they?"

"All over the city. Taverns, mostly; they didn't like the way we gathered, most of all." Rafe's face reflected the unease he'd mentioned earlier. "You're going to . . ." His voice trailed off, as though unsure what he was going to ask Isobel.

"You're no longer a marshal," she said in return. "Unless you've a care to pick up the sigil again?"

He swallowed, fingers tapping faster now. "No."

"No," Isobel echoed, and Gabriel could hear "I didn't think so" in that one word as clearly as if she'd actually said it. "So, that leaves me."

FOUR

They left Bernal's office a little while later, the weight of what they'd learned weighing on both of them.

"So much for rest," Isobel said, her tone a forced sort of cheerfulness. "I suppose I should—"

"Isobel."

She paused in the hallway, turning her chin just enough that she could look up at him. The dim lamps in the hallway cast more shadows than light, but he could tell the lines of her eyes and the stretch of her mouth at midnight on a moonless night by now. "Stop."

"I can't—I need to speak with the hunters Rafe mentioned, and—"

"We've been on the road for months, long enough we've nearly forgotten how to walk rather than ride. Take the morning to find your boots again, learn what the town feels like rather than the road, before you dash into anything. Trust me, a few hours breathing now will help you later."

He could see her hand open and close, fingers curling around the sigil, and her shoulders slipped a little, her chin dipping again. "I'm not even certain what *is* happening," she admitted. "It may be a matter for marshals, when one eventually rides through, or whatever justice this town works out on its own. But—"

"You need to rest. You don't have to sleep, if you're not tired. Write in your journal, send your clothes out to be laundered, make up a list of all the things you want to buy when your pay catches up with you. We can visit another saloon, talk to people tonight, after they've a few ales in them and are less cautious around strangers."

He could see her considering that, weighing her own exhaustion against her worry. "What are you going to do?"

"Stretch my legs. Check on the animals. Maybe find the blacksmith and have him put a new edge on my blades."

Her eyes narrowed, her gaze going inward for an instant, before she nodded. "If you do, take mine."

He watched her walk to their door, waiting until she shot him a look over her shoulder—telling him as clear as words that she knew she was being coddled and wasn't happy about it—and shut the door firmly between them.

He hoped she truly was going to rest; when she caught the bit between her teeth, she could run, but for now . . . His thought trailed off, not entirely sure where he'd been going with it, or how well she would take to being compared to a horse.

"Could be worse," he told himself, rueful. "You could have compared her to the mule."

Another guest came out of his room just then, a lean, angular man with sailor's ink covering the visible skin of his hands and neck, and gave Gabriel an odd look before turning to walk down the stairs to the main hall. The sound of the door to the street opening and closing reminded him that he had things to do as well.

Fortunately, he'd taken his jacket with him to breakfast, so there was no need to go back to the room. The sun was well up into the sky, making it mid-morning, and the storefronts were open, voices calling and hammers clattering, the occasional sound of a wagon being pulled by. It was a smaller, softer scale than Philadelphia, but some familiarity of it remained. After the long, open silences of the prairies and mountains, Gabriel felt the noise like a long-denied itch finally being scratched.

He hadn't realized he'd missed this.

He was painfully aware of the river pressing against his awareness the moment he left the building, but he'd a lifetime of telling it no, and today would be no different.

Still, he hesitated, his face turned toward the river, before turning sharply on his heel and striding in the opposite direction. He had no business with the waterfront today.

His mood fouled, Gabriel picked the first likely-looking mercantile and did a quick browse of what they had on their shelves. Flour, molasses, coffee; prices had gone up since they last restocked. He eyed a new pair of boots and spent some time lingering over a matched set of newfangled dueling pistols that cost more than he'd made in his entire life.

He would ask Bernal if there was anywhere cheaper, but he suspected there would be no bargains to be found for what they needed. Grabbing what looked to be the latest news broadsheets from back east, he headed to the nearest blacksmith, who sent him on to a knife maker, who took a long look at the blades presented to him and shook his head sorrowfully. Gabriel, who had been honing his own blades since he was a boy, waited patiently until the man quoted him a reasonable price, then handed over the coin and blades without hesitation. A whetstone was good enough while they were on the Road, but good tools deserved proper care when it was available.

The man slipped the coins into the pocket of his leather apron and told him to come back in an hour.

Gabriel went back out into the street, thinking he would stop somewhere for something to eat, mayhap overhear talk that might be useful. Instead, he found himself walking back toward the eastern edge of town, as though something else controlled his strides.

"No," he said sharply, and turned around, forcing himself to walk faster than usual, as though not quite trusting his own legs.

Horses, he thought. He needed to check on Steady. The stablemaster had also been a blacksmith; he should see if the man could check their gear and repair anything that looked over-worn or set to fray.

The blacksmith was nowhere to be seen. Steady and Uvnee were tucked into their stalls, drowsing sleepily in the afternoon sunlight slanting through the open doorway. Gabriel hadn't truly had any doubts that they were being well cared for, but it never hurt to let the stable boys know that you were keeping an eye on them. He checked to make sure the horses' water was clean, skimming a finger over the surface, then crunching a handful of the hay in their trough. No rot or dampness, no sign of rodents. There were greenish rinds on the ground by the trough, with indentations the clear shape and size of horse teeth in what remained of the flesh.

"Bet you enjoyed that," he said, slapping the bay's neck affectionately. The gelding snorted, his tail flicking once as though the human were as annoying as the blackflies buzzing around its ears and eyes, and dropped its head again as though to say, "Leave me alone; can't you see we're sleeping?"

Dismissed, Gabriel went out to check on the mule, who had been turned out into a fenced yard with a handful of other mules, and a pair of donkeys who stayed to the far side of the yard, as though irritated by the invasion of their space.

"They don't want to play with the others, huh?" he said, when Flatfoot trotted over to see if Gabriel had brought him a treat. Nobody had given them any melon that he could see; then again, they would likely have eaten the rinds, as well.

"Chee doesn't like anyone except Roy," a voice said behind him.

Gabriel, who hadn't heard the man come up behind him, eased his hand away from the sheath where his knife would normally be, and nodded in greeting. "They yours?"

"They don't belong to nobody 'cept themselves," the man said, coming to lean against the fence next to Gabriel, one boot up against the rail. "But they allow me to hitch 'em to harness every now and again, earn their keep."

Gabriel chuckled at that, scratching the mule between the ears. "Sounds about right. I've got to negotiate with this one on a regular basis, just to keep it from dumping our packs and bolting when it gets the urge. But they're tough little beasts, good companions on the road."

"Never been," the man said. He was balding, tufts of grey hair along his jawline and poking out of his ear, his head as round and white as a river stone. "Born here, planning on dying here. Never felt the urge you riders do to see anywhere else."

Gabriel rubbed at his clean-shaven chin. "That obvious?"

"You boys get that look to you. I seen it a few times. Get to my age, watching other folk is about all the entertainment I've got."

"So, you know this area—and the people in it—well, then."

"As well as anyone, I suppose. You got a question, boy, spit it out. Old man like me doesn't have forever to wait on your hemming and hedging."

Gabriel let out a laugh; for a moment, the old man had reminded him of one of his professors standing at the lectern ready to tear the hide off a feckless student.

"Fair enough. I'm wondering if you've noted maybe something's off, not feeling quite right? People, maybe, or the feel of a place that was fine before? But you can't lay a finger on what's off, not exactly?"

The old man narrowed his eyes, frowning a moment as he considered the question. "Can't say as I have, boy."

"No." Gabriel studied the mules, nudging and nipping at each other. "I don't suppose you have." He had spent too long with the uncanny; he'd forgotten that even in the Territory, not everyone spent their lives looking for it. And riding with the Hand had likely made him more aware than most.

They stood in silence, watching the mules, while the old man's mouth moved as though silently chewing something bitter. "I'll give you some advice, and you do with it whatever you care to. Whatever it is that's chewing on your tail, only so long you've got before it's reached your backside. And once it's got its teeth in there, it don't never let go."

"Voice of experience?"

"Like I said, watchin' people's all I've got now." The old man turned his head and spat, the phlegm thick and yellow where it landed on the winter-pale grass. "And I've never seen it be anything that wouldn't have been better faced." The old man slapped one hand down on Gabriel's shoulder, consolation or commiseration or simply in farewell, and walked away without another word.

Gabriel raised a hand in return, but his gaze, although fastened on the donkeys, was seeing something else entirely. Himself: younger, paler, sicker. And the shadow of a figure, lit by fire and moon at her back.

"I can't remember." Who he was, where he'd been, why he was still alive.

"You had the fever, boy." A woman's voice, dry and scratchy as leaves. *"Not surprising things have gone away."*

"But . . ." He knew that wasn't right, although he couldn't say how he knew. *"I remember things, too."*

Leaving the Territory. Spending years in the States, another life, another *person*. Ignoring the empty echoing within him, trying to fill it with other things, until it left him gasping, twisting, burning up with pain. . . .

"Let them come and let them go," the voice advised. *"Stop fighting so hard, boy. This is what you are."*

He had let them go and kept them gone. But at moments like this, he could taste them lingering on his tongue, ringing in his ears like the after shot of a cannon or the crack of thunder. When the lines between the above-world and the spirit-world faded as though it were high noon, shadows casting too long both in front and behind him, the swirl of something unhealthy rising . . .

He'd felt it before, and no matter how far or long he rode, it was always there when he stopped.

Water don't like being boxed up.

"I don't particularly care what it likes or wants," he said out loud, cutting each word off sharply. "I thought I'd made that perfectly clear." He might be trapped within the Territory, he might have come to terms with that, but he would not let it own him.

He would swear he felt the river laughing at him, and realized that he was glaring at the donkeys as though they'd been the author of his unrest. He let out an exasperated *pfhagh* that made a nearby crow startle into the air.

"Sorry, little cousin," he said, then looked up, craning his neck to catch sight of the sun over the rooftops. It had been long enough; he could swing back around to the knife maker and be back to Isobel before she started to wonder what had happened to him.

Before he started to wonder himself.

Isobel had gone back to their room intending to do as Gabriel had suggested: update her journal, maybe unpack her kit, ask around about a barber, and a seamstress for all the repairs she'd not been skillful enough to make. But the moment the door closed behind her, the pillow and coverlet called to her, a sweetly seductive croon, only aided by the way the sunlight fell through the window, making the linens look warm and inviting.

She slipped her boots off and set them aside, then lay down on the bed, intending only to take a short nap, before . . . doing all the other things she meant to be doing.

Sissssssster.

She knew it was a dream, knew that no snake had slipped into the room, onto her raised bed. And when she opened her eyes, the blue sky overhead, rather than the whitewashed pine of the ceiling, proved her right.

Sisssssster.

"Cousin," she corrected it, groggy as if she had in fact been woken by its hiss. "Cousin" was the proper term between human and spirit animal.

The snake laughed at her, and she came full awake, remembering that the Reaper hawk had called her that as well. *Little sister.*

She swallowed down the sudden fear and sat up slowly, not wanting to startle the snake, whose long brown-and-cream body was coiled alongside her pillow, stretching down the length of the bed. Three yards, she estimated. Maybe more. Large enough to kill her with one bite if it so desired, and she didn't fool herself into thinking that a dream-snake couldn't kill her just as easy. Maybe easier.

"All right," she said, reminding herself to be polite despite the incredibly unwise urge to shove it off the bed, simply to see how it would react. "You have my attention. What incredibly useless bit of advice or vague warning do you have to share this time?"

That was not polite, she could hear Gabriel say in the back of her head. But the snake hissed its laughter again, the rattle at the end of its massive length remaining still.

I cannot sssssimply ssssssay hello?

That would be even worse than useless or vague warnings, she decided, if spirit animals were simply dropping into her dreams to say hello. Worse than calling her "sister." Worse, period.

She waited.

Thisssss isssss not a sssafe place for you.

"This house? Or Red Stick?" Isobel instinctively reached for the knife at her thigh before remembering that it was not there. Not that anything could harm her here, save the snake-spirit allowed it. "Are you telling me to leave?"

You cannot. Sssssso, you mussst be careful.

Isobel woke with a start, gasping for air. Her left hand reached out, slapping the mattress as though half-expecting something to be there beside her, but encountering only warm air and wash-softened sheets.

"Oh." Her skin was sticky, strands of her hair sticking to her face and neck until she peeled them off, grimacing at the feeling of sweat despite her bathing earlier. She pushed the coverlet away and cast another glance at the side of the bed.

Still empty. But the snake's words lingered.

She had been visited by spirit animals before, in person and in dreams, although never before under a roof. She trusted none of them to give her a direct answer; that was not who or what they were, and she did not think it was possible for them to speak directly, but although their advice had been confusing and often conflicting, they had never lied to her.

It was her responsibility to determine what they meant, hopefully before whatever she was being warned of came to pass.

Her hand traced the length of the mattress, as though some further advice might have been left there, then she gave up, forcing herself to sit up, the floor cool under her bare feet. She had likely slept longer than intended but felt less rested than she had previously, which she felt was terribly unfair.

There was fresh water in the basin; someone must have refilled it when they were out. Or someone had come in while she slept, but Isobel thought she would have woken up had that happened. She had never been a deep sleeper, and months on the road had done nothing to change that. Gabriel's snores and the horses stamping and shifting, she could ignore, but not a stranger moving near her.

She used the towel to wash her face and hands, unlacing her top to reach between her breasts. "The mercantile, and a seamstress," she decided, remembering the lighter-looking fabrics the women on the street had been wearing. "As soon as my pay arrives." Or sooner, if she could find someone who would take the devil's credit. Gabriel had said they had enough left to pay their shot for room and board, but she would not borrow his coin for things she should be able to pay for herself.

She draped the towel across the bar on the side of the basin to dry and sat down on the single straight-back chair in the room. Her toes peeped out from under her skirt, and she frowned, lifting one foot up as though she'd not seen it before. The skin of her foot and calf was pale compared to the skin of her hands and face, and she could practically hear Peggy *tsk*ing at how her complexion had coarsened.

"Like there was anything I could do to stop it," she told the memory of the older woman, shaking out her sleep-mussed braid, suddenly far more aware of how her fingers caught against each strand rather than sliding smoothly against them. Eggs, she thought. She could get some eggs and make a poultice for her hair. Find more powder to ease her courses, a dressmaker to fix her seams . . .

"First things first." Braid sorted, she felt suddenly restless. Crossing the room, she opened the shutters over the small window and leaned out enough to note that the sun had lifted above the rooftops. Nearly mid-day, then. She could hear the clatter of wheels and lift of voices from the street, despite the room being at the back of the building. She took a deep breath, unable to identify the rich, sweet smell rising from the profusion of pink and white flowers growing everywhere in the small garden below, their leaves a glossy green, as though they did not know it was winter.

Isobel took another deep breath, savoring the unexpected sweetness, then pulled her body back inside, reluctantly closing the shutters again. Going to her pack, she closed her fingers around the worn leather of her journal, pulling it out with a sense of guilt. She should have updated it the night before, or better yet two nights ago, when everything she had learned from the Acadian boys and the confederacy chieftains had been fresh in her thoughts.

Distraction was not an excuse. The boss expected better of her.

She fetched the last stub of her pencil from the bottom of the pack, noting that she would need to replace that, too, when they replenished their supplies, and sat cross-legged on the bed to write an entry.

She wrote a brief mention of the encounter with the boys on the road, describing their reaction to her, and everything else she could recall. She licked a finger and used it to turn the page. *The next evening, we camped outside the village of the confederacy, and in the morning, were invited by an elder the name of Xaquin*—she paused to consider how his name was actually spelled, then went with the best approximation she could manage—*to pass within their wards.*

That written, Isobel realized that she had no idea what to write about their stay in the village. Usually, the journal documented things she had seen or heard, or done; a record less of her travels than her duties. She would then condense them into a report for the boss, although she suspected he would want to see the journal as well when she returned. Either he or Marie had left the journal for her to take, after all; it was theirs to reclaim when she was done.

But she could not find the words to describe what she had experienced there. This was not a record of fears or suspicions, or vague possibilities, and "they spoke a great deal but said nothing" sounded foolish enough in her thoughts, much less on the page.

But no: the boss had taught her to read people, to judge their truth less by their words than their actions and movements, their expressions and glances.

They hosted a feast, and spoke of the history of their people along the Mudwater, of the Agreement and how their children grew from it. And yet, there was uncertainty in their gestures, and worry in their tones, although they would not speak of it openly.

Later, a young chieftain by the name of Bitter Storm came to us—and she scratched that out and went on—*came to me, speaking more directly of unease and uncertainty, of an unshaped concern as to what was occurring among the people of Red Stick and surrounding areas.*

On arrival in Red Stick, it seems as though his fears have basis, although the unease here seems to be turned against one another rather than the tribes themselves.

She considered adding in the faint memories of her dream, then decided she wanted to think about it more first.

Replacing the journal in her bag, she pulled on her stockings and boots once again, and—since Gabriel had not yet returned—went in search of a pair of shears with which to trim her hair rather than pay a barber with money she did not yet have.

Ana, found in the kitchen, directed her to another young girl, possibly a cousin from her looks, working in the laundry. That girl was able to produce a pair of durable shears from her pocket, the steel blades finger-length and sharp, then gave Isobel equally sharp consideration.

"Do you want me to do for you?"

"I. . . ." Isobel's first instinct had been to retreat back to her room, to do it herself, but common sense won over, and she handed the shears back to the girl with a smile. "If you would?"

Which was how she ended up sitting in the front parlor, having her hair trimmed, while Ana brought them tea and crackers.

"Oh, you should absolutely go to Miz Richardson." The girl's name was Beatrice, and if her uncle didn't pay much attention to what went on beyond his hostería, she went the opposite direction, seeming to know everyone who lived within the city wards. "Her dresses aren't fussy, like some, but they do suit the body, and her prices are reasonable. And if we ask her nice-like, she could alter something for you quick enough, I'm thinking. Especially if you had a story to tell her. Miz Richardson loves her stories."

"Iz has a few of those," Gabriel said from the doorway, making all three of them jump. Thankfully, Beatrice had finished with Isobel's hair by then, and the shears had been laid down on the table. Gabriel was bareheaded, she noted, his dark curls freshly combed, so he'd likely gone up to their room before coming down in search of her. His gaze skimmed the hair scattered on the floor around Isobel, then lifted his eyes back to her face. "Haircut. Not a bad idea. Don't suppose she could take care of me, too?"

It turned out Beatrice could.

There were only a half-dozen people in the dining area when they came down for dinner a few hours later, not including Ana, who was busy refilling the platters, but Isobel had been trained to read a room the moment she entered it, to tell who had a good hand and who was bluffing, and every instinct she had told her they were being watched, as easily as she'd known a demon followed them on the trail.

She told herself she was imagining it, that it was merely being among so many people again that was making her uneasy, but by the time they'd filled their plates and sat down to eat, she had become more uncomfortable than she'd been as the focus of attention in the native village three nights before.

Isobel knew that they'd been looking Road-worn, but simply having their hair trimmed shouldn't have been enough to cause this reaction.

"Are they staring at us?"

Gabriel looked up from his plate, knife halfway to his mouth, and blinked at her, then glanced around. Suddenly, every soul there was otherwise occupied, as conspicuous in their not-looking as they had been previously in their looking.

"No more than any newcomer likely gets a once-over. Most of these folk weren't here for breakfast, so we're newest-come. Isobel, what's wrong?"

"Nothing." She shook her head, reapplying herself to the roast chicken and peas. "Nothing."

She'd managed to almost convince herself that she was imagining it, when Gabriel left to use the necessary, and came back with his face set in an odd expression.

"What?"

He shook his head, sitting back down and adjusting his napkin with almost fussy exactness.

"Gabriel."

His mouth worked over the words, and she waited impatiently until he found the right ones. "Someone stopped me in the hallway. Asked if it was true you were a magician."

Isobel put her knife down on her plate with a muted clatter. "What?"

He shrugged, and she could see, barely, the edges of laughter around his worry. "That's what has them all on edge. Someone's spreading rumors. Most folk have never met a magician—"

"And they should be thankful for that," Isobel muttered.

"—and they don't properly know what it is except something to be wary of. You, apparently, they think they should be wary of."

"Whatever gave them—" They both stopped, and turned to look at the table at the far side of the room, where Ana had been last serving. Her cousin had joined her, and when they saw Isobel looking at them, both girls flushed, and ducked their heads.

"This is why Marie frowned on gossip," Isobel said, her voice promising dire things for the two girls when she caught up with them.

"Mayhap it won't be too bad," Gabriel said, although without much hope in his voice. "If all they did was repeat some of the stories you told them, even mis-told, it won't go too far. . . ."

Except that those were exactly the sort of stories that did go far, she knew. And get more outrageous with each retelling. The Devil's Hand was supposed to be respected and welcomed, not feared. How was she to learn the people there if they supposed she was a madwoman?

Had that been what the snake had meant with its warning?

"Has there ever been a woman magician?" Isobel asked, suddenly curious. The few she'd met—*destroyed*, a voice whispered in her head—had all been male.

"I . . ." Gabriel stopped dead at the thought. "I have no idea, honestly, Isobel. Stands to reason there would be, but I have no idea. I've never heard of one, but—"

"But sane folk run when they see a magician coming; they don't stop to chat," she finished for him. "It's all right," she said, picking up her knife again. "If I don't do anything shocking, they will find something else to gossip about. Even in Flood, there was something new every week; a place this size, surely there will be something new tomorrow."

Whatever Gabriel thought of that plan, he just nodded and went back to eating. They finished their meal in cautious silence, cleared their plates, and stood to leave. Isobel was thinking that she would find the girls and suggest to them that they not speak further about her—with as quiet a menace as she could show, they were only children—when their exit from the dining room was blocked.

"Is it true?" A man stood in front of her, his fists clenched, although he had no other air of threat around him. Tension, yes, but no threat, and Isobel put a hand out to keep Gabriel from doing anything in response. The muscles of his arm tensed, but he stayed still. Isobel drew on years of serving occasionally over-intoxicated guests, as a young girl, and tilted her head and widened her eyes to display innocent confusion. "Is what true, sir?"

The man—not much older than Gabriel, his face the same mixed pattern of sun-darkening showing where facial hair had been, did not seem to even notice her expression. "Is he coming here? The devil. Is he coming here?"

Isobel's thoughts stuttered to a halt. Of all the things the man might have asked her, she had not expected that. The boss? Coming here?

Suddenly, all the things she needed to ask, the things she needed to say to him, had been asking in her journal, rose up and near-choked her before she shoved them down again. A question had been given to her. It wasn't a request, but she felt the obligation of it press on her, nonetheless.

Was the devil coming here?

Ignore the words, she heard the boss say quietly, the way he'd taught her. *Ignore the words and look at the speaker. What does he truly want to know?*

His hands were clenched. Thumbs outside, curling around his fingers. The same way her hand clenched when the sigil burned. His shirtsleeves were rolled neatly to his elbows, not shoved back in agitation, and the cords of his neck were loose, not tight, his jaw rotating slightly, not hard. His eyes . . . She could not read his eyes. He had experience in hiding them. Not the way a cardplayer might but the way a frightened man might, afraid of what others might see, what he might see in others if he looked at them directly.

If they had met him on the road, Isobel thought she might be looking for an ambush—that he was either bait or victim. But here, within the structure of the hostería, protected by the bounds of hospitality?

The man's voice rose, both in volume and in pitch. "Is he coming here? You're the Hand; you must know!"

Her palm itched but did not flare. Every other nerve she had, however, was alight. Had the girls mentioned her title as well as spreading foolish rumors? Rafe was the only other who knew, but he had no reason to speak of it, nor did she think he would—

He would, if he were trying to ease his guests' worries and decided the truth would do less harm than rumor. Especially since she had not given Rafe reason *not* to confirm if asked directly.

And in truth, what did it matter? She would not hide what she was, not for any reason.

The man must have seen acknowledgement in her face, for he pressed on. "I need to know!"

His agitation made her reach out, her left hand catching his, stilling it. Next to her, she could feel Gabriel tense, practically hear the swearing in his thoughts, although he remained silent for now. They'd attracted attention; the whole of the dining room had stilled, looking at them. Waiting.

"I am the Devil's Hand," she agreed. "If you have need of me, I am here. But if there is something you wish to ask the devil himself, you know where he lives."

The boss came to the table when there were players, but he did not look for them. He had no need to.

"I . . . No. No. You're here, though. I saw you last night, in the saloon, and heard . . ." His voice lowered, as though he suddenly realized he'd been near-shouting and rude. "You . . . you are his Hand. And you're here."

Isobel felt her left palm itch, the desperate hope, the need in those words finally rousing the sigil.

"Do you ask for my aid within the bounds of the Agreement?"

His eyes, panicked, flicked to Gabriel, then back to her. "I need protection!"

FIVE

John Harold gave the impression of a man constantly in motion, although he sat perfectly still in the chair Gabriel had steered him to, his hands resting on his knees, elbows tucked against his ribs, shoulders squared and back straight, his chin dipped slightly to his chest. It had less to do with his physical presence and more to do with the air of agitated concern that surrounded him.

"I need protection," he said again, this time less a plea or demand than a quiet statement of fact, the fourth—or perhaps fifth—time he had said it.

"From who, and because of what?" Isobel had asked three times before, and each time, he had merely shaken his head, lips pressed together as though afraid of something escaping without his consent.

Isobel pressed her fingers into the marks of the sigil in her palm and stilled her own breathing, waiting for something to rise. There was a sense of worry, of tension reeling up within her, but nothing else, nothing more than she had been feeling for days now.

She was beginning to wonder if she had ever felt anything else, if there had ever been anything else.

"Isobel." Gabriel's voice, low, from the door of Rafe's study, where he had ushered them when the man began to make a scene. She gave Harold another quick glance, then joined her mentor.

"He's requested aid," she said, before he could say anything. "But if he won't tell me how, or why, I can't tell for certain if it's a thing I can do."

The sigil was interested, but it wasn't *directing* her yet. And the whisper that had sometimes plagued her was silent. Thankfully. Isobel was not entirely certain she trusted the whisper, for all that it had steered her well before.

Gabriel turned to study John Harold, his expression shifting from calm concern to something more calculating. "Can you tell this: is he asking for protection against someone who has wish to harm him, or from someone he has harmed?"

Her lips parted around a small indrawn breath; she had not considered the latter possibility, and felt foolish a heartbeat after that she had not. Not that it mattered: innocence or guilt was a matter for judges, not her.

The Agreement was a simple thing, for all its breadth, and she was bound by it. If a settler had an argument with another settler, a marshal would mediate, or bring them before a judge if needed, to settle the matter. Isobel could do nothing more than bear witness. If the man had given offense to a native tribe and feared reprisal, Isobel could do nothing for him: her obligation was only to ensure such punishment was carried out, if the tribe offended against chose to do so.

The few times she had been drawn into direct intervention, it had been from a threat aimed at the Territory itself, not individuals.

"Do you want me to speak with him?" Gabriel's offer was almost diffident, but something lay underneath, sharp-edged and cool. "Man to man?"

Isobel supposed she should feel offended, likely would have been offended, save for the itching, stinging sensation of worry filling her palm. The work did not care who did it, only that it was done. And yet, below all that she could feel the boil of rage at the idea that he was trying to undermine her authority, her competence.

Gabriel waited for her response. Only a fool refused help for the sake of pride. Isobel nodded once. "Yes." Then she added, "Please. Thank you."

Her mentor's hand was warm around her wrist, gently pulling and moving her to one side. She allowed him to direct her the same way he'd guided her hand on the carbine when training her, the same way he lifted the reins to shift Steady to another trail, his manner clear instruction to stay still and quiet now.

She leaned against the wall, just inside the door, her arms crossed over her chest, and waited.

"So. Master Harold."

"John."

"John," Gabriel said, nodding agreeably as he approached the other man. Rather than taking the chair Isobel had been using, he leaned one hip against the table, crossing his arms across his chest and looking down at the man, his head cocked slightly to the side. Now trimmed, his hair no longer fell across his eyes when he did that, and Isobel had a flash of how he might have looked when he was younger, arguing law in the States. "You're a wheelwright, yes?"

"Yes."

"Rafe says you've been living in Red Stick most of your life?"

"Since I was a boy. My folks came upriver, opened the shop. I took over for them when they died." He swallowed, and his fingers clenched slightly on his knees.

"It's good to have roots," Gabriel said, approvingly. "Sink 'em deep, and nothing can move you unless you want it to."

"I . . . Yes." He sounded uncertain, as though he wasn't quite sure what he was agreeing to. Isobel thought she could see the pattern Gabriel was weaving, and held her breath, afraid to do anything that might disturb it.

"But roots go both ways," Gabriel went on. "You sink deep enough, you start to feel protective, like this is yours, anyone who hurts it, hurts you."

"I suppose?" Isobel watched Harold's shoulders curl in, his entire body sliding shut like a possum trying to play dead, and she knew, the way she knew such things, that he was protecting more than himself; he was holding some secret inside, even as it tried to work its way out.

"That's how the Territory works, isn't it?" Gabriel's tone shifted, from questioning to conversational, as though they were two old friends talking of inconsequential things. "We protect it, and it protects us. That's what the Agreement is all about, learning how to protect what keeps us safe."

"Yes." There was such relief in the man's voice, Isobel felt her knees nearly buckle under the weight of it. "Yes, you understand." He lifted his head, his gaze meeting Isobel's, as though he had been speaking to her all along. "You understand we had no choice. We had to protect it!"

It took all of Gabriel's skills, plus a mug of Rafe's coffee, to calm John Harold—"Johnny, they call me Johnny"—back down before his story came out, stuttering and shuddering but reasonably clear.

He had been witness to the murders Rafe had told them of. More than witness; a participant, if unwilling after the fact.

"We were just minding ourselves, having a drink after a long day. Six, no seven, Louis came in late, and we were minding our own business when they came in. . . ."

"Who?"

"Two of those frothing gospel-sharp types, been ranting in the streets for weeks now. Telling us we'd taken vipers to our breasts; that was her exact words. Told us we'd poisoned the land, disgraced ourselves, brought damnation on us all, that sort of nonsense. And we'd been hearing it for so long, it should have just slid off our backs, but... something went worse, then."

He shuddered, took another deep sip of his whiskeyed-up coffee, and went on.

"I don't know who brought out the rope, who got the chairs. I . . . can't remember. I think I looked away, didn't want to see, but . . . I remember what it sounded like, the side of the chair across the floor and the . . . the crack of his neck first. The way her skirts flapped around her legs, and how she wasn't shouting at us anymore. The stink of piss in the air, 'cause they'd soiled themselves when the rope dropped.

"It was their own fault." His voice changed, as though he was repeating something he'd said, over and over again, or maybe had told to him. "Nobody wanted it; it didn't set well with any of us. But how long can a body listen to someone telling 'em the how we live our lives is wrong, telling us all this, everything we have, is wrong, and the only way proper is to cut down everything we've built, everything we've made of this town, and never build it up again? That we're supposed to cut ties with kin across the river, just because they're across a river?"

He shook his head and downed the remainder of the mug. "But ever since then . . . I've been having dreams. Piss and blood, all around me, and something with scales creeping up my leg, coming after me. . . . and it's quiet, so quiet, and all I can hear is how quiet everything is after it's dead."

Rafe had arranged for two young men to escort John Harold to his home, with instructions to ensure that he spoke with no one outside his own family until further notice, then reclaimed his seat behind the desk, his mouth a thin, grim line as Gabriel recounted what they had learned.

"He killed them? The two who were hung, he did it?"

Gabriel looked to Isobel, ceding the floor to her.

"He was present, at the very least. I'm not certain he remembers what he did or didn't do, only that it was done and he was there." Isobel sighed, pressing her fingers under her eyes in hopes that would make the faint headache go away, before continuing. "The mind can break like a bone sometimes. Or splinter, and the shards stick unpleasantly, making part of them mad and other parts sane. The blacksmith's first apprentice went that way, after the forge threw such a spark the hearth near-exploded, knocking her head over bootheels. She seemed fine, save that she remembered things that had never happened and forgot some things that had."

Isobel felt more than saw Gabriel wince, and looked at him curiously, but he shook his head, making a hand motion for her to continue.

She frowned at him, her eyes promising that they would come back to that, and went on. "But clearly, he believes that the action he took part in, or observed, has left him vulnerable to harm in turn, that something haunts him, threatening him. He simply cannot identify the source."

Rafe frowned at her words. "Cannot, or will not?"

Isobel exhaled, then made trade-sign for a feeling of uncertainty, coupled with frustration.

"The tribes are dreaming of red water," Gabriel said quietly, almost to himself. "They say the wind and the water are uneasy. A man who may not be in full possession of his senses, taking part in a murder and fearing unknown reprisals in a dream . . ."

"It's all connected," Isobel agreed. "All of it. But how—and what it means . . ." The headache intensified, as did the feeling that she was missing something still. Dreams did not come from nothing, not dreams like those. Something had to drive them . . .

"We will need to speak with the medicine folk living within the wards, learn what they've seen."

"They won't speak with you," Rafe said, then snapped his jaw shut when Isobel turned to stare at him.

"They will speak to me," she said, and there was no option for dissent.

❧ ❧ ❧

Rafe had been able to name a handful of medicine folk who lived within the city proper, and another few who had places outside the wards. "They're none of them particularly welcoming to outsiders," he warned them. "And they all keep peculiar hours. You'll want to wait until the morning to be certain of catching them at home, if not awake."

She'd been near-certain he'd added something under his breath about it not being his fault if they came back frogs, but hadn't asked him to repeat himself.

There had been a packet outside their door when they retired for the night. Wrapped in thick brown paper and a string, unfolded it had revealed a long-sleeved but lightweight blouse, dyed a dark blue, with a banded collar not unlike those of Gabriel's shirts, but a decidedly feminine line. There was no note, but she suspected Beatrice's hand in this, likely in apology for her hand in stirring the gossip.

The fabric felt oddly smooth and almost slick, but she could tell the difference between it and her more durable wool; the air could move through it to reach her skin, rather than being blocked from it.

"I need two more of these," she said. "Or three."

Gabriel looked at her with amusement clear in his expression. "Don't show such eagerness," he said, "or you'll end up paying far more than anyone else in town for the same work."

"I'm not twelve," she shot back. "I know how to bargain." But, to herself, she admitted that he might have a point about her enthusiasm.

"Wear it tomorrow," Gabriel advised, as she folded the dress away carefully. "Looking respectable is oft half the battle. And it may well be that the gossip will serve us well, this once," he added, solemn-faced. "They will be so relieved you are not, in fact, a wind-mad magician, they will be willing to tell you anything."

Isobel threw her pillow at him and got ready for bed.

It rained overnight, making everything glisten slightly on leaf and board, tamping the dust of the road down to comfortable levels, even when a heavy draft horse pulled its sledge past them, the driver seemingly half-asleep at the rein. Isobel had draped her shawl over her shoulders, pleased to note that the dark blue cover nearly matched the dye of her new blouse, wishing idly for a blue hatband to complete the ensemble.

Gabriel had also dressed up, wearing a pinstriped shirt she couldn't remember seeing before, his newly shorn hair neatly slicked back under his hat. He offered her his arm as they stepped onto the front porch, making a show of walking along the street-side to protect her from splashes.

Her mouth twitched a little, remembering how splattered with mud and less savory fluids they'd been over the past months, but allowed him to play the gallant.

"You have the list," he reminded her. "Where to first?"

She didn't need to consult the scrap in her pocket; she had let instinct move her, choosing a name not entirely at random. "Down by the docks," she said. "Then we can move back through town and hopefully finish close to home rather than having to walk all the way back again."

"Practical as ever," he said, but there was a tone in his voice that made her doubt her decision, wondering what about it he disliked.

"Do you think we should do it differently?"

He snorted, sounding so much like Flatfoot for an instant, she almost looked around for the mule. "No. Your instinct says go there, we go there."

The hostería had been built in the heart of the north-central part of town, where the buildings seemed to almost lean against each other, rising two or three stories above the street. Isobel noted with interest how the road they started on curved into another rather than turning, and then curved into yet another. It made for a slightly dizzying experience but, she quickly realized, avoided creating legitimate crossroads where power might accidentally pool. Someone would still need to clean up anything that did accumulate, of course—no doubt one of the names on the list Rafe had given them, since there was no marshal in town—but a spiral was much safer than a square.

"Clever," Gabriel said when she pointed it out, but his attention seemed distracted, a faint frown creasing his forehead, under the brim of his hat.

"It's like the river," she said on a hunch. "All sliding soft curves, the power runs in flows. Takes it into itself with the tributaries but doesn't have to share it with anything or get bunched up anywhere."

"I suppose."

Something was definitely wrong; his response was curt, almost as though he hadn't truly heard her. She firmed her hold on his arm, but left him to his thoughts, instead turning her head to study the building they were passing. Unlike the storefronts, this was a long, low structure, with a flat roof and barn-style doors, heavy chains at either end that were clearly used to pull them open. A few men were hanging about the side, having a quiet but intense discussion, while several more men were entering another similar structure a few doors down, laughing loudly amongst themselves.

"Shipwright's shop," Gabriel said, suddenly noting her interest. "Canoes, whatnot, they can be fixed on the banks. But anything larger, you need space for repairs. They're likely arguing over a fee now, those three."

"Larger?" She didn't particularly care, but it was better than him being lost in his own thoughts.

"Barges," Gabriel said. "Big, flat, move things up and down the river. And across, too. River's wide, Isobel. Horses can't ford it; wagons can't cross on their own."

"Oh." She knew that, or she would have known that if she'd thought about it. "Up the river?" She tried to imagine that, but her knowledge of the Mudwater was limited to *very long and marks the eastern edge of the Territory*, as she'd seen on Gabriel's maps.

"River flows down into Spanish lands," he reminded her. "And the States on the other bank. And Liberdad at the end, with all the freebooters taking advantage as best they can. The devil's utter disinterest in things like excise taxes makes the Territory a good stopping point. Pay off the locals, set up shop, show off what you can bring someone if only they'll hand over their coin. Or did you think the stick candy you like so much came from around here?"

Isobel flushed. She did know better; she'd been there when the wagons had unloaded supplies, Ree keeping careful stock of what went where and how much had been paid. She just hadn't thought about how it got into the wagon before. That had been Marie's domain: the Right Hand was the granting and receiving, the *care* of the Territory.

"The molasses comes . . . from Spain, yes?"

"Spanish territories . . . Places where they've only ever heard of us. Where the Territory is just a story they tell to shock the civilized." The thought seemed to amuse him. "But goods come and go, and they're hauled up the Mudwater, dropped off and taken inland. They pull the barges into dock down there"—and he gestured eastward—"and drag 'em down the road to here for fixing, then drag 'em back."

She couldn't imagine what might break on a barge, but she wasn't quite sure she was imagining a barge right, either. "Why didn't they build it closer to the river?"

"Remember what I told you about flooding. River has moods." His expression changed, subtle enough that even looking at him she almost missed it, amusement flickering into something that looked like fondness, then pain, then smoothing out into the mask she now recognized he had been wearing for several days now. She wanted to pull the mask off, to force him to tell her what was wrong.

"Come spring, sometimes in winter, it'll rise up over the banks, come into town like someone called it for supper," he went on. "Nothing's built on the riverside you plan to have last more than a season."

The moment was lost, his facade firmly in place again. She looked eastward, although she already knew he was right: the only structures past the shipwright's shop and a warehouse were shacks that looked as ready to fall over as they were to stand up, and a couple of low, muddy pens that were currently empty of livestock.

"Brewhouses," Gabriel said. "Take a whiff."

She took a deeper breath and coughed. "It smells like bread," she said. Except the smell was thicker than she remembered, clogging in her throat.

"And there you have Red Stick's other claim to fame," Gabriel said, falling back into what she considered his "mentor voice." "Back when the town was barely that, fellow by the name of Delassus came downriver on a barge. Story had it he was fleeing a family dispute, and carried with him his pack, his name, and the recipe for beer that was better than anything the locals had been able to make." Gabriel laughed. "He picked the right place to settle. Combine strong beer and trade access, that makes for wealth. Or at least power."

"Power to do what?"

"Whatever he wanted, within reason. Fortunately, what he seemed to want was a quiet town with uninterrupted trade." He waved an arm, she presumed to indicate the entire city. "And this is what grew from that. It's not quite Boston or Liberdad, but Red Stick does all right for itself."

Isobel was going to ask him more about this Delassus, who sounded interesting, when her attention was pulled away from the discussion, almost as though someone had yanked at her arm. Her gaze passed over the two nearest buildings without hesitation, lingered on the third, then crossed the narrowing street to come to rest on a fourth, standing slightly apart from the others.

Other than that, it was unremarkable: two stories high, windows on the upper level, but only the now-familiar archway for a front door, shutters flung open to catch even a hint of breeze. A sign hung over the arch, painted red, the lettering unreadable from that distance.

A saloon, or a brewhouse, Gabriel said. There was no whisper in her ears this time; no sense of being led to a destination, no urgency or worry particularly, and the sigil in her palm did not itch with the sense of intent or purpose. And yet, something drew her attention.

She took a step forward, then another, aware that Gabriel had stopped speaking and was following her. A glance at his expression showed no surprise or doubt, only a calm expectation and readiness.

"They're here," she told him. "They're waiting for us."

Gabriel could feel himself tensing, every step closer to the river they went. If he had been alone, he would have turned on his heel and gone the other way, names on a list be damned.

But he wasn't alone, and this was more important than his own discomfort.

Normally, the devil wouldn't pay attention to the taking of a few lives: the Master of the Territory had far greater concerns, despite what some folk wanted to believe. But there were threads being wound around those lives that even Gabriel could feel, tightening at throat and wrist.

Although he wasn't certain if he trusted his own nerves just then. The last time he'd come this close to the river, he'd nearly lost himself, and it was only the feel of Isobel's hand on his arm that kept him grounded now, overrode the stink of the river lingering in his nostrils and on his skin, no matter how often he scrubbed himself clean.

"They're waiting for us," she said, and stepped away from him, her fingers slipping off his sleeve.

He thought of the river reaching for him that morning, of the tides turning red, and as Isobel started walking away from him, his hand slipped to the sheath on his thigh, loosening the ties, feeling the bone handle cool against his palm. Not enough, not walking into an unknown danger. There was another knife in his boot, but by the time he reached it—

His gaze slipped over the scene, calculating attacks, defensives, potential traps. By the door, there was a stack of firewood; he identified several pieces that would be the right size to use as a cudgel, assuming they hadn't dried into fragility already.

She was already at the door, and he stretched his legs to catch up with her. "Isobel, wait—"

She didn't. Cursing under his breath, Gabriel pulled the knife all the way from its sheath and followed her.

Inside, the smells were far stronger and stale, as though no breeze had stirred the room in weeks. The light was dim enough after the daylight outside that it took him a moment to regain his sight, all his other senses snapping forward to assure himself that there was no threat.

"No need for that sort of cutlery here, young sir," a woman's voice said, her cheer scraping across Gabriel's nerves and making him itch to bury the knife in something merely in reaction. He controlled it, sliding the tip back into the sheath but not letting go of the handle. The woman coming out of the shadows was tall and pale, dressed in drab homespun, an apron wrapped twice around her waist and a cloth tossed over one shoulder, as though she'd been interrupted cleaning dishes. A handsome woman, Gabriel noted, of the sort he thought Isobel would grow into: tough and stern. The near-panic that had gripped him outside faded to an almost-painful alertness, even as he slipped the knife back all the way into its sheath.

"Our apologies," Isobel said, taking the lead in his silence as though they'd planned for exactly this. "We'd heard this was a good place to catch a proper gossip. Just ridden in, y'see, and still finding our ground."

The woman gave them both a once-over, taking in everything from their boots to their hats. Gabriel, suddenly reminded of his manners, reached up to take his off, and the woman gave a grim nod. "Been on the Road awhile, have you, then?"

"Long enough to wear calluses on my backside where it used to be smooth," Isobel said, her tone dry as desert grass. "And get right tired of the sound of each other's voices."

The words were casual, their bodies speaking of polite back-and-forth, but Gabriel could feel something rising in the space between them, sharp and heavy, and if he'd been a horse or a cat or a thing with any sense whatsoever, he would have given in to that urge and taken a number of steps back.

But he held by Isobel's side and waited until they'd finished sizing each other up.

"So, you came to hear a touch of mine?" There was a drawl to the woman's voice that reminded Gabriel of the flowers that clung to some of the buildings, their perfume almost overpowering when you walked directly underneath.

"If you'd be so kind," Isobel responded.

"Kindness has no play in this, and you know that better than most, I'm thinking." The woman reached up to wipe her hand on the cloth over her shoulder, then offered that hand to Isobel. "I'm known hereabout as Sarah."

"Isobel of Flood."

"Of Flood but not in Flood," Sarah said. "Been a while since the Master of the Territory sent one of his own all the way down here. How did we happen to catch his eye?"

"Funny enough, word is you could mayhap tell us that. Word is, you've been noting things stirring previous, enough to take action to scry for it."

Medicine woman. That's what Isobel had meant, that they were waiting for her. Gabriel exhaled but could not convince his muscles to ease, or his hand to move from the knife's hilt.

"Word's been talking mayhap too much," Sarah replied. "Though I suppose you'd have sussed me and mine out on your own just as easy if they hadn't."

Isobel gave a faint shrug but otherwise stood still, a calm readiness filling her.

"Oh, enough of this posing and posturing," Sarah said. "The both of you, bless. Come in, already, come in and sit yourselves down; it doesn't take a lick of wisdom to know that this is going to take too long for standing."

She led them not to one of the tables out front but through the shadows she'd emerged from, into a back room lit by an open hearth giving off a clear white light and a notable lack of heat. If it were a coalstone, it was the largest Gabriel had ever seen, larger than any he'd ever heard of, and would be worth more than everything he owned. If it wasn't . . .

Fire was not so changeable as wind, nor did it claim so high price, but he'd only ever run into one practitioner before, and he'd been . . . volatile. He tried to think of a way to warn Isobel, but short of giving blatant offense to their host—a thing to be avoided—he could not.

"Sit." And it wasn't a request. Isobel gathered her skirts and settled on a heavy carved chair, leaving the choice of another chair near the hearth, or a long bench farther away. He chose the bench, and the woman laughed at him.

"It won't bite you, not unless I say so. And I suspect your companion might have opinions about me doing so."

Gabriel gave in. He had no place to be telling a medicine woman of any stripe what she might or might not do, and they both well knew it.

This time, the fire laughed at him too, leaping and sparking in a near-audible chuckle. Isobel seemed oblivious to it all, her dark eyes trained on Sarah as though intending to memorize her entire.

"So, devil's girl. You know there's something wrong here. You wouldn't be searching me out if you didn't. Does your master feel it too? All the way in his spider's nest, does he feel the trembling of threads, even here?"

Isobel licked her lips, mouth parting as though to speak, and then instead offered her left palm as though for inspection. The medicine woman glanced at it but seemed unmoved.

"It itches me when something is awry, something needs resettling. It burns when something is wrong and needs fixing. It harries me when there is a place I need be."

"And it does these things here?"

"No." Isobel closed her fingers over her palm and dropped her hand back to her lap. "But it worries at me all the more with every soul I speak to. Something is wrong, but it does not seem to fall within my contract to mend.

"And yet," Isobel went on, before either Sarah or Gabriel could say anything, "everyone we meet seems to think the devil *should* be paying mind. So, tell me, if you will, what happened to the man and woman who died in this place?"

Gabriel felt as though he'd been gut-slapped, and from the expression on Sarah's face, more quickly hidden, she had been caught off-guard as well.

"Were they friends of yours?" And Sarah's voice cracked with something colder than river ice, heavy and capable of crushing the unwary swimming between.

Isobel let out a short laugh. "I suspect I'd have walked silver-bare through a crossroads to avoid them, if the stories told are true. People that angry, they're not restful to be around."

"'Not restful,' that's a good way of putting it." Sarah seemed to come to a decision, pulling the other chair over and sitting down in it as though standing was too much effort. "I'm here, more nights than not, but I wasn't when those two died. If I had been, I might've been able to stop it, although I can't swear to that, either. Can't swear I would have stopped it. Those people, they had a way of riling folk up to do damage, and I've made it my place to keep this town safe."

Isobel shifted in her chair, the slightest rearrangement of her bones into something more alert. "Those people, you say. You knew the entire group?"

"The ones I saw, anyhow. Five of them, two women and three men, all old enough to know better and young enough to still embrace foolishness like a lover. I'd already been uneasy, mind you, well before they came. Salted and smudged and did every other trick I could think of, to make sure nothing evil-minded could come in. And yet they did."

"Evil-minded?"

"As a goblin pup. The words that dripped from their tongues were venom and bile, hidden underneath flowers and moss."

"You didn't like them," Gabriel ventured.

"Not particularly, no." The woman's drawl deepened. "Would you much like a soul as thinks you're living all wrong, you and everyone around you?"

"Not particularly," Isobel agreed. "That's what they were angry about? Judgmental type?"

"Worse than a preacher-man scorned in love. All that one, the woman, lacked was a Bible to thump or a pail of brimstone to rattle."

Isobel's lips twitched, and Sarah raised her chin as though offended. "You find that amusing?"

"Gospel-sharp tried that once, where I'm from," Isobel said. "Boss let him rant a bit, then set his book on fire."

Gabriel suddenly wished, very hard, that he'd been there to see that.

"First good thing I've heard of your boss ever," Sarah said. "Not that I'm against his works," she added. "But you can know a thing is useful and still not like the fact that it exists. And last time his Hand came thisaway, well, a lot of people suffered for it. But I suspect my dislike of him bothers him not one whit."

"He doesn't much care," Isobel agreed. "Tell me more about what happened when they first came to town. When you first felt unease."

Sarah frowned. "Unlikely I can explain it to you, what I felt. Not in ways you'll understand. You've both got the Territory touching your bones, I can tell, but that's a thing different entire from how I was learned, and I'm not sure it's ever translated proper."

Isobel lifted her chin, and Gabriel pinched the bridge of his nose, knowing what was coming. "Show me, then. Fire holds no fear for me."

Sarah laughed at her request, a pealing noise that had no humor in it, but Isobel merely waited until the sound died away, and repeated, "Show me."

"No." There was no laughter then but a flicker of anger. "You may fear nothing, but I am not so foolish. I wish you only well in this, Isobel Devil's Hand, but I will not share what you have not earned, nor tell you things you've no right to know. Not with you, and certainly not with the devil himself."

"But—" Isobel dropped her gaze first, and Gabriel let out a silent sigh of relief, even as he followed suit, just in case the woman looked to him. "I regret if I gave offense," she said. "If you determine there is more you may share, we are staying at the Bernal hostería."

Sarah nodded once, that flicker of anger tucked away again, but he could feel her gaze between his shoulder blades until the door closed behind them. And possibly, he would not swear oath otherwise, even after.

The sun had passed overhead while they were inside, but if anything, the air felt warmer, not cooler. Gabriel settled his hat back on his head and tried to ignore the trickles of sweat along his hairline and under his collar, unable to pretend it had anything to do with the weather.

"You knew she wouldn't show you what she knew. She couldn't. But you pushed her anyway." Isobel might be nearly done with her mentorship ride, but nearly was not entirely, and she had been foolhardy there.

"I wanted to see what cards she was holding. Surprising her seemed the only way to do it."

He played a decent hand of cards, but Isobel had been raised in the devil's house, learned how to read the players, read *people*, from the master of lies himself. It made her actions no less foolhardy but did increase her chances of success.

He waited as they walked, her hand resting lightly on his arm in the perfect pattern of a well-bred young lady out for a stroll; whatever she wanted to tell him, she would. Eventually.

There was more of a crowd on the street now: workers leaving their jobs, the occasional better-dressed man, and a scattering of women, most dressed rough but respectably. At least two of the houses were fancy, he noted, although only one of them showed activity this early in the day.

"She was lying."

And that wasn't a surprise at all. "About what?"

"I don't know." Isobel frowned, the muscles of her hand tightening on his arm. "Maybe about not being there that day, about being uneasy, all of it. Even her offense at the end. I don't think her anger was about my asking—that would have warranted a refusal and maybe a sharp scolding at most."

So, Isobel had known what she was doing. Gabriel wasn't certain if that made it better or worse.

"I can say this: the only whole truth in her cloth was that she truly didn't like the ones who died. She didn't like any of them."

Gabriel didn't pretend to understand how Isobel could read a body like that, not someone she'd only just met, in such dim light, but he didn't question her certainty. He tried to think like an advocate again, sorting through evidence. "So, she was lying. Why? Because she was part of the murders? Or she knew who was?"

"I don't know. I couldn't ask her straightaway, could I?"

She certainly could have: invoke her authority as the Hand, and . . .

And what then? If the woman continued to lie, what would Isobel do then? Either walk away or . . .

Or what? There was the sticking point, and the thing that had made him reach for his blade, useless though it would have been. Pitting power against power was a portion of what the Agreement had been designed to *prevent*.

He steered them around a man who was leaning against a wall, stinking of piss and ale, arguing with himself. "Did you learn anything useful other than how to give me grey hairs?"

"The murders were settler against settler, and likely provoked. A judge might be able to determine if there should be punishment, but not without someone to speak for the dead."

"And the sigil?"

"Nothing. And there . . ." Her voice trailed off, then returned. "There wasn't any whisper."

The sigil flared when something needed the Hand's attention, but the whisper, as she called it, was something newer. Neither of them were quite certain where or what it came from, which made him twitchy as a rabbit on an open plain, but Isobel trusted it, and Gabriel didn't have much say in the matter after that.

"So, we go on to the next name—"

"I want to try something," she said suddenly. "Hold up."

He already didn't like whatever she had planned, but followed her into a narrow alley, out of the way, and waited, keeping one eye out for anyone who might stumble, drunkenly or otherwise, upon them. She knelt in the dirt, and Gabriel took a step back, all too aware of how it might look to anyone who happened to glance down the alley. Isobel didn't notice, her hands palm down on the ground, head tilted up, her eyes closed.

"Here?"

"Too many people, deeper in town," she said impatiently. "I'm betting that's why all the medicine folk are on the outskirts too. Now hush. Please."

She'd tried to explain to him what happened when she reached for the bones, but all he understood of it was that she lost herself for a little bit, and so every time she did this, he clung to the sense of her that he knew, the entirety that was Isobel née Lacoyo Távora, as though it were a light in the window to bring her home if she were to lose her way back.

It had worked so many times, it took him too long to realize that this time, it hadn't.

"Isobel?" Her eyes were wide open, but they were hazed, their normal warm brown color gone milky. "Iz? Isobel!"

He reached down to grab her shoulders. The instant he touched her, she fell forward, limp as a cloth doll.

PART THREE

DEEPER DOWN

ONE

She was home, the familiar creek, the rolling hills, the weathered grey buildings of Flood itself all spread out in front of her, and she was driven to her knees with the sudden longing that filled her. The tall grass prickled her palms, and the smell of sun-warmed dirt filled her nose.

Sssssss.

The heavy muscled body of a snake slithered over one hand, the cool black weight of it a shock. The snake slithered away from her, and in its trail the grass caught fire, thick red flames catching on low winds and spreading impossibly fast across the plains. She stared, rapt, until she realized it had caught her as well, the air becoming nothing but flame and heat. She turned, intending to run, but her legs were gone, her arms gone; there was nothing but a rolling, molten heat, sluggish in veins, charring bones, singeing hide and hair. The aftermath of a lightning strike, the rolling ash of a prairie blaze, the swirling boil of steaming hot springs stinking of rot and rebirth, and deep within all that, the knotted scream of something else, something not-of-heat, something burning charring crumbling even as the fire reforged it, over and over and over. . . .

Isobel.

The whisper hurt too much to hear.

Isobel.

Not a whisper now: a shout, a scream, a howl. Shredding itself out of the flames, wind wrapping itself around stones tumbling in water, green roots sprouting and burning and sprouting, wrapping themselves around wind around flame the heat bound in cool and it was

Isobel.

The whisper did not fade but became separate threads, unwinding and reforming into stone and water, fire and bone, and was

Isobel.

"No!"

She could breathe. That was her first thought: that she could breathe, and the air was warm but did not burn her throat. Her second thought was that she had a throat.

Her third thought was that she was lying down. Her hand reached out and encountered not cold dirt, nor the softness of sheets, but a dry, scratchy crumble. She lifted her hand and identified the brown bits and flakes falling through her fingers as the remains of dried leaves, crushed by her touch.

She was lying in a pile of dried leaves, in a room with whitewashed log walls and a ceiling of grey fog.

"This is a dream." Her voice sounded the same as it ever did, and she wondered what she had been expecting. She didn't think she had ever dreamed like this before, or if she had, she didn't remember when she woke up, not the way a dream-talker would.

She wished now she'd had time to really speak with Calls Thunder, back in De Plata all those months ago. But she hadn't know what to ask, hadn't known she *could* ask. . . .

Moving. She should try that. Maybe.

The leaves crackled under her, giving no support, and she wondered uneasily how deep they went, if there was ground or floor below her at all, or dried leaves all the way down. Down to where? She tried to contemplate that and shuddered. Even in dreams, there were some things best not thought of.

"Particularly in dreams," a voice agreed, and she turned her head to see a tiny, dun-colored bird sitting on the sill of a window that hadn't been there before. Not the bird, not the sill, nor the open window.

"Why not dreams?" she asked, and the tiny bird cocked its head, red-brown wings fluffed, the hook-like beak flashing gold despite the fog.

"The bone world, things are . . . solid. Set. You can change them, but slowly, tick by tick. Here, all you need to do is think, and things shift. Try not to do that. You're not good at it."

Despite herself, Isobel almost smiled. The one consistency she had found, speaking with spirit animals, was their need to insult whoever they were speaking to. She shifted, trying to ignore the crackling, but the sound and the feel of the dried leaves under her skin made her realize suddenly that she was bare as the day she'd been born, hair loose down her back, skin glimmering golden-brown the same way the bird's beak had.

She felt no embarrassment, no shame; the only thing there to see her was the spirit bird, and she suspected it cared not at all if she wore cloth or skin or feathers. But she was curious what had happened to her clothing.

"They burned off," the bird said, and the memory swept over her, the pain muted this time but still enough to make her skin flinch and sweat in response.

"It forgets, sometimes," the bird said, and she might have thought it nearly apologetic. "It needs you too badly. You need to be brave, be careful, and remember."

"Remember what?"

"What you are," the bird said, and with a lift of its wings, it was in motion, a blurring flutter, diving directly at Isobel before she could flinch, and the hooked beak was suddenly much larger, tearing open the skin of her stomach, and *she was falling back into the crackling brown leaves, burning hot and searing the flesh from her once again* . . .

When Isobel fell, Gabriel had panicked. Her skin had been clammy with sweat, her face slack as though insensible, her breathing slow and labored, shoulders tight but her fingers and elbows loose, dangling as though something had cut all strings connecting them.

"Isobel. Iz!" He dared not shake her but cradled her in his arms, calling urgently, hoping against all reason that she could hear him.

Wherever the bones had taken her, his voice could not reach, or she could not respond.

"Isobel, please."

"Hurry, young fool." The voice was not Isobel's, was not familiar, sibilant in a way that made him instinctively look to the ground for a snake. He discovered not scaled muscle but the toes of battered leather boots, a dark blue skirt-hem dusting over them. His gaze lifted and found a woman glaring down at him, her fists set at her broad hips, the wide-brimmed hat hiding her features. "I said hurry. Bring her, before she is seen."

Gabriel had been ordered about in that tone of voice before and learned the hard way not to argue. He secured Isobel in his arms and stood, following the woman down the alleyway, away from the main street, and through a dark-painted wooden door into a narrow structure he was reasonable sure hadn't been there before.

"Put her there," the woman directed, pointing at the narrow cot in the corner of the room. Gabriel fought back the memories of seeing her on another, similar cot not too many months before, and obeyed, carefully disentangling the cord of her hat from her neck before doing so, then tucking the braid over her shoulder so she wasn't lying on it, as though that small comfort might make any difference.

"Step away, you clod," the woman said, and he moved back,

reluctant, Isobel's hat still clenched in his hands. He was responsible for her, his responsibility to protect her. Never mind that he knew this was nothing he could have protected her from, that even the devil could not have expected him to do so; *he* demanded it of himself, and he had failed again.

He closed his eyes, and the red water washed over him, choking him. It took effort to force it away again, to remember that he stood on dry ground, that there was air in his chest, not river-blood.

"Open your eyes, fool," the woman barked, and he jolted back to wakefulness, hand pressed against his chest as though to reassure himself he could still breathe.

The woman had opened the neck of Isobel's blouse, placing cloths there and at her wrists, slipping off her boots and placing a bolster under her ankles, raising her feet off the cot. "Poor thing," she crooned in a softer voice as she did so. "Poor thing, we'll take care of this for you; never you worry."

"What happened to her?" He finally found his voice, realizing after the fact that demanding answers might not have been his wisest act in a lifetime of unwise acts. But the woman ignored him, patting Isobel's cheek before turning away to mess with the table of bottles and bowls scattered among bundles of dried plants and oddly shaped stones.

"Please," he added, placing Isobel's hat carefully on one of the chairs lining the walls. "You know what is happening to her?"

"Nobody knows save the Hand," the woman said. "Only she. You have your own worries to worry on, water-child."

"Don't call me that." His rejection was instinctive, and sharp, and the woman laughed at him.

"You think saying no makes it not so? You've learned nothing, for all your know-how. And yet still you come here, you come right up to the banks of Herself, and think you can refuse to hear?"

River waters rising red. Swirling currents, and he looked down to see great silvery fish flicking their fins, mouths gaping open at him, dead eyes rolling, and his own eyes rolled back, falling backward, water in his mouth, skin sodden and heavy until it sloughed off entire, and he flowed, trapped, surrounded and consumed.

"No." He gasped it, hands shoving away some invisible weight. "I'm not . . ."

The woman merely *tsk*ed at him. "Of course you're not, and never will be so long as you refuse. Stubborn, broken boy." She picked up a scrap of paper from the table. "You're of no use to her, standing there dry-drowning. Make yourself useful and fetch these things for me, then, but don't stand there like a fish flopping on the bank."

He took the paper in numb fingers, barely glancing at the dry brown ink-scratchings. Isobel was too still on the cot, her face slack, her chest barely rising, caught somewhere deep in the bones.

"But Isobel . . ."

"You'd do what, drag her back to your resthouse? Or tie her to your horses and ride her out of town?"

He had no response to that; both thoughts were mockeries.

The woman's voice softened slightly. "She needs to stay here, where none can find her, until she is able to return. I can protect her body until then. But we cannot force her, cannot rush it, any more than the earth itself will be rushed."

He could do nothing for her.

He folded the paper carefully and slipped it into his waistcoat pocket. "What are you called?"

"Auntie," she said. "They call me Auntie. Now go, already."

He left.

It took him three passers-by and an actual signpost high on the corner of a building to find the shop on Auntie's list, not the mercantile he had poked his nose into earlier but a smaller, dustier place. The man behind the long wooden counter looked up when Gabriel entered, sunlight through the open door gleaming on his bald pate.

"Afternoon. How can I help you?" His voice carried a hint of Acadian to it, but his posture was nothing but polite shopkeep, attentive to a possible customer's needs.

"Auntie sent me?"

"Ah." The man's expression didn't change, but his spine straightened slightly. Clearly, Auntie was a known customer. "You have a list?"

While the man moved from one glass jar to another, measuring and scooping, Gabriel wandered around the shop. In addition to the usual dry goods—bolts of cloth and ready-made clothing, soaps and shaving tools—there was a row of tins containing teas and coffee, and Gabriel paused to sniff at them, then check the price scrawled on a placard next to each. "Pricy," he said, surprised. Even more expensive than the larger mercantile he'd checked. Red Stick was a trade stop; he'd expect it to be less expensive, not more, than what he'd seen in smaller towns.

"That's the good stuff," the shopkeep called back, and Gabriel winced slightly. The man had the ears of an owl. "You want cheap, go to Donaldson's. I carry quality goods here."

"My apologies," Gabriel said, but the man waved him off, busy measuring something into a brown sack. "The other things Auntie needs are in the back. I'll be gone only a minute."

Gabriel nodded and kept browsing, noting the pile of broadsheets on the counter, and moving to investigate. He'd not had a chance to read the last ones he'd picked up, folded, and left on his bed. He'd hoped they carried some news of what was happening in the States, if President Jefferson was making any public movements toward the Territory to match the covert ones he and Isobel had uncovered.

News beyond the Americas dominated the pages, however: The Barbary pirates were still attacking ships, and Congress had sent a Commodore Preble, along with a number of warships, to deal with the matter, while England gathered Ireland and Scotland together under one flag, even as the English continued a series of military victories elsewhere. Gabriel drummed his fingers against the broadsheet spread out on the counter, frowning at the print. It had not been so long since the States had won their freedom; if England were gathering forces again, the States would be wary. But would that make them focus their attention on their vulnerable eastern shores, trusting the Territory to not be a threat, or look to expand their holdings west as a preventative? And if the latter . . .

What had previously been an intellectual exercise, a way to keep his thinking sharp, had become a practical matter. "If the devil's driven to action, Isobel will be the horse he rides," he muttered, running a hand through his hair. She was only one soul, only so strong; the devil would break her if he used her too hard.

He wondered if that was what had happened to the first Hand, the one who had roused such ire here, generations before. If the devil had asked too much . . .

"Ah, here we are, all packed up and good for use." The shopkeep came back out, several small, brown-wrapped packages in his hand. He dropped them into a burlap sack with the others and held it up for Gabriel to take.

"I've put it on her account, as ever," the man said. "A pleasure serving her needs; if she's anything else to request, we are ready to oblige."

Gabriel nodded, tucking the sack under one arm, and exited the mercantile. The question of just who—and what—Auntie was prodded at his brain, and he fretted over leaving Isobel with her.

But still, the woman seemed to be an ally, and Isobel needed every one they could get.

The sun made his eyes water, and he reached up to adjust the brim of his hat, ducking his head and walking briskly down the street. It was only when the smell of the river touched his nose that he realized he'd turned and walked in the wrong direction.

The red waters rose up, swirled around him, slid inside him and made him—

"No," he breathed. "No, I will not."

—made him into something else, dissolved and scattered, subject to tide and storm—

He set his jaw and pivoted on one heel, his only thought to get away from the river, away from its reach. Auntie's place. It was likely warded, same as the other medicine woman's place had been. He needed to—

Chin tucked into his chest and thoughts tumbling, he couldn't see where he was going, crashing into a man who had been walking a bit behind him. The man grabbed his free arm to steady him, and Gabriel heard a wet gasp, even as those fingers bit into the flesh of his arm.

"You stink of him," the man said, the words dripping with something Gabriel could not identify, carried on sour breath he could identify all too well: rotgut and eel. "Are you his dog too? Do you carry new orders, then? Have you been hunting me? I've been right here, in this heat-cursed stinkhole where he kenneled me."

"Hands off," Gabriel managed to get out even as the man's grip tightened. "Get your hands off me before I cut them off."

His voice must have conveyed his willingness to do exactly that, because the man released him, nearly springing away in his haste to obey. Gabriel rubbed at his arm, eying the man cautiously. Reed thin and pasty white, the blanched bones of a locust, even his eyes red-rimmed and veined, his brown shirt neatly tucked into trou, tab collar unbuttoned and sleeves rolled to the elbow; a working man, from the corded muscles visible and the grip he'd shown.

"You're not one of his," the man said, his tone half relief, half disappointment, and Gabriel swallowed his own relief. "You've the stink but not the collar."

"The devil sent you here?" Immediate wariness faded, only to be replaced by a sudden odd drop in his gut, that the devil had sent someone to replace him.

"Sent and stuck." He cast a sideways glance, as though to check for anyone eavesdropping, then went on. "I was to fetch a thing from a man. But the man hasn't shown, and I've no orders past fetch and return. If I do not fetch, I may not return."

Another Jack. The devil had a full deck of them, Isobel'd said, but odd luck, to encounter one here. "Who do you wait for?"

The Jack grimaced, as though waiting to be punished, and then when no blow landed, went on, bitter as chicory, "A bandi, come upriver from the bayou, and from before there I don't know and don't care. If you've half a wit left, you'll wash that stink off and get out. And don't you look back. Flames are coming, scour this place clean."

"Red Stick?" Isobel's worries about fire rang again in his memory, as did his own reassurances.

"We could be so fortunate, this place alone be wiped from the earth. No, fool, the Territory itself." The Jack spat, yellow phlegm puddling in the dirt before it was absorbed, leaving not even a dampness behind. "I can feel it, through him. Bloody flames feeding on every damned soul of us, and the devil laughing as it consumes him first."

Gabriel had met madmen before, had heard them rant and froth, and all he had felt before was pity. But the sensation of water pushing into his skin was too close, the sensation of drowning in his own breath too close, and the man's words did nothing to push them away.

Fire and water were two sides of a coin, and that coin too often bought destruction.

"Get out," the Jack said, almost pleading with him. "Get out if you can."

"I don't abandon my obligations," Gabriel said curtly.

"An obligation that drowns you is a death sentence."

Gabriel started at that choice of words—how could he know? How had he known?—then shook his head. "Tell me where these flames come from. Who spreads them?"

The Jack laughed then and hawked another glob of phlegm, this time to the side of Gabriel's boots. "They come from us. We spread them. We are them. Every choice we made chars us that much more, every bargain we make sets us to the fire, and we carry it everywhere we go."

The man was mad, but Gabriel had been taught to respect madness, even as he was cautious of it. Madness opened a way to true dreaming. But without a guide to navigate, to teach him what was truth and what delusion, the man was doomed.

"Come back with me," Gabriel said, offering a hand as one would a cringing dog, slow and cautious. "My companion—"

His companion could do nothing to offer ease, he remembered with a sick and sudden shock, and it was enough time for the other man to step back, twisting away as though Gabriel had offered to brand him, instead.

"I need to wait. Here. For the package." His words took on a strained quality, as though he'd said them so many times, they no longer made sense. "I cannot go. I must wait."

And Gabriel needed to go back. He reached into his pocket, thinking to give the man a coin, at least—the devil's money to sustain the devil's Jack—but when he looked up again, he stood alone.

TWO

Someone hummed an off-key melody. Isobel followed the sound, pushing through layers of confusion as though a thick fog had settled along the river's basin, obscuring her way and making it impossible to tell where the sound came from, making it difficult to tell where her own body began and ended.

There was a woman, moving around a room, her upper body swaying to the melody as she mixed, pounded, scraped, and stirred, bending over a battered wooden workbench, her hands moving with delicate surety over bottles and vials, picking up heavy bowls and pestles as though they weighed nothing.

"I know you can hear me, bone-child," she said, and her voice still carried an echo of her humming. "You're not listening to me right now, but you can hear me, and maybe you'll remember what I've said, later, when you need it. Or maybe you won't; there's no telling and that's a pity. But if we knew, then we wouldn't have to go through all to find out the ending, would we? And some days, that would be a pity, too."

Seemingly satisfied with the mixture in the bowl she was holding, she put it down, then went over to a cot in the corner of the room where a body lay still under a thin blanket, and lifted its right hand, catching a dab of blood on the edge of a small silver knife.

"Gonna cover you up good," she said, balancing the knife so that none of the blood slid off, and returning to her workbench. "Anyone come looking for the Hand, they just gonna find a girl, no more out of the ordinary than any other girl, and pass right over you, mmm hmmm." She tipped the blade, and the drop of red shivered, then fell into the bowl, resting on top of the other ingredients until the woman licked her index finger and then pressed it into the mixture. "Simple lessons are the best, don't try to pretend to be something you're not, just show 'em what they're not looking for. Men don't learn that; they bluster and they be found. But your devil, he know. He know, and I know, and now you know, if you be remembering what I tell you."

Isobel watched over her shoulder, fascinated, as the mixture become a paste, then stepped back as the woman pressed a stripe of it across the bridge of the sleeping girl's nose, then across her bared back, and again, lifting her skirts to where her unmentionables had already been removed, across her lower belly, and down each leg to her ankle.

"Remember that girl," the woman said, her long braids dancing around her shoulders as she moved, the tie-beads clanking and clattering against each other. "You aren't her anymore, but you remember her. She's there; everything you ever been is there. Let them see that, and they pass right over you."

The fog was thickening again; Isobel could no longer see the walls, with their bundles of drying herbs and chair rails, or the floor, with its inlaid patterns that were almost but not quite recognizable, a dance step she could follow, if she could only hear the right music. . . .

Drawing the skirts back down and smoothing the coverlet over the body again, the woman put the bowl on the table, then went to the other side of the room to where a pot of water boiled on a fatbelly stove. She fixed a cup of tea from it, frowning at the tea leaves until they swirled and settled at the bottom of the dainty ceramic cup, and then took a seat in the chair opposite the cot, holding the cup and saucer carefully until the tea cooled enough to sip.

"Your boy best come back soon," she said, but her voice was fading into the mist too. "I didn't take him for a malingerer, but there are things I need to do I can't do without what he's fetching. The living silver's nothing to play about with, not even for one such as you. Precautions need to be taken. You remember that next time, too, yeah?"

Isobel.

That voice was different. Familiar. She turned in the mist, trying to find it.

You're trying too hard.

Her nostrils flared, the familiar voice shading into an even more familiar scent: unlit tobacco, whiskey, brimstone, and pine.

Boss. The word was filled with relief and frustration, and more than a little ire.

Laughter did not soothe her, and she moved forward, trying to find the source, but the grey fog surrounded her, dried leaves crunching underfoot, confusing her sense of direction, and finally, exasperated, she stopped and waited.

Isobel Devil's Hand. Do you regret your Bargain?

Of all the things she might have thought to hear, it had never been that. Her instinctive denial was checked, knowing that he asked nothing without purpose, and she rolled the question in her mouth before allowing an answer to form. She remembered the feeling of discovering plague-ridden farms and empty towns, too late to help. Of the expressions of the mixed-family village living under the shadow of the ancient spirit, knowing that they had only themselves to depend on, that she could not change their fate. She felt again the horror of the magicians' spirits shredded and fading under her touch, although she could not remember even now what she had done or how.

She remembered learning how to kill. To destroy.

But, too, she remembered old woman Caron, giving them shelter and comfort when her menses came while on the road. The stern comfort of Judge Pike, and the whimsical, dangerous, but somehow soothing madness of Farron Easterly. The children of that mixed-blood village, playing without thought as to why the ground trembled under their feet, secure that their parents would protect them. She remembered throwing up when she dreamed of the slaughtered buffalo, and Gabriel holding her hair back, not speaking, not offering comforting words, but letting her know that there was no shame in weakness, that his confidence in her was not broken.

Gabriel. Steadfast, calm Gabriel.

No, she said. *I do not regret making my Bargain. I do regret not shaking more information out of you, though, before we left. You couldn't even see me off?*

That wasn't fair; she knew that. Marie had seen her off. Right Hand and Left. But she wasn't feeling particularly fair, not with the memory of her bones melting inside her skin still lingering, the touch of molten heat flickering behind her eyes.

And you couldn't do this, she gestured irritably, *earlier?*

The laughter faded, the fog swirling more thickly around her.

You are me. My Hand. My power within the Territory. But the Territory—the bones of it—existed before me. It allows me here because it chooses to allow me. The boss's voice was soft as the fog, the sound a memory of sleepy late nights and slow mornings when he told them things they did not know to ask but needed to learn.

The Territory . . . is alive. She meant to say it as a question, but it came as a statement, understanding unfolding like a newborn calf getting up on wobbly legs for the first time. The things she had felt, the whispers . . . *The burning.*

You went too far, too deep. The boss sounded almost . . . worried? *Don't do that, Isobel. I almost couldn't pull you out.*

Into the Territory. The molten heat of it licked at her again, drawing her down into it.

Isobel. His voice became a blade, cutting her back to attention. *You need to wake soon. Be wary of the Territory. Gabriel knows the danger. That's why I chose him.*

Knows what? But the fog was thinning, the crackling leaves underfoot softening, her body forming around her again, and with it a terrible, searing ache. . . .

"Isobel."

She didn't know that voice. It wasn't a bad voice, she thought, but she didn't know it and saw no need to follow it out of the hazy fog. Except the fog was fading, leaving her wrapped in darkness deeper than any night she could remember, without stars or moon overhead or glimmering coals at her feet, and she did not want to stay there, not alone.

Still. She did not know that voice, and something lingered, telling her to be wary.

"Bone-child. Come to the surface; you're not meant to dig and tunnel with cousin mole."

She was the bone-child. She could feel it in her self, warm to the touch and flaking with char. But she was not certain she wanted to do what the voice said; the dark was terrifying, but it knew her, held her.

"Izzy, we don't have time for this," a different voice said. "Auntie says you're awake; you just have to, I don't know, wake *up*."

She was not supposed to argue with that voice, though she wanted to. But to argue with it, she had to meet it, and that meant rising to the surface.

She supposed she could do that.

There was something heavy over her eyes. She raised a hand to remove it and had her hand caught and held. "Leave it be," a woman's voice said. "You've been asleep for a while now; the light might be hurtful. Hold just a moment, all right?"

"All right." Her voice; was that her own voice? She felt it vibrate in her throat, so it must be, but it sounded like a croaking frog, a scornful crow. There was movement: the scratch of a chair, the scrape of pottery across a table, the swish of cloth against cloth, and then the hand returned, lifting the damp weight from her eyes.

"Slowly, Iz. Find your seat before you gallop off."

Her eyes were gummed shut. It took her a few heartbeats to raise her hand again; it felt as though it had been remade from cold iron weights, stiff and clumsy and far heavier than flesh and bone should be. But when it finally reached her eye, the touch was soft, warm, and the flakes of sleep crumbled from her lashes enough that she could open her eyes slowly.

A low, dark ceiling met her gaze, and Isobel felt a vague sense of relief.

"Iz."

Her head turned on the flat pillow to see a blurry shape leaning in toward her. She blinked again and could make out Gabriel from the shadows, hatless, his shirtsleeves rolled up, his expression . . .

"What happened?" she asked him.

"You don't remember?"

"Na't to me," she said, dry-mouthed, trying for asperity and failing. "To you."

He made a scoffing noise. "You're the one who fell insensible. You need to stop doing that, Isobel. My nerves can't take it."

This time, it was her turn to scoff. Gabriel Kasun's nerves were the stuff of legend, or should have been. Times when she'd barely been able to draw breath for fear, he'd gone on calm as anything. And he'd ridden *alone* for years; she couldn't imagine that.

They glared at each other, then he sighed and looked away.

There was a noise, and Isobel turned her head again, wincing a little at the ache in her neck and shoulders, to see another figure looming at the foot of her bed. The woman who had been speaking earlier. Her hair was plaited tightly against her scalp in dozens of braids, making a pattern Isobel could not quite make out, the strands falling to a thick tangle to her shoulders and swaying gently as she moved.

"You gave your boy a scare there, bone-girl. Won't lie, made me a bit worried, too. Didn't your boss teach you not to mess with papa fire?"

"I . . . What?"

"That would be a no," Gabriel said, and the dryness of his voice didn't mask his relief, although Isobel still didn't know why he'd be so worried when he was the one who looked like he'd been kicked hard twice in the gut.

"Papa fire," the woman said. "The one who formed us, gave us our go. You tangled with him, bone-girl, and he tangled right back, tried to take you for his own. But you're back with us now, and nobody knows you were gone, 'cause Auntie was close by when you called."

"I . . . What?" Isobel asked, at the same moment Gabriel turned his head to stare at the woman. "What?"

"Pffft. I'm good but not that good. I heard you call, and I came. You've got a good loud shout on you; that's good. I've no patience for girls with tiny shouts."

"This is Auntie," Gabriel said, turning back to Isobel. "She . . . You . . . I'm not sure that was a faint, what you did, but you hit the ground and I wasn't sure you were even breathing. She got us here, took care of you."

There was something he wasn't saying, but Isobel felt too tired to push. It wasn't only her hand that felt too heavy just then. Everything did, from her toes to her brows.

"Thank you," she said to the woman, instead.

"Bone-child comes into my town, tangles with papa fire, even if I didn't care 'bout nothing else, it's my own interest to know what's going on," the woman said, waving a long-fingered hand as though to dismiss Isobel's gratitude. "And you traveling with a water-child, that makes me doubly curious."

"Don't call me that," Gabriel said sharply, but the hand merely waved in his direction, equally dismissive, and Isobel would have giggled at his expression if she had the strength. "You don't tell me I don't know what I know. I've not got the Touch, maybe, but that don't mean I don't have sight, and I see what I know."

Isobel caught at something the woman had said earlier. "What do you mean with all that, 'water-child'? 'Bone-child'? And 'papa fire.'"

The woman—Auntie—looked over at Gabriel, an expression on her face Isobel could read even in the dim light, having seen it often enough on the faces of the women at the saloon: the look of a woman who was just proven right about something.

"He had his reasons," Gabriel said with a shrug. "You expected me to question it?"

"Might be a better thing if people did," Auntie said. "Boy's gone far too long, nobody questioning him."

Gabriel choked on air, then shook his head, an odd smile curving his face. "I'll tell you what," he said. "You do it, and I'll watch."

"If it wouldn't be too much trouble," Isobel said, trying to remember exactly how Marie did it, the tone that got even the boss to pay attention, "answers would be nice."

Auntie pulled a stool from off the wall—only then did Isobel note that there was a row of them hanging off hooks along the far wall, like horses waiting in stalls—and set it next to Isobel's cot, the sway of her skirts nearly brushing Gabriel's leg. "Fair enough, since you're finally asking for them."

Isobel bit down her impulse to protest: offending the woman who had cared for her was bad enough, but offending someone willing to *explain* would be pure foolishness.

"There're those who're born with the Territory's touch on 'em. You know that much, at least?"

Isobel merely nodded. Her childhood friend April, who could grow things better for just touching them. Gabriel, who could find water even underground. Possum, who understood sigils like most folk understood breathing. Little skills, the things you didn't need to learn but were born knowing.

"Bone and water, they give us those. Same as wind gives power to the fools who chase it hard enough. They claim you, put their mark on you."

"But—" Isobel started to protest the comparison to magicians, and Auntie glared her back to silence.

"Way I was told, it happens to people everywhere if they listen long enough. Only, here it comes out stronger."

"Because the Territory's . . . alive." Her head hurt, trying to chase something deeper, some memory unfolding. "Because the boss makes us learn it, to live here."

"Mmmm. Maybe so. Or maybe not. Not sure I know and not sure it matters more than what is. But the thing that is, it's not just given. Everything's got a price; what matters is how you pay it."

"The Agreement." Her parents hadn't been willing to pay the price to stay, but they'd been willing to pay the price—her—to leave.

"Everything's an agreement, bone-child. Else it's something else, less pretty, less kind, and far less binding. But your boy there's a water-child. River runs in him, deep as deep is, no matter that he won't swim it."

Gabriel made a discontented noise and resettled himself in his chair, but didn't interrupt.

"And . . . 'bone-child'?" But Isobel knew already. When she reached to the Territory, touched the Road, she heard more than Gabriel did. She felt the wide deepness of the earth, the cold dry sound of the bones of the earth itself. She had thought it was the devil's power, moving through her, but not all of it?

"What does it mean?"

"I don't know, child. Not sure anyone does, not for sure and certain. But for certain, while you're riding the Road, the Road's been riding you, too."

It was too much to consider just then. Isobel let her head rest against the pillow and closed her eyes, wishing everything away, just for a little while.

Auntie had let Isobel rest a while longer, while fixing up a packet of herbs, giving it to Gabriel with strict instruction on how long it was to steep, and how often Isobel was to drink it.

"She needs to rest more, at least another day before she's strong again. Wherever she went, it took more out of her than she's remembering. And don't let her go poking at any other folk. They can't help her; she already has everything she needs, wrapped up in that stubborn head of hers. I may not be much on the devil, but he's never picked wrong, not even once.

"And you, boy."

He didn't bother to protest the term, suspecting now that she was far older than she appeared.

"You're broken, boy, crazed all the way through and down." She poked a finger at his chest, hard enough to bruise even through his shirt and jacket. "You need to do something about that."

Gabriel had not been able to get the woman's words out of his head, the feel of that finger poking him, long after he'd escorted a still-shaky Isobel back to the hostería and watched as she shed her shoes and skirt and climbed into bed.

She could tell something was wrong, crossing her arms over her chest and fixing him with a glare that would have done Old Woman proud. "Something happened to you while I was . . . whatever I was."

It wasn't a question, so Gabriel didn't answer, earning himself a deeper glare and an equally heavy sigh. "Gabriel. You've been odd ever since . . . ever since we headed south. But it's worse now. What happened?"

There were times he could still feel like her mentor, her guide. This was not one of those times. But this wasn't the Devil's Hand, demanding an accounting, either. She was concerned. Rider to rider. And it was that person he answered, at least partially.

"Auntie sent me to fetch ingredients for her. While I was out, I was accosted by someone who . . . Did you know that Jacks could sense someone who's made a bargain?"

She was diverted for an instant, then he could see her recognizing the diversion for what it was and regathering her original intent. "There's a Jack here?"

Jacks were the devil's dogs: messengers and errand-runners, scouts and the devil alone knew what else, tied to his will through bargain or, more often, a loss at the tables they could not otherwise repay. Isobel could likely command one, if she so chose; her status was as far above theirs as a farmer's was to a pig's.

They'd only encountered one before; Gabriel had no idea how many there were wandering the Territory.

"He didn't know you were in town," he said. "Didn't know who I was, only that he could tell I'd done business with your boss." Or, possibly, Isobel herself. Gabriel hadn't thought about that before, but could a Jack tell the difference between the devil and his Hands? The one they'd met before had known he was with her, but that Jack had seen Isobel previously. . . .

Suddenly, his own problems seemed mild, compared to what those poor bastards dealt with.

"And he said something to upset you. Or that you think would upset me."

"He said . . . upsetting things," Gabriel told her slowly. "That the Territory was in danger, that there were flames coming to scour it clean."

Isobel's expression didn't change, but he could read her almost as well as she could read others now, and he saw the shadow cross, the faint narrowing of her eyes and the twitch of her jaw. Subtle tells, but as good as a shout after months together on the Road. "What about that is familiar, Isobel?"

She shook her head, not ignoring his question but pushing it aside. "What did he say, exactly?"

He'd been trained to remember the words of witnesses, to repeat them near-perfectly for a jury. This was no different. "He said . . . '*The flames come from us. We spread them. We are them.*'" He paused a moment, trying to capture the inflection as well as the words themselves, the bitter resignation the Jack had carried. "'*Every choice we made chars us that much more, every bargain we make sets us to the fire, and we carry it everywhere we go.*'" He finished, then recalled his attention to Isobel, who had managed to sit up in the bed as he spoke, supporting herself on her elbows. "That means something to you."

"No." She frowned. "But it feels like it should. It's like piecing together a dress the first time. You know all the fabric goes together, makes something, but there's just too much cloth in the way and you can't tell what that something *is*."

"Well, we maybe need to learn how to sew, fast," Gabriel said, then cursed himself when Isobel's eyes narrowed again.

"There's more. Something you're still not telling me."

His jaw clenched, the words locking in his throat.

"Gabriel."

"The entire trip down here . . . I'd forgotten. How loud the Mudwater is, compared to everything else. I haven't . . . I've avoided it since I came back," he admitted. "Since . . . And I forgot."

He wasn't talking about the sound of the water itself, and from the expression on her face, she understood that.

"And then, the first morning we were here. I went for a walk, before you woke. I . . . found myself near the river, and it ran red. The way the tribal chiefs spoke of."

Her forehead creased, concern overriding curiosity. "A waking dream."

He nodded. In sleep, dreams could be anything. Visions while awake were either extreme deprivation—sleep, water, hunger—or a direct slap to the face from the spirit worlds. And he'd been neither thirsty nor tired when the river tried to drown him.

"Exactly the way he described it?"

"I was watching from the banks." *The sensation of tendrils wrapped around him, pulling him forward, urging him into the currents themselves.* "It was the current, faster than it should have been, rising to flood. The water swirled, and . . . steamed, and the red was like clay, not fire or blood." He didn't want to remember, had tried not to remember, but what he could deny for his own sake, he would remember for hers.

"A fish on the shore, an owl covered in snow, and the river waters rising red," Isobel quoted, her memory as good as his own. "Were there fish? Or an owl?"

"No." And that had been different from past dreams, he realized. No fish darting at his feet, nothing soaring overhead. "Nothing overhead but empty sky. Nothing in the water . . ." The moment he spoke the words, he knew, even before Isobel said it for him.

"A fish on the shore. That's you, Gabriel."

THREE

In the morning, rather than being refreshed, Isobel's skin was clammy, her hair sweat-matted, and there was an ashen tone to her face that sent Gabriel down the stairs to Bernal's office.

Instead he found Ana and, after a few terse words, told her to fetch Auntie. He hoped that he had told the girl to ask politely rather than demand the woman's attendance, but he couldn't remember.

Rather than stand in the chamber and stare at her uselessly, he paced in the hallway, his boots too loud on the wooden floor, the brush of his trouser legs too soft for the echo they left, his breath too harsh for indoors. When the door from the street finally opened, he spun as though expecting an attack and let out a sigh of relief when he saw Auntie come inside, Ana a shadow behind her.

"What, then, she didn't sleep?"

"She slept," Gabriel said. "I threatened to tie her to the bed if she didn't. But when she woke this morning, she was feverish, like the girl told you." He glared at Ana as though she might have forgotten to tell the woman that. "And she won't wake up now, not even when I wash her down with water."

"Is she speaking?" Auntie asked, heading for the stairs as though she knew exactly where Isobel was, and for all Gabriel knew, she did.

"No. She hasn't said a word, not even a mumble."

Ana started toward the door underneath the stairs that led to the kitchen, then stopped when Gabriel put one hand on her shoulder.

"Sir?"

"You and I should have a talk about gossip, young miss." He knew taking his frustration out on the girl was not fair, but he could not go up those stairs, not to stand by and feel helpless yet again. "Where is your cousin?"

Ana paled and swallowed, her eyes going wide. "She's in the still-room."

"Fine. We'll—" Gabriel's plan to give the girls an education in why gossiping about folk was a bad idea was interrupted by "Get out of my way!" coming from upstairs.

Auntie, sounding like she was about to smite something. Or someone. Gabriel lifted a finger to Ana's face, letting her know things had been delayed, not forgotten, and trotted up the stairs, flicking the strap off the handle of his knife but not drawing it as he came to the hallway landing and saw Auntie facing up against Rafe. They each stood with fists on hips, bull-shouldered and glaring.

"You'll not bring your nonsense into this house," Rafe said, his voice low and angry. "I'll not have it."

"I've been invited, John Rafe Bernal, so stand you aside."

Rafe looked up and saw Gabriel standing there. "Is that true? Did you bring her here?"

"She helped us before; she knows what's wrong with Isobel." He wouldn't trust a chirurgeon he didn't know; in his experience, they were good for setting bones and pulling teeth but not much else. "Is there a problem?" Auntie had not been on the list of names he had given them of medicine folk in Red Stick, he suddenly remembered.

Rafe turned to glare at Auntie again. "She's a river witch. Near bad as a magician, maybe worse, some ways."

"Not wind-touched, you know full well," she scowled. "And able to take care of that girl *or* stand out here all day jawing you to sense. What's it to be?" But she was looking at Gabriel when she said it, not Rafe.

"Please."

She nodded once, her braids jouncing, and moved past Rafe to the door to their room, opening it without hesitation.

"She's dangerous," Rafe said.

"So is Isobel. What's a river witch?"

"Liberdad medicine. Talks to spirits, seen trees bend right to her hand, she asks them to. Folk say she can make the bones speak if she speaks to them first."

Isobel had communicated with the ancient spirit, and the haints of dead magicians. He'd never seen trees bend to her, but there hadn't been many trees up where she'd grown; maybe she'd just never tried. Point was, nothing Rafe described sounded like Auntie would be a threat to Isobel. Except she was ill. . . .

"Do you have cause to think that Auntie is involved in the murders? Or . . . anything else?"

Rafe looked sideways, then shook his head—reluctantly, if Gabriel was half a judge. "No. She'd have no cause to love them, and they'd no cause to love her, for certain, but I've never heard of her going to that part of town, and certainly never entering a saloon. She wouldn't have been there."

That wasn't quite the same thing as not being involved, but Gabriel let it go.

Inside the room, Auntie was staring down at Isobel, her arms folded across her chest and a stern expression on her face. Gabriel closed the door behind him and leaned against it, aware that he'd made enough noise that she would have heard him, but willing to be ignored for the moment.

River witch. He'd seen oddness in his day; there wasn't a rider worth their salt who hadn't, and twice as much just in the time he'd been mentoring Isobel. But he'd never heard of a river witch before. Likely because he'd made a point not to spend too much time near the great rivers.

If she took her power from the Mudwater . . .

He bit back a shudder at the thought. Just because he chose not to let it take him under didn't mean it wasn't right for others. And she'd shown no sign of being anything other than an ally.

"Rafe says you've no love for the folk who were killed, day back. The ones that were hanged."

He couldn't see her face, but he could tell she was rolling her eyes. "They were foolish children, trying to push the sun back from rising, or the tree from dying. Ain't a one of us who can do that, not even her boss. Best we can do is stave it off a bit or pull the cover over our eyes and pretend. I don't respect a soul who spends their life under a blanket, pretending it's the sky, and even less if they shout at me to do the same.

"But I didn't kill 'em. Not with these hands, not with these skills. That's not what I do."

"What do you do?"

She looked at him then. "Told you. I keep this place safe." She looked back at Isobel. "Same as her boss tries to do, in his own way. We both know we're gonna fail, but we do it anyway."

Her words were a gut-punch. "The devil will fail?"

"Always was gonna. Question was what would happen before he did. Your girl's pushed herself too hard too long, is all, I think. Don't let that fool of a leech near her; he thinks the cure for everything's drain a body of its vigor. Had my way, I'd've drained *him* years back."

He let her redirect the conversation. "Is that what Rafe meant by your 'nonsense'?"

"Ah." Auntie waved away the accusation with a careless hand. "He's sore because I give the girls love charms." She smiled, a thin smirk. "No such thing as a true charm, water-child; no need to look so worried. But girls will fancy themselves in love no matter what, and boys the same, and children have a habit of appearing when they're not wanted."

"You—" Gabriel started to speak, then realized he had nothing to say and shut his mouth again. Then, "Not Ana!"

"If she came to me, I'd smack her backside and send her on home," Auntie agreed. "No, was the young woman who used to keep his books. Pretty girl, finally married herself off last year, and her husband wisely took her with him on his barge. Can't say the new one's half as attractive, and certainly hasn't been to me for . . . anything."

Remembering the woman who had entered them into the hostería's log book, Gabriel decided he had nothing to say to that, either. He gathered his scattered thoughts in hand and focused on the only important thing.

"But Isobel is all right?"

"Of course she isn't," Auntie snapped at him, shaking her head. "She was worn thin already and then stretched herself further, let papa fire burn her to a crisp. She's a fever in her bones, and they're fighting it out."

Gabriel had the sudden sense of water swirling within his own bones, dizzying and nauseating, and Auntie gave him a sharp glance. "There you are. You know some of it, some small manner. Decisions to be made, water-child, for each and everyone. Devil can't protect the Territory forever. Too many parts now, roots sunk in too deep."

He had no idea what she was talking about and, still slightly queasy, didn't have the desire to ask.

She clicked her tongue at him, then tucked a sprig of something under Isobel's head, smoothing her hair on the pillow before reaching into the pocket of her skirt and taking out a jar the size of her finger, stoppered with knot of cloth. The smell of something briny and sweet, half-familiar to Gabriel's nose, filled the room when she pulled the stopper.

Using a finger to open Isobel's sleep-slack mouth, she swiped a finger of lotion from the jar across her tongue. "That should help," she said, her head tilted as she looked at Isobel again. "We just have to wait."

The fog was back. This time, Isobel waited patiently—she thought she was patient, anyways, although she had a sense her body was trembling, what little she could sense of it. When the scent of tobacco and whiskey reached her, it came from behind, trailing over her shoulder like a brush run through her braid.

"Been visiting with snakes," she said. "They keep setting themselves on fire."

"Snakes will do that."

She waited, and his breath came, warm as a touch. "You went too deep, Isobel. Need to not do that. It's hungry and won't ever be satisfied. And I've first claim on you."

"Yes." She could feel the sigil in her hand, even though she couldn't feel her hand, particularly, softened and spreading in the fog. But there was fire below it, and where the black lines touched red, she could feel something molten and warm, and familiar as her own breath.

"He was supposed to teach you better." The boss's voice sounded . . . frustrated? Distant, as though he were fading. She would have grabbed at him, at the sense of him, but she could not move. "He knows better; that's why I chose him. You're mine, Isobel, bound and bargained. Wake *up*."

"Oh. Good afternoon, you."

Isobel turned her head slightly, seeing Ana slide in through the door that hadn't been there . . . had it? It had been grey, not whitewashed, and there had been a window, no, no window, a bird? A flash of brightness, and fire, and something she was supposed to remember . . .

"I've some soup for you." Ana placed the tray down on the sideboard that had appeared in their room, the clatter of bowl and spoon almost too loud for Isobel to bear. She rubbed a hand irritably over her face, disgusted when it came away both shaking and wet with sweat.

"What's wrong with me?" Even her voice was shaking.

"You've a fever," Ana told her. "It came on again yesterday morning. You don't remember anything of the day?"

"No."

"That's normal as can be," the girl reassured her, as though Isobel hadn't sat with others with a fever before, as though she knew nothing, was a child younger than Ana herself. "But you need to eat some of this soup before we can let you sleep again; Auntie said so."

"Auntie." The name recalled something, someone. A voice, a sharp chin, and a tangle of blue-black braids.

"Your companion fetched her when you took feverish again. Wouldn't let you be bled, talked your companion down from near a panic as I've ever seen in a man." Ana's voice was somewhere between awed and amused. "Papa and she, Auntie, that is, had a huge row in the hallway. Auntie always wins; I don't know why he keeps even bothering."

"About me?"

"Oh, no, not exactly. He doesn't hold with Auntie's"—and Ana waved the hand not holding a soup spoon as though to indicate something—"medicine. Says it's not suiting."

Auntie. The woman who had cared for her earlier. The root-worker.

"Your papa is wrong," Isobel agreed, reaching up to capture the spoon before the girl spilled anything on the coverlet. "They argue often?"

"They used to walk together," Ana said. "After we came here. And then they didn't."

The two seemed an unlikely couple, but Isobel had less interest in old gossip than the fact that she had fallen ill again, badly enough for

Gabriel to call for aid. This had never happened before, not simply from reaching for the bones. Was there something about Red Stick itself? Or maybe the Mudwater?

She managed seven spoons of the soup, a thick broth with some bits of unidentifiable meat floating at the bottom, and then left the utensil in the bowl, allowing her body to sink back against the pillows.

"Enough."

"More later," Ana said, sounding so much like Peggy back at the saloon that Isobel's eyes prickled with sudden, unexpected tears. She hadn't been this ill since she was younger than Ana, had almost forgotten what it felt like to be coddled, to be allowed to simply *rest*.

It was a pity she didn't have time to enjoy it. The thought pinched her. Snakes, and fire, fish and birds, and the faint echo of a familiar whisper tucked behind her ear: *be careful. remember what you are.*

"What does that mean?" she asked, only realizing she said it out loud when Ana asked, "What does what mean?"

"Nothing. I was . . . thinking out loud. I would like to rest now."

Ana looked as though she was going to argue, so she narrowed her eyes and tilted her head, staring until the girl took the hint and excused herself, closing the door behind her.

Isobel waited until she heard Ana move away from the door, then reached over to turn off the lamp, as though she were in fact going to sleep. The afternoon light coming in through the window was muted, casting soft shadows around the room. Stripes of soft grey and dappled gold, moving slowly, like river grass in a current.

Isobel shifted, fighting off a somnolent urge to close her eyes, and carefully eased herself out of bed, drawing the coverlet back up over the flat pillow. She considered placing her pack under the coverlet to create the illusion that someone was still in the bed, but decided that Gabriel, if he were to check, would be more upset by that than her simply not being there. So, she only dressed, ignoring the way her body shook with the effort, and, boots laced together and draped over her shoulder, crawled up onto the ledge of the window and looked out.

There was, as she'd remembered, a ledge just below the window barely a handspan wide and running the length of the building, ending at the dovecote at the corner. She'd wondered at it earlier, until she remembered the iron bars on the rooftops they had seen up north, to keep ice from falling on the heads of those below, and surmised this might serve the same purpose for heavy rain. Whatever its actual purpose, she was counting on it to support her weight briefly.

It did. She didn't linger to be thankful but slid carefully along the ledge, both hands pressing against the weathered planking for balance. She didn't let herself look down or look up to gauge how much farther she had to go, but kept taking one step after another until she came to the edge of the dovecote. The smell of it this close made her wrinkle her nose, but she'd smelled—and cleaned—worse in her chores at the saloon. Thankfully, none of the birds felt inclined to drive her out, merely setting off slightly alarmed coos, and she was unmolested as she found the ladder alongside the cote and crawled down it.

When her stockinged feet touched the ground, she untied the laces of her boots and put them on, moving swiftly before someone passing by on the street saw her and wondered why she was standing there in stocking feet.

No one noticed. She supposed that was a city thing: so many people, it would be difficult to notice just one person if you weren't looking for them. For a moment, she felt the urge to forget about everything, to simply wander the streets, discover every nook and corner of Red Stick, until she knew it as well as she knew Flood.

But there was no time for that. Not just then.

Isobel made it halfway to her destination before realizing that her entire body was coated in sweat—cold and clammy, rather than the warm sweat she'd expected from the damp air. Too, her legs had begun to wobble, similar to the way they felt after she'd been riding all day, but unlike then, her arms and shoulders joined in, until she worried that she might simply crumple where she was.

"Easy, now," a voice said, and she felt an arm come around her waist from behind, far too close and familiar for public behavior, but Isobel couldn't find it in herself to care, even as people stopped to glance at them—and, in one instance, glare—before hurrying on their way, shaking heads and pursing lips in disapproval. Steadied, she felt some of the strength return to her body, although the cold sweat remained, making her feel vaguely disgusting.

"How did you . . ."

Gabriel snorted, taking a step forward and moving her with him. "I know you, Isobel Devil's Hand. Also, Ana saw you leaving and came to fetch me."

"That is not how she wins my forgiveness for gossiping," Isobel muttered, but she reluctantly admitted that maybe Ana'd been right to send help.

"She and I have already had words about that," Gabriel assured her. "Where are we going?"

"To the river," she said, not surprised to feel the body next to hers stiffen slightly, as though instinctively readying a protest. If he too was dreaming of rising water . . .

"The visions, the dreams . . . it all seems to come from the river, Gabriel. But I can't feel it the way you can. I need to see it. Touch it."

"I'd love to say that's a terrible idea, but it's likely a very good one. That doesn't mean I like it." A pause. "Just be careful. You may be able to swim, after a fashion, but there are currents there deeper and faster than any you've forded before. And I'd rather not have to dive in to save you."

She smiled quietly, letting herself rest a little more against his arm. "But you would."

"Probably. Possibly. After I took my boots and jacket off."

The teasing eased some of the chills she'd been feeling, and she was able to stand more securely on her own, although he kept a firm grip on her elbow, allowing enough space between them that they no longer caught odd glances from others on the street.

Although, Isobel admitted, that might have had more to do with where they were: if the rumors about her being a magician had spread at all, they would likely have gotten odd glances anyway. Red Stick was large, but not so large that her description wouldn't have spread with the rumor. Fortunately, most were too preoccupied with their own errands or chores to do more than glance.

Two men, however, did linger with their eyes, their conversation trailing off as the riders went by. Isobel noted them more from habit than interest. One was older, his face weather-worn and aged but his hair thick and silvery-white. The other was taller, with a narrower frame and a brown, balding pate that glinted with sweat. They both wore nondescript clothing similar to Gabriel's, but she didn't think they were riders: something about the way they stood, held themselves. Clerks, perhaps, or farmers, men who spent little time in the saddle and none sleeping under the skies.

"Keep moving," Gabriel said softly. He had noted them as well. "If they start to follow, let me take care of it."

She wanted to protest, but the truth they both knew was that walking took all her strength just then. If these men intended trouble, she might be more hindrance than help.

The balding man had left his companion and was indeed walking after them. Isobel felt Gabriel shift, knowing that he was moving his hand closer to the knife sheathed at his belt; city or Road, he would no sooner go without it than he would his boots or hat. The only time she had ever seen him unarmed was in the devil's saloon, where not even the boss carried a weapon.

They had nearly reached the end of the street; another curved off it, and if she concentrated, Isobel could feel the shimmer of the wardings below her feet, tracing the tickle of it to a nearby building.

She had seen buildings warded, here and there; was that common, rather than a boundary warding? That might make sense; Gabriel had said the Mudwater flooded its banks, and running water was sovereign against most wards. She tried to imagine one strong enough to withstand the weight of the Mudwater, those countless miles of restless streams gathering and turning, and could not.

"You!" The bald man shouted, causing other pedestrians to turn around them and then, when they realized he was not looking at them, to turn away again. Isobel would have been amused at how swiftly even rough-looking dock workers moved away once they realized a confrontation was building, eager not to be noticed, save the fact that the bald man had clearly been speaking to *them*.

"Have you no decency? Have you no thought?"

Isobel started to respond—how, she hadn't yet thought—when she realized that the man was not, in fact, speaking to her. Indeed, his gaze had passed over her with an almost-dismissive mien, directing his ire at Gabriel. His hand still rested on her arm, the steady pressure both support and warning. She clamped her jaw shut, unhappily, and waited.

"Spare me your protestations of innocence," the man went on, although Gabriel had not said a word. "You of all folk should know better. You've gone and returned; we can read it on your soul. You've seen what waits on the other side; you know what the world is."

"Have we met, sir?" Gabriel's voice over her head was cold as river ice, sharp as thunder, and crackled with threat. The stranger ignored it.

"We have not, sir, but we know you. We know your sort." Bald Man had a nose like a Reaper hawk's beak, Isobel thought, but his eyes were like a fish's: round and dead. Her heart raced, her limbs trembling with the need to do *something*, although she had no idea what: the man had offered no threat, only words.

She hadn't felt this helpless since the native boy had counted coup on her during her first days on the Road. Exhausted, empty, driven by something she couldn't name, she was trapped between this man and her mentor, and only Gabriel's hands now on her shoulders kept her upright.

"You know this cannot hold," the bald man went on. "The center is rotted, the skin diseased. We must peel it away in order for the flesh to survive."

The image was confusing but revolting.

"And who is the flesh, sir?" Gabriel asked, still cold. "You?"

"Those who would claim, not be claimed by!" The bald man seemed to have reached the end of his tether; Isobel would not swear he was frothing at the mouth, but the way he swung his head back and forth, as though it were suddenly too heavy for his neck, reminded her of a dog with water-madness. "To be born of this mud, it destroys us, piece by piece. The sin-speakers were right in that much, at least. We must break its hold, chain it to our bidding, or be overrun."

"They may have been run out of town, but they left their message behind," Gabriel said, his voice grim, and low enough for only her to hear. "Or more some such nonsense."

She shook her head but not to disagree. "Born of this mud"—she had heard that phrase before but could not remember where, or when, or what it meant. Why was she so weak, so memory-fogged? It was almost as though her body were at war with itself, her flesh its battle-ground.

"You're mad and a fool." Gabriel raised his voice in command, not seeming to care, or indeed notice, that they had gained a small band of observers, standing well clear but watching avidly. Isobel would have hissed them away, but she dared not move, suddenly aware that Gabriel's hands were shaking far more than her own limbs, that her shoulders underneath his palms might be all that was holding *him* upright.

"This is our land, ours to do with as we will, not—"

"Mad, a fool, and ignorant as a pig," Gabriel went on, cutting each word off the way a seamstress would thread, sharp and lean. "He is talking about those with the Touch, Isobel. He thinks that it gives him domain." He raised his voice again, the words carrying clearly. "Your stench offends me. Get gone before I speed your leaving with my boot."

"The end of his rule is coming," the bald man spat, and this time, Isobel knew they were directed at her. "The end is coming."

Never before had Isobel wished for the power the boss wielded so casually, that a flicker of his eyes could quell a snarling dog, four-legged or two. But the sigil in her palm remained cool, no aid whatsoever, and something warned her against touching the bones again just yet. Not when there was no risk to her, or others, save being splattered by the man's ire.

But, she thought, she was more than just the devil's power, or the heat of the bones beneath her. Isobel née Lacoyo Távora was the sum of *all* her parts.

Never lose your hold on the room. Marie, the first week Isobel had been allowed to work the saloon floor, rather than simply running errands for the others. *Let them think they are powerful, if they need that, but remember that you are who decides what is allowed and when it ends.*

It was simpler when she knew that Iktan was behind the bar with a cudgel, if needed, and the boss's presence hung over the saloon, even when he was nowhere in sight. But she lifted her chin and squared her shoulders, feeling Gabriel's fingers tighten deep enough to bruise the flesh underneath.

"If you have news of a threat to the Territory, or cause to believe one comes, then speak if it, plainly, and without useless rantings. If not, then as the rider says, get thee gone." The words rolled in her mouth like clean water, soothing the ache in her throat and nose, the weariness within her lungs, and the skin of her left palm tingled: not the burning of the sigil wakening but of something soothed and eased.

"The center is rotted," the bald man repeated. "All this"—he cast an arm out to include, she supposed, all of Red Stick, or perhaps all the Territory—"must be cleansed, or the devil's Agreement will ruin us all!"

Something rumbled within her, low and dangerous, and she shushed it, never taking her attention off the man.

"There is nothing that demands you stay. If you would rather live under the Spanish rule, or the States, or go north into the Wilds, then do so."

"We cannot!" Bald Man roared it, then drooped, as though the noise had sucked the strength from his back. "We cannot. Ask him. He knows. We are bound like slaves, worse than slaves, because we are told we are free."

He shook his head, then seemed to glance around as though only now realizing where he was and what he had done. "Ask him," he repeated, and turned to walk away, stiff-legged and slow.

Isobel exhaled, feeling her knees wobble. She wiped the back of her hand across her mouth as though to wipe away the taste of the man's words, then shook her head. "This entire town's mad," she said. "Gabriel, what did he mean by 'your sort'? What am I supposed to ask you?"

Gabriel's fingers still dug into her shoulders, and she realized only now that it hurt. "Gabriel?"

It took effort to break his hold, turning to face him. His eyes were glassy, his breathing shallow, and the skin under his eyes had an unpleasantly green tinge.

The sound of her hand hitting flesh sounded louder than it should have. But his eyes cleared, even as the red flush faded from his cheek.

"Iz?" He focused on where the bald man had been, then looked down at her. Then he spun around, staggered to the edge of the street, and went to his knees, retching into the gutter.

FOUR

His mouth tasted like spoiled possum, and his boots were splattered with spew, his hands stinging from the press of pebbles and grit into the skin, and he suspected that he'd bruised his knees, falling to the ground the way he had. And for all that, Gabriel thought, he still felt better than he had before, as though vomiting had expelled whatever weight had lodged within him.

He did not let himself believe it would be that easy.

Red waters rising. A scrap of poetry slid into his thoughts, remnant of a long-ago class or reading: *We must all die, as water spilled, and may not be gathered up.*

A scrap of cloth fluttered at the side of his vision, and he sat back on his heels to see Isobel next to him, offering a kerchief. He took it, realizing that it was the same one he had given her months before, laundered and carried with her.

He wiped his mouth, then turned his head and spat into the dirt away from where she was sitting. The spittle was laced with red, and the color made his breath hitch. *Red water, a fish on the banks . . . A fish with dead eyes, human eyes . . .*

"Gabriel." The word was sharp, demanding his attention.

"I'm—" The lie caught in his craw. He wasn't all right. The man's anger—no, his *loathing*—had struck something in him, some reciprocal nerve, and memories had swamped him.

Near death, though he was physically hale, clinging to the rail of the tiny boat, the current below him both easement and agony, whispering a promise if he could only just make it to the other side, even as he heard the hollow wooden clang of cell doors closing behind him, locking away all freedom . . .

Old Woman Who Never Dies might not have done him a favor, bringing him back to the world, but she had been honest with him. He had never thought he was free, only half a step ahead of the jailor.

Movement caught at the corner of his eye, and they both tensed. The man who had been approaching halted, then raised his elbows to the side, showing he was no threat, but neither one of them eased. Something metal glinted in his right hand.

"Thought you could use a rinse," he said to Gabriel, slowly offering the flask.

Gabriel hesitated a heartbeat, then reached up and took it. The whiskey stung the inside of his mouth, but the burn did the trick, and when he spat the mouthful out, he took another sip, this time letting the fire burn down his throat.

The newcomer was the other man, the older, grey-haired one.

"Isiah, he's . . . Not all of us feel that way," the man said, accepting the flask back and recapping it. "About what he said, about being slaves." He licked his lips, glancing at the flask as though considering a sip himself.

"But you think the . . . center is rotted?" Isobel's voice was low, her body canted toward Gabriel as though to protect him if this stranger so much as twitched in their direction.

"Oh, things are . . . wrong. Near everyone can feel that, at least hereabouts. Maybe it's been like that since the Mud and we just pretended otherwise. Maybe deeper in, it's different. But being this close to the river and knowing we daren't cross . . .

"We don't all blame him. We know he did his best."

"He" meaning the devil, Gabriel assumed.

"Not blaming the local folk, neither. They're not bad, overall. And the Agreement . . . yeah, we didn't get to choose it, maybe, but I never heard anyone spin a better way that might've worked, not for everyone. Way I figure, fault's us, not anything else, maybe. That's what I think, anyway. We're the stuff that's rotten, not native and not other, and it was always going to end this way."

The man was babbling. Gabriel closed his eyes, trying to remember the sharp burn of earlier, to center himself around that. If he could feel that, he didn't have to feel anything else. Not the loss, not the *need*. Not the call of water flowing just below their feet.

Beside him, he could feel Isobel thinking, could imagine the squint of her eyes, the way one side of her mouth turned out when she chased some understanding down, plucking facts and braiding them together the way she would her hair. He didn't think she could understand, not this.

"Why here?" she asked, finally. "Why now?"

There was silence, then the feel of the flask being taken out of Gabriel's hand, the sound of the man rising to his feet. "I'm just a carpenter," he said, the tone of a man who has said as much as he will, or may. "Wood, you cut it, you season it, you plane it, and sometimes it splinters anyway. People seem to be much the same."

Isobel was silent as well, then sighed, and Gabriel could feel her turning her attention back to him. "Can you stand?"

He could, if shakily, rolling on the balls of his feet until he felt steady again. The man with the flask had gone by then, the few pedestrians making a wide circuit around the two of them.

"Why now, that's the question; that has to hold the answer, too," Isobel said. "The devil only calls a Left Hand when there's need. That's why there hasn't been one, that's why . . . why things have *felt* wrong. The unease . . . it's everywhere, not only one place. Could it be the last remnants of the Spanish spell, spread thin?"

Isobel was talking to herself, so he waited, folding the kerchief to contain the stained bits and putting it into his pocket with a grimace. "We hadn't found any more sign of it; I'd thought we'd done with it, but . . . the visions here have all been of water, of fish, and birds. Water, and air. And fire only in my dreams . . ."

Gabriel shuddered, he couldn't help it, and she turned to him immediately, hands at his elbows. "Gabriel?"

"It's all right." It still wasn't, but it had to be.

Her gaze took him in, head to boots and then back again, and he could tell she was not convinced. "If something's threatening the Agreement . . . Something might be trying to breach the Mudwater. I need to see it. Really see it. But if you . . ."

He shook his head, giving her a reassuring grin, every inch of the devil-may-care facade he hadn't needed for months dusted off and put up for show, as though the very thought of going to the river again didn't make him want to spew his now-empty stomach all over again.

He had to be strong for her, for just a little while longer.

"The River's worth seeing up close, anyroad," he agreed, trying for as normal a tone as he could manage. "Although the Old Man didn't make his stand here. That was up farther north, near Yorun land, I think. They still have stories about that day, full of thunder and smoke, and a ghost-cat made of flowers."

"Of flowers." Her tone was dry and disbelieving, and if she was playing to him, he played back to her, and when her hand slid into the crook of his elbow again, he couldn't have said who was comforting whom.

Isobel knew when they were close to the riverbanks, not only because the houses and storefronts gave way to one-story buildings and then ramshackle structures clearly showing signs of abandonment and underuse, or because even the few workmen who had been out and about disappeared, but because of the unease dancing along her skin, pinpricks of unease and uncertainty migrating from inside to out, as though she were caught too close to a lightning storm or within the workings of a magician's spell.

And even if she had seen or felt none of those things, she would have known from the way Gabriel's body closed in on itself, even as he tried to pretend all was well.

She didn't understand; if he was a water-child, shouldn't the river welcome him? But he had told her a little of his return from the States, how ill he had fallen. Perhaps it was only that, bad memories. That, and the man Isiah's words, and the murders . . .

When this was done, she decided, they would visit Liberdad. No matter what Gabriel had said earlier, it would be a good change to go a place where neither of them had responsibilities, if only for a day or three. A place where she was not the Hand . . .

And then there were no more buildings, no more road in front of them. Only the river.

Despite Gabriel's tension, despite having seen it at a distance, Isobel was not prepared for seeing the Mudwater up close, for the shock of it like icy water, or a lightning bolt too close to the ground.

Beside her, Gabriel stumbled, catching himself with a wordless mutter; she did the only thing she could think would help, and pretended not to notice. The urge to turn away, to go to her knees, to apologize for something she didn't even know she'd done, scored at her like claws, but instead, she pushed herself to take another step forward, then another, until she was close enough to skip a stone well into its width. At that point, mud squelching around the toes of her boots, she stopped, forced herself to forget what she knew, for a breath, and simply looked.

It was a river. It was a glorious river, she would admit, even in winter: broad and flat under sloped banks, and she could imagine that with the spring rains, it would rise and speed in the way of all rivers. And yet, she'd expected something more, somehow, from the border that marked the edge of the Territory, that had kept others out for hundred of years, ever since the devil stood on these banks and refused entrance to would-be conquistadors.

She tried to imagine it, tried to imagine standing with the boss, tried to imagine what he might have seen, what they might have seen looking back at him. But there was nothing.

The river was so broad here, with a gentle curve to its shape, she could only just see the shape of the American fort on the other bank just upriver, flags hanging limp without wind, the thick line of trees rising beyond that. She took that in, then moved her attention away from the unknown shore, instead studying the rivulets of water streaming just past her toes. It was shallow there and the sunlight angled just so that she could see the flicker of tiny fish, the glitter of something deeper in the current, the shadow of things deeper still, waiting just out of reach.

They called it the Mudwater, but it shone like silver, alternating polished and tarnished.

"Maybe I'd have to be where he was," she said out loud. "Maybe that's it." Or maybe what it was, was hidden deep, not laid on the surface.

She stepped closer, careful where she placed her boots, feeling the firm mud squelch deeper under her soles. It lacked the steady pulse of the Road when she reached gently for it, fluttering instead, like the wings of a young bird in her hand. She felt the urge to reach deeper but held it in check, breathing through her nose and letting her gaze scan the surface of the river, across to the other side.

She did not dare kneel, not with the ground so slippery-wet, but she opened her hand, the palm facing toward the water, and—despite her exhaustion, despite the toll it had taken on her—tried to reach for the bones, thinking they might help her see better.

The Road, distant. The bones, still. All she could hear was the rushing of not-wind, the gurgle of a thousand streamlets, the slow grinding turn of rocks deep within the currents, the urgent deadly tumble of whitecaps, the press of so much life, slow and fast, flickering and turning within . . .

And a faint sense of wrongness, of . . . disappointment, and anger and damage done, bound into a rock that could not surface. The desire to apologize clawed at her again, and she felt her lungs lose air, flailing in panic until her fingers found bone and root, and pulled herself clear.

She turned to speak to Gabriel and saw he had sunk to his heels, hands resting on his knees, his hat pulled down over his forehead so she couldn't see his face.

It tore her to leave him be, but a greater need drove her now. The Mudwater was the first protection the Territory had, its waters, like the Mother's Knife, a barrier against harmful intent. If something were wrong, if something threatened it, she needed to know.

When she looked down again, although she did not remember moving forward, the water was lapping over the toes of her boots, the tiny school of fish flicking away, deeper into the river. The ground below her felt softer, not like mud but sucking her in, as though it would like to consume her, but Isobel did not back away.

A breath, then another, and a third, until she felt calm, in control, and she tried to imagine being on one of the barges Gabriel had described, traveling up and down the river, trusting those currents to carry her safely. She wondered what it felt like, to feel water under her like that, if the motion would be like crossing on horseback, or something else entirely.

The river was a guardian, an ally. It was running water, broad and strong enough to break any magic that tried to pass it. She had to trust it to keep the Territory safe, as she trusted the devil to keep the Territory in Agreement.

"My name is Isobel," she told the deeper currents. "Isobel of Flood. Isobel Devil's Hand." And she reached down with her left hand and placed her palm against the surface of the water.

Cool, and softer than she'd expected. Dampness, then a soft caress, as though the water were touching her back, sliding across her palm.

The sigil hummed, not the sparking pain she felt when it meant to warn her, not the itching awareness of trouble, although she recognized, dimly, that both were there, waiting deeper beneath her skin. This was more . . . the way Uvnee would lean into her touch when she brushed the mare's coat out in the evening. Something living, aware.

The River recognized her.

"Hello," she said, although she was not certain she spoke the word out loud. Half-expecting a response, she was not disappointed to hear only silence, the constant lapping splash and chuckle of the river sound enough, filling her ears until nothing else existed.

Something familiar slid against her then, like a fish underwater, or a snake in the tall grasses. She braced herself for the mocking voice of a spirit animal, even as she knew that none would come to her there, within this no-place, no-time. This was unlike anything else, even the deepest bones. She was within herself, within the river, within everything. . . .

The River was not like the Knife, with its pulsing veins of living silver. It was not like the ancient spirits or the spirit animals, or anything else she knew. This might be what magicians sensed before the winds swept them away, and the thought made her tense.

But she had faced magicians and survived. She was the devil's silver. Running water was her ally, not her foe.

Her hand slipped farther underwater, encased in wet.

Nothing. Not even the awareness of nothing, but the not-awareness of nothing. Ice ran in bones that were no longer there, and something *snapped*, flipping her from the depths to where she could almost feel herself again, the sense of something massive moving around her, pushing her . . .

And behind her eyelids a map unfolded, the inked lines expanding and etching, until the whole of the Territory spread before her, filled with shades of brown and grey and blue and green, colored dots shimmering and moving as though the entire map breathed and shifted under her watch.

She touched the map, and no-place wrapped itself around her, pushing her through.

Worry. Regret. *Things shift. Things change. I cannot stop them, only slow the process. And I do not know if it will be enough.*

This time, there was no fog to blind her, but she still could not see him, even as she knew he was there. It was a sense, a memory that wasn't memory; she had never been in this room before, the map behind her eyes on the wall in front of her, the colors more distinct, the two realities blurring until she could not tell what was within her and what was without, or if there was in truth any difference between the two.

Boss?

She did not fear the presence forming around her, had never feared him; his anger had been that of a blizzard, or a fire, something that existed not to harm but to express, his sternness and his kindnesses one and the same to the child she had been. She had made Bargain, taken contract.

And yet, so too had the Jacks, in their own way. More, their contract had a term; when they had paid their debt, they would be free to die. Hers had no ending, no point at which her service would be done. What made her so different; what made her think she too would not become pained, lost, miserable?

The presence gave her no answer, though she felt certain it knew her hesitation, heard her question, merely spread its . . . arms? A sensation of arms . . . and enfolded them around her, sinking into her, or she sank into them. There was no comfort there, no safety, only cold truths.

She had always known the boss wasn't . . . like them. But it had been a thing so well known, she had never thought to think of it. Never thought what it meant.

Too late now.

Look, he said now, spreading her across the map. *Look.*

She looked.

FIVE

Isobel had spent her entire life, before taking the Road, in a saloon. Whiskey and rye and gin were as familiar to her as water and juice. But she'd never been on this side of the bottle before.

The whiskey burned as it went down, starting in her throat and lingering all the way into her belly. She understood now why some called it firewater, and why Marie had advised the girls working in the saloon to hold with tea, saying it was fine for men to make fools of themselves, but a woman never should.

That proscription felt terribly unfair now. Why shouldn't Isobel be allowed to do whatever it was men did when they got liquored up?

"He didn't tell me anything," she said, more to the glass than to Gabriel sitting across the table from her. "He never tells us anything, he just"—and she waved her right hand aimlessly—"sends us out and says things that make no sense, and . . . Did you know he's not human?"

Gabriel's eyes met hers directly, the shadows under them likely a mirror of her own. "I'd a suspicion, yes."

She took another drink, making a face at the taste, knowing that her sense of betrayal was ridiculous, utter nonsense, but it still hurt, and she didn't understand why. "He's not human. And we trust him, even when we don't trust magicians who were human once, even when we don't trust spirit animals."

"Except when we do," Gabriel said. Which wasn't fair; they'd listened, but they hadn't trusted. Because only a fool wouldn't listen but only a fool would trust, and—

"And that's not the point, the point is . . ." She didn't remember what the point was.

Look, he had told her. And she had seen . . .

Hate. Fear. Love. Desire. Need. Rage. Loneliness. Hunger. Shifting and stabbing against each other, *needing* things they did not have, willing to do anything to ease the aches, and the boss felt each and every one, watched them on that map, held them under his skin. Every soul within the Territory.

Master of the Territory, they called him. Not master—keeper.

She lifted the glass again and let the rest of it slide down her throat, then pushed the glass forward for the bartender to refill. She didn't miss how the barkeep slid his glance to Gabriel, waiting for his nod, before pouring another shot, and the injustice of that burned under her skin as well.

Gabriel had been quiet, letting her ramble. Too quiet: there was something painful shifting within him, too, she could see it, but her own turmoil made her bitter and selfish. She would feel guilty about it in the morning, she decided.

The River was not an ally. The devil had made Bargain with it when he stood on the banks and claimed the Territory for himself. It had recognized her, not as herself, not as Isobel, but only an extension of him.

She'd given everything away; when did she get something back?

Power, she'd thought she would get. Respect. But the power was his, all his, and there was no respect, only men who spit in the street, and others who demanded she *do* and *fix*.

She knew she was being foolish, a child; knew she was being selfish, and for just that moment, she didn't care.

"Everyone here, everyone in the entire Territory. They either hate me or they want me to solve all their problems. And I don't even know what their problems *are* but they expect me to know that, too.

"I hate this place. I hate everything about it."

Gabriel accepted another drink from the barkeep as well and tipped the edge of his glass to hers. "To hating everything," he said, and they drank.

"I hate you."

"I know you do."

Isobel leaned back, away from the basin, and wiped her mouth with the back of her hand, grimacing at the feel of her skin, then grimacing at the feel of her head, which seemed both two sizes too large and two sizes too small. Gabriel's hand combed gently through her hair, moving the strands out of the way in case she felt the need to vomit again.

She had no memory of going to sleep the night before, and only a vague memory of leaving the saloon. She had a deep suspicion, however, that she had made a fool of herself exactly the way Marie had warned against.

"Drink this."

The thought of putting anything into her stomach made Isobel try to refuse the cup, but Gabriel pushed it back at her, and she gave in rather than argue further.

The water was cool, and wet, and she let it linger in her mouth, savoring that sensation, before swallowing. She was wearing her night rail but couldn't find it in herself to be embarrassed, or wonder if Gabriel had fetched the girls to help ready her for bed; he'd seen her soaked to the skin by rain, covered in mud, and half out of her head with fever before; there likely wasn't much she could do to disappoint him at this point. But she was still cautious as she raised her head to catch his eye.

"Welcome to your first morning after," he said, and while his words were even, the smile he gave her was gently mocking. Isobel thought to be angry, for a moment, then accepted it as her due. But she needed to know:

"Did I do anything particularly foolish?"

"Not particularly." He helped her up off the floor and back onto the bed she'd abandoned in her race for the basin. "No more than any, and far less than most. Drink the rest of the water. It will help."

"I shouldn't have . . ."

"Iz." His eyes were still mocking, but his face had taken the "mentor speaking" expression she'd come to know far too well, even if she hadn't seen it much recently. "The past few days . . . winds take it, the last few months, I've been waiting for you to break. Coming here . . . I'd hoped we'd have time for you to breathe, just be. I don't know, be a sixteen-year-old girl again."

"Almost seventeen." She didn't know why she said it; some stubborn desire to not be that girl anymore, maybe.

"Almost seventeen. I'd hoped—I shouldn't hope; it always ends badly." He tried to smile at her and failed, and her heart twisted awkwardly at the pain in it.

"It was my decision to take you into that establishment; if you're feeling a need to cast blame, cast it my way. But you weren't responding to me at the river, you were shaking, and I thought you'd . . . Well, and I wasn't much better, if we're being honest."

She knew that, had seen that, and hadn't pushed him on it. On why he'd reacted that way, becoming violently ill . . . Was he ill? Was something wrong that he hadn't told her? A flutter of panic beat against her ribcage. "Are you—"

"It's all right," he reassured her, resting a gentle hand against her cheek briefly. "The River . . . it's powerful strong. I'd forgotten, is all."

"You'd intentionally forgotten," she said, and he winced, dropping his hand and sitting back.

"Do you think you could stomach something to eat now?"

Isobel groaned as her stomach tried to revolt against the water she'd given it. "I hate you," she repeated in response, easing herself back down to the pillow and pulling the coverlet over her head.

She heard his breathing, soft, over her, then the sound of boot-heels on the floor, and the door gently opening and closing. Only then, her head pounding and her throat sore and sick from vomiting, did she let tears fall.

Drinking had been foolish; she wouldn't make that mistake ever again. Marie had been right in that it gave no clarity, only a temporary escape. And she had no time for that. No time for it, and no right to it.

They claim you, Auntie had said. *They put their mark on you. Everything's an agreement.* She was as bad as the wapiti, or the snake, telling Isobel things that were important but not *explaining* them.

Isobel reached a hand up from under the flattened pillow, wiping her nose, grimacing at the wet feel of snot on her skin. An agreement was supposed to . . . It was a contract. It had *rules.*

She shoved her face back down into the pillow until she couldn't breathe, then turned to the side and shoved the blanket away, gulping air that sounded too much like sobs. Her stomach heaved a warn-ing, then she rolled half-off the bed and vomited again into the basin Gabriel had thoughtfully left by her side, her body shaking and her head ringing with the effort.

You need to be brave, and remember.

Remember what?

What you are.

The exchange echoed in her head, a flutter of fire-red and blue and gold.

What she was? She was the Hand. The cold eye and the final word.

It didn't matter what she didn't understand. She never under-stood, not until she had a solution, and sometimes not even then, but it had always worked out. She just had to . . . trust the devil. He *needed* her.

∾ ∾ ∾

"She's sleeping?"

Gabriel nodded at the resthouse keeper's quiet inquiry.

"First hangover," he said, forcing a grin. "Not sure how I over-looked that part of her training before this."

"On the Road's no place to be grogged," Rafe said, clearly with a memory of his own in mind. "A bed and pillow, and a door that closes, makes it easier. I'll have Ana come by in a few hours with water and coffee?"

Gabriel hesitated, then nodded. As much as he wanted to wait by her side, he was not sure it would be helpful to either of them. "Thank you."

The other man nodded and moved down the hallway, checking open doors, presumably to ensure that the girls had cleaned them properly before new guests arrived.

Gabriel stood in front of the door, torn between opposing urges. Eventually, he forced himself down the stairs, out past the sour-faced woman who once again sat at the desk, her attention on the pen and ledger on front of her, not guests who left.

He'd get some fresh air, he thought. Mayhap go check on the horses again, mayhap do the restocking, since Isobel wasn't going to be good for much the rest of the day. And, he admitted to himself, a long walk wouldn't hurt him, either. He might not have gotten drunk the night before, but it had been a while since he'd had that much whiskey in his gut.

Rafe was right: you didn't overindulge on the Road. Just wasn't wise, for so many reasons. But normally he didn't indulge in town, either, and Isobel's obvious distress should have been reason for him to stick to coffee, not spirits. So, why had he matched her, shot for shot?

The moment he stepped onto the porch, out from under the wards etched in the doorway, Gabriel remembered. Tiny bone fishhooks

lodged themselves in his flesh like the lip of a trout, setting and tugging him to turn, to walk, to *move.*

Come to me, the water said.

"No." He'd said it out loud, but not loud enough for anyone else
to hear. What he spoke to could hear him nonetheless, and tugged
harder, a sense of urgency, of desperation, of need.

Water-child, Auntie had called him. Old Woman Who Never Dies
had warned him, years before: water does not take well to being
refused. But he'd done it anyway, used the Touch and thought he
could put it away after, as though it were nothing more than silver
and salt.

But he had known. Looking back now, the choices he'd made, the
roads he'd ridden, they had kept him in-Territory, riding the high
plains and hills, skirting the northern borders, staying far from the
east. And if he'd never ridden on a moment's curiosity into Flood,
thinking briefly to test himself against the devil's table, he might have
done so the remainder of his life.

But Isobel had needed to know Red Stick, the same as she knew
every major region in the Territory. She needed to know the River,
the same way she'd learned the Mother's Knife, the ends and begin-
nings of the Territory, the barriers that kept them safe. He'd had no
choice but to take her here, and the devil, damn him, had known it.

He'd sat in that chair, across from the devil behind his desk, watching the skin shift over his face, shape and shade never the same each
time he looked, but always those eyes, darkly golden and intent.

He heard his own voice echo in memory: *You're asking me my
price?*

I'm saying I would . . . owe you your price. If you would do this.

*All I want is something you can't give, Old Man. Quiet. Peace. An
end to all this.*

The devil had laughed. *If that was what you wanted, Gabriel Kasun,
you had only to take it.*

Gabriel had thought the Old Man'd meant death—and he'd

thought about it, and each time something in him rejected it. He'd fought too hard for his freedom to give it up that easily—to death or to the Territory. He'd refused both. Or thought he had, anyway.

But the moment he'd looked up into the wide brown eyes of a girl with potential writ deep in her bones, mayhap he'd known how this would end.

The devil had given him the thing he'd never thought to want. A reason. A purpose past simply staying alive. But the bald man had been right, if foolish. To be born of Territory mud was to be destroyed by it.

Earlier dreams had been of clear waters, and silver fish flashing and turning at his ankles. Now the fish were on the banks, the rivers churning red.

Old Woman Who Never Dies had warned him: he could never outrun what he was. Not within the Territory, and not by leaving it. Eventually, receipts would have to be paid.

But for now, he had supplies to buy and a Hand to take care of. He could hold it off until then.

PART FOUR

AGREEMENTS

ONE

Isobel woke the next morning feeling jumpy and hot, her legs twitching restlessly until she'd thrown back the covers, staggering down the hallway to the washroom, where she'd recklessly, selfishly used as much hot water as she pleased until she felt close to respectable again.

When she got back, Gabriel was awake, although he was still in bed, staring up at the ceiling. She sat on the edge of her bed, soles of her feet brushing against the floor, and asked him, "Do you ever feel like your skin is too tight around your body?"

He sighed, turning onto his side toward her, and propping his head up on his hand. "And your thoughts are a tangle of knots it would be easier to set on fire than unsort?"

"Yes. Exactly that." She'd known he would understand. "How do you stop that?"

He sighed. "Not by burrowing in here like a kwuské. Give me a minute to get dressed."

❧ ❧ ❧

Outside, the sky had clouded over and the air was sticky-wet again, dampening the fabric of her blouse and forming a line of sweat under the brim of her hat, trickling down the side of her face. But the air smelled better than it had in their room, where the scent of sick and sweat lingered despite Ana's having changed the sheets and brought in a beeswax candle to clear the air.

Gabriel studied the sky for a long moment, then said, "Come on."

She scowled but followed. There seemed to be more people moving about, going in and out of buildings, than even the busiest market day Flood had ever held, and despite their earlier forays into the city, she was not certain she could find her way back to the hostería once it was out of sight, if Gabriel hadn't been with her.

Then they curved around a side street, and she realized they were at the stable where the horses had been left.

Something in her chest twisted, but it wasn't until she went inside and saw Uvnee's familiar head sticking out over a gate that Isobel realized how much she had *not* been enjoying living inside four walls and under a roof.

"Me too," Gabriel said, going to greet Steady, who had crowded forward in the stall next to Uvnee, stretching his neck out over the rope gate in greeting.

It didn't cure everything, but some slight sense of *lost* slid away as she wrapped her arms around the mare's neck and rested her forehead against warm flesh, breathing deeply of smells that should have been unpleasant and instead spoke of home and comfort. Gabriel had told her once before, and been right: it helped.

"Hello, girl," she murmured. "Did you miss me?"

The mare turned her neck, pushing Isobel closer in her own version of a hug, and Isobel thought maybe the mare had.

Gabriel had leaned his own forehead against Steady's square head, one hand reaching up to scratch tufted ears, even as the gelding lowered his head for easier reach. He said something in a tongue she didn't recognize, and the horse nickered as though in response.

"Excuse me—oh." She turned her head to see a young boy standing there. "Sorry, I just, I'm not supposed to let people touch the horses."

Native, Isobel noted, with some surprise, although he was wearing a settler-style trou and shirt, with boots and belt. His features weren't the same she'd seen in the local villages, but the shade of his skin and hair suggested he was full-blood, even if not local.

"Dusty, right?" Gabriel was saying, reaching out to shake the boy's hand the way he would a grown man's.

"Yes, sir, you came in earlier; I remember you now." The boy's face flushed lightly, the gaze he turned on Gabriel nothing short of awestruck, and Isobel felt a giggle rise up inside her: there was a boy who'd likely find himself on the Road when he reached majority, if nothing distracted him before then. She hoped he'd be better prepared for it that she was, but she was beginning to think there was nothing that truly could prepare you, not usefully.

"It's good you come in," the boy said, as though suddenly remembering a thing. "Someone was in looking for you just last night. They'd been checking all the stables, they said, which was foolishness; ours is the only place a rider would keep their cattle." He announced that with such matter-of-factness, Isobel had no choice but to take it as true.

"What did he look like?" Gabriel asked, and the boy shrugged.

"Pale all over, old clothes, good horse, probably Spanish-bred but none of the nervous ways some of 'em have, lean but not lathered. He took good care of it."

"A courier," Gabriel said.

"He asked where you was staying, but I didn't know." The boy's gaze flickered to the left, as though trying to decide something, and Isobel tensed, expecting bad news or some new worry. "And he didn't want to leave the packet at the post-drop, said he had to give it to a person. So, Yonnan said we would hold it for you. You want I should go fetch it?"

The thing turned out to be an oilcloth packet with Isobel and Gabriel's names both written in careful writing on the outside. Isobel recognized the writing immediately.

"Marie. It's from Marie."

Gabriel's hand closed over hers when she would have opened it, and she nodded, understanding his caution. Whatever was inside had come from Flood, which meant even though it was addressed to them, it was still the boss's business. They would wait until they were in private.

"We did right, taking it?" The boy, Dusty, was watching them anxiously.

Isobel smiled and fished a quarter-coin out of her skirt pocket to give to him. "You did, thank you. And you're keeping good care of the horses, I can tell."

Dusty closed his fingers around the bit of coin before making it disappear into his own pocket, then added, with the air of one clearly determined to be entirely truthful, "The horses, they're easy. Your mule . . ." He shrugged, a "what can you do" expression on his face. "He's not bad, just . . ."

"Stubborn?" Gabriel asked, serious in the face of the boy's seriousness.

"Ornery," Dusty said. "He's eating fine but won't let no one groom him or check his hooves, and . . . he's taken to nipping at anyone who brings him feed."

Gabriel lifted his face to the stable's roof, as though asking for patience, but she could see the corners of his mouth tipping upward as well. "Let's go have a word with him, then, shall we?"

Flatfoot looked to be in excellent spirits, lounging in a pen with several other mules, and if his coat was coated with dust and there was straw in his mane, Isobel couldn't really see where it was hurting him. But Gabriel sighed and then made a clicking noise with his tongue.

Isobel would swear to her grave that the mule sighed as well, in the exact same tone, before ambling over to the fence where they stood and allowing Isobel to pick the straw out of his mane.

"Causing trouble again, are you?" Gabriel said. "I should have named you Bother or Fuss."

The mule snorted wetly, and Gabriel made a face, wiping mule-snot off the front of his shirt. "I haven't missed you at all, either."

Sometimes, Isobel forgot that Gabriel had traveled with his horse and his mule for maybe even years, before she and Uvnee had joined them.

"He gives you any more trouble, just drop a bucket of water over him," Gabriel told the boy, slapping the mule affectionately on the neck, as though in apology for the instructions. "He'll sulk for a while, but he won't give you any more sass."

Outside the stable, the clouds had thickened, the wind picking up slightly, blowing scattered leaves and dust down the street. There were fewer people out and about; they were either done for the day or taking shelter from the threatening rain. Isobel noted all this, estimating the likelihood that rain would begin to fall before they returned to the hostería, but her main thoughts were less on physical discomfort than the scene they'd only just left.

The package was a hot weight in her hands, making her itch with curiosity, and so to distract herself, she asked, "Can animals truly miss us?"

Gabriel shrugged. "All I know is what I've seen. A creature spends time with you, has its own sort of fondness for you, it will greet you when you return—or at least tolerate your greeting them. Is that actually missing? I'm pleased to say I've no ability to understand creatures, but I think so, yes."

There had been animals in Flood, of course, but she'd had little interaction with them, save tossing scraps for the cats that lived behind the kitchen, or occasionally petting the dogs that trotted in at the heels of herders and farmers. And horses had just been . . . horses.

They pulled wagons, or carried riders, or sometimes hauled a plow.

"Do you think—"

"Hand! Devil's Hand!"

Isobel swung, mid-sentence, her right hand falling to where the hilt of her knife would be if she were riding, cursing the fact that she'd fallen out of the habit already of attaching it to her belt when she dressed. Gabriel had no such problem, the blade already halfway from its sheath even as he shifted to step halfway in front of her, then stopping as though realizing what he'd just done.

The man who had called out stood in the middle of the street what few other folk were around quickly clearing a space around him or disappearing into storefront doors. He did not seem dangerous or threatening, his chest heaving as though he'd run a long distance, his brown trou splattered with mud and his face red with exertion.

"You are the Hand?" He seemed uncertain now, his gaze flicking from one to the other, as though expecting one of them to suddenly grow extra limbs or maybe a pair of horns like some of the gospel sharps said the boss had.

"I am," she said, stepping forward, trusting Gabriel to keep his knife ready in case there was need.

The man sagged in clear relief, his entire body near-collapsing off his shoulders. "Calico Zac said you'd be here. You need to come."

Gabriel left Isobel with the stranger, ducking back into the stable to get the horses, while Isobel sat with the man in the shadow of the doorway, the man's walleyed pony resting with its head low to the ground, as sweat-flecked as its rider, getting them both to take cautious sips of water.

"He all right?"

She looked at the man, who nodded. "I took too much time finding you. We need to get back. I will explain . . . as we ride."

Gabriel didn't like it, didn't like going blind into anything. But

Isobel nodded, and he followed. He had left his carbine at the hostería, but he'd borrowed a battered musket from the stable owner—with a silver coin slipped to Dusty to assure its return—and loaded it with shot before saddling up. It might be risky, riding with a loaded weapon at his hip. But if they were riding into a trap, the time it took to load might be time they didn't have.

Not that he thought they were riding into a trap. Not really. He was merely being cautious in light of recent events.

Once they'd cleared the entrance gate and could mount up again, Isobel pushed Uvnee alongside the man's pony, reins looped loose over her hand, her hat pulled forward and a determined lift to her chin. "Tell me again what happened."

The man's walleyed pony looked like it spent more time in harness than under saddle, although to be fair, the awkward way the man sat the saddle suggested neither of them were well used to it.

"We—my brothers and I—we took up land just off the Curve, where the river turns?—near on five years back. Spent a season living with the Horned Rabbit folk when we came. My little brother Jordan, he married one of their girls, got two kids now, they spend most of their time with her people, but the rest of us, we've been farming. Land's rich as god's gift here; you just have to look at it and things grow, like it *likes* us being here. And everything was sweet as honey until last spring, when new folk decided to settle a patch near us. We didn't think anything of it; there are folk coming and going all the time. But they—" The man shook his head, his jaw working as he clearly tried to consider his words.

"You said there was trouble," Isobel prompted.

"Not at first. But over the summer, it was as though the hotter it got, the meaner they got, to where even extending a hand was as like to have it bitten off as shaken, if you take my meaning. Which we wouldn't have paid mind to, being busy, except Jordan's wife said they'd done the same to the village in particular when croup hit us all. Medicine woman there, she's a fine hand at healing. Never turned a request away, neither, not from anyone. 'Cept they weren't asking for help; they were demanding. Told her to treat them first or she'd be sorry."

Croup could be deadly if it wasn't treated; the cough could sweep through a household seemingly overnight, especially children. Gabriel could understand parents panicking, but insulting the ones who might ease it seemed foolish, if not quite cause for hauling the Hand out months later.

"She helped 'em, more gracious than I would've, tell you that. And they made the right gifts, after, if grudging—we sent 'em a she-goat and kid, us. So, we thought they'd learned their lesson, things would settle down. And then last month, they went and cleared another field, without permission."

Gabriel almost choked on air. The first thing every settler learned, within days of coming to the Territory, was that they had no right to claim land without agreement of the nearest tribes, even if they weren't using it themselves. Tribes had the right to say no if they didn't like the cut of your cloth. Isobel's own parents had tried to build without permission and gotten burnt out for it, trading their only daughter to the devil for passage out of the Territory. He wondered, briefly, what her life would have been like had they taken her with them, instead.

"And how did the tribe respond?" Isobel's voice had shifted, only a bit, only enough that Gabriel could notice, likely, but it was there: the gentle curiosity replaced by a touch of delicate, smoke-filled frost. He wondered if she was thinking of her parents as well.

"Better'n I would have," the man admitted. "They sent a delegation to the farm. High-ranking folk, too. Nothing insulting. Asked 'em to step away, that they hadn't been given leave to farm there, or, you know, make an offering for the worth of the field, as was only proper. So, we all thought that would be it. You either step back, or you start bargaining and make it a good offer, 'cause you're already on the wrong foot, yeah?"

Gabriel already knew it hadn't ended well, else the man wouldn't have needed to fetch Isobel, but he pushed Steady forward a little, caught up in the story.

"What happened, instead?" Isobel asked.

"They put up a fence!" The man's indignation was still wound about with shock. "Overnight, practically. A *fence*."

Isobel didn't have to ask how that had been taken. It wasn't that fencing was forbidden, not exactly—there were places where penning cattle was only good manners, so they didn't trample crops or have to be fetched out of someone's yard—but in this instance, it was rude, a shove when a handshake would have been expected.

A provocation.

"That was a morning ago," the man went on. "They've been staring at each other since, things getting quieter and quieter, the way things do before someone throws a swing and starts a brawl, you know? But Zac had ridden through, said you were heading into Stick, and I thought maybe you could . . ."

"You did the right thing," Isobel reassured him, not-so-subtly urging her mare to move faster.

Gabriel only wondered if they'd arrive in time.

As it turned out, they did, though Gabriel wasn't sure that was due to anything save luck and weather: the overcast sky had started to drizzle as they neared the settlements, and the ground turned muddy under hoof, not good conditions for anything save staying put.

The fence in question was, to his eye, a shoddy thing that a decent wind would knock over, but he acknowledged that the quality of construction wasn't the issue at hand.

Their guide rode on ahead, joining the miserable-looking huddle of people standing under an open-sided shed, next to an impressive stack of firewood.

"Do you have a plan?" he asked Isobel, reining Steady alongside Uvnee.

"No," she admitted, the fingers of her left hand clenched over her palm. "The sigil's been itching, the closer we get; I'm hoping it will tell me something when they start speaking."

Gabriel nodded even as he marshaled his own knowledge of law and procedure if she needed to draw on it.

The thought of trying to present this to a judge in a courtroom back East made his head ache, and he forced the image down before he broke into laughter that would only be half a step away from hysteria.

"Truth is, there's no defense for their behavior," Isobel said, and that smoky tone had deepened, another voice layering hers, shaping her words. He felt a chill at his spine, and any desire to laugh fled as abruptly as it'd arrived. "But I will hear them out nonetheless."

"All you can do," he agreed, leaning forward in his saddle and watching as she dismounted in a smooth action, one hand setting her skirts to rights, then adjusting her hat so others could see her face while the brim kept the drizzle out of her eyes. She walked like a rider, he noted not for the first time, lacking only the long coat over her skirts. She would need one for winter traveling. And new boots. Her stipend would cover that and more.

That reminded him of the bundle they'd been given, and he looked back to make sure it was still latched securely to his saddle. It was. Too large simply for coins; what else had the devil needed her to have? His fingers itched to find out, through sheer curiosity, and he forced that thought down, too.

When he looked back, he noted that the group of people had spread out a bit and Isobel was already speaking with one of them, an older white male. He slid from the saddle, took the reins of both horses in hand and looped them around a nearby post, and hurried to join her.

The man was strong-backed and weather-beaten the way only a farmer got, with a sour look to his mouth and lines that could be either anger or exhaustion—or indigestion—etched on his skin, causing his eyes to drop at the corners and his jaw to look tighter than it might have been otherwise. In short, he looked like a man ready and willing to fight, and the words out of his mouth did not dispel that impression.

"They've no right to keep us from using the land to feed ourselves! We haven't gone near lands they're using, haven't touched their waters or anything marked; it's just sitting there, waiting to be planted."

Gabriel bit the inside of his mouth. He'd heard those arguments before: if land wasn't being used, it should be free for the taking, that the needs of a young nation were measured in land farmed and towns built. That was the argument they used in the halls of governance from Philadelphia to Boston, and likely elsewhere as well, to justify taking lands from tribes that didn't know how to best use them and moving them elsewhere, as though one place were just the same as another. It was, he suspected, at the heart of Jefferson's sending surveyors and scouts into the Territory, with an eye toward expanding the United States' hold.

Two hundred years ago, the colonists had accepted the devil's claim to the Territory, because they'd had neither need nor ability to push further west. But even when Gabriel had lived in the States, he had heard discussion: how could one negotiate with a land that had no government, no visible ruler? And without negotiation, without a treaty . . .

"Was the Agreement explained to you when you came here?" Isobel's voice had gone from frost to ice. "Was there anything within it that was unclear?"

The older man, if possible, looked even more sour. "We understand keeping the peace," he said. "We may not like 'em, but we're not going to do anything stupid."

"Too late," someone said sotto voce next to Gabriel, for his ears only, or perhaps not even that. He spared a glance sideways to find a young girl standing beside him, her clothing covered in a leather apron like a farrier's or blacksmith's, her auburn hair pulled into a plait away from her face. "He thinks he's smarter'n anyone else, but the truth is he just sits and broods until something knocks him loose."

Not so young, Gabriel reconsidered; Isobel's age, or thereabouts. And with, he suspected, the same gift of observing. "And something knocked him loose?"

The girl nodded, her pointed chin rising and lowering once. "Someone's buying up grain, up and down the river. So, he got to thinking he should be making more than he was, and, hey scout! There's a parcel of land, and never mind it wasn't given him originally to farm it."

There were days Gabriel wondered why they didn't just hand everything over to women and be done with it. "You know him well?"

She looked at him then with a wry twist to her mouth. "He's my da. Those're my brothers, and those two with Callum, who fetched you, are his brothers, the McCallisters from the next farm over. They 'n my da never got along. They think like natives, Da says, not proper men."

Gabriel closed his eyes for an instant, wishing a flood to wash all fools from the earth, then opened them again as though afraid that a breath of inattention—or too powerful a wish—might cause someone to do something even more spectacularly foolish.

Isobel was trying very hard to keep her temper, but it was difficult with her palm itching fit to be on fire and a fool square in her face. The man's bitter-faced argument, that he had the right to anything not nailed into place, made her want to bite at the finger he was poking toward her. Only Marie's constant training in how to handle rowdies in the saloon kept her still and her face calm.

"Of course you wouldn't do something stupid, George," she said, smiling gently at him, and had the satisfaction of seeing two of the men standing behind their leader take a sudden, surprised step back, their spines straightening as though a mule had just bitten their backsides.

She might be smiling, but that did not mean her voice was mild nor her smile sweet. "For it would be the act of a very foolish man indeed who would think that breaking the devil's Agreement would be overlooked, or winked at, even this far from Flood."

The man finally paled and looked as though he too would have liked to've taken a step back, though his words remained stubbornly foolish and foolishly stubborn. Whatever had happened the last time a Hand rode through there, it was good to know it left proper respect for the devil as well as anger.

"It was not broken. I gave no offense, did not take their belongings nor intrude in their daily lives. They asked for payment for these lands, and we paid it, willingly and without complaint—four young horses and saddles, plus half the yield of our first harvest."

A fair and manageable price, save for one fact. "It is my understanding that this field was not included in that price." She offered him the chance to argue it, to catch himself in a net of his own lies, and settle this quickly.

George shook his head, rain splashing from his hair, a drop dangling distractingly from the beak of his nose. "They weren't not! They said we should plow what we needed."

The men behind him—his sons, Isobel decided, from their age and appearance, muttered agreement, while two others, standing to the side as though to indicate they were not part of this mess, looked hesitant. They were well aware they stood on uncertain ground with that claim. Things that are understood might as easily be misunderstood if it suits a man's need.

The devil knew how to look into a man and see what he needed, what he desired. Isobel could only read the surface, and she had never adjudged a usage dispute before. She wanted desperately to ask Gabriel's opinion, gain his experience in such matters, but could think of no way to do so without appearing to defer to him before these men, and that she could not do. She was the Hand, not him.

She cast her gaze over the crowd again, searching for something, although she was unsure yet what. Then she frowned. "Is there no one here who speaks for the affected tribe?"

"Why do you need—" The question was cut off by a grunt, likely applied by someone else's elbow.

Isobel identified the speaker and narrowed her eyes at him. "Were you kicked in the head by your horse at some point, or were you born a fool?"

"How dare you—"

This time, the elbow was obvious, connected to the arm that wrapped around the speaker's mouth, yanking him backward.

"My mother dropped him on his head as a babe," the yanker said, easily keeping his brother in check. "We try not to let him speak in public. Apologies, Hand."

The sharp burn of the sigil reminded her of the glitter of reaction in the boss's eyes when someone challenged him, and she repressed a shudder at the violent urge that accompanied it.

No, she told it. She would handle this her way.

"Keep him silent," she said. "And fetch someone of the tribe who can speak for their people. Please."

"I'll go," a voice said, and a girl stepped out from behind the taller men. She was perhaps the same age as Isobel, or slightly younger, dressed similar to the men around her, save in skirts rather than trou. The girl looked first to Isobel, then to the older man—her father, Isobel determined, from the similarity in their faces. "I can run fast," she added, "and they know me."

And like her, her expression suggested.

When he nodded, curtly, giving permission, Isobel began to hope, as the girl ran down the road, the rain barely seeming to touch her, that they might settle this without further offense.

"You gentlemen might want to settle down to wait," Gabriel said, coming up alongside her, the musket he'd taken from the stable held in one hand. "Nothing's going to happen for a bit yet, and it would pain me only somewhat to shoot someone in the knee while we're waiting."

Isobel's eyes widened, and she felt Gabriel's free hand come up against her back, a gently firm touch of reassurance. "And trust me," he added, staring down the man who'd been muffled earlier, "me shooting you would be preferable to what she might do if you give her further sass."

TWO

An uneasy truce fell into place, the two groups of men huddled around the fence, occasionally glaring at it, or each other, none of them seemingly willing to trust the others unsupervised. Isobel and Gabriel moved off to the side, trying to watch both groups without looking particularly worried, waiting for a representative from the village to arrive. Their guide had said the main village was only a short walk away, that there was a clear—and oft-used—path between, and Isobel understood that they would not rush back immediately, that such things would take discussion and preparation, but she couldn't help but stare at the sky, the sun hidden behind thick clouds, and wish she had less time to think her own thoughts that Gabriel could not ease. She was revisiting every decision made and word uttered, the itch in her palm growing no worse, but not fading, either.

"You shoulda—"

"Don't you speak—"

"Enough!" That was one of the McCallister brothers, Gabriel had told her. One of three, the third being Callum, who had fetched them. The speaker—yeller—was more slender than his brother and, she thought younger, but he had a set of lungs and a voice on him that would shame a rooster: high and piercing.

After a glance at Gabriel, who had pulled his hat forward over his eyes to shield them from the light rain but was otherwise intent on watching the men, she tilted her head to the side, telling him that she would be moving away for a bit and not to fret. He didn't nod or otherwise indicate he understood, but when she stepped away, he did not follow.

She moved to the road, ignoring the curious looks of the two men who stood with their guide, then crouched, placing her hand to the ground, tentatively, the pads of her fingers first, then the palm coming to rest, feather-light.

Hello, she thought to it, and something stirred deep below. But it did not rise to meet her, and she did not feel herself descend.

She sat there, quietly breathing, waiting. Letting her thoughts cool. She was the Devil's Hand. The cold eye and the final word. She would hear both sides and pass judgment. That was what she had been sent there to do.

That was something she *could* do.

"The last Hand to walk these trails did not understand."

Isobel had heard the steps coming closer but thought it was Gabriel. So, she managed to jolt only slightly when a stranger sat next to her, legs crossing underneath him.

"What?" She winced at how young, surprised, her voice sounded.

"The last Hand did not understand," he repeated. "But you, I think, do. Or will."

His hair was easily as long as hers, shorn on the sides and braided in a dozen or more plaits, and he wore a settler-style shirt over leggings, his feet shod in comfortable-looking hide moccasins without any adornment whatsoever. He looked to be about Gabriel's age, or older, though there was no silver visible in his hair that she could see in the cloud-dark light.

He placed his hand next to hers, not quite touching the ground but barely a sliver of air between it. His fingers were long and slender, the knuckles scraped with scabs Isobel recognized from the fisticuffs some of the saloon regulars used to indulge in. "They tell stories of you. That the land listens through your eyes. That it speaks on your tongue."

"I don't know what you mean."

"Yes, you do. You only don't know it yet." He patted the back of her hand once and then turned his attention to the now-larger group of people standing by the shelter. Far more than before. All male, save for the girl darting back and forth between the two groups, until her father caught her by the shoulder and sent her to stand with her brothers.

The local tribe hadn't sent a representative: they had sent a delegation.

Gabriel was leaning against the fence, watching, a steady presence that seemed to have a sobering effect on them all, if the way they milled about, looked at him, and then checked themselves was proof.

Before she could respond, the stranger stood, as graceful as he'd sat down, and extended his hand to her. "It's time."

Her breath caught, echoes of something else rippling out from those two words, but she had no opportunity to follow them: there was a judgment to be made.

She tried not to count, but there had to be at least two dozen people gathered now, split into three clumps: one mostly native, two settlers. Word must have spread to neighboring farms, Isobel thought. This affected them all, one way or another, she supposed. It made sense they would come to watch.

Knowing that didn't help settle her nerves any. Isobel had never done this before, had no idea, even as she walked toward the group waiting, what to expect, what to do. Some memory of the judge in Andreas came to her, the way he'd heard testimony, the way Gabriel and she had told of what they'd observed, but it felt wrong somehow for here, and she discarded the idea. Before she was ready, she found herself standing just outside the shelter, the misty air worse than sweat on her skin, the eyes of too many people upon her.

Her right hand reached up to touch the two feathers knotted into her braid. The edges were ragged now, between road-wear and weather, but she still took comfort in them, the gift of a dream-walker back when she was still green and uncertain. Her toes wiggled inside her boots, flexing as though to dig deep into the wet soil beneath her soles, and although she had not dropped into the bones, she felt them nonetheless, their power reaching up like sprouts in the spring, pale white tendrils wrapping around her ankles, sliding up and into her legs.

It should have been a disturbing sensation; instead, it brought clarity, and the words came from her mouth with surprising ease.

"These people have called upon the Master of the Territory to mediate the Agreement. Is this acceptable to you?"

The man who had spoken with her slipped into position at the shoulder of their leader, an older man with pock-marked skin, his hair brushed into a stiff quill down the back of his head. He glanced briefly at the man at his side, who nodded once, then looked back at Isobel and nodded as well. "We accept the Old Man's mediation." His English was impeccable, making Isobel blink; she was tempted to switch into Spanish, convinced that he would flow naturally along with her.

"I am Isobel of Flood, the Devil's Hand, and I speak for him."

"I am called Maika. We have heard of you, Hand, and accept your judgment."

The first man had said that as well, that they had heard of her. She wondered if Calico Zac had spoken to them, too, what he had said, then shut those thoughts off firmly. Now was not the time.

She turned to the settlers, searching out the man she had spoken with earlier, waiting for him to step forward. He did so, his mouth working like he tasted something unpleasant but meeting her eyes squarely this time.

He had already given her his name, but she waited for him to join her judgment formally. "George Peralta." His eyes were tired, she thought, his greying hair plastered to his forehead by rain, slicked back by an impatient hand. "We'll abide by your decision."

She looked around the rest, seeing from their nods that they had heard and witnessed that. If anyone went back on their word, all of Red Stick and the surrounding farms would likely know within days.

"Two winters back, the Peralta family made agreement with the Moons Confederacy, to settle this land and farm it. May I know the wording of those terms?"

One of Peralta's sons started to speak, and she waved them silent, waiting for one of the native party to respond before hearing any rebuttal.

She'd been worried about following the arguments, about paying attention to who said what, to how and where they disagreed, but as the two men spoke, kept civil by her presence, Isobel felt their voices fade to a background hum, the rhythm overlaid by the soothing *flickerthwack* of the devil laying down his cards. It was not about the words; words could mislead, could misdirect. Instead, she focused on how they stood, tilted their heads, moved their hands; how those around them reacted.

A warm sensation emanated from within her, as though a hot spring bubbled up within her veins. Not the touch she'd felt before, not the whisper that had led her before, but something similar, not so much subdued as contained, sharpening her sight even as time passed and the dim cloud-light turned into true dusk, figures moving and speaking softly around them.

"Enough," she said, rising out of the half-dreaming state she'd fallen into, and someone took the opportunity to strike a firestarter and light a series of lanterns, bringing some illumination to the scene.

Neither man had been lying. None of their followers had reacted as though they had heard a lie or been keeping one. But that did not mean that one or the other was speaking the truth, only that they *believed* they were speaking the truth. If the hot spring bubbling within her could sigh, she thought it might have.

"We don't serve our own whims . . . We play the devil's tune, and he calls it as he will." Those had been Marie's last words to her as she left the saloon. He had taught her how to do this, used the gambling tables to hone what skill she had, and sent her to work his will. She was the Hand, the cold eye and the final word.

But she was also a rider on the Dust Roads, with mud on her boots and blood on her hands. She had seen the map of the Territory and all it contained.

"This is our observation. The terms of the Agreement were set and met. In that time, the Peraltas have lived by the letter of the Agreement, if not the spirit." Thinking of the way they had greeted her, the things she had heard from their original summoner, she added, "I would advise them to mind their manners, as befits good neighbors, that I need not look this way again." Rudeness was not the same as offense, but she could feel the distaste pulsing within them, the feelings of heated superiority, and the echoes to that of the boys on the road made her doubt it was tied to only this one incident. The smug smile not quite hidden on some of their faces as she was speaking gave weight to that fear.

"The Moons Confederacy did not set limits on the land that was to be taken." Peralta had been correct: by the letter of the Agreement, that meant the settlers had done no wrong, given no offense. Again, by the letter, but not the spirit. She lifted her gaze to catch Gabriel's and saw the faintest nod of his head. Suddenly, she understood all the hours he'd spent telling her about his education in the States, the people he had worked with, there and here, as an advocate. Not to tell her about himself, as she'd thought, but about what the law meant. Or what it *should* mean.

There was more here than the devil's will. What she would decide would be carried forward. People would hear about it, think about it, before they did something like this again. What she decided would change how they behaved. The Territory would live and grow by what she did there.

Even generations after she was dust on the road, there would be people who would know the results of what she had done.

"That said," she continued, and saw the smug smiles fade, even in the dim light, "it is also our observation that the Peraltas were full-aware of what they did, pushing the Agreement to include gifts not expressly given nor traded for, and that the erecting of a fence was done with the intent to give deliberate offense. For that, the lands are forfeit and must be given back."

George merely looked stricken and, she thought, possibly regret-ful, but another voice raised in objection. "They didn't claim offense! You can't claim it for them!"

Isobel met the angry shout with a calm facade, even as every Road-trained instinct told her to reach for her knife, even as the heated springs within her gave way to something icy-hot shimmering out of her bones, radiating through her skin. "I am the Devil's Hand and his voice, the cold eye cast on the Territory. I am the final word. You would challenge me?"

There was a snarl as anger won over common sense, and the man lunged for her, but Gabriel was there, a hand coming down hard, breaking the man's arm with a sharp, green snap. A saw-edged knife the length of Isobel's hand clattered to the dirt as the man howled, its blade glinting in the lamplight.

The would-be attacker dropped to his knees, his wrist still in Gabriel's hold, and there was a breath of stunned silence.

"You scabby son of a whore!" someone howled, and suddenly Isobel was in the center of a windstorm of limbs and fists, voices raised as the tension she'd felt earlier was given physical expression. She could find no reason or pattern behind it; they were not fighting to defeat some-thing, only to show anger, frustration. She ducked, and felt something brush her face, reacting instinctively; she was not carrying her knife, and the longer blade was still attached to her saddle sheath, but the flat of her hand hit something with a solid *thunk*, and she felt immense satisfaction, even as she realized that his was her first true fight beyond Gabriel's training.

She felt the earlier heat shimmer more intensely within her, telling her to end this, here and now. She pushed it back fiercely, ignoring the whisper that licked through her thoughts, brimstone and lightning. Her muscles sang with effort, her teeth pulled back in a grin as her fist connected with a rib and she felt someone stagger back. Gabriel had taught her how to throw a punch at the same time he taught her how to duck one, but she had never been given cause to use either skill before.

She had not realized how good it could feel to put force behind her swing

Someone landed a blow to her ribs that made her stagger, knocking her back-to-back with someone, her hat falling forward over her eyes and blinding her until she shoved it back impatiently, feeling something catch and pull on her braid. She reached up instinctively, grabbing a hand holding a knife and yanking forward hard enough that her assailant fell forward, folding in two and meeting the ground head first.

"I am getting very tired of people around here coming at me with knives," she said, her teeth gritted.

"Be glad someone's not tried to trample you," Gabriel said, yanking her back as someone new waded in with a stick, thick around as a fist and fluttering with braided leather and feathers. "Dad's here, fun's over."

Panting, she leaned against Gabriel, tasting blood on her lip and in the back of her throat as she watched the newcomer lay into the crowd with his staff, sending native and settler alike to their knees or backsides.

The heat within her, rather than subsiding, surged back, and her vision flickered, until she could have sworn that the newcomer was limned in lightning, the *thwack* of his staff the crack of thunder.

"Enough!" he shouted finally. Or Isobel assumed from the tone that this was what he said; she did not recognize the language. Those around him clearly did, however, even the ones he hadn't laid out falling to their knees, hands raised in surrender. Then he turned to glare at Isobel, and even in the dark she could feel the dressing down he was preparing to give her, making her feel seven years old and useless again.

It was the man who had spoken with her, at the first, the stick in his hand making him seem fiercer, nearly unrecognizable until now. With the stick down, placed on the ground in front of him, she could identify him once again.

Isobel pushed back against the way his glare had made her feel, pushing away physically from Gabriel's support, and meeting the glare head on. She had not started the fight, but she would not apologize nor be scolded for defending herself.

Her right hand reached up to touch her feathers, familiar reassurance, but no delicate flutter met her fingertips. She pulled the braid forward, gaze sliding sideways, only to find tattered, bare spines that, when she touched them again, slid out of her braid as though they'd given up all hope.

"No . . ." She wasn't sure what she was denying, but the exclamation of disgust from the newcomer brought her attention back up to him.

"Do you feel better now?" he asked, his glare encompassing everyone, not only Isobel. "Did this solve anything, make you feel more a man, more a warrior?"

Even in the darkness, she could feel the silent, resentful embarrassment coming from them all.

"While you—" He looked at her specifically, and she braced herself. "You waste time with foolishness, and things worsen." He looked at her, and for a heartbeat his eyes were puzzled, worried. "Do you not hear it?"

The heat within her flared, and her left hand clenched instinctively at the thorn-sharp pain it inflicted, but the molten whisper deep within suggested that he was right, even though she did not know why, or about what.

"I know something's wrong. That's why I came here," she spat out, her own resentment rising. "But I don't know what to *do* about it!"

She probably shouldn't have said that, shouldn't have admitted helplessness, ignorance in front of these people. But none of them seemed to hear, and none of them mattered in the face of that burning pain and the look in the man's eyes.

"I told you. The land sees with your eyes, speaks with your tongue. You touched deep and brought it back with you, and now it rides you the way a magician rides the winds."

She ignored the others, slowly picking themselves up, withdrawing, leaving the two of them facing each other.

"The whisper's gone—" She didn't doubt he would know what she meant about the whisper, the voice she'd tried and failed to explain to Gabriel, the ribbon of urgency that had driven her before.

His only response to that was to snort and plant the decorated staff firmly in the dirt at his feet. "You are not listening."

"I don't—" *understand*, she wanted to say, and heard that echo of earlier conversations in her words. The spirit animals' warnings. Auntie's comments. The devil's cautions, his words about going too deep.

The bird in her dream, telling her to remember who she was.

What she was.

"No." But it was not a denial, and the man merely watched her, the worry in his eyes now tempered with sympathy not unlike Auntie's rough concern.

They knew. Whatever had happened to her, whatever the devil had feared, they knew.

She had to know too.

Isobel took a deep breath and tried to open herself to the heat she'd felt before, the quiet strength that had wrapped around, licked through her bones, given her clarity.

It hurt, far more than when she'd fallen off Uvnee's back and jarred her spine into agony, far more than any cramp or megrim she'd ever experienced, and part of her wanted to tear it out, to dig with a knife until it was out, thrown aside. But she breathed through it, the way she breathed through a cramp, her gaze set on the long, pale feather tied to the staff, fluttering without a breeze, breathing in and out as it moved.

Something waited. Lingered.

It came from the River, swirling in the no-place. She'd half-expected to feel the same unpleasantly sticky tendrils of the spell the Spanish had set on the territory, that it had reached this far south, sinking itself into the Territory, creating ripples that she needed to burn out—or bind. But this wasn't that. Nor was it the burning rage of the ancient spirit that had been woken up north by meddling, maddened magicians, that had sent the land itself into tremors, trying to contain it. This was . . . softer, cooler, sick and slick like snot in the back of her throat.

The lines set in her palm flared, a warning, and she clenched her hand, nails biting into the flesh as though to dig the sigil out or force it to still. She had to *listen*.

THREE

Gabriel had been keeping half his attention on the fighters, not entirely certain that a wrong look from one of them wouldn't start the brawl over again, and the other half on Isobel, who—after exchanging words with the native with the thump-staff—had sunk to her knees, taking a position he at least recognized. The expressions on some of the faces around him would have been amusing under any other situation and with better lighting; a little fear, a little confusion, and some awe. All he felt was concern.

"Is she—" he started, and the man held up a hand, trade-signing, "Wait, be silent."

Gabriel didn't like it, didn't like any of this, but he waited, watching her carefully. Any sign of distress, any indication she felt threatened, and he would kill whoever got between them and her safety.

His breathing steadied, the vigor that had sustained him during the fight was sliding from his limbs now, leaving him unpleasantly loose. To distract himself, he broke down Isobel's ruling in his thoughts, as though he were writing a judgment.

Her ruling had been split. *Prima facie,* she had chosen for the settlers. He hadn't expected that. The native tribes had always had the final decision; that was the very nature of the Agreement, why they had accepted it in the first place. Would the confederation accept it? If they did not . . .

But she had ruled the Peraltas had also given offense, deliberately and with probable malice, and a penalty incurred.

And she was the final word. No amount of fisticuffs could change that, for all that it had likely felt good for everyone to let out some of their anger and frustration that way. It certainly had settled some of his upset.

And she had given near as good as she'd gotten. He didn't deny a flare of pride about that.

Until she lurched forward and started vomiting red onto the ground.

"You need to stop doing this."

Isobel managed to glare at him with only one eye, squinted half-shut. "It wasn't intentional."

Gabriel grinned down at her, a lopsided shape of a smile, then handed her a canteen of water and watched carefully while she swished a mouthful, then turned her head to spit it out. There were still streaks of red in her spittle but far less than had been previously. She made a face, then something shifted in her expression, and she struggled to sit up, managing it only when he helped her.

"Where is it?"

She wasn't asking him but the man who had helped carry her into the Peraltas' farmhouse, a surprisingly cozy building with furnishings that wouldn't have been out of place in Philadelphia. He supposed being within carting distance of the Mudwater made such things easier to transport than having to hump them over high plains or through forests, loaded up in wagons or on muleback.

They hadn't had to kill anyone, either; those who lingered had moved out of their way as though she were made entire of silver and were on fire as well.

"Blue Cloud, where is it?"

He didn't remember the man having given a name, when he was breaking up the fight or after, but he admitted he might have been distracted and missed it. He wanted to know what "it" she was talking about, but knew better than to interrupt to ask.

"The River," Blue Cloud said. His staff rested across his lap now, both hands folded over it, and Gabriel spent a few minutes studying both it and the man. Short, by the standards of the others of his tribe Gabriel had seen, and mid-aged, with his hair shorn on the sides close to his scalp. His face was thin, as though he'd been ill, although his skin was firm and his movements steady and full of health. His face was marked with dark colors around his eyes, same as they'd seen on some others, and Gabriel wondered if it was some variant of war paint, or a permanent marking, and what it meant.

Gabriel didn't interrupt to ask that, either.

"It is in the River," he said again. "It has been there for ages, deep in the mud. Sleeping, or merely ignoring us, I do not know. But it is awake now."

"It's poison," she said, her voice still a scratchy whisper from the trauma inflicted on her throat, and she wiped her mouth as though in memory, although he'd made sure her face was clean. "I felt it . . . when I tried to listen. If that was what I touched, it's poison."

Blue Cloud made a slight gesture with his fingers without lifting the hand from the staff across his lap. "Some things carry poison within them without poisoning themselves. And not all poison makes us ill."

Gabriel recognized that voice; he'd used it on her himself. The "you know better than that, show me what you know" mentoring voice. And Isobel, well trained, rose to it.

"It's been here . . . It's part of the Territory. But people are only dreaming of it now?" Her voice took a more considering quality, softer and lower. "It's always been here. But it's rising now. Why? Would this"—she gestured, taking in the house around them, the people outside, the events of the day—"have happened before it rose?"

Blue Cloud shrugged, the gesture clear despite Gabriel not seeing his shoulders actually move. "Does the wing rise or fall first, that the bird may fly?"

"Don't," Isobel said, and a quick smile graced his face at her scolding, softening the marks around his eyes.

"The dreamers say only that it is here now, that it demands to be acknowledged." The smile disappeared then. "There are some among my people—and among yours, I suspect—who claim it is here, it wakes, because we have spent too long among each other. Some of my people are not pleased with the confederation. They think that there is too much . . . comfort between the tribes, as well as with the whites."

"They think a river spirit is judging them for living in peace?" Gabriel wished he found that harder to believe.

Blue Cloud let his fingers tap against the wood of the staff before responding. "Interpreting what the spirits wish of us is . . . difficult even in the calmest of times."

A river spirit. Worse, a spirit of *that* river. Gabriel's gut hurt, and his chest felt squeezed tight, too large for his rib cage. He rested a hand on Isobel's shoulder, seeking something solid to hold on to.

"All this," Isobel said, reaching up with her right hand to cover his own, the warm touch reassuring both of them. "The anger, the frustration, the killings . . . You think the river spirit is warning us of them, of whatever causes it, not the cause itself?"

Her doubt had basis: their experiences had been with monsters and beasts causing trouble; even the spirit animals that they'd encountered had seemed more prone to stirring trouble rather than easing it. Blue Cloud seemed to take it in stride, neither frowning nor mocking her question.

"Perhaps you need to ask it."

❧ ❧ ❧

Isobel had been prepared to travel to the river's edge immediately, but Gabriel put his boots down: whatever had been going on had clearly been happening for months now, and if there was no immediate danger to anyone that Isobel could prevent, then there was no reason for them to rush anywhere, much less to the edge of the Mudwater, in the darkness.

Blue Cloud had sided with Gabriel, and she found herself tucked into a bunk in the farmhouse, with a cup of water and a slice of bread thickly slathered with fresh butter, which Gabriel watched her eat before turning down the lamp and telling her to get some sleep.

It was ridiculous. Infuriating, even, to have two men decide what she should do, and even more so to have to acknowledge that they had been right.

She had stared at the dark shape of the ceiling above her, feeling deeply put-upon, convinced that she would never be able to sleep with the remnants of everything still shimmering under her skin, until she opened her eyes again and the ceiling was visible in all its whitewashed glory, and she could hear voices and people moving outside her room.

A cautious stretch of her limbs told her that a night's sleep had done away with the aches and cramps she'd felt the night before, the muddled haze gone from her thinking.

"Bah." She hated when Gabriel was right.

Rising, she found her clothing folded over a straight-backed chair, the skirt hem neatly mended, and smelling of fresh clover-rose, her boots cleaned and polished, and stockings she didn't recognize. They were deep blue rather than the grey hers had faded to, and she realized they picked up the threads of blue used in the stitching of her blouse.

Somehow, she couldn't connect this with any of the men she had met the night before, although she admitted that she hadn't seen them, perhaps, at their best. The girl who had gone to fetch the others, perhaps. Those were likely her stockings. Isobel would need to thank her before they left.

Dressed, she started to re-braid her hair, looking around for the feathers to braid into the plait, when her hand stilled in memory.

They had been destroyed in the fight.

Isobel sat down hard on the now-bare chair, not even wincing at the ache that ran up her spine, proof that she wasn't as recovered as she'd thought. It was foolish to feel so devastated by the loss of such simple things, and yet she couldn't name it any other way. Calls Thunder had gifted her with those feathers when they'd met, when she'd only been on the Road a little while, uncertain and half-afraid. The feathers had been a reminder that they'd seen something in her, something they respected.

And now they were gone.

Her fingers lingered on the plait, then finished and tied it off with brisk practicality. She had lost things before and survived. There were more important things to worry about. Things she could do something about.

Going to the river. Confronting what she had felt before. She swallowed, forcing panic down. This wasn't Andreas, or Clear Rock, or De Plata. For once, she knew what she would be facing before she was required to make a decision. Surely that should make this easier, not more difficult?

The farmhouse was empty. She pushed open the door to the outside and found the site of the previous confrontation had been replaced with a long wooden table, where half a dozen people were seated, eating breakfast.

Gabriel was among them, but as she watched, he looked up and tilted his head at her, indicating the empty space left on the bench next to him.

As she sat down, someone dropped a platter in front of her, filled with fried egg and greens, and another slice of that thick bread she'd had the night before, and a slab of yellow cheese. She looked up to see a man with a sling holding one arm tight to his body. Her eyes widened, and he made a face, then shrugged.

"Cookie duty until my arm heals," he said. "My da says it's no more'n I deserve, and probably a lot less than I should have gotten."

She was the final word. A settler might argue with a marshal, or petition a judge, but the devil's word was final.

She thought of the bald man who had accosted Gabriel, the anger in his voice, and thought, *For now, at least.*

"Eat fast," Gabriel said. "We leave as soon as you're done."

There were four horses waiting outside: Steady and Uvnee, plus a deep-chested dun and a smaller but equally sturdy-looking paint, neither of whom wore anything more than a bridle and blanket. Blue Cloud claimed the dun, swinging up onto its back with an ease Isobel could never have managed without stirrups, while one of the other young men who'd been eating with them mounted the paint.

"That's Jordan McCallister," Gabriel told her, and the name stirred a memory, but she couldn't quite place it.

"Brother to the fellow who fetched us, married into the tribe," Gabriel prompted her, and she nodded, the names and faces sliding back into place. Admittedly, she had been more concerned with the Peraltas the night before.

Blue Cloud reined his dun onto the road, and the other three followed. It felt odd to be riding without the mule tagging alongside, but Isobel found herself distracted, observing her companions.

On the surface, everything seemed fine; Gabriel was speaking quietly with the other two men, using trade-sign when a word failed one of them, discussing what other settlements were along this side of the river, and how often they'd spotted men from the American fort, what sort of raft they used, how many men were on it, and details of that nature. Isobel supposed that she should have been taking part in this conversation as well, but she hung back instead, observing all three men, her curiosity—and worry—engaged.

Blue Cloud, for all his ease on horseback, kept shifting, as though he could not make himself comfortable. She tried to consider what he must be thinking: he was not a medicine worker, not, as far as she could tell, touched by the Territory. And yet, all this . . . if it was disturbing her, it must certainly be disturbing him.

Jordan, on the other hand, behaved as though they were simply out for a social call. She was unsure if that were ignorance or bravado, or if it mattered.

But Gabriel. Her hands tightened on the reins unconsciously, making Uvnee half-halt before she realized what she was doing and eased up again with an apology to the mare. Gabriel wasn't worried the same way Blue Cloud was. His discomfort was deeper. It was what she'd been sensing in him for days now, but worse now, more . . . obvious.

Maybe it was being out of Red Stick that allowed her to see it.

The river was powerful, he'd said. It pulled at him, made him uncomfortable. And she kept dragging him closer to it.

She wanted to pull him aside, gnaw at him until he told her what he was thinking, what was wrong, what she could do to help. To tell him to ride inland again and wait for her, if that was what he needed. But if she even tried now, he would shut himself up again, pretend that nothing was wrong, both for her sake and because others might see. Better to wait until they were alone. Ideally, on the road, by a campfire: he spoke more freely, more easily when they weren't boxed in by walls and a roof.

But there might not be a chance for that anytime soon, and she thought maybe time was important now.

Then Blue Cloud clicked his fingers to get her attention and gestured ahead, to where the banks of the river had come into view. The trees here were sparser and scrub-like, the dirt a darker red, and the shores, rather than sloping to the water, fell sharply off steep banks.

"Our village is downriver. The American fortification is there." He nodded his chin toward the grey-brown walls clearly visible on the other side of the river. "Their boats come from there."

She had seen the fortification; it had seemed farther away, viewed from town. But the bend in the river might have confused her judgment, or maybe distances by water were different from those on land.

"They never attempt to cross and land?" She studied the walls, then the flow of the water, broad and smooth. Water this wide and deep, no ward could remain, not even the boss's work. The Mudwater's current washed everything clean. All that had kept the Americans on that side was fear of the devil. But now they were sending spies and surveyors, poking at the Territory's defenses. Watching from their fortification. Waiting?

The Spanish had attempted to use their magic against the territory and it had failed, but had the consequences been enough to keep them from trying again? Isobel suspected not.

Waters rising. Isobel could practically feel them lapping at her own feet.

"Do you feel anything?" Gabriel asked her, and she shook her head, dismissing the sensation.

"Not . . ." Not the way he meant. There was no sensation of anything watching. Not even the feeling of no-place she'd gotten before. "Unease, but I'm thinking I've forgotten what it feels like to not feel uneasy." She tried to smile and knew she was making a bad job of it. "You?"

"Me?" Gabriel looked surprised, but she read more than that in his reactions. Surprised, and worried, and . . . afraid? No. Not fear. Something deeper, worse than that. "It's running water," he said, cracking a smile at her. "Deep and wide and much of it. Of course I feel something."

His smile was good: warm and amused and slightly mocking, the facade of the cardsharp he'd used on her once before, when they first met, and again when he needed to pretend that everything was all right, that there was no reason to worry. She had thought they'd gone past that now.

"Are you all right?"

His smile softened, less bravado, more fondness. "I'm fine, Iz. You worry about what you need to do."

There was a finality in his words she needed to accept, that he needed her to accept. Isobel bit back the argument that rose to her tongue, studying him, then sighed and nodded. When she looked back toward the river, Blue Cloud, who had slid off his horse by now, was clearly waiting for her to join him by the banks. She dismounted and, unsure how long they'd be there, loosed Uvnee's saddle band for comfort, and looped the reins before giving her the command to stay, then walked slowly to join him on the steep bank overlooking the Mudwater.

This close, the river smelled different than it had in town. Greener, and darker. Isobel breathed in, the air so different from what she had grown up with, and yet as though these smells had always lain within her, waiting until now to come forward.

She said as much, and Blue Cloud huffed in amusement.

"You have ridden the Territory. You never thought it might also be riding you?"

"I've been scolded by dream-walkers and spirit animals," Isobel told him tartly. "You think you'll be the one who's going to impress me?"

His laughter was high and warm, and his entire body shook with it, while Jordan, still in the saddle and firmly staying on the road, leaned forward against his pony's neck and shook his head, brushing tangled locks out of his face. "You're all mad as magicians," he said, loud enough to carry. "If you don't need us for whatever it is you're fixed on doing, I'll be out there"—he waved his arm vaguely back onto the road—"scouting around, make sure you stay undisturbed."

Isobel nodded. "Go with him," she said to Gabriel. "I need to be here, but you don't."

He studied her, and she could feel the doubt in him, then he pursed his lips and the doubt flattened into acceptance. "No need to tell me twice," he said, reining Steady to follow the paint pony as it left the narrow dirt trail they'd been following and made its way across the soft ground, the horses' hooves sinking deep as they went.

Isobel watched them go, feeling an odd mixture of loss and relief, then turned to Blue Cloud. "What now?"

"Now you sing up the river spirit."

"Oh." Isobel blinked, licked her lips, started to say something more, then shut her mouth and nodded, looking back out over the surface of the water. It was grey and smooth as a mirror now, reflecting the sky overhead. "What . . . what do you want me to do?"

He looked sideways, and she was reasonably certain that smile on his lips was mocking her. "How is your singing?"

"Terrible," she told him.

"Stand here." He put a hand on her shoulder, pushing her a little until she found a place that suited him. "And call."

"Call what?"

"Whatever you hear."

Realizing that she wasn't going to get further instruction, grumbling at him in her thoughts, Isobel took a steady breath, then exhaled, shaking the tension out of her body as best she could. Some of this she'd learned from Gabriel; some she'd learned on her own. Start at the top, a sense of light pressure, a soft hand working from the crown of her head down past her ears, pushing down her shoulders, spreading across her ribs and hips, pressing into her thighs and knees, until all obstructions flowed into her heels, pooled, and flowed past her toes, spreading like a puddle of milk into the ground, and was soaked in and disappeared, the earth taking whatever she had, leaving her clear and nearly weightless.

Only then did she realize how quiet it was. No birds, no wind. No sound of humans speaking or splashing of waves against the shore, no rustle or crackle; the entire world suspended on an indrawn breath.

She exhaled, and sound returned.

Blue Cloud was chanting, his voice low and soft, the words indistinguishable even if she'd known the language he was speaking—no, singing, the syllables fluid as birdcall, as deep as the lowing of cows. He was not a medicine worker, he'd said, but the sounds were soothing, encouraging.

She was supposed to call . . . what? *Call what you hear*, he had said.

She listened, closing her eyes against his motions, closing her eyes against the sight of the river, the ground, the grass, the sky. Only listening, only seeing the call.

The notes vibrated within her, heat rising and pooling where she'd emptied herself out, something liquid and thick, weighing her down and filling her with effortless motion. . . .

This was nothing like the devil's power. This came from elsewhere, else-who, and Isobel would have panicked, fought, save that she knew this, knew the sensation, the presence, though there was no name to place it. Molten but not burning. Smooth and strong and terrifying.

The bones . . . no. The Territory. Her ribcage pressed in, or something inside pressed out, something fluttering like a frantic bird, her skin hot and tight, her eyes watering.

Call what you hear.

She could not sing, did not know how to sing, not the way Blue Cloud meant. She had no ritual, no medicine to call on, and the sigil in her hand was dark and cool as though it'd been painted on rather than branded from within.

"Help me," she told it, her whisper fierce and sharp. "You sent me out here to do this; now *help me*."

As though her words had stung, the sigil flared, cool heat washing across her palm, meeting the heat within her veins and the collision shattering her bones as though someone had hit her again.

The damp flavor of whiskey and the dry scent of an unlit cigar, the texture of pasteboard cards underhand, *flickerthwack flickerthwack* against green felt, the soft susurrating sigh of markers moved along a map, the sweep of skirts and pants as they pace, bootheels and slippers against polished wooden floors. Isobel knew where she was, knew who she was, but in that heartbeat, she was also the boss and Marie, back in

Flood, back in the Saloon, looking at a map filled with slow-dancing lights, flickering and going out.

Isobel.

Izzy.

They did not welcome her so much as enfold her and unwrap her, awareness expanding until it was too much to contain, spreading her across the map, the colors lighting within her, the supple calfskin her own hide.

Isobel. Worry, then, and concern, the devil's hand reaching for her, slipping against her when she would have grasped it in return. Then, understanding, resignation, affection: *Possibly inevitable. Potentially useful. But the Bargain remains.*

Before she could ask what he meant, something rose beneath her, sluggish and thick, traveling not directly but side to side as though blind, rising. . . .

Isobel did not open her eyes, but she could see it nonetheless, the great blunt head breaking the surface, flat as a skipping-rock, streams of water running off its sleek grey skin, whiskers twitching as it turned toward the sound of the song, its own rising in return. No monster, this, and no spirit animal, but something more and greater; she could feel the medicine within it, deep and steady as the Mudwater itself, ancient and unchanging, roused by tremors that reached even the deep dark waters below.

Names came to her, not in words but knowing, in memories not her own. *Bone-snake. Earth-turner. Moon-eater.*

Powerful and slow, the great head turned to her, grey skin rimmed with scales that glinted silver around a half-clouded eye filled with sorrow that dropped her to her knees.

Creature of the first water, old as the bones and stones, born when the winds and fire split creation itself. She had so many questions to ask it, answers to demand, but the words did not shape themselves. It was too much, too deep and too quiet, to disturb with more noise of such fleeting mortal concerns.

And yet they had, enough to rouse it this far already.

"Forgive me," she whispered, and asked them nonetheless: all that she was, all that she feared, all that she cared, pushed into the dark, still water, and left to sink and be eaten.

what am I supposed to do?

how am I to do it?

what am I?

The great whiskers twitched, tracking the ripples, and then the wide flat mouth opened and swallowed her questions whole. And then it sank back below the surface, into the murky depths, until even the last remaining swirls of its passing faded into the slow, steady rush downstream.

Isobel opened her eyes, half-expecting the air to be murky as the river, only to see Blue Cloud staring back at her, his expression still, his eyes stricken.

"What?" she started to ask, stopping when the word cracked in her mouth.

He stepped forward and reached for her left hand, turning it palm up. She looked down when he did, seeing nothing new: her hand, the palm still sigil-marked, her nails still raw-edged and bitten where they weren't broken, finger pads callused from months holding reins. Then he placed his other hand on her chin, gently tipping her head up so he could look under the brim of her hat. Whatever he saw there did not seem to ease his concern.

"What?" she asked him, the word holding steady in her mouth this time. She knew that she should feel worried about his worry, but it was only that, an awareness of what she should be feeling; in truth, her mind felt wrapped in batting, muffled and dry.

"There is more within you than expected, more even than you expected or know." His eyes were so dark, eyebrows pulled down in a frown. "I wonder that you contain it all, and how long that will remain."

Now some measure of concern stirred within her. The boss had said something . . . *Possibly inevitable. Potentially useful. But the Bargain remains.*

"Contain what?" She could hear voices behind them: Gabriel and Jordan were returning.

"Most choose their roads, but some few have it chosen for them. Those who are touched, who hear the singing of the winds, the pull of the water, or the chanting of the bones. My people find them societies to learn from. Yours . . . I do not know what yours do."

"Mentors," Gabriel said, clearly having heard the last bit of conversation, at least. "We find them mentors."

Blue Cloud nodded, and she could see him tucking that word away in his memory. "But where do you belong, Territory-child?"

Gabriel was her mentor, but Isobel didn't think that was what Blue Cloud meant. Water-child. Bone-child. *Territory-child.*

"I made Bargain with the devil," she said, the concern turning to the first flutterings of panic, her free right hand reaching for the feathers that were no longer there. "I am the Hand." The boss said the Bargain remained.

Blue Cloud nodded again. "You are; the sigil claims you." Her relief lasted only a heartbeat, as he continued. "But the oldest ones speak to you. They see their blood in you, the . . . ah, how do you call it? The living silver."

Isobel's eyes widened, the panic becoming a full-sized wing slamming against her rib cage, making her need to vomit. No. What he had—no. Silver was mined and shaped to protect, to cleanse. The deepest veins of silver, the darkest glitter of the mines—they were dangerous, best left in the ground, but that was all. It did not, could not . . .

It was. She knew it, had known it months before. The molten whisper, pushing and pulling her. The power that was less and more than what the devil fed her. The devil had tried to warn her, too late. She had gone too deep, too many times, and she had been noticed. Living silver, wrapped in her bones. The blood of the Territory, trying to claim her for its own.

"Is it dangerous to her?" Gabriel came up behind her, his hands resting lightly on her shoulders, their warmth making her aware that her skin was chilled far beyond what the damp air could explain. She clung to that warmth, imagining it soothing the panic, calming the bird within her chest, allowing her to breathe again.

Blue Cloud looked thoughtful, then let go of her hand. "I do not know. I do not know anyone who could tell her that."

Possibly inevitable. Potentially useful. But the Bargain remains. She was still the Left Hand. Still the devil's tool.

And if she was the Territory's tool as well . . . the spirit animals had warned her, in their own way, the wapiti and the Reaper hawk, even the snake. Protect herself, or follow her obligations.

Telling me what I was protecting myself from *would have been help-ful,* she thought irritably, as though her thoughts were a lance she could throw at spirit-beings. But she could not bring herself to regret any of what she had done.

The flutter of wings in her chest settled slightly at that acceptance, and her breath caught, the entirety of a dream flooding back to her. The bird of her vision, stealing her away from the fire, telling her . . . what? What had it told her?

You need to be brave. Remember what you are.

The bird had thought she already knew. So had the Moon-eater.

You need to be brave.

She did not feel brave. She felt tired, and sore, and weighed down at every joint. But there were things she had to do.

"Did the river tell you anything?" Jordan had been silent until now, unlike Gabriel still on horseback, keeping a distance between himself and the other three, but the way his gaze anxiously flitted between them all told Isobel that whatever they said would be spread through-out the farming settlements by nightfall, for good or for ill.

The problem was, she still didn't know what to tell him. Or if she should speak of it at all.

"A spirit of the river has been woken by something in the water," Blue Cloud said, as though that explained anything at all.

To Jordan, it seemed to, or he trusted the other man enough to let it be. "The Americans disturbed it, coming on the waters the way they have?" His expression grew dark. "Is it a danger to anyone on this shore?"

Isobel remembered that wide, flat mouth, large enough to take in the leg or arm of an unwary swimmer if they ventured too close. "It might." She thought of the quietness within it, the slow steady sameness, and shuddered to think of being consumed by that, to disappear into the quiet. "It might, but not of malice." There was no malice within it, nothing of any emotion save existence. "It prefers the deeper, slower waters. The sooner we ease it, the sooner it will sink below again."

From the still-dark expression on Jordan's face, he did not find that comforting.

Looking out over the flat surface of the Mudwater, the murky depths keeping their secrets, Isobel could not blame him for doubts. She had more than enough for them all.

FOUR

They rode away from the riverbank, but Isobel did not feel ease, even when the horses' hooves touched the Road once more.

"What does it mean, what you said? That . . . that the living silver is in me?" Even saying it, Isobel felt an odd shiver, but from heat rather than cold, the touch of that molten finger on her bones.

Blue Cloud looked up at the sky, or maybe the trees rising overhead, as though they would offer an answer. "It is nothing evil," he said. "Nor is it good. Simply power."

"Like magicians, and the wind?" That was not reassuring: the wind gave power, but stripped sanity in payment.

"Like, unlike, as cousins are like and unlike." She squinted her displeasure at him, and Blue Cloud looked down, making a face at her. "I am not a dream-walker or lodge elder, to understand such things. It may be that had you not chosen the path you did, it would have laid still in your bones, unwoken. Or it might have roared out, untamed, untrained, and consumed you." He touched two fingers to her right cheekbone, a steady pressure. "It may still, Little Sharp Beak. It seems the Master of the Territory draws you one path, and the Silver agrees.

But it may not, always. Paths diverge, and only one may be walked at a time."

She thought of the whisper driving her toward the slaughtered buffalo, telling her how to find—and destroy—the magicians. The sigil and the whisper; she had thought them one and the same, at first. The devil and the Territory. People thought of them together, but the boss . . .she had never wondered, before, where he came from originally. There weren't any myths or stories about him, not before he stood against the banks of the Mudwater the first time.

Even how he'd set the Agreement wasn't really a story, just . . . something you knew happened. She opened her mouth to ask Blue Cloud if he knew any stories about that, when Gabriel interrupted.

"Did you learn anything useful at all? Because right now it feels as though we've been handed the leads on half a dozen horses, and each one's itching to gallop off in a different direction. Which leaves us with a broken arm and no answers."

His voice was tight, and his body screamed at her that something was wrong. She wanted to shake him, to demand he talk to her, but it could not be done, not there and then.

"The creature . . ." and her thoughts hitched midway and the words changed in her mouth. "The creature was responding to what's happening, that the Territory itself is distressed."

"But it's not the source?"

She shook her head, certain of that, of nothing more. "No."

"So all this leaves us . . .where?" Exasperation joined his distress, a layer of snow over thin ice. "Spirits waking and dream-walkers uneasy, and people getting killed for it, but we don't have the first clue what it is?"

Isobel flinched. She knew that Gabriel wasn't the sort to poke an open sore, but it felt as though he were doing exactly that, and flicking salt into it as well.

No. She reined herself in the way she would Uvnee when she spooked. It wasn't her Gabriel was upset at. He was tetchy and twitchy being this close to the river, he'd told her so. She needed to get him farther away—but they couldn't leave.

She moved Uvnee over so that she was riding alongside Steady, and lowered her voice for only Gabriel to hear. "Is it better for you in Red Stick or here?" She didn't pretend he wouldn't know what she was asking.

He took a deep breath, visibly settling himself back inside his skin, and shook his head, although not to say no. "In town, I think. There are too many people there, but all those bodies help . . . quiet it, a little."

"Jordan." Blue Cloud, behind them, did not raise his voice, but all three of them jumped slightly, as though stung. "Will your people listen to you?"

"Depends on which of my people you mean." Isobel looked back to see him lean forward in the saddle, and despite his height, it was clear to Isobel that he was submitting to Blue Cloud's authority, not challenging it. "But yeah, enough will. What do you want me to do?"

"Tell them the River rises."

The phrase meant nothing to Isobel. But Jordan's jaw-clench suggested that there was meaning deeper than it seemed.

"You think it's come to that?"

"Come to what?" Gabriel asked, frowning at the other men as though they'd willfully withheld evidence from him.

"There is a story," Blue Cloud said. "A very old story, that came before my people had a name, when another tribe lived on these lands. That there was no river, no water, no hills; only plains as far as the eye could see. Until the people became too many, and their words were filled with argument over where to hunt, how to live.

"The spirits were disturbed by this noise, and sent dreams to tell them how to behave."

"But they did not listen," Gabriel said, because they all knew that was how these stories went.

"They argued over what the dreams meant, over who was to lead, over what color the sky was and which direction the wind blew and how the water flowed. And the wind cared nothing for what the people thought, but the waters, hearing this nonsense, rose up in disgust, to show them exactly how it flowed. And it flowed over them, washing them from these lands, before returning—not entirely below the ground, but running through it, a reminder to those who would make camp here."

"A reminder of what?"

"That we are not the masters of this land, but live at its sufferance," Isobel said quietly, feeling the weight of it settle in her breast. "The beating heart of the devil's Agreement."

Gabriel had gone with Jordan when Blue Cloud told him to, not because he thought he'd be useful, not to keep an eye on the young settler, but because the need to move had him nearly bursting out of his skin, making him useless to Isobel just then.

He had spent his entire life aware of water around him, the soft whisper of creeks and the contented hum of rain, the crackle of it trapped in ice, and the sleeping dreams of deep-stone pools. It hadn't been until he crossed the Mudwater the first time, lived in the States where the sound of water was muted under the press of so many feet and voices, that he'd realized how *noisy* water was.

But he'd no memories of the Mudwater itself. The first crossing, he'd been too nervous, too distracted, and taken it far too much for granted. And returning . . .

Returning, it had been too much, too loud, too intense. He had panicked, fighting it, until he'd woken with Old Woman Who Never Dies crooning in his ear, wiping his brow with a cloth that dripped with moisture, and nothing but the faint trickle of streams in his soul.

She had taken him away from the River, to heal. And he had not been near it since, always finding reasons to stay inland, afraid that if he went too close, his life's battle to remain himself, to not give in to that pull, would be for naught.

He had been wiser than he knew. Since coming close to it again . . .

The thought of being that helpless, that lost again, terrified him.

"You think it's all connected?"

"What?" Forcing his attention back to his companion had taken more effort than it should have.

"Everything that's happening down here," Jordan said. "The squabbles over land, the way the townsfolk keep eyeing us like we're some new creature, the village being all on edge . . . and now this?" He gestured carefully at the river, as though not wanting to attract its attention. "You think it's all connected?"

Gabriel did, yes. If there was one thing he'd learned, riding the Dust Road, it was that everything was connected if you looked deep enough. Just like the Road itself: things doubled back and looped around, and you rode over the same ground more than once, in a lifetime.

That thought made him check himself: there was no tendril of the Road underfoot, not within his ability to feel. Isobel could likely find it: he suspected she could find the Road anywhere within the Territory by now, simply by asking for it.

That thought stung his pride, and he pushed harder, trying to find the reassuring song of the Road under the thrum of the River.

Come. Come. Come.

He pulled back, hasty and inelegant as though a snake had just nipped his ankle. That was *not* the Road; it did not speak, was not aware, was merely the gathered power of every soul that rode it, straight-running, where it wasn't bound up by a crossroad or warding.

He felt the urge rise up to turn and face it, to shout his defiance, to tear off his boot and throw it at the river the way one would at a particularly loud cat in the middle of the night. He didn't have time for this. He'd tried to leave the Territory once and been dragged back, ill and defeated. He'd accepted that, accepted his fate, but he would not allow it to consume him.

The devil had promised him peace, if he brought Isobel through her mentorship ride intact. He only needed to ride a little longer.

"Leave me alone," he warned the voice, then coughed when Jordan turned to look at him, curious.

"Yes," he'd said, ignoring his odd look. "I do think it's connected. We just don't know how, yet. Or who."

"I can tell you that," Jordan said, with grim certainty. "The Americans. All this started when they built that fort, across the river, like they wanted us to see them gathering their troops, waiting just outside the border. You think the Agreement will keep them out, if they decide to come?"

"The devil's stopped them before," Gabriel said.

"They were fewer, before. And they didn't want us so much, then."

There wasn't anything Gabriel could say to that. It was all true.

Hearing Blue Cloud's story did not ease Gabriel's mood. He was a man who liked challenges, nobody could say otherwise, but this was becoming . . . dispiriting.

"If I tell folk the waters are rising, it will cause panic," Jordan protested. "We'll have another Mud. Or worse."

Gabriel flinched, and Blue Cloud nodded. "If we have roused the river-spirit enough that it rises to the surface, then the evil words have already done their harm. You know your people better than I: What would you suggest?"

Jordan ran a hand across his chin, gaze distant, looking up at nothing in particular. "We need to give 'em something to do, if we're giving 'em bad news. Leaving 'em to sit and think never ends happy. Do your folk have, I don't know, a ritual, a dance, anything, they could take part in?"

Blue Cloud's expression would have made Gabriel laugh at any other point, but Isobel's left fingers were clenching over her palm again; Gabriel knew what that meant. He leaned forward, his voice meant for her alone. "What's it telling you?"

"Nothing." Her voice was low, directed toward her hands, not him. "It's itching, but not giving me anything to ride on."

He narrowed his eyes, knowing that she would notice that he didn't believe her.

She made a face, suddenly seeming very young again. "The boss . . . he said it wasn't entirely unexpected. Whatever's happening. But I'm still supposed to . . ." Her voice cracked, and she had to start again, her throat clenching around the words. "How can I trust anything I do, anything that happens?"

"Isobel, stop. Breathe, can you do that? Just breathe, like learning how to find the Road again, all right?"

Her eyes focused on him again, and she nodded once, too jerkily for his liking, but in control of herself once again.

"They say, they're saying... the living silver, in me. The whisper I've been hearing, it's . . ." He saw her take a breath, steadying her thoughts, bringing her nerves under rein. "The boss told me to be wary of the Territory. But it's . . . I'm walking two paths, and maybe they're going to split, maybe even soon. What if I choose the wrong one?"

"You won't."

She might. Everything human was fallible. But she needed him to be confident this moment, and so he was.

"You're smart, and you think things through," he went on, ticking them off on his fingers. "That's rarer than it should be, and probably part of why the devil picked you in the first place."

"That, and I offered myself up like a lamb at shearing," she said, but the tight-wound sound of her voice had eased slightly, and she didn't look as though she would shake out of her own skin at any moment, now.

"That too. Listen to me, Isobel. As your mentor, I'm giving my judgment." He waited until she looked up, dark eyes steady on him. "The girl you were, she might have assumed she knew everything. But the Road shook her out; that's what the Road does. She isn't you, not any more.

"You're cautious without letting caution rule you; you look at things cold and clear, and you don't assume everything's how it looks on the surface. Even this whisper—I've seen you work it. You listen, but you poke at it, pull it, see where it's leading you, and don't rush headlong just at its say-so."

Again; that wasn't entirely true, but he willed it to be so, so she would believe it, and *make* it so. He didn't question why it was so important that she heed him, just then, but it was.

Her gaze wavered, looking inward to something he couldn't see. "But what if—"

"No doubts, Isobel. Consider the evidence, and make a judgment."

He waited, watching, until something shifted in her clear brown eyes, the skin of her face easing into smoother lines.

"Blue Cloud," she said over her shoulder. "Have you and Jordan determined how to handle your people?"

"Possibly. The fight may have some use after all," he said with reluctance. "Men who have fought each other are more willing to sit together at a fire and tell stories of their bravery. We will bring others in, tell the story of how the Devil's Hand slapped sense into both encampments, and speak of the tension between our people, and how it must end.

"It may not aid in your workings, but it will distract those who would cause trouble, either from anger or mischief."

Isobel had winced at the mention of stories to be told, but nodded when he finished. "That should work. Thank you. Gabriel and I will return to Red Stick, and find the *source* of all this. And root it out, once and for all."

He had given her back that confidence. Gabriel just wished he'd kept some of it for himself.

PART FIVE

RED WATERS RISING

ONE

The Road turned on itself, Gabriel said. You never said goodbye to another rider, because you might encounter them again, farther down the Road. Like the devil's sigil of twisted loops that had neither beginning nor end.

It was a pretty thought. But Isobel could see too many loose threads in the weave, too many paths that never joined the Road but wandered off until they simply stopped, too many events that made no sense, did not fit into anything else, and if there was a connection, she could not see it.

Not everything tied up neatly. She had never been more than competent at sewing, and an utter failure at weaving, but she knew that the more bits there were, the more difficult it was to keep them in order. Random threads, numbering in the hundreds, perhaps even thousands? If not impossible, certainly unlikely.

And yet.

Isobel could feel the itch in her palm, could feel, if she reached for it, the subtle simmer of molten heat deep in her bones. If she stretched, she could hear the hum of the Road below her and, further from that, feel the shifting lights from the boss's map the way she could feel Uvnee's muscles flex and release under her, or her own breath rising and falling in her chest.

Connected.

Too many sensations, too much pressing against her, within her, and yet at the same time she felt numb, all those things happening to a body alongside hers, not her own.

A shudder ran though her. Was this how Gabriel felt about his water-sense? How April felt about her grow-sense? It couldn't be; she could not imagine them using it so casually, if it were so.

Auntie's worried expression came back to her, the boss's words, the dream-bird's warning to be brave. What was happening to her—had *happened* to her—was more than all that.

Worse.

"What are you thinking, Isobel?" Gabriel was loose in the saddle beside her, reins lax in his hands, broad shoulders eased, hat tipped back to allow the sun to touch his face, highlighting the scruff that had begun to sprout again. Hints of grey glinted at points on his chin and cheeks, new since she had met him, and she wondered if they were her doing, and if Gabriel minded.

"Iz?" He didn't look at her, keeping his eyes on the road ahead of them, the soft dirt puffing up around the horse's hooves, the familiar pattern of *clop-clop* thrown off by the lack of the mule behind them and the addition of the two shorter-legged horses ahead of them.

She thought of the bodies strung up to die and then discarded like refuse rather than burned or buried as was decent. Of the men—and herself—swinging fists and sticks because of nothing but frustration. Of the former marshal-turned-innkeeper, who wanted only to keep his daughter and niece safe, and discovered that putting his badge away had not kept trouble from his town. Of Bitter Storm standing before her, breaking his pride to ask for help.

Isobel had learned from the time she was knee-high to read

the people who came into the saloon, in the way people spoke or were silent, in the shifts of their bodies and the expressions they let slip. Greed and love, fear and worry; she knew how to discern them even when they were held tight to the ribs, protected and coddled like a babe. The boss had trained those skills; she had always thought he'd *given* them to her, but maybe they had been hers to start.

She didn't know how to ignore them. She didn't know if she could. *Save yourself. You have a duty. Remember what you are. Be brave.*

Spirit animals did not care about the devil one way or the other. They had existed before he came; they would likely exist if he were to leave. They were creatures of the Territory itself.

And Gabriel had said he'd rarely encountered them before riding with Isobel.

"Once upon a time, I thought a Spanish curse the worst I would ever need to face," she said, more for Uvnee's ears than anyone else's. The mare twitched one ear back at her but offered no advice or consolation.

"It may be that's what started all this," Gabriel said. "The working they did, you said the Territory absorbed it, changed it."

She nodded, reaching up to adjust the bend of her hat's brim, more for something to do than any real need. The felted fabric was slick under her fingertips, the nap smoothed down by sun and rain and wear. "Some of it, anyway." The Mother's Knife had shredded the working as it passed over the range, slicing it into ribbons. She had *seen* that in her dreams. Some of those ribbons had been changed—the giant otter-beast that had attacked Gabriel had been shaped from a ribbon of that spell, combined with the mud and bones of the Territory. But other ribbons had slipped free.

But the magicians she had stopped had been manipulated by a man from the United States government. It could not be connected to the efforts of the Spanish king. Could it? Isobel did not understand the world beyond the Territory, had never *wanted* to understand it. But it pressed against her, against the Territory, everywhere she turned.

"The devil doesn't believe in coincidence," she said, and Gabriel, thankfully, followed her thoughts.

"Sometimes it's not coincidence, and it's not conspiracy," he said. "It's just . . ." He shrugged, and exhaled, a tired-sounding sigh. "It's just . . . politics."

She looked her question at him, aware that the other two men had reined in their horses, drawn by the conversation.

"Men with power want more power," Gabriel said. "Men with land want more land. But also, men without power want any power they can grab, and likewise with land, which they see as a form of power. Same as happened here, putting up that fence. Spain and the United States both, they've got too many people now who want to put up fences, and not enough land for them all. Not enough power. And then there's the Territory sitting there, welcoming settlers but telling their military, their government, no, you can't come in.

"And if there are too many settlers, if there are . . . problems. The Agreement gives the tribes the ability to refuse to allow settlers to farm land, build towns. But if the Agreement's broken . . ." His gaze flicked to Blue Cloud, who looked down, then back up at Isobel.

"It's not," Isobel said, fiercely. "It's not broken. It will not be broken."

The silence from the three men around her was not comforting.

The road split soon after, and the four parted ways, the locals heading back to their people, and the riders going on toward Red Stick.

Isobel's thoughts meanwhile had gone still and deep, the memory of that giant fish rising lingering within her. The wide, flat mouth opened again, and this time it was Isobel herself that it swallowed, encasing her in a damp, silent darkness.

"I wish we'd never come here," she said, a surge of something violent overwhelming the sadness. "That's terrible of me, isn't it?"

"To wish for a quieter life, if only for a few days?" Gabriel sounded like he was laughing, although his face was solemn when she looked. "You're allowed to be tired, Isobel. The devil may drive you, but your flesh is only that: flesh. It needs to rest."

"I'm not sure I even remember what rest is," she admitted, and they rode for a while longer in silence, before Gabriel finally did laugh.

"Neither am I," he admitted, as though it were a secret the two of them shared.

Another rider came toward them from the opposite direction on the road, tipping his hat but not slowing or speaking. He wore a sleeveless leather coat and had leather sacks tied to his saddle, and Isobel belatedly realized he must be the post-rider who had brought her package—had it been only the day before?

If the packet was her payment from the boss, as Gabriel thought, she thought she might spend some of it not only for new clothing to replace the things worn down by the road, but something foolish and vain as well. Ribbons, perhaps, or something made of lace. Or candy. There had to be a sweets maker in a place this large, certainly, and if not, someone traded in them.

The last time she'd had store-bought candy was on her birthday, the sugar-stick Iktan had given her. She wondered if she still liked them.

"Do you ever think that maybe we shouldn't be here?"

He looked over his shoulder at the rider disappearing around the bend, then back at her, as though he must have misheard. "What?"

"Here. The Territory. Did you ever think that maybe we shouldn't be here at all? Settlers, I mean. Do you ever wonder what it would be like if we weren't?"

"No." His voice was definite, then he sighed. "My mother's mother's people have been here since the mountains raised up from the sea, Isobel. Her father, my father, they came here thinking to make their fortune in furs and go home, but never left again. This was where they belonged. If we weren't meant to be here, you think the Territory would have let us stay?"

"My parents didn't," she reminded him.

"They chose to leave; from the story you've told, they weren't meant to be here. But you had a choice and stayed."

She thought about that, then said, softly, "You left."

He grimaced. "I did. And I was miserable. That's how I know. I have to be here. So do you. It's who we are, what we are." There was such deep resignation in him that Isobel regretted ever raising the matter. But Gabriel went on. "And people like Jordan? Could you imagine him anywhere else?"

"No." He was as solid as the Mother's Knife, and made of the same stuff. "I just—"

She stopped at the same moment Gabriel reined Steady in, his entire body going on alert.

Something giggled around them, and Isobel glanced down at the ring on her little finger, checking to see if the silver had tarnished since she'd polished it that morning, a now-daily habit, same as checking her boots for spiders.

The silver glinted dully under the sunlight, and she could hear Gabriel swearing under his breath.

"Demon?"

Gabriel shook his head. "I've never heard of one coming down this low. They like it higher and dryer." His gaze was flitting across the shaggy-barked trees lining the road, looking for the source of that noise. Tarnish meant something was gathering power; a crossroads— but the trail they were on was straight and hadn't been used nearly enough to gather power worth worry—or a creature of power.

"Not a magician," she said. She remembered what that felt like. "And it's gone." Isobel knew the moment it disappeared, even though she hadn't felt it arrive. Or maybe they had arrived at it. That thought made her feel slightly better, especially as it hadn't lingered. Still . . . "We should keep moving."

The horses seemed to agree, picking up their pace without urging. The sun was nearly direct overhead, and Isobel was aware, even more than the sweat against her brow and running down the line of her spine, that high noon, like dusk and dawn, was a dangerous time. And the knowledge that she bore the devil's sigil did not carry the same reassurance it once had.

They might need to be there, as Gabriel said, but they weren't the only ones there. And some were less hospitable than others.

She had no sooner thought that thought than a voice rang out from ahead of them.

"Do it!"

It was a man's voice, filled with defiance and no little fear, and had Isobel goading Uvnee into a fast lope before she'd identified the words, Steady hard on her hooves. It was foolishness to rush into possible trouble, and she could feel Gabriel swearing at her back, but she could no sooner have hung back than she could have spread wings and flown.

The trail opened into a flat clearing, the river hidden from sight by a thick copse. She took the scene in at a glance: the dry expanse of grass, and the handful of men gathered there, circled around another man who crouched, hands on his knees, bareheaded and bleeding.

"Do it," the crouching man cried again. "Finish it. Or don't you have the guts?"

A rock caught him in the ribs, and he bent forward around it but then straightened again, a mocking sneer on his bloodied face. "*Ta mère. Mon tabarnak.* Is that the best you can do?"

"Hold!" Isobel's voice rang out over whatever the men might have said in return, even as another stone cut through the air, this time catching the man in the face, just under one eye. "I said, hold!"

She might as well have been whispering; one of the men turned to look at her, but the others were too busy picking rocks from the piles at their feet and pelting their victim, as though they had simply been waiting for that final taunt as invitation.

Steady pushed past her, riding straight into the cluster of attackers and scattering them even as Gabriel slid out of the saddle and placed himself between victim and attackers. "Try that again," he said, and his knife was in his hand, the silver of its hilt still gleaming despite a layer of tarnish. "Try that again and see what happens."

TWO

A mob, Isobel, a mob is the worst of what we are, given a single voice. You can control them, but if you lose that control, they will tear you apart. Isobel had no memory of the boss ever telling her that, no thought as to when it might have been discussed, but the memory was clear in her mind as Gabriel stared down the men surrounding him, the knife in his hand nowhere near enough if they chose to rush him. Not even Steady's hooves, deadly though they were, could defend Gabriel and the bleeding man behind him, not against a mob.

One of the men spat at Gabriel's feet, although he did not move to threaten him otherwise. "You don't know what you're defending."

Gabriel showed his teeth in something that was in no way a smile. "So, tell me."

"What business is it of yours?"

Gabriel straightened, his face gone hard and cold. "I've made it my business. Tell me what crime this man has committed and who set you to be his jury."

The first day they had ridden together, they had encountered a posse of four men hunting a fetch. Gabriel had stood like that then, between her and them, the green girl and the hunters. But she was not green now, and she could taste power gathering.

If you lose that control, they will tear you apart.

While they were all focused on Gabriel, Isobel slid from Uvnee's back, moving slow enough to not seem a threat, but not so slow as to seem as though she were trying to hide. Seven men, all around Gabriel's age, as best she could tell. Boots and trou, shirts open-necked but rough, sleeves unrolled, some turned up at the wrist; none wearing jackets, although two sported waistcoats of an oddly muddy yellow fabric. Some were clean-shaven, others had facial hair, and none of them shared similar enough features or coloring to be siblings, at a hurried glance.

And none of them showed the sigil of a posse, authorized to bring someone before a judge, or the tree-and-circle of a Territory marshal.

"He used magic," one of the men blurted.

Isobel stopped cold, her focus turning from the attackers to their victim.

"He's a magician?" Gabriel managed to convene utter incredulity in three words. "And you cornered him with rocks?"

Impossible. Isobel had faced off against magicians and barely survived. These men . . . a magician might toy with them, but not to this point. Not unless he was using them to set a trap.

"We bound him," the man said, his voice both arrogant and afraid. "Used his name to set him still."

"No magician is fool enough to give you his true name, assuming he even remembers it. And even if he did, there's no binding that could hold him through high noon, not unless he wanted to be held." Gabriel glanced over his shoulder. "You a magician, sir?"

"If I were, they would already be dead." The man spat, the sputum bloody and thick, and started to chant something, low and unfamiliar, the syllables harsh but liquid, stinking like fresh rotgut. Isobel felt the air change, thickening the way it did before a storm, but the sky remained clear, the wind still. But two of the men facing him gasped, hands reaching to their chests, one dropping to his knees, his forehead touching the dirt.

The others, rather than going to their companions' aid, hurled another volley of rocks at him, narrowly missing Gabriel as they did so.

"Stop that," he said, then half-turned. "And you, shut up."

The man glanced up at him, and Isobel's breath caught; the gleam in his eye should not have been so bright, the flash of it under the direct sun molten-hot, untarnished and *alive*.

Bone-child. She had never met another, but she knew him, and he knew her.

"*Vrásei ta ostá tous sto aíma tous plénoun tis stáchtes tous apó aftí ti gi.*" The words were clearer now, hurt her ears less, but she could not recognize them at all, could find nothing familiar in them. She was halted, held; her gaze on his, his words filling her ears, trying to find a way inside.

Another man went down, and another rock flew. Gabriel growled, striding forward to grab the offender by the arm, yanking him down to his knees. But that simply allowed the remaining three to continue their attack, one well-placed stone taking the man square in the forehead. His head rocked backward, breaking his hold on her before he looked up at her again, his mouth still shaping words, but no noise emerging. She watched, no longer frozen but still unable to move as the silver gleam faded and his body pitched forward, landing facedown on the ground.

She didn't need Gabriel's confirmation to tell her that the man was dead.

"I'm sorry," she whispered, even as she knew, somehow, that death had been a release for him, not something he feared. But his last words rang in her ears, and she had to force herself not to rub at them, as though the sounds were dirt to be washed out.

"We were within our rights," the man Gabriel had pulled to his knees was saying, even as he was standing up, ostentatiously dusting off his trousers, shaking his arm free from Gabriel's hold. He had oversized ears under a bad haircut, Isobel noted. And a small nose. It wasn't a good combination. "He was using magic—"

Isobel turned on him, feeling her skin prickle with misplaced rage. "And what business of that was yours?"

"It was wrong." That was one of the remaining men, less brave or perhaps less foolhardy than his fellows, since he took a step backward when Isobel and Gabriel both turned to look at him. "We . . . we all felt it. We came on him here, just . . . doing something. And the words he was saying, they weren't words any of us knew, and it wasn't no tribe words, either."

Isobel hadn't recognized the words either. She had no idea what the man had been trying to do, or why, or to whom. For all she knew, the power he'd been reaching for would have been used against them, not only his attackers; and he'd been goading them on when she and Gabriel arrived. He might have been the victim, but he'd had a hand in his own death.

They had every right to defend themselves, if he were a threat, and the tarnished silver was proof enough.

But he was still dead, seven against one. Those odds did not sit well with her. Or, from the look on his face, with Gabriel.

"I see seven cowards in front of me," her mentor said now, each word low and precise, the knife still in his hand, point angled toward them. "Seven cowards who can say nothing more than 'I didn't understand' as excuse for why they just killed a man."

"He wasn't no man!" The third man left standing, shorter than the others, bald-pated but with skin smooth as fresh butter, and much the same color. "You could tell it about him. There was something off in him and the medicine he carried. It wasn't healthy, wasn't *right*."

The rage went from prickle to searing pain, forcing the words out of her like steam from a kettle. They would say the same of her if they were frightened enough. "And so, you took it upon yourself to judge and execute."

Something in her words dragged their attention away from Gabriel, despite his being the one with the knife in hand, and they stared at her, gawking like half-grown crows.

Gabriel stepped backward, standing by the body, an abandoned doll, crumpled and broken. She had seen the dead before; they did not look like dolls, not like that. They looked like bodies, abandoned unwillingly, pulled out by force. This . . . was an empty snake-hole after the inhabitants had left.

They had not been wrong: whatever had driven the shell in front of them had not been like them. Had not been a man.

Bone-child. Silver Eyes.

It did not matter. Could not matter. The glint of silver in his eyes had been malicious, but it had not been foreign. They had the right of defense, but the Territory knew its own. *Isobel* knew her own.

They had no idea who she was, what she was. But they knew they were in trouble.

Her palm did not itch, it did not burn, but she knew without looking at it that the sigil in her flesh was glowing brightly, even as she lifted it to show them. But more than that, beyond that, something burned hotly within her, something molten and silver.

She was filled with certainty, as she had not been for days. "You usurped rights that were not yours. And the Territory claims offense."

"Hand." Gabriel's voice, still cool, cutting through the heated fog of her thoughts. "Hand, enough."

She blinked, focusing on him, then at the ground around her, where five figures were crumpled, blood streaming from their mouths and noses. Five. There had been seven before.

Before . . .

Screaming, terrified and pained, and she studied them, read their culpability, their lack of regret, dragged invisible claws made of silver through their innards and scratched the names of their sins within them.

The sigil flared, and something deep within her responded, two elements for once in sympathy, in concert.

This life had another purpose. It had not been theirs to take.

Then there was a deep, bloody pop, not a clap like thunder too close, or the snap of a cinder from a bonfire, a thousand times louder than it could have been, and then another—

Isobel felt bile rise in her throat, filling her mouth, and she turned away quickly to vomit into the grass.

She came back to herself, her back against the wide, rough surface of a tree, dry grass under her legs, sweat and grime drying on her skin, making her feel dirty, disgusting.

This was what had happened with the magicians before. She had not remembered then. It had been too much to remember.

What did it make her now, that she *could* remember?

A shadow fell over her, and Gabriel knelt by her side, one warm hand resting briefly against her cheek, fingers brushing against her cheekbone before pushing a strand of sweat-slick hair off her forehead. "You did the right thing. I know that doesn't help now, but you did."

She shook her head, not denying it but unable to hear his words, not just then. His hand came back, holding a canteen, which she took, her own hand unerringly steady. A swig of water, spat back onto the ground, rinsed her mouth and a damp cloth took care of her hands and face, but Isobel still felt blackened and burnt, filthy as though she'd rolled in the embers of a fire.

She exhaled and leaned back against the tree again, suddenly aware that she was no longer wearing her jacket, that it had been removed and folded to form a cushion for her backside. She tried to remember removing it, or Gabriel removing it, but there was only a blankness in her memory she thought it might be better not to probe. They were alone, only the horses nearby, familiar warm noises. She had a vague memory of men leaving, loud voices and Gabriel's louder over them, but the memory faded into wisps of the Spanish monks dragging their dead, the remains of the magicians scattered on the dark earthen floor of the warded cabin, the felt-topped tables set up on the gleaming wooden floors of the saloon.

Gabriel took the canteen from her, then the cloth, and moved away. She felt a flash of uncertainty, the silent maw of the fish rising up to swallow her again. "The boss used to say that mobs were the worst of our guts strangling our hearts."

"The devil has a way with words. The stories get that right, anyway."

For a heartbeat, Isobel though she could smell tobacco and whiskey and brimstone, could feel the boss hovering behind her. But then a breeze of cool, mossy water brushed it away, and she was alone again.

No. Not alone. "They should have left him alone, left him be. Whatever he was doing, was it worth dying for?"

Gabriel squatted down next to her, resting his elbows on his knees. She didn't look at him, couldn't tell if he was looking at her or not, but the familiar feel of him next to her helped a little. "You know better 'n that, Isobel. People are scared, and when people are scared, they do foolish things, mostly against people who make 'em feel more scared. We rode in here, and the first thing that happened was someone attacked you."

"Because I was the Devil's Hand."

"Because you were the Hand, because you had power they didn't, because you were different. Because something made 'em scared, and being scared makes 'em angry. And scared and angry people are fools, even if they weren't born that way."

He wasn't wrong. And yet, it felt wrong. "I killed them." She still wouldn't, couldn't look at him, couldn't look behind her at the spaces where the seven men had been before the survivors fled in fear. Where the shell of the man she hadn't saved still waited for her.

Gabriel sighed. "You made a Bargain, and part of that Bargain was an obligation. Your anger . . . It doesn't just belong to you. The cold eye saw, and issued the final word. Let it be, Isobel."

She didn't want what he said to make sense. But it did. Far more than he knew.

Because that anger hadn't only been hers, or the boss's. It had been the Territory, too.

And it hadn't only been anger. It had been fear.

Fear of what was rising.

THREE

Gabriel knew that he was many things, not all of them pleasant. But by Territorial standards, he had always been ordinary. Touched, yes, but of no interest to the spirit worlds. Even when he'd gone across the River into the States, the world of steam engines and streetlights, of universities and courtrooms, where his water-sense made him odd, unwanted, uncanny, he had told himself that he could cut his ties to the Territory without anything taking notice.

He had been wrong.

But even when he'd woken once again on the Territory side of the Mudwater, wrapped in deerskin and sweating out spirit-dreams, tended to by the oldest woman he'd ever met, with eyes the color of stars, he'd believed that he was merely caught up in these things, that he was not a part of them. He was *of* the Territory, but it did not own him. Did not decide his path or his destiny.

Old Woman had mocked him, gently, and sent him to Graciendo, who had grumbled but advised him.

And in the end, none of it had mattered, when he offered to mentor the girl-child who would become the Devil's Left Hand.

Gabriel Kasun, Two Voices, Rider on the Dust Roads, had thus become resigned to magicians sharing his road, to spirit animals offering useless advice, and dreams catching him out of time.

But he still didn't like any of it.

Especially not the dreaming.

The water flowed past him, knee-deep and dark red. He dipped a hand in, letting the scoop of water flow back into the current, noting that it was clearer then but still tinged with red, as though morning storm clouds passed through it.

"It's not blood," he said. Blood stained the hands; it didn't slip off, drop by drop, without a trace.

The fish in the current mocked him soundlessly, flicking fins and tails as they moved past him, swimming upstream.

He frowned at the water. It wasn't flowing downstream. Or, rather, it was, except where it wasn't. It shifted as the fish shifted, a school of silver-flecked tails going one direction, a single red-finned monster driving the other direction, seemingly pulling the waters along with it. And it was higher on his legs than it had been a breath ago.

"You still look for order where there is none," a voice said behind him. Gabriel straightened, letting the last of the water drop from his hand, but did not turn.

"The world is built around order," he said. "It merely takes time to find it."

Graciendo scoffed, and Gabriel heard the sound of something heavy dropping into the water with a wet splash, the smell of musky fur reaching his nose, and making it wrinkle in disgust.

"Why are you here, old bear?" he asked. "You saw me just months ago." They had delivered a package to Graciendo's cabin, up in the mountains near De Plata. The recluse had taken one sniff of Isobel, and the magician who had traveled with them, and sent them off without Gabriel's usual overnight stay. That had been rude, even by the old bear's usual lack of standards.

There was a low grumble, then the slap of a paw hitting water, and chewing. Then: "I told you to stay clear. You can't avoid trouble when you're in the middle of it."

"You told me. You told me many times. But it just doesn't seem to be in my cards. So, why are you here now?" Dragging him into dreamwalk, he meant but didn't bother saying. Graciendo had never had any trouble hearing his thoughts, if he'd a mind to. Unlike Old Woman, he rarely had a mind to.

"Who's to say I am? Who's to say you didn't drag me here? Or make me up out of your own dreaming? Who's to say I ever was, at all?"

"Now you sound like Old Woman," Gabriel said, and did turn, the water turning with him, reversing its flow to follow. Graciendo looked the same as ever, despite the smell of wet fur that lingered in the air around him: bronzed skin and broad cheekbones, the same glossy brown hair that ran from his scalp down to his shoulders, then up again over his chin, curling wild. But he was bare to the waist, and his eyes were deep red, too small for his face, the nose somehow wrong-shaped, although at first glance it looked perfectly normal.

In dreamwalk, Gabriel had learned, the true shape of things always came through. He'd wondered more than once what he himself looked like, but never enough to find a mirror or ask.

"Maybe she's me, or maybe I'm her, or maybe we're both you, or nobody at all."

Now the old bear was mocking him, Gabriel knew. They'd played those games on late winter nights, the fire burning warm enough to make him sweat under furs, the shadows dark and heavy against the walls. Graciendo didn't walk the world willingly, and worked to wean Gabriel from it, as well.

There had been a time that such a weaning was what he'd wanted, or had thought that was what he wanted: to pass lightly over the land, without hook or binding. To refuse the thing that ran in his blood and his bones, the Touch that bound him to the Territory.

"It's too late." Gabriel shoved his hands into the pockets of his jacket, worn and familiar, and stared at anything save the water, rising now to his thighs, or the figure looming, broad and tall and shaggier than before, in front of him. "It was too late the moment I chose to return and live." Gabriel could not remember much of what had happened, the last days on the other side, the first days after he'd returned, but he remembered that, the desire, the *need* to not die.

Everything since then had been the choice to survive.

"If it was too late, the water would be in your mouth." Graciendo—the shape of Graciendo—looked down to where the red-tinged water now lapped over Gabriel's hips. "Don't wait too much longer, rider."

"Gabriel? Are you all right?"

He turned, unsurprised to be crouched by the side of the creek, the canteen still in his hand, half-filled, the other resting by the bank. He met Isobel's worried look square, without hesitation. "Thinking," he said, even as he moved his hand to rest against the fabric of his trou, relieved and surprised to find it bone-dry. He wouldn't have put it past . . . anything to have left him damp as a reminder.

"We should go," she said, clearly not believing him but unwilling to push further.

It had been a long . . . a long few days, for both of them. Right now, they needed to believe the other was all right, even if they both knew it was a lie.

"Let me finish this," he said, turning back to the creek. This time, when the water touched his knuckles, pressed tight against the side of the canteen, he resisted.

He was too close to the Mudwater; it had noticed him, and even the side creeks and swamps were not safe.

❧ ❧ ❧

The canteens filled and hooked back into place, Gabriel reached for Steady's reins when Isobel held them out, then swung up into the saddle, feeling his legs and buttocks adjust to the press of leather and wood, his fingers settling themselves along the reins, his heels fitting into the stirrups and his spine settling into his shoulders. There was familiarity and comfort here, a thing anchoring him to the land, keeping him grounded, focused. The ground did not flow, did not ease. It fought and it pushed and it carried dangers he could not sense.

Come to me, the water sang. *Let me in.*

Gabriel put his heels to Steady's sides and focused on the Road.

The ride back to town seemed to take longer than Gabriel remembered. Odd, that: typically, the journey back felt shorter than the one out. But then, they'd been focused on the worry of what they might face, then. Now . . . well, they still had the worry of what they faced.

"The man they killed." Isobel's tone was too casual; even if he'd only just met her, he wouldn't be taken by it. She wasn't asking a question, so he merely tilted his head toward her, to show he was listening, and waited.

"He wasn't a magician."

"No." Gabriel thought of the magicians they had met—three, which was three more than any sane man should ever have to deal with. Two of them had been unconscious for most of their journey, but he had still felt the power—and the madness—like the stink of old sweat clinging to their skin. And Farron . . .

Farron Easterly had been mad as well, mad as every magician was, but he'd also been dangerously charming, and the madness had been less a stink than a perfume. But proximity had made Gabriel's hackles rise nonetheless. The man he had tried to protect had caused no such reaction. He had felt . . . pity.

"I think he was like me."

Gabriel blinked, and turned in his saddle to stare at her. "What?"

"In his eyes. You couldn't see it"—he'd had his back to the man most of the time—"but there was something in his eyes. Like silver."

Gabriel wanted to reassure her, to tell her that anything she had seen had been a trick of the light, a delusion, a hallucination. That when he'd called her the Devil's Silver, he'd meant it only as a metaphor. But the words stuck in his throat, and all the water in the west wouldn't wash them clear. In the exhaustion of dealing with the settlers, Gabriel had almost been able to forget what Auntie had said, but clearly, Isobel had not.

"If there is something . . . something of the Territory in you," he said finally, aware that he'd been silent too long, "then maybe it's like what you saw in him. But that doesn't make you like him. I told you that. You haven't changed, not who you are."

Except, if that were true, why did he run from the water's call? If going deep into the touch did not change who you were . . . why had he spent his entire life resisting it?

But Isobel was different. The devil himself had put his mark on her. He'd seen her pull power from the bones before, seen the sigil in her palm channel what no human flesh should hold. And she'd done things. . . . Things that would weigh heavily on even the hardest of souls.

He'd never wanted that for her; had thought, when he first offered to mentor the bold, slyly laughing girl he'd seen in the saloon, to temper the hardness of the Road, show her how to soften those blows, not take them so to heart. But the devil'd put his mark on her, and there'd been no turning back from that.

No matter what his own heart had wished for her.

"He wanted them to kill him," Isobel said, bone-certain. "Do you think . . . maybe he couldn't bear the weight any longer? That whatever was inside him, it was too much?"

"Mayhap." Gabriel couldn't think about his answer too long, not when she asked questions in that tone of voice. "Could be he tried to handle it wrong and it broke him. Or it could be something else entire. You've no idea what goes in a man's life when you meet him at the end of it, Isobel. Speculating without facts won't win a case, ever."

She made a face at him, the way she often did when he slipped into saying things like that, things he'd thought he'd left behind on the cobbled streets of Philadelphia. But it was true enough, and he didn't know a better way to put it.

"You're not that, Iz. Whatever he was, you're not that." And then, thinking it might distract her, he added almost as an afterthought, "I'm more curious about what he was saying at the end. It sounded like a curse, but—"

She took the bait, exactly as intended. "You understood what he was saying?"

"Not a word of it," he admitted. "I thought at first it might be Latin, but the sound of it was wrong, and it wasn't any other tongue I've ever encountered. But the tone, Isobel. Think about his tone." The words had been set out precisely, shaped in anger, not fear.

The kind of anger that came from being wronged, not threatened.

From the way Isobel was nodding slowly to herself, she was remembering the same thing he'd seen. "That might explain why he provoked them. A curse, with your dying breath. That's powerful medicine."

Especially if Isobel were right, and the man's medicine was, somehow, impossibly, taken from living silver. The men Isobel hadn't killed, who'd run from the scene . . . they might not be able to run far enough to evade what had been brought down on them.

"Takes a particular kind of man to do that"—and by "particular," he meant "mad as a magician." "Question is, you think he was random, or connected to what's been going on?"

She looked at him as though it had been a foolish question, and he bit back an utterly inappropriate grin.

"If we're right about what's happening here, even a little bit right," she said, and the tone of asperity in her voice was a relief to hear, "then there's nothing happening with anyone that's random. The answer is in the crossroads where they meet."

He waited.

Isobel reached forward to pet Uvnee's neck, running her hand under the mare's mane.

"I think I need to speak to that Jack you met. I've some questions to put to him."

FOUR

The noise and hustle of Red Stick's streets struck Isobel like an open-handed slap, if possible even worse than the first time she walked through its gates, as though leaving and coming back had made things worse.

It helped that she had a plan this time. But first, they returned the horses to the stable, taking time to reassure the mule that they'd returned, that they hadn't abandoned him.

"Idiot beast," Gabriel said, ruffling the poll between the mule's long ears with rough affection, while Isobel let him lip at her open hand, wide wet tongue swiping at her skin even though he knew full well she didn't have a treat for him.

But when Gabriel started to walk back toward the hostería, she put a hand on his arm, halting him.

"I told you. I need to find the Jack."

"In a town this size?" Gabriel took off his hat and ran a hand through his hair, fluffing the sweat-dampened curls, then shoved his hat back down on his head. "I wouldn't even know where to look, save the last place I saw him, and I don't know that that's where he'll be."

"I will find him," she said, and knew it was true.

❦ ❦ ❦

It took longer than she'd thought, and Gabriel was thin-lipped and sallow-faced by the time she finally took down a narrow alley that curved around a warehouse by the docks, but she knew the Jack when she saw him, even from the back. His shoulders were thin and his walk was hunched, but like called to like, and she could feel the devil's leash on him, as though she were holding it herself.

"Face me, Jack," she called, and he halted, then turned as though every bone in his body ached.

"You."

Isobel crossed her arms across her chest, suddenly aware again of the dampness under her arms and breasts where sweat made the material cling unpleasantly.

"Me," she agreed. It didn't matter how she looked or what tone she used; she'd run into a Jack before and they didn't like her. Not that she could blame them for that, truly. As much as she'd turned her entire life over to the boss's tune, she'd gotten something out of it in turn. They'd played cards with the devil and lost, for stakes likely long forgotten by now, and had to pay until the boss called the debt paid, for seven times seven years, and then seven more again.

They'd played of their own free choice, true, but that was a steep price for foolishness.

"Devil has a thing for sending little girls to do his dirty work."

Isobel kept her face still, although she felt the urge to roll her eyes at the attempt to anger her. "Maybe because we're better at it than men. If that's the best you have, can we be done now?"

Something flickered on the man's face, under the bitter exhaustion, and to her shock, he grinned at her. A small grin, crooked and wry, but all she could read from him in that moment was humor.

"Well-hit," he said. "And what can I do for you, then, Hand of my Master?"

Until that moment, she hadn't been certain. The man Gabriel

had described to her had been broken, his mind shredded under the demands the boss had made on him. But this man . . . there was still iron in him, for the devil's forging. Iron for her using.

She studied him, the earlier conversation with Gabriel resting in her mind, and made a decision. "You know what's been happening."

"In town?"

"In the Territory."

His grin faded, but his eyes remained bright and dark. "Aye. I've heard some. Kept my nose clean of it, but my ears aren't dead yet."

"Then you know about the folk who were strung up, few days back."

"Aye. Ran their traps in the wrong places, to the wrong folk, and got 'em shut with a handsome bit of necktie." He didn't sound too broken up about it, but neither was he gleeful. Merely . . . matter-fact, she decided. As though what happened to other people didn't much matter to him.

Seven times seven years, then another seven, she reminded herself. They'd no way of knowing how long he'd served yet of that time. A fair amount, she suspected.

"I need you to find them."

The look he gave her made it clear he was silently doubting her sanity. "They're dead."

Her fault for not being clear. "The ones who are left. Their companions. Find them, wherever they scattered, and bring them back."

He let out a bark of laughter, harsh and broken. "No way they're going to want to come back. They did their best to save this town, and it made it clear it didn't wanna be saved."

"You will find them, at least one of them, and bring them back here." Her words left no room for discussion: she was not making a request but giving a command. And from the way his jawline stilled and his eyes shuttered, he recognized it full well.

"You think I can just find 'em, like that?"

"They came from a settlement downriver; they will likely have gone back that way, to lick their wounds. I doubt they were careful to cover their tracks when they fled."

The Jack looked skeptical. "And what of the orders I am already under? The bandi I am to wait for?"

Isobel took a breath. She had never contravened any order of the boss's before, had never been in a position where it came to play, much less might be required.

"I am the Left Hand, the cold eye and the final word." The words shaped themselves clearly in her mouth, dropping with quiet certainty into the air between them. "I am the devil's reach into the Territory, and I say that this is the chore you are to perform."

There was an almost-inaudible sigh, and she saw his shoulders slump, then straighten again, the faint sense of disrepair replaced by a sturdier purpose, and she could not regret her decision. It *was* important that she speak with one of those who survived; she felt that in her own bones. But it was also important that the Jack not be so worn down by a chore he could not complete that he became useless. The boss wasn't here, he couldn't see it, but she could, and did.

"As you say, Hand." The tone was mocking, the expression drawn and dubious, but she could feel the Jack gathering strength he hadn't known he had, settling himself into his debt.

"This is the last task we will ask of you," she said quietly, and his gaze jerked up to meet hers, startled and warily hopeful. She nodded, and his gaze was shuttered again, but the wary hope remained.

The bandi be damned; if he hadn't arrived by now, he might be dead, and she would not hold the Jack there forever. The Left Hand needed to carry mercy as well as judgment.

She watched as he shuffled off, aware of Gabriel at her shoulder, practically quivering with words he was not saying.

"What?"

"What makes you think he'll come back, now you've given him permission to leave?"

Isobel closed her eyes, feeling the pinprick pain of a headache boring behind her eyes. "He'll come back," she said. "It's the only way to be free."

"But—"

"Leave it be, Gabriel," she said. "He will do what I asked, and he will come back."

She only hoped he was able to complete his task quickly. Because the moment she'd made her decision, she had felt a pressure, something ticking in the back of her head the way the chiming clock in the saloon had ticked away the hours, calling out the marks, one after another.

They had arrived too late, or maybe only just in time; she didn't know. Her body ached, bruises from the fight only now making themselves known, and a deeper weariness she suspected sleep would do nothing to erase.

"What now?" Gabriel asked.

"Dinner," she said. "A hot meal, and sitting down. I'm so tired, I can barely think."

And thinking was exactly what she needed to do.

FIVE

By the time they made it back to the street they were staying on, she wasn't sure she'd be able to stay awake long enough to take her boots off, much less eat dinner.

"Iz?"

She liked it when he called her that. She'd been Izzy once, then Isobel, but Iz belonged just to Gabriel. But he only used it when he was worried. She had to stop worrying him. Oh. He'd called her name again.

"Mmmm?"

"You're asleep on your feet. Come on, just a little longer."

His arm went over her shoulder, and she sighed, the heat of his body uncomfortable but the support welcome. "I can—"

"I know you can," he said. "But you don't have to."

"Bossy-boots," she grumbled.

"Guilty as charged, your honor." She saw him tip his hat to someone, then turn her smoothly down a corner, and she could recognize the blue-painted storefront of the building, and then the resthouse a few steps past that. "Up you go, just a few steps more . . ."

"Isobel! Gabriel, you're back!"

Ana had flung open the door, but she looked less happy to see them than worried. Isobel straightened, feeling Gabriel's arm slip away from her shoulders as he too readied himself.

"What is it?"

"Auntie stopped by this morning, looking for you. She was right unhappy you'd left, says you need to see her right away. And Papa needs to talk with you too, he says. I don't know about what, before you even ask." She sounded deeply put out by that.

Isobel bit back a groan, the promise of rest stripped away just before she could grab it. "Is it urgent?"

Ana's indignation took a deeper tone. "I don't know?"

Isobel sighed. "Let me wash off the road, and I'll be down straight away," she promised.

The girl sized the two of them up, and offered, "I'll fetch you something hot from the kitchen, while you wash?"

"That would be lovely, thank you."

Isobel watched as Ana turned in the doorway and dashed down the hallway, reminded once again of the days when she had been that girl, running errands and clearing tables, waiting and watching and hoping for a chance to do something more.

It felt a lifetime ago, not less than a year.

When they made it to the haven of their room, the door shut firmly behind them, Gabriel dropped his pack off his shoulder and onto the bed, where it landed with a faint thump. Unlacing the flap, he reached in and pulled out a small, square packet, then handed it to her. She stared at it numbly before remembering: Marie had sent it from Flood. He'd carried it with them, all this time. And she'd utterly forgotten about it.

In her defense, much had happened.

They were needed elsewhere, yet curiosity overrode her.

Isobel sat down on the bed and untied the string, unfolding the leather envelope to reveal a flat cloth purse, and another object, wrapped in fabric.

The purse was filled with silver coins, shining dimly when she spilled them out onto the coverlet. Her pay for the past months on the Road. The fabric-wrapped object turned out to be a leather-bound journal, similar to the one she'd been given when she left Flood, but with fresh, blank pages, and a cover that was not showing the wear of a hundred nights packed in a kit and too much handling by a campsite fire.

She flipped open the front cover again, then the back, then thumbed through the pages, then searched the wrappings again, spreading the coins out onto the coverlet, ignoring their soft clinking in favor of checking the inside of the purse for anything she might have missed.

But other than the name on the outside, in Marie's still-familiar handwriting, there was nothing. No note. No message.

Isobel hadn't realized how much she had been depending on one being there, until there was none.

"Is it all there?"

Isobel started; she was so tired, she had forgotten Gabriel was in the room. She blinked at him, trying to parse his words, and then realized that he meant the coins.

"I don't know?" She shrugged, a little embarrassed. "I don't remember how much there was supposed to be."

His lips twitched, she bit her lip, he looked away, she rolled her eyes, and then the both of them were giggling helplessly, Gabriel dropping down onto the bed next to her, making the coins bounce a little on the spread, and that set them off again, as though her utter ignorance of her own contract was the funniest thing either of them had ever heard.

Finally, wiping his eyes, Gabriel reached over and sorted through the coins, the silver edges tumbling over his fingers; full coins and halves, and the occasional quarter, the edges cut clean.

She remembered seeing the boss snipping coins at the table, his fingers deft and sure. What others needed a shears to do, he did with a touch, taking his percentage and pushing the remainder back across the felt. Silver coins, quartered and eighthed.

Silver was the Territory's currency. It was used elsewhere, too. Spain, the Americas, the British, they all carried silver coins.

But it was different here. Silver mined from the mountains of the Mother's Knife could sense power, cleanse crossroads. The silver within the Mother's Knife had taken the Spanish magic and turned it into something else, kept the Spaniards from reaching into the heart of the Territory.

Silver protected. There was no evil in it. No wrongness in the whisper that had guided her.

But she thought of the glint that she had seen in that not-man's eyes, that afternoon before he died, and wondered with a shudder what she might see in her own eyes if she were to look in the mirror. She wondered what Gabriel saw when he looked at her.

Her limbs felt heavy and soft, her thoughts muddled and puddling like over-ripe apples. "The only silver mines are to the west, right?"

Gabriel stopped counting, scooping the coins up, plucking the one from her fingers, and pouring them back into the purse. "There's some small deposits've been found elsewhere, mostly back East, across the River. Nothing significant, though. Stories claim there's a bounty down south, among the Aztecan, but if so, they're not trading much of it up north." He made a face. "Not that they would, if it's like ours."

"It's not like that, back East, or in the North, or anywhere not here." She'd heard the boss say that, more than once, and Gabriel, too. That silver was just a metal there, like iron or gold. "Because there isn't enough?"

"Maybe. Or maybe there isn't enough because the mines died. I've never inquired too close."

A vein of living silver could destroy entire mines if it were disturbed. Miners learned to sense it, avoided it if they could.

Isobel felt the skin on her arms and neck prickle. She'd merely walked past the open mouth of a mine back in De Plata, and it had made her want to run. But she'd not been certain if she'd meant to run away or into.

Had it been in her before then? Had it slid into her then?

"Blue Cloud said he didn't think it was dangerous to me. But am I dangerous with it?"

Gabriel put the packet away and draped an arm over her shoulders, drawing her close. He wasn't a hugger, Gabriel wasn't, but it felt natural to rest her head against his shoulder, his heartbeat a reassuring thump in her ear.

"I'm no medicine worker or dream walker, to ask those things, Isobel. You know that. All I can tell you is what I've seen or heard."

And what he'd heard, he'd told her. She worried at a thumbnail, tearing the edge of it with her teeth before realizing what she was doing. "Do you think Auntie would know?"

"I think that woman knows more than she tells, even if not as much as she wants people to think she knows," Gabriel said. "But I'm not the one who needs to be asking her." He touched his nose with two fingers, then pointed at her with one. Trade-sign: identifying her as the one who would make the final deal.

"And since she wants to see you, you'll have the chance to ask her. But before you do that, we need to visit with our host, hopefully before he raises our tariff for the additional work we've made for him. Are you ready?"

"No." She let her head rest for a heartbeat longer, then sighed and pushed herself up off the bed, her body protesting.

A splash of water on her face and a towel run under her blouse helped a little, but Isobel would have wrassled a ghost-cat for a cup of Gabriel's camp-coffee. Thankfully, Rafe had a pot waiting for them in his office, hot and black, if not quite as strong as she needed it.

The older man looked as tired as she felt, the shadows under his eyes more pronounced, with the creases that told her he was fighting off a headache. He watched as they helped themselves to the coffee, his own mug abandoned on his desk along with a half-eaten leg of chicken on a plate. Isobel found herself hoping that whatever Ana brought them to eat looked more appetizing than that.

Rafe didn't waste time with pleasantries. "You realize that everyone in town is buzzing with gossip. And they're blaming me for everything you've done, somehow."

"What have we done?" Isobel might still be exhausted, but her confusion was honest. When she looked over at Gabriel to see if he were following the conversation any better, he had his face down, one hand massaging the bridge of his nose.

"Your little set-to in the street with one of our finer locals?" Rafe prompted. "Shouting at each other like fishwives? Or how about your getting Auntie's attention and stirring *her* up?"

"I hardly think we're to blame for her," Gabriel muttered, his head still down.

"And now I hear that you beat the snot out of some of our admittedly less-than-stellar residents—"

Isobel had a breath of relief that there had been survivors, then only felt annoyance. They must have started howling the moment they crossed under the gate, for rumors to have spread already. "Did they tell you they killed a man?"

Rafe's body stiffened, and she practically heard a click in the air as his attention focused on her. "They did not. You have a name, or a body?"

"Neither," Isobel said. "He did not give a name before he died, and the survivors ran before we could learn anything more from them."

"Survivors." A deeper crease formed between Rafe's eyes, just over the bridge of his nose, and he leaned backward in his chair. "Tell me everything, from the beginning."

"We came across them—"

"No," Rafe interrupted. "From the *beginning*."

Was he serious? She bit her lip and considered starting at the very beginning, with that birthday meeting with the boss in his study so many months ago. It would serve the former marshal right—but they would be there all day and possibly all week if she started with that.

"The devil offered me a place, a position, as his Left Hand." Rafe's eyebrow raised, indicating that yes, he knew all this, get on with it. But he had requested from the beginning, and he would get it, within reason.

"This is my mentorship ride. I had never left Flood before, and the boss felt that I should familiarize myself with the people and places of the Territory, that I would know them and they me." She swallowed, thinking of those difficult, confusing first few weeks, the things she'd faced, the things she hadn't *known* she needed to know. "And to learn the extent of what I am and what I must do."

Rafe had been a marshal; he knew some of what she was and might do by the nature of the oath he had taken.

"It has not been an easy ride," she went on. "Spain moves against our borders, with both greedy intent and magics sanctioned by church and king." She thought briefly of the monks who, reluctantly, horrified at what their leaders had done, had helped them subdue one manifestation of that spell. "The United States abuses their access, sending men of war and politics across the border, to stir unrest among . . ." It still terrified her to say it. ". . . among magicians."

Rafe's eyes narrowed. "Magicians. Magicians are not restful at the best of times."

"They're dead now," Gabriel said, not even pretending to be helpful.

Rafe looked at her. "Your doing?"

Isobel nodded, stiffly.

"Good."

"Good?" Whatever she had expected, it hadn't been the satisfaction filling every line of his body.

"Good. Knowing there's someone sane who can take on a magician and win? May be the best news I've been given in years."

Isobel wasn't quite certain his definition of "sane" and hers would match, but chose not to argue the point.

"You're sure they're all dead?"

She nodded. What she had done, she was certain they would not be returning from. And the others . . . they were still trapped in the mountains, tangled in the bones with the ancient spirit they had tried to control. The Territory had protected its own.

"And then, with all that, you came here. Why?"

"Gabriel wanted to avoid the snows."

Behind her, her mentor snorted.

"And no other reason?"

Her patience, already strained, broke. "We've been over this before, Rafe, when we first arrived."

A muscle in his jaw popped. "And since then, people have died."

"People died before we came here. Or have you already forgotten? You were the one who told us." Her tone sharpened, cutting through the protests he might have been forming. "Nothing that is happening was caused solely by our arrival. The tensions among settlers, the way the native villages look to you with caution now rather than ease? That has been growing for months. Maybe longer."

Maybe the same length of time since the devil decided he needed a new Left Hand, and Isobel presented herself to him, ready-made and full of foolishness. She reached up to touch her braid, fingers shocked anew to not feel the feathers tucked there.

"The river-spirits are rising, Rafe. I've seen it. I've *felt* it. Do you understand what that means?"

From the way he blanched, he did. The River meant life and trade to a port town, but it could also mean destruction and death, all ugly, and often quick. The Mud had been within his lifetime; he remembered.

"So, don't ask me why I'm here. You know be-damned well why

I'm here, likely better even than I did from the start. Either mount up, or get out of my way."

She didn't remember standing, but she was, feet planted square, shoulders down, and she could feel her jaw jutting forward in what Peggy used to tell her was a most unfeminine pose. There was silence around her, as though the winds themselves were holding their breath, then Rafe sighed.

"Quiet times. That's all I wanted for my girls. Just a nice, quiet life."

He reached down, opening the drawer of his desk and withdrawing something wrapped in grey cloth. Unwrapped, it revealed a brightly polished object glinting in the lamplight. "But I suppose I always knew there was a reason I kept it 'stead of having it melted down to something useful."

He pinned the sigil to his lapel and paused, fingers resting on the bright surface.

"I'm not doing this for you. I'm not taking your side in anything, not just yet. Your being the Hand doesn't buy you more than tolerance. I'm here for my oath and my town. To keep them safe."

The urge to remind him that it had been members of *his* town that had killed those people bubbled under her tongue, but she swallowed it back down. He looked a half-score older than he had just moments ago, the weight of that badge bearing down on him already. Instead, she offered her hand across the desk, waiting until he stood as well and took it. "That is all we expect of you, Marshal," she said, and watched his gaze flicker down, then back again in acknowledgement of the title.

Not every marshal was a good man. But a good man made a better marshal, and that was what Red Stick needed just now.

PART SIX

THE DEVIL'S HAND

ONE

Stepping across the threshold, down into Auntie's lair, Isobel felt the lack of someone beside her more keenly than she'd expected. But Gabriel had suggested that she go alone, that whatever Auntie had to say, she would likely prefer it to be directly to Isobel, without a man lingering about.

Isobel didn't think the presence of anyone would keep Auntie from speaking her mind, but she let him be. He had reasons of his own for sending her alone; she could read that easily, and just as easily read that she would dig it out of him unwillingly, if at all. So, she left him sitting in Rafe's office, telling him only that if she did not return by nightfall, he should come rescue her. He'd laughed, but she hadn't been joshing. Not entirely.

She trusted Auntie, within reason. But she also remembered that Rafe did not trust her, not entirely. There were uneven and uneasy threads in this town, and they could trip her if she was not careful.

Also, Auntie had strong medicine, a power perhaps not as strong as the devil's, nor as deep, but not to be dismissed, either. And she had thought there was something to hide Isobel from when Isobel had gone too deep. . . .

She'd fallen ill again before she could ask Auntie about that. About so many things. But she was well now. So long as she didn't become misdirected or put off her road . . .

"There you are." Auntie had been seated at her worktable, spinning slowly on the stool to look at Isobel as she came down the steps. The space seemed larger than Isobel remembered it, the ceilings higher than they should be, the air brighter than it could be from the dim lamps and small windows. "Have you been avoiding me, bone-girl?"

Isobel let out a surprised half-laugh. "I've been elsewhere," she said. "The which you already know if you spoke with anyone, since half the town seems set on keeping a finger on me."

Auntie squinted at her, flipping a handful of thin braids over her shoulder before pointing to the other chair in clear command. "And the other half would lay an actual finger on you if they only dared, no doubt."

"No doubt." Isobel went to the chair—the only one in the room not covered with books or hides or sacks of things unknown—and sat down, gathering her skirt underneath her as neatly as she'd learned to do in the saddle, the toes of her boots peeping out from under the hem. She looked down and noted that the toes were sadly scuffed, the leather discolored from wear. She had money now; she could replace everything that needed replacing. And buy extras, as well. Gabriel had counted the coins, not her, but she suspected it would be more than adequate to her needs.

Although she had no idea what prices were there. Simple things had surprisingly high costs, she had discovered. She would need to ask Gabriel; he had visited the mercantile already, he'd said, and would likely know.

A rough and pointed cough recalled her to the room.

"I am here now," she said. "As you requested."

"Mmm, so you are." The older woman seemed in no hurry to get to whatever she'd meant to say, however, her back turned to Isobel while she moved objects on her workbench, taking a pinch of this and a crumble of that, stoppering jars and sealing paper packets. Isobel waited, not at all put out. It wasn't as though she didn't know how to wait. The boss had deigned to notice you, no matter who you were, when he was well and ready to and not a breath before. Marie would sometimes make you wait in the chair for what seemed like forever, until she was ready to speak—or, at least one time, had calmed down enough to speak without yelling. And since then, Isobel had spent hours in the saddle with her own thoughts, even with Gabriel riding beside her. She could wait.

Finally, Auntie spoke. "You're dawdling."

"What?"

"You heard me, bone-child. Bone-touched, devil-touched. Way I'd heard of you, I'd expected you to ride into town and sort things out before high sun. Instead, you've been dragging your heels and making like you never felt the sting of power in your veins. What are you waiting for?"

"You heard of me?" Isobel's thoughts had gotten stuck on that, everything else she'd thought to ask dropped by the roadside. Had Calico Zac ridden into town, as well as seemingly every settlement along the river? Or were other folk talking, and if so, what were they saying?

Auntie turned then, rolling her eyes. She had a smear of white dust across one cheek where she'd obviously swiped the back of her hand, but her eyes were fierce enough that Isobel decided not to mention it just then. "And now you're playing the fool. You think the Hand doesn't ride out, shake the Road up something good, and the whisper won't tell?"

The last time Isobel had fallen off a horse—Uvnee had spooked when they rode over a haint's resting place—she'd landed badly and felt a painful shock along her entire spine. She felt a shadow of that now.

"Child, what—" Auntie snapped her mouth shut and narrowed her eyes at Isobel, then reached behind her and grabbed a ladderback chair, settling herself on it so close in front of Isobel, their knees nearly touched. "You been hearing the whisper, feeling it hot in your veins, and not a clue what it means, haven't you? Oh, child."

Isobel heard the pity in her voice and felt a heartbeat's urge to throw something in sheer rage, things she'd thought settled rushing back like a storm wind. The boss had sent her out without any instruction; she'd had to learn everything by doing, fitting together what she was, what she could do, after she'd already done it.

Isobel couldn't argue it hadn't been effective, and most days she understood why he'd done it, but just then, she battled rage and tears at the thought that something could have been explained and saved her some confusion.

"It's the living silver. You said, but I thought . . ." She shook her head violently, feeling her own braid twitch, painfully aware of the lack of feathers fluttering against her skin. "Everyone can hear it?"

"Not everyone, no. Not even most folk. We're born to it when we're born to the Territory, but most folk don't hear the wind around their ears, much less anything so quiet and deep."

"I thought . . . I thought it was the boss at first, but it wasn't. It's loud sometimes when the sigil's quiet, and it says things, sends me places. . . ."

It had woken her out of a sound sleep, sent her to witness the massacre of buffalo, led her to the magicians who'd tangled with the ancient spirit and lost. And she had known, had *known* it was something deeper. Had felt it, even before Auntie said anything, even before Blue Cloud said anything, but hadn't wanted to know. Because it was impossible, because it was unthinkable. Because nothing with that sort of power that she had ever seen stayed sane.

"Not your boss, no. Older even than him. Not silver, not the way we know it, the thing that's shapeable, usable. It's deeper and colder, though I suspect they've the same dust at their core."

Auntie took Isobel's hands between her own, the press of warm flesh startling, making Isobel realize she was shaking. "You're hearing the first voice, bone-child. The sound of stars-fell-to-earth, and moon-rose-from-water."

The story of the Stars That Fell to Earth, Isobel knew: she'd heard it as a child, when shooting stars filled the summer skies, and one of the older children told the younger ones about the sky-spirits that had seen the earth when it was young and found it too interesting to remain distant, casting off their burning robes as they fell to earth, to have adventures with Bear and Otter and Raven, and all the First Animals, long before people were there. But—

"Auntie, I do not know the story of Moon Rose from Water."

Auntie shook her head, braids clacking, and reached forward to touch one long finger to Isobel's nose before pulling back. "Then listen, child, and learn. In the time when there was no land, before Badger pulled the mountains from the deeps and Crow dragged the sky to cover it, the moon lived deep in the waters, cool and perfect . . . and very alone. But when Frog dove to fetch flat land for the people to stand on, the moon was curious. It followed Frog until it reached the surface and saw the sky, and felt a great longing to be there. But what it had weighed in the water was too much to rise into the sky, and so it had to shed itself of some of that weight. It peeled as much of itself as it could spare, bits and scrapes falling into the dirt and trying to dig their way back into the deeps, until it was pale and light enough to rise. And so it has remained—but bits of it lingered within the earth, tied to the medicine of the bones that housed it, shaping itself to it, but still glimmering in memory of what was lost."

Isobel realized she'd been holding her breath when an ache pressed against her chest, and she had to gasp to ease it.

"Silver."

Auntie made a gesture with one hand that could have been agreement or disagreement, or somewhere in-between. "We call it that, living silver, or dreaming dust, or a dozen things beside, depending on who you ask. Naming things is tricky and not always wise."

"And when I touch the bones . . . I'm touching that?" Isobel felt slightly nauseated.

"Your boss should be taken out and tanned," Auntie muttered. "Marking you like that and letting you go out, when he knew full well you were a bone-child. . . . Oh, I know what he was up to; card-players are like that, always thinking they've a trick up their sleeve, a card they can turn at the last hand, but, ah, *fah!*" She made that gesture again, then clenched her hand into a fist and shook it twice. "All the old ones, they play us the way they play all else, with rules they break even in the making.

"Listen to me, bone-child, and you listen well, because I'll only tell you this once. There is power in this land; there has always been power in this land, and the foolish take it for their due, think it will always be there, always answer to them, a thing to be used, its pelt to be worn, its meat to be eaten, its bones to be shaped into weapons or decorations. But it is not. It is deep and it is fierce and it may care for us, but it will consume us without thought, because it does not *understand.*"

The nausea remained, but Isobel felt something click inside. "Like the winds consume magicians."

"Worse. More."

"But . . . it's in us. Me. You?" Isobel thought of every time she'd reached deep, every time she'd felt the surge of the bones, every time she'd heard the whisper wind itself through her, and shuddered as though a haint had just touched her skin. "I saw . . . On the way back to Red Stick, we ran into a group of men; they'd caught another man they said was a magician. He wasn't. But he called power, using a language I'd never heard before."

Auntie raised one eyebrow, looking unimpressed. "Many languages, bone-child. Many ways to call power."

Isobel knew that; that wasn't what she'd been reaching for. "His eyes . . . before they killed him. They were silver."

Auntie stilled, even her braids resting quietly. "He is dead?"

Isobel nodded.

"You are certain?"

Isobel hesitated, then nodded again. She had seen death enough to know when it filled a body.

"Fool boy," Auntie muttered, her stillness gone as though it had never been. "And the body?"

"Buried," Isobel said. "Should it have been burned?"

"Burned would have been better, burned and broken to ash, make sure nothing got out, but you've more to worry at now."

"About whatever is happening here, I know. But I don't know what—"

"*Phaugh.*" Auntie turned her head as though to spit, then suddenly recalled that she was in her own workspace, and changed it to a head-shake. "You know why it happens, why it's happening now. You've just sold yourself too hard to one view; you won't let yourself see the others."

Isobel would have taken insult, save that she'd been told often enough by enough folk that she knew something she would have sworn she did not, that she'd learned to pause before rebutting.

"All I have are pieces, Auntie," she said, and the older woman leaned back, arms crossed over her chest, as though Isobel'd just proven her point, exactly.

Isobel ticked the things she knew off on her fingers, beginning with her thumb. "The Americans are poking at our defenses. Nothing the boss can act against; they've learned how to sneak. But Gabriel says their new president has to prove himself, and that makes men take risks. And the Spaniards—they used spellwork against us, even though their Church says it's a sin."

The monks she'd met had been horrified by the use of spells but not by the idea that they should claim the Territory. The US marshal who had caused such trouble, he had been saddened by what happened, but he'd warned them he would not be the only one sent—and others would not fail.

"They need our lands, both of them. And the devil stands in their way."

She had not stopped either attempt, only eased the damages. The Territory had done more. . . . The Territory had used *her* to do more. The same way the boss had. Still, after all this time, she was nothing more than a tool.

"You're bone-touched and devil-touched," Auntie said, as though seeing her thoughts writ on her face. "That gives you the strength to go deep and come back again different. But you don't have to."

"What?"

"There are other folk who're silver-touched, bone-child. Always have been, every age and every skin. Some do something with it, some don't. Some build, some break, some spread good, and others . . . well, I don't judge, but some folk do leave a mess behind."

A mess, Auntie called it. The last Hand? Was that why people were still angry, all these years later?

"People are being killed." She looked down at her hands, as though expecting them to be bloody. But they were clean, the nails still ragged, but a healthy pink below. "I have to do something."

"People always gonna be getting killed," Auntie said, blunt as a stone. "Here, there, anywhere, and likely everywhere. We don't have a fondness for folk speaking things that upset us, and that bunch, they were upsetting."

And she'd sent the Jack to bring them back, to be upsetting all over again. But there was something else, something important she needed to ask Auntie before they got distracted again.

"Why did you protect me? When I fell, after . . . after touching too deep. Why did you help me? And what were you hiding me *from?*"

Auntie sighed, lifting her hands in a gesture Isobel could not read. "Everything, mostly. You were too open, too deep. That's not good for anyone. There're things hungry for what you carry, even though it would do them no good to take it. That sigil protects you from most of 'em but not when you were like that."

Auntie studied her face, then touched one slender, harsh-knuckled finger to Isobel's nose.

"Listen to what I tell you, bone-child. There's a mark on your palm says you entered into an agreement most wouldn't ever be offered and, if they were, would be wise enough to run from. But you took it up, dropped your blood on a contract and bound yourself to it."

Isobel waited; so far, the woman hadn't said anything she didn't already know.

"But the devil, he knows the Territory, and the Territory, it knows him. They're neither of them as solid as they seem, and they both play a long, long game. But you, bone-child. You're solid as they come. And you're in the now-and-here, under this sun and the next, and that's all we get to know for sure."

Isobel's gaze flicked up to Auntie's face, thinking how the devil's face changed every time you looked at it, with only his eyes ever remaining the same. She'd never thought of it, never thought oddly of it; it just *was*. But Auntie's words now made her think of that suddenly. "I know how your boss works; he don't ask anyone, but waits until they ask him, yeah? You asked *him* for something to do."

"I said I wanted to work for him. With him."

"Mmmm." Auntie reached out again, taking Isobel by the wrist and turning her palm up so the sigil showed to them both, the thick black lines inked on her skin by some means she'd never been able to determine, appearing and deepening, darkening. "You wanted the job. Wanted power. You took it. Got more than expected. And now you—only you, bone-child, not him—got to decide what all that means."

Gabriel stretched his legs out in front of him, making himself obviously at home despite the fact that the newly repinned marshal was clearly about to ask him to leave.

"Is there something more you feel the need to say?" His tone was even, although the man clearly would have preferred something less polite from the glare he was subjecting Gabriel's legs to. Isobel had left a few minutes before, grimly determined to get some sort of answers from the witch-woman, and Rafe clearly thought that was the end of his involvement.

"Just a few things left to discuss, if you don't mind." And even if he did, Gabriel's tone conveyed.

Gabriel studied the other man as he seated himself behind his desk again, trying to see any difference between the hostería keeper they'd met and the marshal he'd been and become again, in the way he sat, or looked, or spoke, and finding nothing in particular different. It wasn't as though the man had scraped one skin off and put another on, the way Isobel had, or even layered one over another. They were both the same skin, same meat, same mind. He'd never cut off that part of him, or denied it, only set the use of it aside for a while.

Gabriel wasn't sure if he admired that or if it unnerved him. Mayhap both.

And mayhap he envied it, more 'n a little.

"So . . ." The marshal spread his hands, inviting Gabriel to keep talking.

"So, what are you planning to do, if it's not to help Isobel?"

"I told you. Protect my town."

"And how you think you're going to do that? You think a rifle and some sharp words'll do it? Threatening to haul them before a judge?"

The marshal folded his hands in front of him, resting them on the desk. "It's a start."

Gabriel nodded. It was a start, that was true, and more than anyone had been doing in this town for a while, it seemed like. He knew there were places that prided themselves on not having rules, or settling things one on one. He'd never seen anything much good come out of that, which was likely what had driven him to the law in the first place. He didn't particularly like rules, but order, order was a good thing.

Although it seemed some days, the Territory itself wasn't so keen on it.

"You ever been out of the Territory?"

If the question startled the marshal, he didn't show it. "Nope.

Skirted it a few times, spent a while riding the river Road, keeping an eye on the currents, but never felt the need to cross. Just more of the same over there, isn't it?"

Gabriel huffed a laugh. "I suppose it is, yeah." No reason to tell him how wrong he was.

"The Americans I've spoken to, and admittedly it's not many, seem to think it's different over here. The way they poke and peer from their fortifications as though we were animals they need be wary of." It was a question, even if not phrased as such.

"They dislike being held at the border," Gabriel said with a shrug, more casual than he felt. "The trickle the devil allows in only whets their appetite for more."

The marshal's gaze flicked up, then off to the side, as though what he was about to say wasn't important at all. "They've an awful lot of men just across the river. More than they did even two years back."

That was interesting, and useful news, were it Gabriel's job to keep track of such things. It was not. They'd trusted the devil's strength to keep invaders out for nearly three centuries now. It seemed hubris to think that would change in their lifetime. And yet. Gabriel had been trained to look at evidence.

People within the Territory were twitchy. The Territory *itself* was twitchy. The Americans were asking questions they shouldn't be asking. And the Left Hand—the one responsible for enforcing the devil's form of justice—was riding again.

As casual as the comment had been made, Gabriel lifted his hands, making trade-sign for "I do not have an answer."

The other man rubbed the bridge of his nose with two fingers, then squinted at Gabriel. "Exciting times we're in."

Gabriel chuckled ruefully. "The number of times I've thought that in the past year . . ."

"And that's all you can tell me."

Gabriel lifted his hands again, this time in a shrug.

"Right. If I'm to do this, might as well do it officially. Might lead to having to knock some heads together." Gabriel thought there might have been a bit of anticipation in the man's voice at that last.

The marshal got up from the chair and reached behind him to pluck a battered, narrow-brim hat from the rack, then looked down at Gabriel still sprawled in his own chair. "You coming with?"

He should, Gabriel knew. Watch the reactions, listen to what wasn't being said when Rafe made it official, that a marshal was back in town, that what passed for law in the Territory was once again being enforced. But he remained in his chair, his bootheels square on the floor. "I've got something else needs taking care of," he said. "You have fun."

Rafe made a rude gesture at him, then settled the hat on his head and went out the door, yelling for Ana as he did so.

A quiet voice watched the marshal leave, then said, *You should not be here.*

"Shut up, old bear."

Graciendo's grumble lingered in his brain despite the dismissal. Like Old Woman Who Never Dies, the mountain recluse had given him good advice that Gabriel had never been able to take, not completely. Stay apart, stay isolated, Graciendo had told him. That was the only way to remain himself. To not lose himself again. But short of holing up in a mountain cabin the way the old bear did, Gabriel didn't see how that was possible. Even as a rider, constantly moving, there were people everywhere; the Territory was filling up, settlement by settlement.

The devil never asks for anything you're not willing to pay, but he always knows what you need.

Gabriel had thought he could balance between it all, the need to be within the Territory, the need to *belong*, but still be himself, to not let the pull of the water drown him. Had thought he could walk the line, remain unconnected without isolation.

And then he had to be a fool and ride into Flood on a whim.

"I have an offer to make you," the devil had said, as casual as he might deal out a new hand, all friends around the table, no cards up his sleeve. "Or perhaps I am accepting your offer. Either way, I think it may be of interest, and of worth, for you to accept."

He had made no offer to the devil, not then or after, only to Isobel. He had not realized, then, that they were already one and the same.

But he was no Jack, bound until the devil tired of him. He had agreed to do one thing: mentor the girl-child Isobel until she was ready to ride on her own.

She was; the past few days had shown him that. And he had nothing left to offer her, not here, not with the River so near.

Old Woman Who Never Dies stood behind him, wizened hand knuckling at his lower back, her breath smelling of dried fish and pine, hot on his neck.

"Time, boy. It's time."

TWO

"What are you saying?"

"Saying what I said." Auntie turned back to her worktable, moving a glass vial over, shifting two small clay pots to where the vial had been. Busy-work, distraction. "Territory and the devil, they hold shape because we need 'em to. We shape 'em just by being here, like water shapes a riverbank."

"But the riverbank directs where the river flows," Isobel said. "We're . . . the riverbank?" But that didn't feel right either.

"We're ourselves, nothing more. Chalk and dust. But there's something that gets into us, makes us more. Silver's what we call it, here and now, because that's what we can see, touch, feel." Auntie made a face, telling Isobel what she thought of those limitations. "We can shape it, control it, use it. Silver—what is it they say? Cleaned the way?"

Isobel nodded, touching her own silver ring resting in her little finger, as though for reassurance. "It tarnishes in the presence of power being used, warns of danger in the crossroads, cleanses the way for safe passage." She frowned in turn. "And it does."

"Not all that it does," Auntie said, and her gaze rested on Isobel's hand, the fingers twisting the silver band without realizing it. Isobel flushed and stopped.

"We shape it, use it," Auntie said. "Seems it does the same to us. Ties us to it. It needs us much as we need it.

"Some folk feel it without knowing, without having it inside them. Some it makes uneasy, like they're always being watched. Some, it makes 'em powerful, sometimes arrogant with it. Your boss knows full well the moment they're born, I'm thinking. And those of us who've bothered to look past what's easy, we see 'em too."

Isobel opened her mouth to refute the suggestion that she'd taken the easy way in anything, then shut her mouth again with a snap at the look Auntie gave her.

Auntie waited to see if Isobel was going to say anything. When she didn't, the medicine woman went on. "We say living silver, and dangerous, and then we push it from our thoughts, nothing we should concern ourselves with so long as miners bring the ore and smiths shape it to something useful. But nothing living should be ignored, and nothing that old and living dare be ignored, not for long."

"Else what happens?" Isobel anticipated being told about some fixed danger, maybe earthquakes or explosions, like living silver'd been blamed for, previous. Miners coming too close to things that shouldn't be touched, not with pickaxe nor hand. But those things only happened deep in the mines. What Auntie was saying sounded worse than that, like it might affect them all.

Like it was already affecting them all.

"Don't know," Auntie admitted, slumping back in her chair, the first easing of her posture Isobel could remember since she'd first woken up on the woman's cot, full of dreams and confusion. "Suspect it's nothing good, though. Ignore something, do it long enough, sometimes it goes away. Had a Nahua medicine teacher once say a mountain without silver had no spirit, no power. Take away the spirit, all that's left is dirt."

"But." Isobel forced her hand to rest on her knee, not touching the ring, not thinking of the silver coins in her pocket or the thin silver bands in Auntie's braids.

"Don't know and don't much care," Auntie said again, as though she knew what Isobel was about to ask, about places where there were no mines of silver, nowhere for that spirit to reside. "I'm just a poor river-witch; I got enough to worry about right here without wasting time on fools elsewhere maybe later." Her head lifted, and her eyes rolled, braids trembling as she shook her head. "And speaking of fools here . . ."

There was a pounding against her door, steady, heavy fists demanding entry.

"You stay put," Auntie said, when Isobel moved to get up. "We are nohow finished talking yet."

Auntie stood in front of the door, her hand on the handle, and shouted, "You hold yourselves; don't go falling on me when I open the door, you hearing me?" She flung open the door before there was an answer, stepping back in time that the people standing outside did not fall on her, though from Isobel's viewpoint there wasn't much difference in how they entered, staggering forward in a mass of arms and torsos.

Then one of the torsos tried to wrench itself free, and the tangle defined itself into three men, two holding the arms of the third, who had a rope halter tied around his neck.

"What have you brought me, and why have you brought it?" Auntie asked, as though this were nothing out of the ordinary for her.

"Found him by the river," one of the men holding him said. "Shouting and raving; had other folk nervous enough to try and quiet him down their own way." He lifted his chin to indicate the rope. "But there was something in his eyes I didn't take a liking to; thought it might be wiser to let you take a look before it got put out."

"That's Patli," Auntie said to Isobel. "One of my less foolish students." The other man started to protest, then subsided when Auntie glared at him. "All right, then, you brought him here for me to see; let me see him."

But at that moment, the bound man's gaze fell on Isobel, and his mouth opened in a pained-sounding shriek that had nothing human in it.

Isobel had not thought the older woman could have moved as quickly as she did, pushing past the three figures to catch at the wooden door, shoving whoever had followed them back up the steps, clearly not caring if she caught a finger or toe in the doorway as she slammed the door shut, then whirled back to face them.

"Bind him with proper rope," she told her students. "And you, bone-child, why am I not at all surprised this has your name smudged all over it?"

"I've never seen him before in my life," Isobel protested, trying to ignore the surge of . . . something she had felt at that noise, at the presence of the man they'd hauled in.

"You think that matters?" Auntie asked, still shaking her head. "Bone-child, stop your foolishness and *listen*."

Isobel didn't want to listen. Didn't want to go anywhere near the man now bound with fabric ropes, pressed down into a high-backed chair and the ropes tied to that, secure enough that he couldn't move arms nor legs. Didn't want to go anywhere near the face that glared at her, with eyes the molten glint of silver.

But she wasn't given a choice. Not with those eyes staring at her.

"Things stir, unease and dis-ease move people like children move toys, and twice now, the silver's filled someone to overflow here, in this town. At a time when *you* walk among us and the whisper knows your name. Is that coincidence, bone-child?"

"Of course not," Isobel replied, finding Marie's tartness in her voice when someone asked a foolish question. "Coincidence is just bad luck we're paying attention to."

The old woman snorted, pointedly turning her back on Isobel to study the figure bound to her chair, cautiously looking over the bindings without touching them, looking for something only she could determine.

Isobel closed her eyes and clenched her fingers into her palm, digging nails into the sigil until the itch of power within her skin reassured her. She was the Devil's Hand, she belonged to the boss, she had a purpose and a meaning that had nothing to do with . . . any of this. No matter what Auntie said or thought.

But if what rode this creature was the source of the unease the people felt, that threatened the Agreement, it was her responsibility to find it and remove it.

Even if every patch of her body wanted to go no closer.

It took several breaths before she could open her eyes again, taking in the scene before her: the figure bound to the chair, Auntie standing behind it, two fingers pressed to her mouth, her students back against the wall, clearly awaiting instruction.

"Salt," she said, her voice steadier than expected. "Two lines, around the chair, one close, and one outside where I will stand."

The two men glanced once at Auntie and, after she jerked her head in a nod, hurried to do Isobel's bidding, each taking up a small brown sack from the worktable and splitting the work between them. Isobel waited until they had poured enough granules in the close circle to make a secure binding, then stepped up to it and let them work behind her. The thing bound in the chair watched her without blinking, no expression on its face, but the eyes still silver-bright.

Come to me.

There was no whisper in her thoughts this time, no push or pull to go anywhere, do anything, merely the memory of walking past the open mouth of the mine up in De Plata, and the shiver of something too large to be seen.

"Who are you?" Names had power. Not as much as some feared, not enough to trap or control, but enough. Enough that she could hold.

The thing smiled at her, sweetly, the bright flicker in its eyes briefly swallowed by brown. "Louis."

She had no way of knowing if that was its actual name or not. The pale skin and shaggy brown hair ruled out a native origin, but she'd met natives with blue eyes and pale skin before, the result of settlers like Jordan, or Gabriel's own grandfather, marrying into the local population and leaving mixed-blood generations to follow.

But when she shaped the name with her own mouth, it slipped over the figure like water over rocks, leaving only a trace of itself behind. Enough to feel; not enough to hold. Cold.

If Auntie was right, nothing human rested within that shell of flesh. Whatever they had been once, they were something else now.

That could be her, if she wasn't careful. If she hadn't had the devil's sigil on her palm, a Bargain tying her to him.

Come to me.

If she had answered, would she be like that? Emptied of all that was Isobel, replete with power that recognized no controls . . .

Fear thrummed in her gut, twisting around her ribs with the need to vomit. She licked her lips, tasting only bitterness there, and forced herself to swallow. The boss had ridden out to deal with the aftermath of a living silver explosion in a mine once. She'd told Gabriel about it, about the boss riding out grim-faced and coming back more tired than she could ever recall. But he had ridden out and come back, and dealt with whatever it was. That meant she could too.

Maybe.

Behind her, someone shifted, cloth scratching against skin. She could hear their breathing, too loud, scratching against her ears, and their very presence irritated her, like a spider crawling on her skin.

"Isobel." Auntie's voice, sounding as though it came from very far away, from another room through a closed door. "Isobel!"

She came back to herself just as her right toe inched over the inner salt line. She gasped and set her foot carefully on the ground, well clear of the salt.

The man who had died earlier that morning had not tried to harm her. Had not tried to harm anyone. Which was more than she could say about herself.

—there was a deep, bloody pop, not a clap like thunder too close, or the snap of a cinder from a bonfire, a thousand times louder than it could have been, and then another—

She had done that. The magicians, ripped apart. The two men earlier that day, gone beyond the finding. Was that what she was? The Left Hand could not heal, was not meant to heal. The Left Hand was the cold eye and the final word, the judgment of the devil. . . .

Isobel's thoughts stuttered to a halt, balking, refusing to go further. She forced them to, just as she would push Uvnee through a river she did not want to ford, careful but unrelenting.

The whisper had spoken to her, directed her. She had felt it, followed it. Had let in within her. It had been what destroyed those magicians, not her. The fact that she had thought it was the boss's voice at first gave her no excuse.

Sigil and whisper had both worked within her, had both used her.

Isobel met the silver-tinted eyes squarely and wondered what it saw within her.

"Louis, then," she said, and was amazed that her voice was calm, conversational, as though she were sitting across a campfire from Gabriel, asking him if dinner was ready yet. "These men say you were raving by the river. That others were trying to silence you with violence." She didn't need to point out the rope, now cast aside on the floor beyond the binding circles: they both knew it was there.

"I was warning them."

"Of what?"

"Of themselves." Louis paused, then grinned at her, and it was like being grinned at by a skull, for all that flesh and skin still covered his bones. "Of what is to come."

"Owl-touched," a voice whispered from behind them, loud as the crash of thunder, and Louis's grin widened even further.

"You should listen to the night-hunters more often," Louis said over her shoulder to whoever had spoken. "The moon shows more than the sun ever would."

Moon. Moon-rose-from-water. The pale light in darkness.

Isobel had been taught that night was when the winds died down, when medicines rested. No rituals she had ever heard of were worked under the moon. . . .

Suddenly, Isobel laughed, the sound breaking into every corner of the room, filling the spaces and shocking everything else into silence. As though she knew anything about rituals or power. As though she knew anything at all.

She only knew one way to learn. The hard way.

"I know what's coming, Louis." Two nations, pressing against the Territory. The devil, trying to push them back, buying time . . . How much time? To do what?

Silver, living in more and more bodies. Owl-touched, the man called him.

Owls, covered with snow. Fish on the banks. Red water rising.

"I know what's coming. Tell me how to stop it."

THREE

"You can't."

Louis's words dropped into the room without an echo. His eyelids dropped, and when they rose again, the pupils within were brown, only a hint of gleam in them. He smiled, licking dry lips with a snake-like flick of his tongue, then shuddered slightly, and his head tilted, lolling to the side as the life slid out of him, leaving the shell behind.

"Typical," Auntie muttered into the silence. "Tell us we got trouble and then flit off and leave the mess behind. Typical."

"Auntie," one of the men started to say, his voice hushed and worried. "Owl-touched said—"

"Owl-touched be crazy. Don't mean he be wrong," the other man said, his voice equally hushed, as though afraid to wake something with his words. "Bad times coming, maybe nothing we can do to stop it."

Isobel reached out, gently righting Louis's head so it looked as though he'd fallen asleep in the chair, only. Nothing *they* could do, no.

"Find out if he had family," she said. "Let them claim the body, give it binding and rest. I need to . . ." Her thoughts flickered over all the things she needed to do, like the devil flipping cards against the felt. "I need fresh air."

Whoever had followed Auntie's students and their captive had dispersed, clearly unwilling to linger and risk the woman's anger. Isobel stood in the narrow street outside the steps and breathed in, then out, feeling the cool, damp air fill her chest until she no longer needed to scream.

Her hand still trembled when she raised it to eye level, though, and her knees felt as wobbly as they had after the first week in the saddle, as though uncertain how to stand on solid ground.

"Gabriel." She needed to talk to Gabriel. And then . . . She felt her fingers press against the lines of the sigil in her palm. And then she would talk to the marshal, make a plan. Get people to calm down. That's what Marie would do; she'd ease fears enough that people didn't feel the need to be rash. No fistfights or hangings or silver-lit power snuffing out the lives carrying it. That's what she would do.

But a voice deep inside reminded her that the Right Hand was for gifting and giving. The Left wasn't for healing. It was for judgment.

Come to me, the whisper had said.

Isobel forced her fingers deeper into the sigil and shook her head once, violently. Silver didn't care about people. Only about staying whole. It would eat her, turn her into something like Louis, like the man on the road. Nothing better than a Jack. *Worse* than a Jack.

"Miss Isobel?"

A voice behind her almost made her jump. She controlled the instinct and turned to see one of the men—Patli, her memory supplied—standing on the top step of Auntie's, looking at her like he'd rather be anywhere else in the world.

"Miss Isobel, Auntie says I'm to walk with you. Run whatever errands you have need of doing."

Isobel had no desire for company and no need of protection, but she remembered the feeling of falling ill before and nodded once, acknowledging the truth of Auntie's concerns. She could not be vulnerable. Not now.

"Thank you," she said, and watched the lines in his face smooth out in relief. He was older than she, but at that moment, she felt ages older.

The walk back to the hostería was completed in silence. Patli kept himself to her right side, as though unconsciously staying as far from the sigil in her palm as was possible without giving offense, and a step behind. It reminded Isobel of how the mule would trail the horses, anxious to be included but unwilling to lead, and felt her lips twitch in a mixture of amusement and aching sadness.

Being on the Road hadn't been any easier, but it had seemed simpler, somehow. Maybe that was why riders chose it.

"Have you ever left Red Stick?"

"A few times." If Patli was surprised by the question, he didn't show it in his voice, and she didn't turn to look at him, instead focusing on the folk going about their business, a team pulling a wagon down the center of the street, storefronts bustling with custom, a group of children gathered over a game of marbles on one porch front, shoving and giggling, while an older girl-child perched on the rail above them, clearly minding the lot. "Been north a few times, running errands. I can ride, so Auntie sends me out a bit."

"Do you miss it?"

"Hate it. Road's empty. I like people around me."

Her lips twitched a bit more at the emphatic tone in his voice then. "Takes all kinds, I suppose," she said.

"Yes'm."

The fact that he had just yes'm'd her should not have been amusing, but somehow it cracked something in her, and she paused, bending forward, the laughter cackling out of her as though she'd gone mad.

"Miss Isobel? Are you all right? Should I—" And he was at her side, her right side, hands fluttering over her arm as though torn between the need to offer comfort, and fear of touching her.

Gabriel would have touched her, she thought, as the laughter kept coming. He wouldn't have hesitated, would have wrapped his arms around her shoulders and probably even laughed with her.

That thought allowed her to collect herself. Gabriel. "I'm fine. I just . . . Please don't ma'am me, Patli. My name is Isobel."

"All right." And she got the feeling that he would have been willing to call her anything if she would only stop laughing.

"There you are." Rafe was standing in the hallway when they entered, and she wondered, fleetingly, if he'd left the house since they'd last spoken, or if he'd been hiding there all that time.

Although, she realized with a shock, it hadn't been that long at all. It only felt so.

"Man came looking for you," Rafe went on, with a curl to his words that told her what he felt about the man who'd come looking, and also told her who it had to have been.

"Was he alone?"

"He was not. They're waiting out back. I didn't want 'em in here where decent folk would have to deal with them."

Isobel bit her lip against what she wanted to say and instead simply nodded. "If you could show Patli to the kitchen, I think he might enjoy a glass of lemonade, and maybe something to eat?" It had to be past noon by now, however off her time-sense might be, and what needed to be done now did not require Patli's observation. "And could you send Gabriel to meet me?"

Rafe checked himself and shook his head. "I haven't seen him for a while. Not since just after you left, in fact. But I'll send one of the girls to look for him and send him on."

She felt a flicker of concern. Gabriel should have been back by now. What was he up to?

"Thank you." She gestured for Patli to follow the marshal, and then went down the hallway he had indicated, where her guests had been tucked away.

The Jack was waiting outside the door, leaning against it as though he didn't have the strength to stand on his own—or as though he were afraid whoever was within might try to get out. His narrow face was drawn, the skin leathery, as though a month had passed since she'd seen him and not barely a day.

"It was as though they were waiting on me," he said before she could say anything. "Just . . . waitin' outside the city walls. Only two of 'em left."

She raised an eyebrow, waiting for him to tell her whatever he clearly needed to say.

"Rest were laid out on the ground, just waiting for flint and steel and a decent pyre."

"Dead?"

"By their own hand, if you can trust what those two inside have to say." There was no judgment in the Jack's voice or on his face, but a trace of envy: a Jack's life was not their own, they had no say over their own death, so long as they owed a debt to the devil.

Isobel licked her lips, feeling them oddly dry under her tongue.

"Hand."

She had said it would be the last thing he would be asked for. That in returning, he would be free.

Once before, a Jack had asked her for release, and she had refused. This time, she reached her left hand out, placing it gently against the man's face, pressing the heel of her palm against his chin, fingers resting just below his eye socket.

"We thank you for your service and return you your name, Thomas Paul."

He exhaled, eyes slipping closed, and she moved past him, opening the door and closing it again behind her, even as flesh dried to leather and leather crumbled into dust.

Inside the room, two men stood, ignoring the straight-back chairs that had been set against the wall. This was no parlor, nor an office, but a storeroom of some kind, and no thought had been given to comfort or hospitality. But those within made it clear that they would have rejected it, had it been offered.

She looked at them, relieved beyond expression to see no glint of anything in their eyes save a weary determination. One was older, slightly built, with strands of white glinting in his dark brown hair, a patch of his chin scruff white as well. The other was younger, his hair a paler brown, but the shape of their jaw and cheek suggested they were related. Father and son, perhaps. Or uncle and nephew.

She nodded at them, removing her hat. "My name is—"

"We know what you are."

Isobel felt her eyebrows rise, but let it go, merely nodding. "And do you know why I had Thomas bring you back here?"

"To kill us, most likely. Thus is ever the fate of prognosticators."

Isobel had no idea what that word meant, making note of it to ask Gabriel later, but suspected it meant "troublemaker" or something of that ilk. She focused, instead, on the first part.

"Do you think I should have cause to kill you?" Her hands wanted something to do, itching for the feel of reins between her fingers, and she forced them to be still. "Have you done something so unforgivable that death is the only answer I might have?"

They glanced at each other as though taken aback by her mild tone, or her words, or both. What, she wondered again, had the last Hand done there that left such a memory? But with her own actions so recent, Isobel did not linger long on the question.

"You speak against the devil, against the Agreement. Yes." She tried to inject the same weariness she saw in them into her voice. "Do you think the Master of the Territory fears your words, that he would send his Hand to wipe you from the air itself?"

The older one scowled, shaking his head. "But you are here."

"Not for you. Or not merely because of you," she amended. "Because you are distressed."

They didn't trust her. Didn't believe her. But they wanted to speak, and she wanted to listen. It would have to be enough.

"Distressed. That is one word for it."

"Tell me." She pulled the third chair away from the wall, sat herself in it, resting her elbows on her knees and her chin in her hands; a portrait of attention.

"What does it matter now? We know the devil's will: that we bend under his whim, until we breathe dirt rather than air."

Isobel bit down her instinctive anger, shaking her head and then tilting it to one side, reaching back to the girl she'd been a year or three before, looking wide-eyed at a gambler itching to show off. "I don't understand?"

His companion shook his head as well as though in response, a tic in his jaw proof how tightly his face was held in check. "The Territory's gone soft, crowded. Folk've let the *Agreement* control them, make them less than masters in their own home, force 'em to share space with outsiders who don't understand, who can't *hear*."

Isobel felt a shiver creep along her spine but controlled it.

"Hear what?"

He gave her a suspicious glare. "This is our land. We were born to it. We understand it. We're supposed to protect it. The whispers said so."

Isobel closed her eyes briefly, pieces shifting in her grasp, and something fluttered at the edges of Isobel's awareness, the rustle of a Reaper hawk's wings overhead, or the scrape of an owl's cry in the dusk.

The bald man's cry echoed in her memory: *To be born of this mud, it destroys us, piece by piece.*

She opened her eyes again, to find the men staring at her. They were mad, though they did not know it, could not know it. Aware enough to know there was danger, but not enough to find the source, to direct themselves to the true threat. And so, they turned on the thing they could see, the enemy they could identify, and in doing so, in riling up their neighbors, they created the very threat they thought to defend against.

And those like the bald man—Isiah his name was, Isiah—who wanted no part of it but were tied the way Gabriel was tied—Gabriel, where was he?—they too were going mad.

And the natives, by proximity, felt the rumblings of that madness as well. Enough that a spirit of the Mudwater itself raised its head to take notice.

FOUR

Isobel closed the door behind her softly, and rubbed her palms against the fabric of her skirt, although they were dry of sweat, almost cool despite the air's warmth. Her flesh felt heavy on her bones, her eyes scratchy and her throat parched and sore. She wanted to crawl into a bath and soak, wanted to crawl into her bed and sleep. Wanted to saddle Uvnee and ride north until there was snow on the hills, follow the whisper of silver all the way until it finally consumed her and she was silent again.

She would do none of those things.

Isobel'd had illusions, once. She'd had dreams, ambitions. But she could see now that they were fever-dreams, the kind that come when you're too tired to see straight, too trusting to question what you're told.

She'd thought becoming the Devil's Hand meant power, authority, respect. She'd learned soon enough that the power was not hers, that she was only the tool. She'd learned that the respect was given to the title, not her.

And authority? She weighed the word in her mouth, the sour-sweet taste of it, like candied fruit peel. Authority wasn't a prize. It was a burden, heavier than anything she carried in her pack.

But she had been sent out to do a job that needed doing. That only the Hand could do. That was why Auntie had protected her, why Gabriel had trained her, why the boss had agreed to take her Bargain. The devil takes nothing you're not willing to pay. He'd known, even if she hadn't, not then. Bone-child, silver-touched, owl-mad. Devil's Hand.

Gabriel. Urgency woke in her again. She needed to talk to him. Needed him to tell her she was right.

"What do you mean, he's gone?"

Isobel stared at Ana, who looked near to tears, her hands fisted in the fabric of her skirt, her shoulders hunched up as though afraid Isobel might strike her. The Hand forced herself into a softer stance, opening her own hands and gentling her voice. "Ana. Where is Gabriel?"

"Gone. His things are gone from your room, and I thought maybe he'd just . . . maybe put them away somewhere else, so I thought, and I went to where you'd stabled your horses, and your mare's there, but his horse is gone, and the boy said he left with all his things hours ago."

The words tumbled out of Ana's mouth as though she was afraid her voice would disappear before she could finish, and when she was done, her jaw snapped shut and she stared at Isobel with wide, frightened eyes.

Isobel drew a slow breath, then let it go, feeling her skin prickle in response. "The mule? Was the mule still there?"

"I . . . I don't know, miss? I didn't know to check."

If Flatfoot was still there, Gabriel would be coming back. Isobel held on to that, tucking it—and worry for what was going on now with Gabriel—into a pocket. If he wasn't there, she would have to go forward without him and catch him up later; that was all.

Isobel forced everything down, breathing through her nose again until calmness settled, the way Gabriel had shown her.

She felt someone come up behind her, pausing an arm's length away.

Boots, heavy tread, but not Gabriel.

"What is it, Marshal?"

"We have a problem.

"Of course we do." She turned to face him, aware that Ana took the opportunity to flee. His oilskin jacket on and hat in his hand, as though he'd either just come in or was about to go out.

"What now?"

"Some folk saw you bring those boys in; they're gathering outside, want an accounting. And . . ."

"And?" She waited, knowing there was more.

"And they're restless, in a bad way. And I don't have a posse, or time to round one up, in case trouble breaks."

He looked as though he regretted pinning the sigil back to his lapel, but she felt a gathered excitement in him, too. Not the coiling of a cat before it springs, but the heartbeat-thudding of buffalo hooves on the plain. You could take the rider off the Road, but they never settled to staying still. Not truly.

"And what do you expect me to do about that? This is your town, Marshal. Your people." His own words, tossed back at him.

"Yah, I figured you'd be saying that. Native riders are here too. Full paint and ponies, four of 'em, looking like they're looking for parley of a serious type."

"What tribes?"

He shook his head. "Confederacy for sure, so that's half a dozen represented, but I don't know any of 'em personal-like. And they're not here for me, that's certain."

"The waters are rising," she said, almost to herself. Running water. Silver warns and cleanses, but running water *breaks* and erases.

"Not an actual flood," she told the marshal, who waited a beat, then shook his head. "Beg pardon?"

"The visions, the warnings. They weren't about an actual flood." Her thoughts were falling over each other, and she forced them to stillness. A breath in through her mouth, and then out through her nose: once, twice. "They were a warning. Something has been chipping at the Agreement."

They spoke of it as though it were a treaty, and it was. But a treaty without power could not have lasted this long, not over so much land and so many people. Not a government, not an army—not even the devil himself, not really. People. Those born and those come; in accepting the Agreement, they enforced it.

But the power was spread out among so many now. So many, and so many with different desires. Different needs. Even without pressure from outside, could it have held much longer?

And outside pressures—Spanish and American and who knew what else—could not have helped either. The devil had held them at the river and the ridge, had kept military forces from invading, but he had not kept out people. Had not kept out ideas.

Isobel pressed her palm to her chest, willing the sigil to tell her something, *anything*. The sigil itched, but there was silence elsewhere. No whispers, no crashing of thunder, no whiff of the boss's scent or echo of his voice. A twinge of abandonment skittered down her spine, like a spider dropping down a web, and was gone.

Save herself, the Reaper hawk had counseled. It was not safe, the snake had warned her. Perform your duty, the wapiti had said. None of them had been wrong, and none of them had contradicted themselves, even when they had. It was not a question of preventing anything—it had never been a question of prevention. She couldn't stop the waters from rising—or keep them from retreating again after the flood. All she could do was channel it, protect the things that needed to be protected. It might be that in the aftermath the Territory would fail, the devil's Agreement be broken, the power of the land fading the way it had elsewhere, used up or ignored until it was gone.

She tried to imagine a Territory where demon did not gather on rock, or magicians wander, where crossroads were merely pathways, and owls did not cry secrets in the night air. Where reaching for the bones would reveal the flow of water underfoot, the stirring of green seeds and worms, and nothing more.

It was easier to imagine than she'd feared.

FIVE

"A problem," the marshal had called it. Isobel could feel them before she heard them, and she heard them before she saw them. But even without that, she would have known something was wrong; the streets were too empty, too quiet, the closer they came to where the mob had gathered, but she could feel eyes on her from every storefront window they passed.

They were milling about in the street, too close to where the corners bent, and she knew the streets had been shaped to not create pools of power, but there were limits to how much you could stave off, and the restless swirl she could *feel* was already too strong.

"Draw silver," she told the marshal, who nodded grimly and touched his gleaming sigil once before sliding a short, thick blade from his boot. Another day, she would have wanted to stop and look at it, admire the work that had clearly gone into its forging, but now she merely nodded in turn. "At my right," she said, and trusted him to fall into place as she strode forward, reaching down into the ground below her, stretching her awareness just enough to scoop the surface, imagining a net tied with glittering silver threads and slowly casting it out, the way native fishers did, standing on the banks.

A fish on the banks. She pushed the image away; now was not the time.

Auntie was in the crowd; she was unmistakable in the net, aware of it, allowing herself to be drawn forward before slipping through the mesh and disappearing, a dark fluke swimming against the tide.

Isobel wanted to pull her back but resisted the urge. Auntie went where Auntie felt she was needed. If she did not stay, Isobel had to trust that there was a reason.

She could feel the bones deep below; the closest she could describe it was agitation, a restless unease that mirrored the crowd still growing in the street, maybe three dozen settlers by now, clumping and shifting in patterns, schools melding and dividing, a steady rumble of voices increasing in volume.

A quick glance at her pinky showed the silver band was almost black with tarnish already, the blade in the Marshal's hand darkening at a slower rate but still steadily. There was power growing, and she could not spare attention to clear it out, not and keep an eye on the crowd as well. If Gabriel had been there . . . but she did not know the marshal well enough yet to trust him that well.

And, off to the side, standing by the wooden walkway, the confederacy representatives the marshal had mentioned: silent, watching. Waiting. Their eyes not on the crowd but her.

Isobel didn't take it personally. They saw her, but they saw past her, to the presence of the boss stitched to her like a shadow. The ground below their feet was uneasy, but it did not rumble.

Yet.

She had to stop this before it did.

"Papa?"

Beside her, the marshal swore, then: "Ana, get back; go inside."

"No."

"There is nothing you can do here, child. Go inside."

Ana was wide-eyed, uncertain, but a glance showed her boots

planted in the dirt the same as her father's, her chin the same determined jut.

"Ana, I said—" He seemed to lose all fury, all at once: Isobel could
read it in him, the resignation, the fear, and no small shape of pride.
"You have your knife?"

And she showed him the length glinting in her hand, silver-chased,
and shaped to her fist: a fighter's knife like the one Gabriel carried that
Isobel had never properly learned to use. From the way it rested in her
grip, Ana had no such hesitations.

She could not spare them any more; the closer they came to the
mob, the more the sense of power gathering grew. Something hid
within, masked, waiting.

"That's the Hand!" someone yelled, and the crowd shifted, too
many eyes gazing at her, too much attention driven at her. Isobel
lifted her chin and kept walking, hands in her pocket, coins tumbling
between her fingers. *Keep them in your hand*, she heard Marie coun-
seling her. *Keep control of the crowd.*

The marshal stayed to her right, half a step behind, a hand resting
easy on his belt, the other holding his blade loose and ready, Ana a step
farther behind him. He was not carrying a rifle, but she would not have
wanted to be the one to test how quickly he could drop the smaller
silver blade and pull one far deadlier from the sheath at his thigh.

The pressure in the crowd was almost visible to her, and she suddenly thought she understood what a magician saw when they looked
through the winds. It seethed and surged, shuddering under its own
weight, crackling ice and searing flame. If it could not be cleansed, it
must be used.

As though that thought drew him from hiding, a figure appeared,
stepping off the wooden walkway into the street, casual as if it were
his own parlor. Bodies moved away without realizing it, clearing a
space in the center of the crowd.

She glanced up toward the sky, trying to determine the sun's position. Noon had come and gone, but the light was bright enough that

they were not yet nearing dusk. But a magician not at full strength was still a thing to be cautious of.

She had killed them before, but at a cost.

"Stop." Her voice carried directly to him, and the magician grinned, a mirthless smile that filled his eyes and did not soften his face. Pale-skinned, pale-haired, hatless, dressed like a rider in dust-covered trou and boots, open-necked shirt, and battered leather coat. Utterly ordinary, until you looked into his eyes. Or felt the power sparking and swirling around him, hungry and quite mad.

Not human, not any longer.

"Who are you to stop me?" he asked, leaning against the air as though it were a solid wall at his back. She had seen Farron do that before; it did not impress her now.

"You know full well who and what I am."

Farron Easterly had known before she had, had smelled it on her. The other magicians, even maddened beyond most, had recognized her. If this one didn't, he was new, and possibly weak. But she did not make the mistake of assuming that as fact.

"My name is Isobel née Lacoyo Távora, also called Little Sharp Beak. I am the Left Hand, the cold eye and the final word." She breathed out, accepting her own words. "I am bone-child, silver-touched. And you?"

She did not expect him to give a name, and he did not.

"I've got the crowd," the marshal said, his voice low and confident, and she nodded, not taking her gaze from the magician, drawn by the power gathering here.

Dust swirled around their ankles, glittering in the light, lifting the ends of the magician's jacket and ruffling Isobel's skirt. Sound was muted, as though she had submerged her head entire in a tub.

Now, a whisper told her.

She felt the edges of the net she'd cast, eased it slightly, then yanked it hard.

The magician felt the net tighten around him too late and tried to take it back from her, feathered claws forming to tear at its knots, the air around him shimmering as he broke a strand, then another, reaching out in counter-blow, scraping the gathered power from around them to use against her.

The winds dropped down, drawn by clash of sigil and wind-medicine, dirt and dust swirling more vigorously around them both.

The magician laughed, clearly thinking their arrival gave him the advantage; Isobel dared not dip into their offering, not without risking the madness he had already embraced.

Isobel did not take her eyes off the human shape before her but directed her words into the swirling winds touching her skin. "This is none of your concern. This is mortal stuff."

A risk, speaking to them directly. The eight winds were as mad as their magicians and curious as demon, but she had been taught they had no care for matters of flesh or blood, and never lingered; not even the devil could hold their interest for long.

Seconds passed as she waited to see if she had made an error. Then the winds faded and were gone, the magician's silent howl shivering through the air as the dust settled back down to the ground.

In his distraction, Isobel *reached*, slipping the net from the magician himself to gather the power the mob had created; she felt it shiver into her bones, crackling painfully, trying to find somewhere to settle, the faint flavor of the devil's cologne-and-smoke smell in her nose before the sparking, burning sensation under her skin simmered down to a bearable itch.

She could not use that power, not the way a magician could, but she could hold it. Prevent him from claiming it.

His teeth bared at her, outraged, a wolf ready to spring.

"Go," she told him through gritted teeth, holding the power where he could see but not reach it, a deliberate taunt, a reminder of who had won. "I bid thee get hence. Get gone. *Váyase!*"

"You're interesting," he said, as though she hadn't spoken. "I think I like you."

The only thing more dangerous than having a magician notice you, Gabriel had once warned her, was having one decide you were interesting. She had been lucky that Farron had been less mad than most; she could not count on that happening again.

"Go, or I will send you," she warned, loosening one hand enough to show him the sigil, now burning darkly red in her hand, and he rolled his eyes, throwing his hands up to the air before the clawed wings appeared around him once more, a showy piece of work, and he dissolved into a north-driven breeze.

She didn't think he was gone, not while power still gathered there, and others might come, but he had backed off for now, and that was all she could hope for until she'd cleared the lure entirely.

"Magician," someone murmured, and her attention was brought sharply back to the crowd around her. She did not think they were talking about the one she had just sent away.

"River-witch," another said, louder, and with more anger than fear. Ana's careless whispers hadn't been banished as easily as the actual magician; she did not know if it was better they fear her for what she wasn't than be angry at her for what she was. . . .

Neither, Gabriel would say. Neither was better.

She took a breath, pulling herself from the corners and crevices of the makeshift crossroads, easing herself away from the gathered power with an almost-physical ache, to stare at the faces staring at her.

The crowd was mostly but not entirely men, older, most looking to be shopkeepers, trousers and polished boots rather than the rougher wear she'd seen closer to the docks. The few women among them were likewise well dressed, the cloth well cut but not fancy or frilled. Not a one of them looked as though they'd be able to last a day in the saddle, or had ever lifted a knife to do more than cut their dinner.

She didn't make the mistake of thinking that meant they were harmless. Not riled up and scared as they were.

The marshal stepped forward, not so much putting himself between her and the crowd as drawing their attention back to him.

"Folk, I'm going to ask you once last time to disperse."

"You think you pin that sigil back on and you can order us around?" The shout came from the back of the crowd, someone well hidden by others, but the marshal didn't even bother looking to see who it was.

"That's exactly what I think, Conrad, and you'd best respect the badge if you're not going to respect me. Or would you rather be the one everyone's demanding answers of? Feel free to pick up the sigil yourself; I'd gladly hand you over to these folk if so."

That seemed to cow Conrad and drew a few chuckles from deep in the crowd: even in their confusion, they were reacting to the soothing presence of law in their midst. This was why there were marshals and judges, Isobel realized, why they traveled the Road, why they needed to be visible. Not to enforce but to reassure.

If there had been a marshal there all along, would things have reached this point? Isobel couldn't know.

"So, tell us, if you've got all the answers!" someone else called, still carrying an edge to their voice. "Why'd that girl bring killers back into town?"

"They're not killers; they're the ones getting killed," a woman in the crowd yelled back. "Because of you people being threatened by them telling the truth!"

"They were the ones who came here and started riling things up!"

Isobel listened as a third voice joined in, turning it into a vocal brawl. "Wasn't them, was the tribes. Look at them, standing there, just waiting like dogs to pick at our scraps!"

"Sweet River Jordan, we're surrounded by idiots," the marshal muttered, and Isobel bit back an entirely inappropriate grin.

Someone pushed forward, a block of a man, his suit dark, his head bare, his expression thunderous. "It's the Hand's fault." He pointed one thick finger at her, like a preacherman finding sin. "We were handling things fine until she showed up. Same as last time. A Hand comes to town and everything goes to the devil! Maybe we don't want to go to him anymore!"

"You don't like it, go cross-river," one of the earlier voices yelled at him, and there were rumbles of agreement. "The Territory doesn't need the likes of you."

"This is my home, too!" he yelled back. "I'm born to the bones, same as you. Maybe more'n you, since I've never heard tell of you having the Touch. So, why don't *you* leave, since you can."

"And they're done," the marshal said, gently moving past Isobel even as he lifted his sigil into the air and bellowed, "Settle *down!*"

Her sigil flared, relaying a sudden request for aid that she recognized, although she'd never felt it before: the Tree calling on the *infinitas*.

Isobel instinctively pulled some of the power-ache out of herself and pushed it into his words, making them echo against the storefronts until the entire crowd was startled into silence.

Satisfactions

Isobel felt the now-familiar whisper curl through her, but she was too busy to listen, trying to find the thread of power the marshal had let loose with his roar, the glinting spark rising like a tree, thick-trunked and many-branched, spreading down and out equally, the symbol of the Territory, roots deep and branches wide. She wove herself around it, looping instinctively, allowing it to bear the weight the way it was designed to, directing the itch until it eased to something bearable, calming and gentling the heartbeats of everyone in the crowd.

This was the power the devil had taken into himself when he first stood on the banks of the Mudwater and claimed it as his own. This was the power the devil had sent into her, into Marie, the strand of otherly medicine mixed within the earth's own, shaped into human form, given to human agents for human purposes.

"Come on, folk." The marshal was moving, moving away from her, and she focused, half-closing her eyes to keep him in better view. "Come on, look at each other. You're friends, most of you. Neighbors. All stuck here together because this is where we live, and nobody wants to go anywhere else, yeah?"

The boss had raised the first wards on the River and the Knife. He had bargained for the Agreement. His Hand watched them, enforced them, defended them. She had shed blood and shredded flesh to keep them safe.

If these people tried to break it, if they chose conflict . . .

She could destroy them. Destroy, to protect. Take their vigor as she had taken the power from the unnamed magician, to prevent greater harm.

You are the final word, the killing blow.

She was. But she would not.

She could feel the gaze of the tribal leaders on her back. Waiting.

She could hear the cards against the green felt, *flickerthwack, flickerthwack*, the echo of hooves on dusty earth, the slow beat of wings, the steady pulse of the bones. The thud of every heart in the crowd.

Flickerthwack.

There had to be another way.

"What do you want?" She placed a hand on the marshal's arm, stepping past him, sensing more than seeing the crowd give way, backing up once for every two steps she took. Her voice carried without her having to lift it. "What is it you wish, people of Red Stick? You could not come to Flood, and so Flood has come to you. What would you ask of the Devil's Hand?'

Fish on the banks. Owl covered with snow. The waters rise. Flood comes. She almost laughed with the obvious simplicity of it now.

There was silence, and then she heard the voices, although not a single mouth moved.

Wealth.

More land.

He needs to stop looking at me like that, like I'm not as good as him.

I want to kill him.

They need to be pushed back, back across the river where they came from.

Why can't everything just be the way it was? I'd give anything for it to be the way it was.

She was not the devil; she could not make Bargains. But she could listen, and she could hear. Not only the wishes but what drove them. Some were ashamed, their desires muffled. Some angry, hot enough to burn everything down. Some were autumn storms, bluster and chill. The sigil itched, burned, feeling the Agreement threatened. The molten flow in her bones pushed forward, not alarmed, not awake, but aware, the unrest reflecting back within itself.

Flickerthwack.

The devil bound them with Agreement. But the Agreement had not been made between settlers and natives but flesh and bone. Mortal and Territory.

To become one and the same.

Do what you do. Auntie's voice, strained from a distance, as though she were pushing through rock. *Do what you are, bone-child, silver-child, devil's child. Isobel. Don't you be afraid.*

Isobel reached, stretching for the shining bright sharpness of the tree-and-circle, the symbol of the Territory itself. It surged to her touch, the scratchy, dry feel of bark against her skin becoming fuel for the burning, then a torch, filling the air with flame.

She could burn it all down, leave nothing but mud and bone behind.

A single thought reached out, touched the flame, curled around it, carried that flicker within. Then another tendril, and a third, until the flame was shared out, gentled and rekindled, not a conflagration but a hundred smaller fires, and Isobel could feel them stretching farther, out along the Road, looping and looping throughout the Territory, until the Road itself was aflame, a wash of red drowning the Territory from River to Knife, and the slow silent beat of carrion wings traveling overhead, the thunder of heartbeat hooves fading into echo as the Territory itself faded and was no more.

She showed it to the mob, a dry, chill dampness of snowfall hissing where it touched the char, and waited, holding the image as snow gathered more thickly, dampened the voices until the fires subsided, glinting darkly the color of clotted blood under snow.

This is you, she warned them. *This is us. The devil never asks for more than you can pay, but the payment is forever. What would you ask of the Devil's Hand?*

The tree was rough at her back, the sigil burning under her feet, and she heard only the snow falling on her wings, the smell of sulphur, tobacco, and whiskey wrapped over her skin.

And then silence, and then nothing.

She opened her eyes to see the marshal's face before her, hatless, worry-creased, dark eyes hooded and shadowed with exhaustion.

"There will be no Mud this time," Isobel said, the only thing she could be certain of. "What else may come, who knows, but there will not be another Mud."

He sat back on his heels, one hand still on her shoulder, and she wasn't sure if he was holding her up, or using her to hold himself up.

"That's good," he said, and his voice sounded a bit faint. "That's . . . good."

"Better than they deserve." Auntie came into view, her braids in disarray, a smudge of something ashy over one cheekbone, and she looked as exhausted as Rafe, as exhausted as Isobel felt.

Isobel felt the heated weight of her veins slowly ease, the dry scrape of her lungs moisten again with each breath she drew. Never had she thought to be thankful for the warm air of Red Stick: had the air been drier, she thought her chest might have shredded.

"It's not over," Auntie went on. "You scared them, but scaring someone only goes so far, and they won't learn. They never do."

"She doesn't think much of the rest of us," Rafe said, and he tried to smile at the both of them.

"That's because I know them, and you do too, *Marshal.*"

"Hope is what we live on, *witch*," he said in return. "Hand?"

She coughed once and took the flask he offered her, wetting her throat with watered-down whiskey. "Yah?"

The marshal was side-eying her, although not, she thought, with fear, which was a pleasant relief. "What happened to the men your Jack brought back?"

"I let them go." They could stay in town or leave; it made no difference now.

She wasn't sure he entirely believed her. "And the Jack himself?"

"I let him go, too."

Something in her voice must have alerted him to the fact that he didn't want to ask further questions, because he nodded once and then jammed the hat back on his head, adjusting the narrow brim. The sigil of the tree-and-circle was pinned to his jacket, in clear view, and she gave in to the urge to reach out and touch it with her fingertips.

He jolted at the spark as the tarnish cleared, but held steady, only the pulse trembling at his throat an indication that it had unnerved him.

She did not tell him that it unnerved her as well.

She could feel both within her, an uneasy balance: the sigil warm in her palm, the silver hot in her bones. They'd used her, but she had used them, too. The devil might call the tune, as Marie had warned her long ago, but she would decide who danced.

She frowned, not certain if that made sense. She would ask Gabriel. After she gave him an earful for not *being* there.

The street had emptied, but she could feel the pressure waiting, from behind walls and under stone, lapping against the shores. She had shown them the cost of what they wished for. But Auntie was right: they would forget if they were not reminded again. And someday, reminders might not be enough.

The Territory was still at risk, and like Auntie, she wasn't certain it could be saved. Not as it was, not forever. But maybe it didn't have to be forever. Maybe just a little longer.

Someday was a problem for another morning. When Gabriel came back. When she could talk to the boss, and Marie, and take a good, hard look at that map of his.

"Lot to do in the here and now," she said. "Are you ready, Marshal?"

"No," he said, with admirable honesty. "But that's never mattered a bit, has it?"

She grinned, feeling its crookedness, and curled her fingers into her palm, curled the whisper around her bones. "Not even ever once."

Gabriel felt a faint, scratching sense of guilt as he left the city's gate behind him, his body tense and his throat tight. But the farther he went from Red Stick, the easier each breath became, his body loosening in the saddle, his chest expanding to take in more air.

Too many people; he'd told Isobel that that many people around made it easier, but that had been a half-truth. Easier to distract himself, easier to close his ears, but the press of people brought back memories of Philadelphia, of the years he'd lived cut off and pretending, unable to sense even the water in a bucket.

That silence had made him ill, eventually. Had driven him back to the Territory. It had taken his dream from him, and handed him stress and sorrow.

The Road had filled the silence with its steady hum, not seeking to pull him in further. But the price was constant movement, a restlessness he'd never asked for.

The devil had promised him peace. That wasn't a thing the devil could guarantee, and they'd both known it. But the devil didn't lie, and so Gabriel had allowed himself to hope, just a little.

Maybe the devil had just sent him to where peace might be found. If so, the irony was elegant.

He directed Steady north and east, following instincts he'd long suppressed. There were no farmsteads here, no marker-posts to indicate that this land was claimed, only empty ground, and the River just over the ridge. Waiting for him.

Old Woman Who Never Dies had told him once that water didn't judge. He hoped she was right.

Something small rustled in the underbrush, as though mocking him for hesitating at this final step. He dismounted, leaving Steady by the side of the road, reins loosely tethered to a sapling. If anything threatened him, the gelding was more than capable of kicking free and heading back to Red Stick where the rest of his herd was.

If Gabriel did not return . . .

A fish on the river's bank for too long, dies. Time to let the waters rise.

He grinned at that, a rattlesnake grin, that he should have known better than to ride into a town called Flood.

He took his pack off Steady's saddle and patted the bay on the neck. "You be good," he said, and the horse turned its head to stare at him, brown eyes accusing.

"Be good," he repeated, and stepped off the Road.

Look for the novella "Gabriel's Road."